A REBEL WITCH

Spellcasters Spy Academy, Grind Year

A MAGIC OF ARCANA UNIVERSE SERIES

ASHLEY MCLEO

Meraki Press

CONTENTS

BEST READING ORDER FOR SPELLCASTERS SPY ACADEMY

A Legacy Witch, Spellcasters #1 - available in audiobook format

A Marked Witch, Spellcasters 1.5 (Eva's point of view) - available in audiobook format

A Rebel Witch, Spellcasters #2 - available in audiobook format

A Crucible Witch, Spellcasters #3 - available in audiobook format

Newsletter subscribers can get A Marked Witch ebook for free! This book will round out your experience in the Spellcasters universe.

fternoon was well underway when my friends and I pulled up to the iron gates of Spellcasters Spy Academy.

Eva gripped my hand as Hunter spoke the password that would allow us entry. "It's different this time, isn't it?" Her eyes, the color of cornflowers, never left the cold metal that surrounded the school.

I leaned back, content to wait as Headmistress Wake's blue magic shimmered and swirled around Hunter's car. It seeped in through the window cracks and car vents, rippling across my skin and lifting every hair follicle in an effort to validate our worthiness.

"Undoubtedly," I replied, watching the academy's prophetess symbol crack in half as the gates opened to allow us entry.

How could it not feel different? So much had changed.

At the start of last year, my peers knew me as the only

witch in the last forty years to claim the legacy route into the academy. Not thinking others would see this as entitled and lazy, I waltzed right into school to find that many people resented my choice.

Now I was one of two head junior spymasters for the Grind-year. While everyone would have bet on Alex, my boyfriend, being a shoo-in for the male head junior spymaster slot, I doubted that many believed I would snag the other position. I barely believed it still.

"Are you ladies nervous to meet with Headmistress Wake?" Hunter asked, his bright green eyes latching onto Eva in the rearview mirror.

"Yeah . . . I'm nervous about that. Who knows what the battle-axe will say?" Eva whispered as she peered out the window.

My heart ached for my best friend. While I'd been through a ton of shit last year, she'd undergone her fair share of traumatizing experiences too.

"You two know that Hunter and I will be with you every step of the way, right?" Alex twisted in his seat, his Caribbean blue gaze hard. "I realize the headmistress didn't ask to see us, but I don't care. I'm not letting either of you deal with this alone."

"Ditto," Hunter said.

For the billionth time since our little group had formed, gratitude overwhelmed me. My three best friends had been my rocks for the last year. As we began our Grind-year—the most difficult level at Spellcasters—I had a feeling I would lean on them even harder in the months to come.

Finally, the cloud of blue magic dissipated, and the gate opened wide enough for us to drive through.

Hunter pressed on the gas. "Took long enough."

He was right. It had taken a long time for the wards surrounding the school to accept us. *Much* longer than last year. After the events of our Culling-year, I was very grateful that Spellcasters had tightened their security. Not that I truly believed any magic could keep out a royal demon determined to break in, but it still made me feel better.

Needing a moment of introspection before my meeting with Headmistress Wake, I gazed out the window. Dense trees lined the miles of drive. Flashes of blue lake and the gold spires topping Merlin Amphitheater—the birthplace of so many of my nightmares—punctuated the greenery.

When the trees finally broke and the academy appeared, I sucked in a breath, as impressed by the school as the first time I'd laid eyes on it. Spellcasters always reminded me of the perfect mix of a gothic cathedral and a German fairytale castle. With its stone gargoyles, beautiful stained-glass windows, and green-topped towers at the four corners of the estate, it was unlike any place I'd ever seen.

Hunter pulled around to the right side of the main building, where the students who kept cars at the academy parked alongside the staff and visitors. Some of our classmates were in the lot, unpacking suitcases from their cars; among them was a girl I hadn't expected to see again.

"Holy crap," I breathed. "Look! It's Phoebe Pudeator. They let her re-enroll!"

Phoebe's parents had insisted that she leave school before our Beltane Trial last year. As she hadn't completed the final trial, everyone assumed she'd been expelled.

"I wonder if Diana had anything to do with that?" Alex mused. "They've been best friends since they were young."

Eva's lips flattened. She didn't like Phoebe much. Not only because the girl was rude to me last year, but because Hunter spilled the beans that he'd messed around with her before he met Eva.

I understood how she felt. I'd experienced jealousy after I'd learned that Alex had kissed Diana before we started dating.

I opened the car door and exited. "Let's go find out what happened."

"Hey, Phoebe," I said once I was close enough for her to hear.

Phoebe had been talking to her mom, and when she turned around, shock flitted across her face.

I supposed her reaction was natural. When she'd left the academy, her best friend and I had still regarded each other as enemies. I'd never have approached Phoebe during our Culling-year.

"We're surprised to see you back," I continued.

Phoebe's eyes darted to her parents. "To be honest, I'm a little surprised to be back."

I opened my mouth to respond, but Phoebe cut me off.

"Can you guys hang on? My parents are about to leave."

We took a handful of steps back to give her privacy, and Phoebe went about saying her goodbyes. A few minutes later, her parents drove away, and Phoebe turned back to us, her face more relaxed than moments before.

"Sorry about that. I didn't mean to sound so short. It's just that Dad is scared to death about the curse of our year. We went to *war* over me returning to Spellcasters. I didn't want him changing his mind last minute."

The curse . . . I'd forgotten that many of my classmates still believed that the curse was real. I wished that I could tell them they were safe—that the so-called curse was really more of a prophecy and only applied to Alex and me, but I couldn't. Telling the truth would mean spilling too many dangerous secrets.

"His concern is understandable," I said.

"Of course it is, but that doesn't mean I'll just accept not being able to follow my dream," Phoebe said. "Especially since after I convinced *him* to let me come back, it took nearly as much debate with the headmistress to make it happen. Like seriously, *so* much work. Thankfully, Di vouched me."

"Did you have to do an internship?" Alex asked, clearly curious about how deep nepotism ran at Spellcasters.

Phoebe nodded. "Kind of." Her eyes flashed to Eva and me and she bit her lip. I assumed she might know a little of what happened during our internship. "Thanks to Dad's connections, a Master Poisoner took me on as an apprentice. Not my first choice, I'll admit, but Headmistress Wake approved it. Beggars can't be choosers."

"What about a Beltane Trial?" Hunter asked.

"I have to take my own mini-Beltane Trial within the

first week of classes," Phoebe shrugged. "It sucks because I don't get a partner, but it'll be worth it."

"Sounds like you lucked out," Eva commented flatly.

"Definitely," Phoebe replied, and then her eyes lit up. She threw her hand into the air to wave at someone behind us. "Hey girl!"

I turned to find Diana, Headmistress Wake's daughter and my once-enemy, approaching. With almost unparalleled self-assurance, an aquiline nose, a statuesque frame, and long, blonde hair, Diana always reminded me of a super model walking the catwalk.

As soon as she reached us, Diana pulled Phoebe into a hug. When they broke apart, the headmistress' daughter faced the rest of us.

"Welcome back. I heard you four experienced an interesting summer internship?"

"That's one word for it," I muttered.

Diana arched an eyebrow, her steely blue eyes latched onto me. "Right. Well, Mother is waiting to speak with you and Eva in her office. You can leave your luggage outside the car, and someone will bring it up. It's all tagged, right?"

We confirmed that it was, and Diana waved for us to follow her. Although I didn't need an escort to the headmistress' office, I said nothing. The only other night I'd been there, Diana's other friend, Tabitha, had been killed. No one wanted to be reminded of that day.

Alex and Hunter trudged behind us, and while Diana shot them a surprised look, she didn't comment or stop them.

We entered through an ivy-concealed side door near the back of the academy. I'd never seen the doorway before, but wasn't shocked by its existence. A place like Spellcasters was sure to have many secrets I hadn't discovered. Some I probably never would.

As we walked down the corridors, a sense of coming home overtook me, and tension that I hadn't realized I'd been holding in my neck dissipated.

Diana spun around to walk backward and face us. "Notice anything different?"

We were passing the main entryway to the school. Two stairwells, with a black and green banner bearing the Spellcasters prophetess mascot hanging between them, curved and climbed up the three primary levels. The hallways led to upper level classrooms and the towers in which the initiates, second-years, academics, and staff lived during term. My gaze climbed upward to the only other distinguishing factor of the entryway—the enormous, circular, stained glass windows that depicted the four elements.

Even though witches didn't use elemental magic—that was a fae characteristic—we still revered nature. After all, our power was just modified energy, and that came from nature too, albeit indirectly.

But as far as I could tell, the windows looked the same.

Unable to deduce what Diana was referring to, I shook my head. "I give up. What changed?"

Her hand twirled in the air, and graceful, thin fingers wiggled. "Wards. They added about two dozen since last term. Half of which were put in place after your internship." She darted a conspiratorial glance left, then right, before locking eyes with me again. "So a fae court is working with the demons, huh? I'm not supposed to know what happened during your internship, but Mother couldn't help but get overexcited when she told Father. I overheard."

"Yeah," I said. "Eva actually discovered it."

Diana's intense stare, so like her mother's, shifted to Eva, who sighed.

"I found fae runes covered in blood all around Portland. Somehow, the combination of blood and fae runes—which don't usually require blood—lets demons into our world."

"Hmmm." Diana chewed her lip, and turned back around, apparently needing a minute to absorb the new information.

Good luck. I barely understand it, and I witnessed everything.

Even before we found ourselves fighting for our lives in the dank Portland underground, everything had been so damn confusing. We hadn't had any idea what the fae runes or blood meant. Or why Eva's demon scars reacted to other demons' presence. As a greater demon had made them, and not a royal of Hell, they shouldn't have been so sensitive. Nothing like mine, which was a curse from Queen Ishtar herself.

Or so we *thought*.

During the battle, we'd discovered that the succubus who had scarred Eva had been carrying King Lucifer's child. His essence and blood ran through the succubus, and now by extension, Eva.

My best friend was demon-touched, just like me. Which meant that she had a target on her back too. And most likely, that we both had a crapload of questions to answer before Headmistress Wake set us loose in the academy.

I inhaled a deep breath, preparing myself for the formidable witch who was the headmistress of our academy. *Let the fun begin.*

CHAPTER TWO

Headmistress Priscilla Wake closed the door, sealing us inside her office. "Take a seat." She gestured to the chairs in front of her desk.

I arched an eyebrow. The only other time I'd been in her office, there had been two wing-backed chairs. Today, there were four. The headmistress had clearly expected Hunter and Alex to join the meeting.

Eva and I claimed the middle seats, and our boyfriends winged us protectively.

Immediately, my best friend began to squirm. I placed a gentle hand on her arm, letting her know that I'd take the lead.

"You wanted to talk about our internships, Headmistress Wake?"

"Yes." The master of our school situated herself in her armchair gracefully and nodded, business as usual. "I'd like a full debriefing of what happened, straight from you two ladies."

"Fine." Not about to lay the burden on Eva, I launched into the story. Nothing I said seemed to faze the headmistress. Not news of the fae runes that had been covered in blood to transport demons into our realm, or the battle we'd fought below the city of Portland. Emotion had no place on her face. And although I recognized that it shouldn't—she was a trained spy, after all—her reaction frustrated me more with each passing minute.

"And that's what happened," I finished and leaned back in my chair, waiting for her to grill me.

Instead, Headmistress Wake rose and went to her liquor cabinet. She plucked a crystal decanter filled with brown liquid from her stash and served herself a two-fingered pour.

As if she'd forgotten that we were there, the headmistress turned to look at us. "After a story such as that, I'd offer you some, but you're underage."

"Makes *total* sense why we take a mixology workshop every year, then," Hunter muttered under his breath.

Wake shot him a glare heated enough to singe the hair off his head, but said nothing before tossing the drink back.

When she returned to her seat, she folded her hands in front of her. "Since last year's Beltane Trials, I've been conducting research on demon-touched witches."

"So, the *two* reported cases," Alex muttered.

The headmistress didn't shift her gaze from Eva and me. "Yes. *Those* cases, Mr. Wardwell." She leaned forward so that her elbows rested on her desk. "It seems that while the afflicted witches shared symptoms, their experiences of being demon-touched varied wildly. Some hypothesize that it comes down to the royal demon's intent when they touch you. All we know is it's not only the act of touching that produces a mark. Otherwise, many black witches could make the claim that they're demon-touched after making a deal with evil. It's because of this . . . individuality in marks that I must ask—are you two in control of your demon marks?"

A deep line formed between my eyebrows. I hadn't expected that question—although, perhaps I should have. If she made her way into this world, Ishtar would be able to control me through my mark. The same could be said for Lucifer and Eva. Thankfully for us, the king and queen of darkness were still in Hell.

I considered Wake's question carefully. So far, my mark had reacted to a demon's presence, but I'd never felt out of control. And until the Hellgate opened and spilled demons into our world, I suspected that it would stay that way.

Or at least, I hoped so.

"I'm in charge," Eva confirmed.

"Me too. We both felt demons in Portland before we saw them—although, like you mentioned, the sensations were different. But I never felt out of control."

"I was hoping you'd say that," the headmistress said. "Clearly, other students know that you have been through difficulties, but they know little else on the matter. I would like to keep it that way." She arched her brows.

Eva and I nodded. I didn't really feel like spreading the word around that Ishtar, the Queen of Hell, could control me, or that Lucifer could control Eva. Or even that we could sense demons in our presence. Only our families, the Paranormal Intelligence Agency, and the Spellcasters instructors knew, which I preferred. Fitting in was already hard enough without being demon-touched.

"I also want you to know that we've enhanced the academy," Headmistress Wake continued. "The number of wards we've set up on the grounds and within the school is unprecedented. As you may have noticed, I've reinforced the boundary gate myself. Visitors will be permitted on school grounds only if they have met certain, stringent requirements. Keep in mind—"

"That's nice and all," Alex said, uncharacteristically cutting her off. "But we're in our Grind-year. We have to undertake missions off academy grounds, so it seems almost pointless to spend all this energy when we'll be in danger, anyway."

"I'll ignore your rude interruption, Mr. Wardwell." Headmistress Wake glared at Alex. "After all, you've been through a trying time, but *don't* let it happen again."

She resumed, addressing primarily Eva and me. "As I was about to say, the wards are not just for your safety. They are for the safety of all the students. We hope that if Mr. Alexander Wardwell and Miss Dane do not go on missions together, that threat will be lessened. As I recall, Alexander, you mentioned that the royals of Hell have made it clear that they want you *and* Miss Dane. Or am I wrong on that point?"

"We can't be separated," Alex said, his tone firm. I could practically feel the frustration vibrating off of him. "Odie and I have to stick together. That means going on our missions together."

Headmistress Wake's lips flattened. "I understand that you are an item and wish to look after one another, but honestly, Mr. Wardwell, I cannot allow such things. It's much too risky—like putting a target on your backs. And seeing as this is your Grind-year, the trials before you will be risky enough." She shook her head. "And then there's another matter, of a *certain event* taking place at Spellcasters this year."

"An event?" Hunter leaned forward, curious as ever. "Like the initiate trials? Or a dance?"

I refrained from rolling my eyes. *Yeah, Hunter. She's talking about a dance.*

"You will learn of them tonight at the Grind and Crucible welcome feast."

"Why can't you tell us now?" Eva asked.

"It would be unfair to the rest of the students." The headmistress looked as though she wished she hadn't said anything at all. "As much as I believe that you—Miss Dane and Mr. Wardwell—are capable witches, on this point, I'm immovable. You will not be sent on missions together, and that is final. As I respect what you've been through, I wanted to be the one to tell you. And inform you that we'll be doing everything in our power to keep you safe."

"But we have to be together!" Alex shot out of his chair.

"Mr. Wardwell! Sit down this instant!"

"You don't understand! Odie and I—"

Before he could press harder, I grabbed his arm and squeezed it tight. "It will be fine. Let's go." My gaze shifted to the headmistress. "Are we excused?"

Headmistress Wake gave an impressed nod at my unusual restraint. "Yes. That will be all."

I stood and pulled a seething Alex behind me.

While it was sweet that he wanted to stay by my side, it would do no good to argue with the headmistress on the matter of our missions. She didn't know that Alex and I were descendants of the famed wizard Merlin and Morgan Le Fay, the notorious witch who some believed was part fae. No one did, except Eva, Hunter, Alex, and me. Even after the Queen of Hell branded me, we hadn't told anyone else. It felt too private, and because we still weren't sure how Morgan and Merlin—or M&M, as I thought of them— were related to all this, we wanted to keep it to ourselves.

At least for now.

CHAPTER THREE

When we exited Headmistress Wake's office, Diana was still waiting outside.

"That was fast." Her eyes darted to each of us in turn.

"Yeah," I glanced at Alex. With his fists clenched and his jaw tightened he looked ready to explode. I shifted my grip from his upper arm to the tight ball of his hand and squeezed. "Most of it, we expected. The rest . . . we'll mull over."

Diana took in the whole interaction with hawk-like intensity. "Right. Well, I guess it's time to show you to your rooms."

My eyebrows pulled together. We all knew the general location of the second year tower. I'd assumed they would label our rooms and entry would be voice-activated, like last year.

"Why do you need to show us the way?" Hunter asked, clearly on my wavelength.

Diana twirled her hands high in the air, once again indicating the wards. "Spymaster-level students have their own floor. Our level includes additional security to prevent jealous pranks from other students."

My stomach dipped at the mention of jealousy. Few people had as much reason for others to be jealous of them as I did. I'd sucked at everything at the start of last year, and completed the term at the top of the class. And then there was the matter of my family's influence and wealth—both often incited envy in others.

"I'm the first spymaster in our year to 'arrive'," Diana placed the word in air quotes because the school was her home, and aside from her summer internship, she'd been here the whole time. "So I get the job of showing the rest of you how to break the wards and gain access to our floor. After that, we use normal voice activation to enter our rooms."

She led us to the entryway and up the stairs to the third floor. We turned the same way we would have gone if we were heading to our old tower, passing paintings of ex-spymasters and celebrated headmasters as we went.

Diana chatted the entire way, which I was sure the rest of us appreciated. It gave us time to think about our meeting with the headmistress. About halfway down the hall, I was snapped out of my musings when we took an unexpected left turn down a narrow side corridor. I cocked my head, lost. I would have passed this hallway daily to get to the initiate tower, but somehow, I didn't remember it at all.

"Where did this corridor come from?" Hunter asked, once again on my level.

Thank the universe I'm not the only confused person here.

Diana's lips curled up in a smile. "It was always here. It's hidden from initiates—a lot of things are. Mother believes that fewer distractions allow us to hone our focus better."

I snorted a laugh because the hallway we found ourselves walking down was the epitome of distraction, lined as it was by old weapons, artifacts of espionage, and accolades that the school had earned from the United States government, and even one from the Irish government.

Each item was interesting and clearly valuable, as they were kept behind sturdy, likely magically-reinforced cases. But one artifact caught my eye more than the others. It was an ancient blade, studded with a ruby handle. I paused long enough to read the name inscribed on the metal.

The Realm Slicer.

A shudder ran up my spine. *That doesn't sound ominous at all.*

We proceeded down the hall for a couple minutes more until the corridor ended. A single door, painted a dark, Spellcasters green stood at the end.

"Why is it green?" The door to the initiate tower had been basic black. From what I remembered, most other doors in the academy were also a neutral hue. But maybe they painted them yearly?

Diana grinned. "The doors to the student, academic, and alumni buildings are all painted Spellcasters colors. The initiate one is black because we're often kept in the dark or clueless at that stage. But as Grind-year students, we've earned green."

Good grief, this school and their freaking symbolism. I wondered how many other things I'd missed when I'd been floundering through my initiate-year. In fact, only one of my friends looked unsurprised—Alex. He'd probably read about the doors in one of the bajillion books he'd devoured.

"What are the other colors?" Eva asked.

"Crucible students get silver," Diana said. "Academics and alumni earn white, since they're the most enlightened. If you ask me—"

"While all that's interesting," I interrupted, "what do you say we get inside? I have to pee." I didn't actually have to use the restroom. But I wanted to avoid a lecture, get to my room, and regroup a little.

"Right," Diana said. "The voice activation on the tower door coincides with your fingerprints. Make sure your right pointer finger is on the handle when you grip it and say your name." She demonstrated, and the door clicked open.

The aroma of coffee filled my nostrils, followed by sage, telling that a staff member had been in the tower to cleanse it before term. Both were scents that I associated with the initiate tower, but another aroma floated around the Grind tower. Something unusual, almost acrid. I tilted my head, unable to place it.

"Rue." Alex wrinkled his nose.

Diana nodded. "An additional measure to ward off demons." She walked through the door.

About half our class was already inside the tower, chatting and catching up with friends they had not seen in weeks.

The Grind tower looked much like the initiate tower, except nicer. They had upgraded our furniture. The tables were all a dark, gleaming wood, and the chairs and couches were a rich brown leather instead of gray cloth. Whereas our old dorm had one fireplace, this tower had two. The change was most welcome; it meant more people could sit in front of the fire during Maine's bitterly cold winter. To my great surprise, there were even a couple entertainment options, like a pool and ping pong tables in the common space, a luxury we didn't have last year. A tightly wound spiral staircase climbed toward the bedrooms. Domed at the apex, a lunette window allowed natural light to stream inside during the day, and would give us a glimpse of the stars at night.

"Wow," I breathed. "It's beautiful. And more welcoming than the initiate tower."

"Mother says the higher we rise, the more privileges we accrue. Wait till you see our rooms." Diana waggled her eyebrows.

A grin spread across my face, only to falter a second later when I realized just how many people were staring at us cooly. My eyebrows knitted together at the cold welcome from students who I considered friends.

"What's up their butts?" Eva whispered, as we walked by a small group of people who blatantly turned away from us.

Diana waited until we'd climbed halfway up the stairwell to answer. "When they arrived, they got their rankings. Some aren't happy with where they're placed."

Oh. Right. The rankings.

"I take it those who looked like they've had the most poo shoved under their noses got emissary spy?" Eva asked.

"Yup. They think they deserve sorcerer spy . . . or maybe even spymaster." Diana arched an eyebrow, which made my stomach twist. "Don't worry. Mother says it happens every year. We're all competitive at Spellcasters, or else we wouldn't be here. Once they realize that being in our good graces is to their advantage, they'll warm up again."

I scoffed. Diana was always so confident and blunt that it took me by surprise. Although, in this instance, I hoped she was right. I'd spent the majority of last year being disliked. I didn't need a repeat.

We climbed to the top floor and came face-to-face with another green door. Diana pivoted to face us. "This is where you need to say the incantation that will allow you passage. Like this."

She extended her hand to hover inches above the gold knob. "*Dominum.*"

Purple magic flowed out of her hand. It shimmered and undulated around the doorknob, which then turned on its own accord and opened.

"It's that simple," she said. "Just be gentle. If you're mad or upset, try to cool it before you open the door. One year, someone spoke the incantation when they were angry, and the door flew off its hinges. Oh, and don't tell anyone the password. Only spymasters up here."

It was no wonder why others were upset they hadn't made spymaster. I doubted that this was the only perk we'd get.

"Thanks. I guess we'll see you at the feast," I said, moving past Diana.

"Yup. Mother says she has a surprise for the whole school." Her blue eyes lit up with excitement.

"Can't wait."

My room was the second one on the right, squished between Diana's and Alex's. After realizing that I wasn't sharing a bathroom with Eva this year, a wave of sadness overtook me.

"We're not roomies." I stuck my lip out. "It's the end of an era."

Eva gave me an understanding smile and wrapped her arm around my shoulder. "I think all the spymaster level bathrooms are private. There's not even a communal toilet on this floor. And judging by all the books and desks, that room over there is a special, spymaster-only library." She pointed to the first room on the opposite side of the stairs. "We probably should have expected that the dorms would be nicer. Remember the King's Castle?"

I nodded. Who could forget the Crucible dorm? That place was off the chain. "Still, it's sad knowing that you won't be barging in on me whenever you want," I said.

Eva chuckled. "Yeah. I'm sure you'll *totally* miss that. But I'll be a few doors away, so have no worries. I'll knock until you let me in. If you don't, well, I think I can do a decent Odie impression. Maybe I'll trick the voice-activation enchantment."

We shared a laugh, and after one last hug from my girlfriend, everyone separated to explore their private spaces.

A plaque bearing my name glimmered on my door. However, this year, the word "spymaster" had been added below. I took in the title with awe, proud of my achievements. When I stepped inside my room, I found that it was at least twice the size of last year's dorm. A private bathroom stood off to the side, already stocked with plush white towels, and smelling of black currant. My desk resembled one that might be in a low-level executive's office.

And then there was the view. Last year, my room had looked out upon the lake, and I'd secretly thought that couldn't be beat. But I'd been wrong.

As I gazed out my window, a vast expanse of the forest swept before me. In the distance, hills rose and fell, and even further away, blue mountains soared toward the heavens. Sunlight dappled the greenery, dancing off the trees. I imagined that in the autumn, the scenery would be spectacular.

I sat on my bed, taking everything in, and my lips curled up. I had earned this. For months, I had been terrible at magic, and it wasn't even my fault. After Alex released the bind on my power, I'd improved drastically. It was like I'd reaped all the benefits of my hard work in mere days.

But the rest of our class didn't know that.

They didn't know that I had been spellbound as a child,

because like Alex and my connection to Morgan and Merlin, I hadn't told them.

I doubt there's a single couple in the academy's history that has more secrets than us.

Unfortunately, I couldn't make our secret public. Not without putting everyone around me in danger.

CHAPTER FOUR

The feast that marked the beginning of the new academic year was held in Agnes Sampson Hall. To mark the occasion, I wore my favorite green maxi dress. Eva dressed up too, sporting fitted black trousers, a white blouse, and oversized emerald jewelry. She looked as though she belonged on Wall Street.

"The green necklace goes amazing with your hair," I said, only a tad envious of my friend's bright red hair.

She wrapped her arm through mine and gave me a grin. "We both look awesome."

The guys had said they'd be in the common space waiting for us. When we reached the bottom of the winding stairs, I spotted them among a crowd of female students.

No surprise there. Eva and I had lucked out snagging the talented, charming, intelligent, and hot-as-hell Wardwell cousins as our boyfriends. People—ladies in particular—couldn't help but be drawn to our guys.

Before we reached Hunter and Alex, someone called my name, and I twisted to find my friend Amethyst approaching.

"Hey girl," I said, relieved to see a friendly face. A few peers, many who had congratulated me at the end of our Culling-year, were definitely serving me some side-eye.

"Hey, ladies! Looking good." Amethyst's brown eyes sparkled nearly as much as the shimmering black skirt she wore. "Are you excited about the feast tonight? I heard Headmistress Wake is going to reveal something huge."

"I heard the same thing," I said. "I guess it's why we were told to come back so early."

A large group of our peers walked by, and yet another person—Kira Johnston—gave me the stink eye. I sighed and Eva, catching the interaction, spoke up.

"The feast will start in a few minutes," she said. "We should get going."

She waved Hunter and Alex over, and the guys joined us. When we reached Agnes Sampson Hall, it was already packed. The staff, Crucibles, and the rest of our class sat waiting at tables. On the stage, Headmistress Wake was chatting with stout Professor Umbra of Conjuring. We were still scoping for open spots when an owl hooted through the halls, proclaiming the hour.

Amethyst said she'd catch us later, and flitted off to sit at a table with Mina Köhler, one of her closest friends. Not wanting to be standing around when the feast started, Alex, Hunter, Eva, and I approached a table on the far side of the room.

"Do you mind if we sit here?" I asked the two Crucible students who were already sitting there. I recognized them vaguely, but didn't know their names.

The guy's dark brown eyes opened wide, but the girl I'd pulled up a chair next to looked less surprised by our approach.

"Sure," she said.

Once we'd settled in, she leaned close to me.

"I see that you're already avoiding your fellow Grind students. Welcome to what it's like to be head junior spymasters. I've been in the top spot for my class two years running, which has made me *incredibly* popular, let me tell you." She rolled her eyes and held out her hand. "I'm Sam Pines. Welcome to the club."

"And I'm Andre Allen. It's my first year as head junior spymaster, but I'm feeling the pain, too." The guy smiled wide, and perfect, white teeth gleamed against his onyx skin.

"Odette," I said, shaking their hands even as my heart sank.

Sam and Andre had been sitting by themselves. I already felt set apart from the rest of my class, and we'd only been here a few hours. Were things only going to get worse?

I didn't have much time to ponder the question, because Headmistress Wake stepped up to the mic and cleared her throat. The gabbing crowd quieted instantly.

"Welcome back to Spellcasters." She spread her arms wide, and everyone applauded. "It's wonderful to see so many familiar faces, all healthy and well. As we embark upon the next academic year, I'm pleased to say that we have exciting surprises in store." She snapped her fingers.

The lights dimmed, and I chuckled. Headmistress Wake was stern and often uptight, but she had a tiny flair for the dramatic.

"Usually, I like to allow our students to feast before the evening speeches, but this year I need to prepare you for what's to come. For *this* year, at the end of the feast, I will ask you to make a choice."

"A choice?" Eva whispered, as a curious murmur flew up from the crowd.

The headmistress clapped, and someone walked out from the side of the stage. I sat up straight in my chair, immediately recognizing the man dressed in a blood red cloak and black suit.

"Headmaster Ezra," I whispered.

"Good evening, students." Headmaster Ezra had stopped to stand next to Headmistress Wake, although his voice boomed over the hall without aid from the microphone. "I thank you for allowing me back to your lovely academy. Myself and Headmistress Wake have exciting news for the Grind and Crucible classes of Spellcasters." He glanced at our headmistress.

She inclined her head. "Please, Ezra, do the honors."

Even from where I sat near the back, the vampire's long canines were visible when he beamed. Since their teeth weren't normally *that* pronounced, I figured he must be showing them off.

Which was kinda gross—and freaky.

"Thank you, Headmistress." The vampire rubbed his hands together as if he were about to give us the treat of our lives. Then he flung his arms wide, and the cloak he wore billowed up behind him. "Ladies and gentlemen! The Society of Spies has been deliberating this event for decades, and has finally permitted the four United States spy schools to make it a reality." He paused dramatically, and his smile grew wider. "I'm pleased to announce that this year, we shall hold the first inaugural Spy Games!"

Every muscle in my body stiffened. All around me, excited chatter rose, but it fell nearly as fast when Headmistress Wake clapped for silence.

Headmaster Ezra continued. "The purpose of the Games is to promote friendly rivalry and forge bonds between the four magical spy schools of the United States—Nightdwellers, Spellcasters, the Fae Academy of Elemental and Arcane Arts, and the Shifter Academy of Spies. But of course, there will be prizes too. Each champion from the winning school will receive $20,000, in addition to another little bonus."

He began to walk around the stage, his eyes piercing the crowd, teasing us as the excitement over what the bonus could be mounted. "As you know, each academy insists that their students undergo internships over the summer. Whoever wins the tournament will have their choice of study, or in the case of graduating students, employment. These internships include *global* opportunities."

A gasp went up from the crowd. That was huge. The

United States was home to many amazing witches, but so were other countries. Especially the European and Asian schools, where witching magic had run in bloodlines for centuries. But the U.S. government didn't allow students to study with non-Americans as part of our curriculum because they needed as much control over us as possible. This was the chance of a lifetime.

"Yes. It's all very exciting, I know. Now, for the bit you might not like to hear," Headmaster Ezra said. "As each school has three academic levels in attendance, the headmasters and headmistresses have decided to select two students from each of the upper classes to take part in the tournament. Whether you will throw your hat into the ring is your choice. But I advise you not to take this lightly. If selected, you must participate in each game, and these games *will* be dangerous."

Around me, a few people murmured excitedly.

"Thank you, Headmaster Ezra, for that rousing invitation," Headmistress Wake said, taking control of the mic.

The vampire bowed, then leapt off the stage and went to sit at the table with Professors Umbra, Tittelbaum, and de Spina.

"As Headmaster Ezra said, two students from both the Grind and Crucible-years are eligible to participate. However, I have made the decision that, for my school, the five Grind and Crucible-year students with the rank of spymaster get first pick. If they decline, I will appraise the other applicants, and select those I believe will best represent our school. You have until the end of dinner to decide whether to submit your name for consideration." The Headmistress paused, and her face became serious. "Be advised that Headmaster Ezra is correct in stating that these games will be dangerous. They will be on par with the missions we send you on. And speaking of, those who take part in the games are *not* exempt from any regular school work, including missions. If a Spy Game event takes place during an exam or on a deadline date, professors will give the school champions extensions, but *not* exemptions. That being said, I will leave you to your decision." She clapped her hands, and waiters rushed out from the sides of the room. "Dinner is served."

Servers began setting massive platters down in the center of the tables so that students could serve themselves family-style. I barely noticed them stopping at ours to deposit plates of chicken, beef, mac and cheese, roasted vegetables, and other delicious smelling dishes. I was too engrossed in what I'd heard.

The waiters left, and still no one at our table had spoken.

And I knew why.

Everyone at our table was ranked spymaster. We had first choice to enter the competition.

The quiet had almost become unbearable when someone bumped into my chair.

"I'm *so* entering. Are you guys?" Diana was breathless with excitement, as if she'd run a mile and not across the room. Her gaze shifted from me to Alex and back.

She would want to know if we were in, because if we

were, as the *head* junior spymasters for the Grind-year, we'd get chosen over her.

Still, no one spoke, and Diana moved on to stare at Hunter and Eva. They were both spymasters, same as her.

Eva shook her head. "I'm not even going to try. Although, I could use the money for college and grad school after Spellcasters."

I wrinkled my nose. Since the day I'd met her, Eva had insisted that she was not going into espionage after Spellcasters. She wanted to be an archeologist, but her parents had bribed her to attend Spellcasters. They'd wanted her to have the clout that being a graduate of Spellcasters assured. After our internships, I'd hoped that she'd changed her mind, but I guess not.

"But the Grind will be hard enough," Eva continued. "And after what happened this summer . . . I don't need the extra stress."

Hunter nodded. "Me either. I'll stick to my studies." He wrapped an arm around Eva's shoulders, and my heart swelled.

Hunter might want to participate in the tournament—knowing him, he probably did—but he was staying for Eva. They were so sweet together.

"Good. Less competition for me." Diana's gaze shot back to me.

I squirmed beneath her intensity.

What does she do, take staring lessons from her Mom or something?

I dropped my eyes to the table. I wanted to enter. The

chance to study with an elite master warper was *incredibly* enticing. I'd studied with a lower level Master for my internship, but there was so much more to learn—like timewalking. If a warper was capable of timewalking, they were the best of the best. There were only a handful of them in the world—and none in the United States.

My thoughts flitted to Master Măriuca, an elder warper in the wild Carpathian Mountains of Romania. It was said that she had time traveled more than any witch in living memory. She took on students, but never for money. Instead, Măriuca taught only those who had proved themselves to be exceptional.

If anyone could teach me to timewalk, it would be her. And if I won this tournament, I'd surely be proving myself exceptional, right? Not only that, but my judging peers could no longer deny that I'd earned my position.

"I'm in. Can't pass up getting first shot at the good jobs, now can I?" Sam said suddenly.

"Me too," Andre agreed a moment later.

"Not me," Alex said. "I have private healing sessions this year with Professor Medulla, in addition to classes. That should keep me plenty busy."

Diana fist pumped the air. "Yes!"

Alex's reasoning was as good as any. Although I suspected that wasn't his only motive for turning down the games.

I bit my lip and decided it was best to get this over with. "I'm going to do it."

Alex's face hardened, but Diana demanded my attention more by slapping me hard on the shoulder.

"Yeah, Dane! It's a good thing we made up last year, huh?"

"Yeah," I agreed. Hell, if we hadn't, I would have insisted that Alex participate so I wouldn't have to partner with Diana. But there was no need for that now.

"Awesome. I can't wait to tell Mother." Diana dashed off and, against my better judgment, my eyes shifted to Alex.

He shook his head, and in the thin set of his lips, I read frustration. He did not agree with my choice.

I inhaled a soft breath. Later, when we were alone, I was sure to be in for quite the talk.

CHAPTER FIVE

t the end of the feast, I hung back to tell Headmistress Wake that I was interested in being the Spellcasters champion. Once I'd been assured a spot, I left Agnes Sampson Hall and had just caught sight of Eva and Hunter, when Alex swooped in.

He wrapped his hand around my wrist. "Can we take a walk?" His eyes blazed with intensity, even though his tone was measured and careful.

I nodded as my stomach twisted into knots.

Across the room, Eva shot me a sympathetic look, but I couldn't say no to him. He was my boyfriend, and even though after eight months we *still* hadn't said it out loud because I was weird about relationships and needed to move slowly, I loved him. Plus, Alex's frustration over my choice was justified.

I'd done the exact opposite of what M&M told us to do.

Even though I realized that about halfway through the feast, I'd stuck by my choice.

In my defense, this wasn't the first time Alex and I would be separated. Our internships had been hours from each other, and after that, we'd lived on opposite coasts for three weeks. We hadn't wanted to part in either instance, but a healing internship with Tiberius Thorn had been too good an opportunity for Alex to pass up. And what would our parents have said if we'd told them we needed to always be together?

It wouldn't have gone over well in my house.

We broke from the crowd, and walked out the front door of the academy, toward the lake. Anxiety bubbled inside me. Alex hadn't spoken a word, but I knew he was angry. Sweat began to trickle down my back as I debated what to say—how to defend my actions.

"Why did you do that?" The question burst from him as we stepped onto the lake path. "Morgan and Merlin said we needed to stick together. We can't help that Head-mistress Wake will separate us on missions, but there's no need for you to leave the safety of Spellcasters outside of those. Especially without me."

A swathe of nerves eased at his statement. I arched an eyebrow. "The 'safety of Spellcasters'? You mean the same place where three of our classmates died last year?" Alex's cheeks darkened, and my tone softened accordingly. "I'm not sure we're safer here than anywhere else, babe."

Alex's lips flattened. "You heard Diana and the head-mistress talking about all the extra precautions. They might be oblivious to what's happening with Morgan and Merlin, but they *know* about the demons."

I bit my lower lip, still not buying it. "I'm sure their wards are all fine and dandy—against a lesser demon. But Ishtar or Lucifer? Or even the Prince and Princesses of Hell? No one has been up against them in living memory."

I paused. My statement was no longer true. Alex, Hunter, and I had gone up against the Queen of Hell just a few weeks ago.

"Well, no one except us," I amended. "And we needed a fair bit of luck to get through that." I patted the spot where my totem, a ruby and moonstone encrusted necklace that had once belonged to Morgan Le Fay, rested beneath the scoop neck of my dress.

At my touch, the totem warmed, as if asking if I needed anything. It was strange how the magical object operated, but it had saved my butt a few times, so while I wished I understood it better, I wasn't about to complain.

"And no offense to the headmistress, but if any of the royals of Hell want to breach the academy wards, they'll figure out a way," I continued. "We already know that they're experimenting with new methods to infiltrate our realm. A few wards won't stop them."

Suddenly, a *crack* rang through the night as Alex turned and slammed his fist into a tree. "Dammit, Odie. Why are you making this so hard? Can't you see you're putting yourself in unnecessary danger?"

I threw up my hands. "Of course I can! But I can't help it! I have something to prove to people. They don't think

I'm good enough for the spymaster position. I want to show them otherwise. You can't judge me for that. Not after taking the internship with Tiberius that was three hours away when there was a perfectly respectable healer in Portland. You can't judge me for wanting the best, because that's what you want too."

He jerked back.

I pressed my lips together hard. Had I gone too far? We'd both agreed that Alex's internship was important, just like mine was. There were things Thorn could teach him that no other healer in the country could. Considering our circumstances having a skilled healer around seemed paramount. And as not a single warper lived in Seattle, separating had been a fair compromise. I still believed that.

So why had I thrown that in his face? It was a dick move.

"This choice might change my future, babe." My voice softened. "Imagine if I won and got to study with a timewalker . . ."

"I understand the draw. And you deserve to study with the best, because I honestly think that, one day, you could be among them." Alex released a long exhale. "But I don't like the idea of you running around other academies alone."

"There will be hundreds of magicals at those games, watching whatever torture the heads of each school cooks up. Three other champions from Spellcasters are going, *and* Headmistress Wake. It's not like I'll be alone. On our missions, we'll only have a partner, but you're not arguing about *those* anymore."

"I'm *not* fine with the arrangements of our missions." Alex clenched his fists at his sides. "I've been pissed as hell all day long that Headmistress Wake won't give in to what we asked. Pissed that I can't just tell her the whole truth because who knows how that could affect our futures. And mostly, I'm furious that I don't know what's happening to us!" He practically roared the last word. Pivoting to face the tree, Alex struck it five more times before his hands fell to his side.

I stepped back, watching his arms tremble. I'd expected anger, but this was a whole new level. He'd mentioned it before—the infamous Wardwell temper—but I'd never witnessed it for myself.

My Alex remained in control, even in the most dire of circumstances.

"Hey," I whispered, "you have to calm down."

Alex's shoulders relaxed. A few seconds later, he turned to me, and I saw tears running down his face.

"How can you say that, Odie? How can I be calm? So much shit is going to happen this year, and I won't be able to watch over you."

"You don't have to," I said. "We're a team. We look out for each other. This isn't a one-sided thing. It never has been. Remember Ishtar?"

His lips quirked up a touch. "How could I forget my girlfriend coming to save me from the Queen of Hell?" Alex shook his head. "But that isn't the point, sweets. I know this isn't one-sided. It's just that . . . I can't bear to lose you. I would break. Shatter. I—" His mouth snapped shut. He gulped and glanced down at his hands. Blood covered them, but he wiped it off on his pants before closing the distance between us to inches.

"Odie, I love you."

My breath hitched.

Long ago, I'd suggested that I be the one to say it first. I was weird with relationships, and had *never* told any guy I loved them. I hadn't wanted to feel pressured to move too fast. Alex had agreed at the time, but apparently, the restriction had been too much.

And honestly, it was kind of silly. Even though he'd been a massive dick the day we'd met, I'd fallen in love with Alex Wardwell right then and there. So why hadn't I been able to tell him in the months since then? Why had I felt the need to wait?

There was too much to lose.

A lump formed in my throat. There was still an enormous amount to lose. If Morgan and Merlin were right, Alex and I were destined to accomplish great things and have an unparalleled love.

I hadn't wanted to risk starting something like that, only to have it all crash to the floor.

But just because I didn't say the words didn't mean that I didn't feel them. For months, love had burned in my soul. It was time that I told him.

My hands dropped to clasp his, and I brought both pairs to my heart, which was thumping hard. They rested against my totem, and the object began to glow bright red. Alex's totem, a ring with a moonstone to match the one in my necklace, lit up the exact same shade. Red light illuminated our faces, making them shine, otherworldly and beautiful in the dimming evening light. My lips tugged upward. The damn totems were so frustrating and mysterious, but they sure knew how to set the mood.

"Odie . . .?"

I realized that I'd been silent for too long. I'd left the poor guy hanging.

I pressed a finger to his lips. "I'm sealing this moment in my memory," I whispered. Removing my finger, I looked deeply into his eyes, and the three tiny words that I'd fretted about for months didn't seem so scary. They felt like the only truth in this world.

"I love you too, Alex."

He didn't even speak, only pulled me close so that our lips crashed together. We kissed hungrily as our hands roamed over each other's body, all the tension of moments before forgotten as if it had never been.

As if the entire world was just us.

CHAPTER SIX

Our free day before classes began flew by. As spymasters, my best friends and I were among the ten upperclassmen tasked with meeting initiates upon their arrival at the academy and showing them to the first-year tower. It took *hours*, but I did my best to make sure that everyone felt welcomed. I didn't want any of the new Culling students feeling like I had at the start of my first year.

It was an unfortunate tradition that the Spellcasters upperclassmen ignored the first-years until after February. The practice stemmed from the belief that it was dumb to waste time on people who may not be around if they didn't pass the Samhain Trial or the Imbolc Challenge.

I thought the practice was idiotic, and that belief was validated as I met the Culling students.

Most of them seemed really cool, and two particular girls, Heidi and Holly, reminded me so much of Eva and me that I ended up giving them a tour of the whole academy.

I was preparing for my first class and reminding myself to introduce Eva to the girls, when someone knocked on my dormitory door.

"You ready?" Alex asked as I opened the door.

Mascara wand in hand, I glanced at the clock as I returned to the bathroom. "But we still have twenty minutes."

His cheeks pinked. "It's a new class for us. New professor, too. We wouldn't want to be late."

I arched an eyebrow. "No, we wouldn't want the healing golden boy to be late for his first Intermediate Healing course." I laughed at Alex's sheepish expression. He was so excited to finally be in a class focused purely on healing that he'd been talking about it for weeks. "It's okay, babe. Even if you don't show up to half the classes, I'm sure Professor Medulla will still think you're the best thing since sliced bread. Remind me, how many *other* students has he recommended that Tiberius Thorn take them on as interns?"

Alex barged into the room, wrapped his arms around my waist, and lifted me up for a kiss. "Yeah, yeah," he said when we broke apart. "You've made your point. We don't have to rush." His hands slid to my hips, and he pressed himself against me.

I waved the mascara wand in front of his face. "Oh no. We don't have to rush, but we definitely don't have time for *that*." I pointed at my face. "That is, unless you want your girlfriend showing up to class with half her face done, and wearing a telling flush."

Alex gave me a roguish smile. "I don't mind."

I whacked him on the shoulder. "Well, I do! Sit down while I finish my makeup."

He obliged, and I went back to applying mascara. When I finished, I peeked out of the bathroom to find him playing with my totem, which I'd left on the bed with my other accessories.

The piece was lighting up at his touch, just as it normally did when our totems were next to each other.

"I wish I knew why they did that," I said.

Alex nodded. "Me too. I'm tempted to ask during our totem workshop, but I know neither of us feel comfortable with that yet."

"Not yet," I agreed. "Hopefully, once we learn a little more, we can share. Don't worry, babe. There are numerous totem workshops on the schedule."

"What *isn't* on the schedule?"

He had a point. We'd received a notice of our full course load yesterday, and boy was it a doozy.

Every day, the Grind students had seven one-hour class sessions, three of which were advanced level magic courses. In addition to regular classes, we had to spend a minimum of six hours in the Physical Conditioning room every week, and attend workshops every other weekend. Eventually, we'd squeeze in specialty tutoring too. Those sessions would be erratic, as they'd depend on our mentors' schedules.

And then there were our three required Grind missions. They were like our initiate trials on steroids and could last up to four days.

There was a reason they called the second year at Spellcasters the Grind. It could wear a person down. While I was excited for it to start, I knew that balancing all that—hell, getting through it alive—would take a crapload of skill. And way more sleepless nights than I wanted to consider.

I sighed and slipped my totem over my head. The moonstone in the center lit up when it touched my skin and cycled through the colors of the rainbow before resuming its regular appearance.

"All ready," I said, grabbing a thin sweater to wear over my t-shirt.

It was July, but the academy was an old, massive, mostly stone building, which meant it was always drafty. Some areas, like the basement where Battle Magic took place, were downright cold. This Californian didn't appreciate freezing her hiney off, so I carried a sweater everywhere.

"Great." Alex glanced at the clock and, seeing that we still had ten minutes, smiled. "We'll be sure to get good seats."

While I'd met Professor Medulla, I'd never seen his healing sanctuary. He'd taught us a bartending workshop in a stark, unused classroom, and I'd expected much the same of the sanctuary. So when I stepped inside it for the first time, the ambiance took me by surprise.

Dozens of amber bottles filled with elixirs lined the walls. Massive bundles of dried herbs and flowers hung from the ceilings. Crystals of all sizes and colors charged on the windowsill. And metal devices, none of which looked reassuring, rested on tables around the room. It even smelled different from most of our other classes, like a meadow, with faint undertones of rubbing alcohol.

"Wow," I exhaled, taking everything in.

"It's something, isn't it?" Alex's eyes shone with excitement as he pulled me to the front of the class.

Surprisingly, Hunter and Eva were already there.

"Hey, early birds," I said as we claimed a table next to them. "What got you two here so quick?"

"Medulla wanted to see Eva and check out her scars before class started," Hunter explained.

I became more confused. Professor Medulla knew of Eva's predicament. He'd been among the many healers who had tried to erase her scars when we thought they were inflicted by a greater demon, and not a more powerful royal. However, he'd since learned otherwise. If he couldn't eliminate the scars back then, why would he think he'd be capable of banishing them now?

"I told him there was no point," Eva shrugged. "But he insisted. And since he's one of our professors this year, I thought it would be stupid to deny him another shot."

"Good call," Alex said. "He's no Tiberius Thorn, but Medulla is prideful."

"Must be a healer trait," I tickled Alex's side.

He scoffed playfully. "Prideful? I resemble that remark."

We all chuckled, but pulled ourselves together the moment tall and portly Professor Medulla waddled into the room.

"This is Intermediate Healing," the red-faced man said. "If you are a Crucible or Culling student, you should not be here. You should also stop by the infirmary and get your eyes checked, because none of these people are in your year, and yet you remained in this classroom."

A hearty laugh boomed from Alex, making me jump. I twisted to look at my boyfriend and arched an eyebrow. It hadn't been *that* funny.

But when Professor Medulla's face lit up at Alex's response, I understood the show. Alex hadn't been joking when he said the healing professor was prideful.

Clearly, Alex wants to keep his Golden Boy status.

"Welcome to your Grind year," Medulla continued. "I trust that all of you are prepared to work hard and learn. If not, you'd better change your frame of mind, as we cover many aspects of healing in this course alone. These are the subjects you will encounter this year."

The professor faced the whiteboard. With a twirl of his hands, words began forming on the surface. I read them as quickly as they appeared.

Syllabus:

Cell biology

Gross anatomy

Herbalism and plant identification

Healing potions

Poisonous substances and their bodily effects

Magical creatures with healing capabilities

Energy healing

Crystal healing

Magical identification of pathogens

Magical elimination of pathogens

A healer's toolkit to battle mental illness

Introduction to surgery

Introduction to midwifery

"Holy hell," I whispered under my breath as I took in the laundry list of things I was expected to stuff into my brain.

Alex didn't look surprised, but then again, he'd sat in on some Grind seminars last year. He might not have been allowed to attend the regular classes, but he'd surely heard the students talking about their schedule.

"We will start with an overview of the basics that you should have already learned. This stage will only last a few days. I'd simply like to know how much you have retained from the survey course Herbalism, Potions, and Poisons. Some of those subcategories can be transferred into healing; most notably, herbalism and potions. Although poisons is not to be dismissed."

"It's all about the dose," Alex chimed in, which made Professor Medulla beam.

I pressed my lips together to keep from laughing. If I didn't know how ecstatic he was about this class, I would have thought Alex was the biggest suck-up to ever live.

"That is correct, Mr. Wardwell. Even for herbs and normally benign potions. After my initial assessment, we'll focus on the hard sciences before learning how to apply magic for healing."

A few people groaned at the mention of hard sciences, but the professor gave a dismissive wave of his hand. "You may not like it. But understanding the biochemical reactions of the body is necessary for healers—even those who only work with magic."

Alex nodded enthusiastically. I rolled my eyes. My boyfriend was such a huge, adorable nerd.

"As for today, we will focus on herbalism." The professor raised his arm, and a swirl of teal magic flew from his hands. I followed the shimmering colors as they wove through the bundles of flowers and herbs above us to untie every ribbon and lower the bundles to the tables below. "Each of these specimens has been numbered. Without talking, I'd like you to walk about the room and identify them."

My heart skipped a beat. All of them? But it was only our first day, and there had to be at least eighty bundles of flowers and herbs on the desks. Sure, some of them were easy—like rosemary and sage—but some of these plants, I had never seen before.

"Best of luck to you." One corner of Professor Medulla's lips lifted as he read the reactions in the room. "Your time starts now."

CHAPTER SEVEN

"*That* was *beyond* ridiculous." Eva threw her hands in the air once we were a fair distance away from the healing sanctuary.

"That's one way to put it." My brain physically hurt from all the stuff Medulla considered an overview.

"Thank goodness you were there, cuz. Otherwise our class would have looked like a bunch of idiots." Hunter punched Alex's shoulder, the way guys do.

Alex beamed. He had correctly listed off every single plant Professor Medulla wanted us to identify and only missed one potion. And thank the universe for his expertise. Judging by my first Intermediate Healing session, I would need some major help to pass the class.

"Studying with Tiberius helped me a lot," Alex said. "I should call and thank him for introducing me to his method of olfactory identification. I never would have gotten that last flower otherwise."

Eva, Hunter, and I glanced at each other and burst out laughing.

"What?" Alex asked, his eyebrows pulled together. "Do I have catchweed on my nose again?" He rubbed at his nose.

"No. We're laughing because you sound like a huge geek," Hunter joked.

Alex scowled, and his eyes swept to me.

Unable to stop laughing, I shrugged. "Sorry, babe. The truth hurts."

Alex stuck out his tongue. "Fine. See if this geek offers to be study buddies with any of you."

We begged for forgiveness all the way to the academy entryway, where the hidden entrance to the Battle Magic classroom was located. We were about to descend the staircase when Headmistress Wake swung around the corner.

"Miss Dane. Might I have a word about the Spy Games?"

"Of course." I turned to my friends. "I'll see you in Battle Magic."

They nodded, and I strode over to join the headmistress.

"I wanted to check that you were still interested in the Games?" Headmistress Wake asked once we were face-to-face. "I know we said that once you announced your interest that you were bound, but all the headmasters and headmistresses involved decided to give their academy champions a couple of days to mull it over. We realize that sometimes decisions take on a new light after the excitement of a new venture wears off. The first event of the Games will occur in late-September, and the other events will follow every two months. Is that a schedule you can commit to?"

I wanted to say yes right away, but Alex's cautions stopped me. Determined to weigh all the pros and cons, I mentally ran through my reasons to enter, and then Alex's reasons not to. To me, the pros far outweighed the cons. The Spy Games offered many opportunities, whereas not entering felt like I was letting the bad guys win. Plus, my missions were sure to be just as dangerous, and there was no getting out of those.

"I'm still interested."

Headmistress Wake smiled. "I can't say I'm surprised. You and Diana are two of the most driven women in your class. With Sam and Andre at your side, the Spellcasters team should do well. Congratulations, then, Miss Dane." She stuck out her hand.

We shook, and the headmistress gave me a brief nod of pride before marching down the corridor.

"Did you tell her you still wanted to be a champion?"

I turned around to find Alex standing in the same place I'd left him. His face was hard and his lips tight. I hadn't realized that he'd been waiting for me.

"I told you I wanted to do it, babe. Why are you so surprised?"

"I thought . . . after our discussion—our *proclamation*, you might've changed your mind."

My lips formed an O. "Babe, I never said I'd changed my mind. I said I love you."

"People who are in love take each other's feelings into account, Odie," Alex said. "I thought you would understand that."

"Excuse me?" I blinked. "What does that even mean?"

"I just—"

"Class starts in one minute. Get yer arses into my classroom now." The thick Scottish brogue of Professor Thrax cut through me, and I twisted to find him walking toward us. "Just because it's the first day dinnae mean you get a break."

"Yes, Professor Thrax," Alex and I said together.

As soon as the professor had vanished down the stairs, I caught Alex's gaze again. "Can we talk about this later—like, *really* talk about it? Maybe tonight?"

Alex didn't respond, just disappeared down the stairs.

My lips parted in surprise. Since we'd been dating, Alex had never turned his back on me. That single gesture told me how pissed off he really was.

During Advanced Battle Magic, Alex's anger only seemed to intensify. Professor Thrax divided us up into groups, and while Alex was not in my group, I watched him closely, and winced as he pummeled José Valdez, Kira Johnston, and Dakota Wily with a ferocity I'd never witnessed before.

If all three of them weren't among the people shunning me for daring to earn the rank of spymaster, I would almost feel bad for them.

"What happened? You're not performing well, and he . . . ." Eva gestured to Alex, who was brooding on the far side of the room while we stopped to get water. "Seems like he wants to tear down the classroom."

I released a sigh. Professor Thrax had already commented on my use of shoddy spellmanship twice. And Jasmine Sahni, another Odie-hater and one of my sparring group members, had also remarked on my lack of prowess with a smug smile. Maybe if I told Eva what was bugging me, I'd be able to concentrate better.

"He doesn't want me to be the champion."

"But I thought you guys worked through that?"

I hadn't mentioned that Alex and I had said the "L" word, but I could see why Eva would think things were all good. We'd been affectionate and carefree the last couple of days. Apparently, because Alex had thought I intended to give in to what he wanted.

"Well, we fought over the games, but ended the fight by saying 'I love you'. I guess, in Alex's mind, that meant that I wasn't taking part in the Spy Games anymore. Even though I *never* said that. It was more that neither of us brought it up again because things were good."

"Oh shit." Eva shook her head.

"Yeah. A classic case of not talking through our issues." I facepalmed myself. "Anyway, Headmistress Wake asked me if I was still up for the Games right before class, and Alex heard." I gestured to where Alex had started fiercely sparring again. "Now he's taking it out on his group."

Eva winced as one of Alex's sizzling spells swept past Kira, and singed off a thin black braid.

"He's definitely being more aggressive than usual." She shook her head and then turned back to me. "Do you want Hunter to talk to him? He remembers last year and sees how people are reacting to you now. He thinks you should compete. Maybe he can work some cousin magic."

My lips tilted up in a smile. "That's sweet, but—"

"I'm serious, Odie. We were there when everyone was treating you like shit. It's not *so* bad this year, but it feels similar." She nodded to Alex. "I think that might be why he doesn't understand. He wasn't there at the start. He was one of the people looking down their noses at you. And even though he loves you now, I don't think he comprehends how hard those first few months were. Or how badly you want to cement your reputation in this society."

Eva was right. How could Alex understand completely? The moment he'd arrived at Spellcasters, he'd been the top student and very popular.

"You think Hunter can smooth it out a little before we talk?" I didn't need him settling my relationship problems, but if he could calm Alex down a bit, I would be grateful.

Eva waved her hand to indicate it would be a piece of cake. "They get each other, you know? I'll tell Hunter to talk to him at lunch." She wrapped her arm through mine.

"You and I will find those two girls you wanted to introduce me to, and we'll have some lady time."

I grinned. Some girl time was well overdue.

"Oh my God, I about died when de Spina showed us our first demon conjuring!" Heidi held a hand over her mouth, and her eyes widened.

I laughed, recalling my very similar reaction all too vividly. "What was it?"

"A wraith!" Holly exclaimed while simultaneously batting away a pigeon that was steering a little too close to where her sandwich lay on the picnic blanket. "So gray and wrinkly and ugly. And all those teeth!"

"It seems as though de Spina doesn't like to deviate much," Eva giggled. "That was the first thing he showed us too. You should have seen Odie's face when it appeared in class."

I tickled her side. "Oh, and you were so tough, Proctor?"

We tossed a few good-natured jabs back and forth before we realized that the younger girls were staring at us with smiles on their faces.

"Sorry," I said, turning my attention to Holly and Heidi. "We got a little carried away."

"Don't be sorry," Heidi said. "I like seeing that you guys are so close. We've heard stories about what you two went through. It's kinda awesome that you have each other to lean on." She glanced at Holly. "I hope we can stay that way too, no matter what this academy throws at us."

My heart grew three sizes. I freaking loved seeing strong sisterhoods. "And I hope you both know you can depend on Eva and me too."

"We appreciate that so much," Holly said.

As our lunch progressed, my anxiety over Alex melted away. By the time Conjuring and Transfiguration rolled around, I felt confident that he needed space.

It seemed that Hunter had worked his magic during lunch, because the moment Alex walked into Professor Umbra's class, I noticed that he appeared less tense. We still didn't talk much, and certainly not about our issues, but he wasn't avoiding me and even passed me a pen after I dropped it. I hadn't expected a miracle right away anyhow.

Our first day of classes stretched on longer than I ever could have expected. When the torture finally ended, I retreated to my room. I had just set my book bag on my bed when a knock came at my door.

When I opened it, Alex stood in the hallway, his messenger bag still sitting on his hip. He hadn't even dropped it off before coming to my room.

"Can we talk?"

"Come on in." I sat on the bed and patted the spot next to me.

"I'm sorry for freaking out on you," Alex blurted as soon as he joined me. "And I'm also sorry for assuming that because we took our relationship to the next level, everything would be fine, and you wouldn't want to participate in the Spy Games."

"Thanks for acknowledging that." Although it was a little jarring, I took Alex's quick and thorough apology in stride. We'd been here before. Swift apologies was how he operated. "But I know just because you regret becoming upset with me, doesn't mean you'll support me fully in this."

I understood where Alex's concern came from, but I didn't agree. Morgan and Merlin were irritatingly vague, and we'd been apart twice already and hadn't keeled over.

He shook his head. "Of course not. I love you, babe. I want you safe and preferably close to me all the time."

"Errr, that's sweet and a little creepy."

One corner of his lips quirked up. "You know what I mean. Not like a stalker. Like a protector. Until we get all of this worked out, I'll feel the need to protect you."

"You realize the feeling is mutual, right? I'm not the only one the demons are after. I'm just the only one they can control if Ishtar makes it to this realm." I frowned.

"I'm aware that they want us both equally, and because of that, I have a proposition for you."

He reached inside his messenger bag and pulled out a small, leather-bound book titled *Magical Objects for Safety and Protection*.

"Do we have to find something to keep us safe?"

Alex shook his head. "There are some rare objects in here that have been enchanted by powerful witches and wizards, but there are also spells to enchant everyday objects too. They'll let you know if your loved ones are safe."

"How did you learn about them?"

"After the Beltane Trials, my parents told me about this book. They wanted to make some of these objects them-selves." His cheeks turned bright red. "I refused."

If we hadn't made up only seconds before, I would've pointed out the hypocrisy in that decision. As it was, I let it slide. I hated arguing with him.

"So you want to make something that lets us know if the other one is safe?"

My gaze caught Alex's ring, and I placed my hand over it. The moonstone began to cycle through the colors of the rainbow before settling on white once again. "If only our totems would do that, we would have less to worry about."

He let out an irritated laugh. "I thought the same thing."

Flipping to a page in the middle of the book, Alex pointed out a spell for protection. "This one responds to your heart rate, which could be a little dicey. The academy likes to scare the shit out of us all the time. But if we cast it so that the enchanted talisman responded to heart rate *and* another factor that we can control, then I think it might be perfect. This way the person in trouble can warn the other person."

My eyes ran down the page. The incantation didn't seem difficult. It didn't even require any unusual ingredi-ents, or magic that Alex and I couldn't perform.

"I say we try it. The worst thing that happens is it

doesn't work. Then we pick something else out of this book, and give it a whirl."

Alex gave me a small smile. "Exactly." He leaned in, and our lips met in a tender kiss. "Thanks for being willing to try this out, sweets. I need something to let me know that you're okay when we can't be in the same place." He closed the book and placed his hands over the top. "Also, I've been thinking that maybe you should try to teach me how to warp."

My eyebrows shot up. That would not have been my next logical train of thought. "Warping? But, babe, you know it's a rare talent."

As soon as the words left my mouth, I realized how snobbish I sounded. Still, I couldn't take it back, because it was true. Warpers were one of the rarest types of witches. So rare that no one knew if the talent was genetic or not. Neither of my parents were warpers, but I suspected that it had been passed through one of them—whichever was the descendant of Morgan Le Fay.

"I know it's rare and difficult," Alex said. "I'm fully prepared to fail. But trying would make me feel as if I'm doing everything that I can. Think about it. What if you're the one in trouble, how am I going to get to you?"

He was right. It was worth a shot. And while I wasn't confident in my teaching abilities at that moment, I had an idea that could work.

"You have a point. My mentorship with Professor Tittel-baum begins in a few days. Apparently, he's also teaching a new warper. I'll take notes on what he says, and when I feel like I can teach you well enough, we'll begin lessons."

"Why not tomorrow?"

"I know this is urgent, but I want to make sure I know what to do and say." I cupped his face. "I'd be pissed if I told you something wrong, and you made some funky warphole that screwed up your pretty face."

Alex snorted. "That would be a shame, wouldn't it?"

"A tragedy," I agreed, and leaned in for one more kiss.

CHAPTER EIGHT

he weeks passed by in a haze of classes, physical conditioning, various spymaster obligations, and long nights filled with studying. Before I knew it, August had arrived, and the first Spy Games event loomed only a month and a half away.

Somewhere in the mire of school work and training, Alex and I had succeed in creating our protection talisman —a small prophetess pendant that Spellcasters had gifted the Culling students at the end of last term. When we'd first received it, neither Alex nor I had known what to do with the charm. But after two failed attempts at enchanting it, the dime-sized emblem now had a fantastic purpose.

Alex hung his around his neck, while I'd opted to make my talisman a bracelet. If we ever found ourselves in serious trouble, all we had to do was touch the pendant and say the word *"suppetia"*. The combination of an elevated heart rate, our touch, and the magic word would cause the charm's twin to glow red-hot, alerting the other wearer to danger.

The moment I clasped the bracelet around my wrist, Alex calmed down. Since then, our relationship had been carefree. Well, mostly. The threat of the royals of Hell always lingered in the back of my mind, and probably Alex's too. But because we couldn't control it, we did our best to ignore it.

Luckily, we had about a billion things on our mind to help us forget our problems. The courses we continued from last year were as challenging as ever, and the new ones were even harder. For me, the most difficult course was definitely Divination and Tarot. Whether we spent the hour reading tea leaves, staring into crystal balls, or sloshing water around a scrying bowl, I was terrible at all aspects of fortune-telling.

In Divination and Tarot, we worked in pairs, so one person could read the other's fortune. Since we were all beginners, I could easily take most of what my peers said with a grain of salt. That is, until the day Professor Videns paired me with Amethyst Rhines.

Amethyst had proven herself gifted in Divination and Tarot from day one. According to Professor Videns, this should have come as no surprise to anyone. The Rhines family excelled at spirit walking and talking, which indicated a predilection to communing with the other side.

As my friend took up the stool on the other side of my table, fear over what she would predict gripped me.

"Do you want to go first, or should I?" Amethyst asked.

I grabbed the cards, determined to perform such a drawn-out reading that Amethyst would never get the chance to read my future. Unfortunately, my plans were foiled rather quickly by Professor Videns claiming it was time to switch moments later.

"Ten cards is the extent of your abilities, Miss Dane." He waved his hands, and the deck reshuffled itself and landed before Amethyst.

"It's time to let Miss Rhines practice," the professor said. "I have yet to feel a jolt from the other side in this room, and I so wish to experience that today." He gave his star pupil a gracious smile before gliding away.

"I thought you did well," Amethyst said kindly.

"Oh please," I gave her a dismissive wave of my hand. "I made all that crap up. Don't put any stock in what I said. I'm a total hack."

Amethyst giggled, and from the corner of my eye, I caught Joseph, a quiet guy in our year, glance over and wink at her. She noticed too, and her cheeks grew red.

I arched an eyebrow and leaned over the table. "Did Joseph wink at you?"

She grabbed the crystal ball and began repositioning it, her cheeks darkening as she did so.

"Girl . . ." My voice dropped low. "Do you have a crush on Joseph?"

Amethyst pressed her lips together. "Maybe."

A giggle rang out of my throat. "You go! He is one hot hunk of a witch."

My partner's face broke out in an embarrassed smile as

she looked up to catch my eye. "I know, right? I had a thing for him last year, but he never noticed me. And to be honest, I was struggling in a lot of classes, so I tried to push it aside. But this year, it's—different."

Amethyst had been struggling? I wouldn't have guessed that. Although the part about this year being different made sense. She'd clearly been practicing over the summer break. And having a new course like Divination and Tarot come easy must have boosted her confidence too.

"Well, he was totally checking you out." I waggled my eyebrows.

"If you two are quite done gossiping . . ." Professor Videns came up behind me once again, and my heart rate spiked. How did he expect anyone to "tap into the other side" when he kept sneaking up on us like that? The man barely made a sound when he moved. "I think you should proceed with your readings. Amethyst?"

Amethyst nodded and stared into the crystal ball. Her hands began sweeping over it, like I'd seen old fortune tellers do in the movies, and her eyes softened. She mumbled a couple incantations to enhance clairvoyance, and then closed her eyes.

Appeased that we were doing what we were supposed to, the professor finally moved on.

The pit in my stomach deepened as I watched Amethyst, dreading what she might predict, and partially in awe over how relaxed she looked behind the crystal ball. I was always squinting and blinking too hard in hopes that something would appear.

The minutes passed, and I'd started to wonder if Amethyst had fallen asleep with her eyes open when her hands flung upward to grasp her throat. Her eyes grew round and wide, and her breathing became ragged, labored, as if her windpipe was obstructed.

"Amethyst! What's going on? Are you okay?" I shot up and pivoted to get help, but my friend grabbed my wrist.

"Do not move or speak, or else the girl dies."

My throat constricted, and my eyes dropped to my ankle, where the demon-touched mark was branded into my skin. Shockingly, it didn't burn or even tingle, but that didn't matter. I would recognize that voice anywhere. Ishtar was speaking through—no, *possessing*—Amethyst.

"Yes, you have identified me correctly, mortal," the Queen of Hell said, pleasure at being recognized obvious in her tone.

"How did you get here?" I squeaked. "Why can't I feel you?"

The second I said it, I realized that I did feel *something*. It was malevolent and cold, but very muted. Nothing like the powerful energy that had rolled off Ishtar the night I met her in New York.

"Did I say you could speak?" Amethyst growled, and her eyes began to glow red around her brown irises.

I didn't answer or move, terrified that either would cause Ishtar to harm my friend.

"That's better. Now, promise not to mention that I'm here, and I won't injure the spirit talker. We're going to have a little chat, queen to queen."

Queen to queen? My lips parted in shock. What did that even mean?

"Promise!" Amethyst hissed in Ishtar's cruel voice.

The sensation of coldness intensified inside me.

Unable to repress it, I shuddered. "I promise."

"Good witch. I'd have hated to destroy the soul who volunteered for this job. Not that he is much of a keeper. No one in Hell is, but still." Amethyst's mouth split in a sinister smile. "They're *my* souls, and I like to keep them around."

A shiver ran through me as understanding dawned. Ishtar wasn't actually here, she wasn't even truly *possessing* Amethyst. She was controlling a ghost—a soul who lived in Hell—to do her dirty work.

And wards conjured specifically to keep out demons didn't do crap against ghosts.

Amethyst cracked her knuckles. "I can see you've caught up. I always knew the blood of Morgan would be intelligent. Merlin got all the credit for his genius and ability. The people of his age revered him," Amethyst snorted. "But truly, Morgan was the gifted one. She would have outshone Merlin, had her time been more receptive to a woman's intelligence."

Amethyst turned her head, and her gaze landed on the far side of the room, where Alex and Kira sat. "They say humans have become more progressive, but really, not that much has changed. You saved that boy and fought a legend for your rank, but few believe you deserve it. Like in the past, the blood of Merlin once again outshines the blood of Morgan."

Anger bubbled inside me at her cheap shot.

"Nice try. Alex and I are a team. You can't come between us."

"I've noticed. Your devotion to one another is quite irritating." Amethyst's eyes darted to my talisman and she wrinkled her nose. "Now that we've covered all the formalities, let's get to business." She gestured to the tarot deck.

I spread the cards out in front of me—albeit shoddily. I simply couldn't find it in myself to care what the cards looked like when the Queen of Hell sat in front of me.

Unfortunately, at that exact moment, Professor Videns passed by again. He glanced down at my pitiful spread and shook his head. He was about to come over to correct my poor tarot work when a hand shot across the table and began reshuffling the spread.

"Nice try, Odette! But you have to be more fluid than that when prepping for a read," Amethyst said in her own voice.

I jerked back, shocked by the shift, and my gaze latched on to her. My friend's eyes were clear, but the tense line of her jaw told me that the demon was still there, hiding inside her and calling the shots.

"Okay," I said, playing along. "Like this?" I grabbed another deck and mimicked her.

"Much better," Amethyst said. She peered down at her spread. "Oh! And I see something interesting! Do you mind if I read your future real quick?"

Appeased, Professor Videns moved on. For the first time

since the term had begun, it disappointed me to see his back.

"Wonderful performance." Ishtar's voice grated me like nails on a chalkboard. "But clearly, you're no ace at Tarot. Perhaps it's better that I ensure no one disturbs us." She pointed to the crystal ball, which lit up. "I realize that you've already met some of my children." Amethyst's eyes glowed red.

I gulped, remembering the tunnels in Portland, and how many demons we'd slaughtered that day.

"However, we've grown since then. Let me show you my clan."

Horrifying images were already unfolding in the crystal ball. Armies of the dead and vicious-looking demons marched down a black, rocky path. Devils with pronounced canines, wide black wings, and glowing eyes flew over-head, shooting fire at their kin down below. Hellfire rained everywhere, and occasionally, an eruption would shoot up from the ground, gobbling up a body in its way.

It was a grotesque sight and how I imagined Hell looked every day.

"As you can see, we've amassed quite the army. Lucifer and I have discovered a way to raise the dead who have joined us, and, as you know, we are procreating." Amethyst placed her hand on her flat belly.

The implication was clear, and a question arose in my mind.

The royal demons of Hell didn't procreate often because every time they did, a bit of their magical essence transferred to their babe. By creating children of her own blood, was Ishtar growing weaker? I hoped so, but didn't dare ask.

"Of course, our minions are still producing children too. We're bolstering our forces in preparation for when we burst through your ancestor's enchantment on the Hellgate."

My mouth went dry. The Hellgate. Its location had been lost for centuries. Although no one knew for sure who had closed it, now I did.

Merlin and Morgan. And if they had been the ones to close it, I guessed that their bloodline had to be the ones to open it. It made perfect sense. We knew that they wanted to enter our realm en mass. If they didn't need the power of our bloodlines then why were the demons so fixated on Alex and me?

"Oh, don't worry," Amethyst said, every syllable dripping with Ishtar's malice. "At first, we thought you two would be necessary to open the gate. But now that we have allies, that's no longer the case."

I snapped out of my revelation, and put on a stoic face so Ishtar didn't think that she had gotten the better of me.

"About those allies," I gritted my teeth. "Are they ever going to show themselves? Or are they just going to keep hiding? You know so much about us, it seems unfair that we're left in the dark."

"In the dark," Ishtar chuckled. "That's rich, coming from someone born on this plane. Someone who drips sunlight from their skin. Someone ignorant to the eternal darkness of Hell." Amethyst shook her head. "No, blood of Morgan, I will not tell you any of our secrets. You shall have to figure them out for yourself."

Suddenly Amethyst gasped and began to tremble violently. My heart went into overdrive. Was Ishtar going back on her promise? Was she harming my friend?

I was seconds from yelling out for help, when Amethyst's hand shot out and gripped my arm.

"Don't! Don't say anything," she begged, her voice once again her own and laced with terror. "If you tell anyone what happened, Ishtar will return. And she swears that if she has to possess me again to speak with you, she won't leave my body alive."

CHAPTER NINE

I was in a pickle.

I desperately wanted to expose Ishtar had a means of breaching Spellcasters' wards, and that the Queen of Hell had said they'd wanted Alex and me to open the Hellgate. But I couldn't because the story put Amethyst in danger.

Of course, there was always the possibility that Ishtar was bluffing, but the risk was too great.

Talking to Amethyst comforted me a little. Well, *talk* might be too soft of a word. For the rest of Divination and during lunch, Amethyst clung to me. Her behavior caught the attention of Alex, Hunter, and Eva, and earned us some funny glances, but I couldn't do anything about that. Telling Amethyst to back off when she needed reassurance would be cruel. And to be honest, the more snippets of conversation Amethyst and I shared, the better I felt.

"My parents have only taught me how to sense spirits

and call them, because that's more than half the battle when you first learn how to interact with ghosts," she'd explained after Alex excused himself to use the restroom as we walked to our next class. "We didn't discuss how to deter them at all. But you'd better believe I'll be asking how to do that now."

"Are spirit walkers and talkers easier to possess?"

"Definitely."

"And are you the strongest spirit walker and talker in the academy?"

Amethyst's cheeks grew red. "I haven't spirit walked yet. And there are five Crucible students taking Spirit Walking and Talking, but it's not in their blood the way it's in mine."

They should be thanking their lucky stars for that.

"What would happen if a ghost possessed someone else? Say, someone who's resistant to ghostly energies?"

Amethyst's eyes widened. "The ghost wouldn't want to."

"Why?"

"Because it would be *terrible*—for the person and the ghost. If the person wasn't at all sensitive to spiritual energies, the ghost might even kill them."

"Yikes."

Silence hung over us as we neared the Conjuring and Transfiguration classroom.

Amethyst stopped as we reached the door. "We're not saying anything, right? Like to anyone? Ever? She was serious when she threatened to come back, I could tell." Her brown eyes bore through me.

"Not a peep," I assured her.

She breathed a sigh of relief. "Thank you. I know that this is as scary for you as it is for me, but the way she felt inside me —" She shuddered. "It wasn't like how my parents described a regular ghost. I *never* want to experience it again."

I nodded, understanding her fear. If Ishtar ever made it to this realm, she'd possess me in a hot second. "I get it. We won't say a thing."

Together, we walked into Conjuring and Transfiguration to find that an array of small items dotted each desk. I sat down, and Amethyst chose the table next to me. Briefly, I wondered if she ever planned on leaving my side again, but I quickly vanquished the unkind thought.

I'd had months to come to terms with the possibility of a demon possessing me. But Amethyst had experienced a possession two hours ago. I needed to cut her some slack.

The owl hooted right before Alex rushed into the classroom alongside Eva and Hunter. He plopped down at my table, and our friends took the one next to him.

"What's so funny?" I asked, gesturing to Hunter, who was laughing so hard tears leaked from his eyes.

Alex rolled his eyes. "We saw your friends, Heidi and Holly, in the corridor. Hunter hadn't met them yet, and one —the blonde, I can't remember which is which—basically fell in love with him."

"That was Heidi. And?"

"And, since Hunter is the biggest flirt *ever*, he used it to his benefit," Eva rolled her eyes. "He regaled them with a story from last year—nothing serious—and then proceeded to scare the ever-living shit out of them when he told them about the Samhain Trial. The girls literally screamed when he impersonated the succubus, and ran away. Hunter thought it was *hilarious*." Eva's lips quirked up in a way that told me she thought it was a little funny too.

Before anyone could say anything more, Professor Umbra called our class to order, and another whirlwind session began.

In our Culling-year, Conjuring had been one of my weaker subjects. Even after a year of study, I still sucked at creating objects out of thin air. And as far as making them move or act alive like Amethyst was capable of doing? Those skills seemed like a distant dream.

But the magical discipline of transfiguration was a whole different story.

Starting with an object made it much easier for me to create another. In fact, I was pretty damn good at it.

I positioned my mug carefully in front of me, and a thrill of possibility that today might be my day to level up ran through me.

"*Mutatio*." I whispered the basic transfiguration spell, and fuchsia magic flew from my hands to wrap around the plain white coffee mug. At twelve ounces it was larger than the last mug I'd managed to transfigure into a wine glass. I squinted my eyes, hoping the spell would work. But after a few seconds, it was clear that today wouldn't be my day.

Instead of transforming into a copper Moscow mule mug, it stopped somewhere in between—half ceramic and half metal.

"Dammit," I swore.

At my side, Alex chuckled. "You're doing awesome. Most people are still working with matchboxes and spools of thread. A coffee mug is ten times that size."

I smiled at him. "Thanks, babe. When I finally turn this into copper, I'll bust out Mom's recipe and make you the best Moscow Mule you've ever had."

"Is that a Medulla-approved concoction?" Alex teased.

"Probably not," I laughed. I had a hunch that Mom's recipe for a Moscow mule, which used starfruit-flavored vodka, would not go over well with the healing professor.

The rest of class flew by, and I was taken by surprise when the owl hooted once more. Our next session was Advanced Faeology, and we were halfway to that classroom when I ran into Professor Tittelbaum.

"Miss Dane!" Tittelbaum clapped his hands together. "Are you prepared for our session tonight?"

I almost groaned but held it inside. I'd *completely* forgotten that my specialty class with Professor Tittelbaum was that evening.

"Of course, Professor," I said, trying to push all the homework that was piling up out of my mind.

"Wonderful." He beamed. "Remember, tonight we will have someone joining us! A Crucible student who recently discovered his warping talent."

Despite the fact that I would rather be sleeping than go

to my lesson, I smiled. Professor Tittelbaum looked like a thin, nerdy academic who never saw sunlight, but once you got to know him, he didn't give off that vibe at all. He had a zest for both of his subjects, Magical Languages and Warping, and that fervor was infectious.

"And you're still not going to tell me who this person is?"

I'd been trying to pry the student's name out of him for the last two weeks, while arrangements were being made for the student to join us. Unlike a lot of private tutoring sessions, warping required lots of bureaucratic hoop-jumping because it was so dangerous.

I hadn't known of *half* the dangers when I'd created my first warphole to banish Ishtar to Hell during the Beltane Trial. But even if I had, I still would have done it. Being pulled into Hell seemed a much worse fate than a couple of missing body parts, or even temporary madness.

Tittelbaum grinned. "If you're going to be a warper, Miss Dane, you must learn to appreciate some mystery in life."

"Right," I said, although I totally disagreed. "Who wouldn't want some of that?"

Perhaps the girl who's up to her eyeballs in mystery at the moment?

"See you tonight, then," the professor said.

"See you tonight," I echoed.

CHAPTER TEN

My feet dragged as I trudged to Alice Kyteler Hall. Every cell in my body yearned for a nap, but the lure of learning the identity of the new warping student kept me going. Although I liked Professor Tittelbaum, it was strange having *so* much attention directed on me. A friend my age in the same tutoring session would be welcome, if only to take the pressure off.

"Andre!" I said as I entered the hall to find the professor and my fellow Spellcasters champion already there and chatting. "This is a great surprise."

"Now you see why I didn't tell you!" Professor Tittelbaum clapped his hands. "Imagine the possibilities! If Andre here can get the hang of warping before the first Spy Game . . . Spellcasters will have an almost certain victory!"

Wow. I wished I had half of Professor Tittelbaum's confidence in our team. The first Spy Games event would take place on Mabon, the witching sabbat in mid-September. But with a little less than a month to get through my never-ending mountain of coursework, and my first spy mission, I wasn't as enthusiastic as the professor. At least not yet.

The tutoring session began, and it quickly became obvious that Andre was a *total* beginner. After only twenty minutes, the professor asked me to demonstrate making warpholes from one side of the room to the other, while he described the intricacies of the magic to Andre.

It was interesting to hear warping taught in this way. I had made my first warphole through sheer force of will, and had never had to think about it in such technical terms. I'd learned during my summer internship that my hands-on experience put me squarely in the minority among warpers. Many preferred a methodical approach, but not me. I always sensed my way through making a warphole.

This personal preference was yet another reason why I wasn't keen on teaching Alex how to create warpholes. He was much more technical. Plus, there was a lot of inherent risk when creating them. What if he tried my method and injured himself? Or worse, lost his mental faculties?

When we'd reached the end of our session, Professor Tittelbaum set the next class for two weeks out, and Andre and I left Alice Kyteler Hall together. As soon as the doors closed behind us, he turned to me.

"You make it look so easy. What's your secret?"

I grinned, pleased by the compliment, even though it wasn't easy at all. It had taken me months to get where I was, and I still found it very difficult to warp to sites unseen. The farther away, the harder it became.

"An amazing summer internship where I practiced, practiced, practiced."

His face fell. "I was afraid you'd say that."

"The best tip I can give you is to listen to your body. Professor Tittelbaum has never mentioned it—he likes to be by the book—but I feel how to warp in my body and soul. I still have a lot of work to do, but each time is a little easier than the last."

Andre sighed. "That's something, I guess."

We made our way down the hall until we reached the corridor where we'd split.

"You did well today," I said. "See you around."

"Thanks for your help." Andre grinned.

I took a few steps up the stairs, only to pause when Andre spoke again.

"Hey! The Crucibles are having a party tomorrow night. Wanna come? Bring your friends too, if you want. I think Diana plans on stopping by. We could talk about the Spy Games a little."

Something in me seized, and it didn't take a genius to understand why. The last time I'd been invited to a party at the King's Castle, the ridiculous name that the Crucibles gave their fancy dorm, a classmate had died.

But surely that wouldn't happen again. Not with all the wards the academy had put in place.

Everything will be fine.

"Sooooo, is that a no?" Andre asked, and I realized that we'd been standing there, him staring at me, and me mentally running through a lot of doom and gloom.

I shook my head. "Sorry. It's a yes. It's just, when you mentioned a party, I—"

"You thought of that kid they found dead in the woods last year," Andre finished for me.

"Yeah." I cocked my head. "Were you there too?"

"I left before all that shit went down. Sam was there, though. She's my best friend and told me about it afterward." He shook his head. "So messed up."

For some reason, maybe because I had hit my max of secrets for the day, the truth burned its way up my throat, and I blurted it out before I could second guess myself.

"That thing that killed Efraim was looking for me . . . or maybe my boyfriend, Alex." I paused, feeling relieved but also slightly dumb because Andre was staring at me with wide eyes. "I thought you should know, since we'll be participating in dangerous games together. Demons want us for . . . reasons."

"Reasons you know?"

I shook my head, which was a partial truth. I knew bits, but not everything.

Andre continued to stare at me, and it was almost to the point of becoming really uncomfortable when he shrugged. "Well, they'll already be hammering us during the Spy Games. What's a few demons added to the pile? I'm sure we can take them on." He flexed ludicrously, making me laugh.

His lips curved up. "That's better. Things were getting a little too serious for my liking." He turned and walked away. "See you tomorrow, Dane. You'd better have your party hat on."

"Will do," I called back, and made my way to the Green Tower.

When I arrived back at the dorm, I found half of my class in the common space, studying. Since we'd started our Grindyear, seeing the study area full of people with their nose buried in books was routine. As was someone tossing a book across the room, or bursting into tears over some horrible assignment.

Kira, José, Jasmine, and Dakota, four of the people who hated me this year, shot me sour looks as I passed. I ignored them. After almost two months of being the recipient of their envy, I didn't have the time or energy to care what they thought anymore.

When I reached the sixth floor, I noticed the door to the spymasters' private study room was open, and familiar voices emanated from within. When I peeked inside, I found my best friends and Diana at various tables with books spread out before them.

"Odie! We were wondering when you'd get done with your tutoring session. Amethyst was looking for you earlier. Did she find you?"

"I'll catch her tomorrow." I was sure she wanted more reassurance that I hadn't blabbed. If it had been serious, she would have waited for me in the common space. "What are you guys studying?"

"Faeology," Eva and Diana called out, seconds before the guys claimed to be working on the Potions and Poisons assignment.

"Awesome. I need to do all of that. I'll get my stuff."

I ran to my room and grabbed my overstuffed book bag. A few minutes later, I was nestling myself into the last free table between Alex and Eva.

"Which are you going to do first?" Alex asked.

"Hmmm, Faeology." Our Potions and Poisons assignment dealt with a lot of science, and my brain couldn't handle that at the moment. "But before I get started, I have something to tell you guys."

Everyone leaned back, and Hunter placed his feet on the table, clearly happy for another break.

"There's a Crucible party tomorrow. We're all invited."

"Yassssss!" Eva shouted. "I *so* need to let loose."

The guys agreed. Diana merely nodded, reminding me that she already knew about the party.

"Have you been talking with Sam and Andre about the Games?" I asked her.

Diana's eyebrows furrowed together. "What? No. Why would we talk about the Games without you?"

My lips parted at the show of thoughtfulness. "I was wondering because Andre told me you already knew about the party."

Diana's creamy complexion took on the slightest hint of pink. "Oh, right. I actually saw him in the hall earlier and he told me then." She spoke hurriedly as if she wanted to move on.

"Well, we should have a brainstorming session at the party."

She nodded and quickly buried her head in her books. I watched her, wondering why she was acting so odd before realizing that my homework wouldn't do itself, and followed in Diana's footsteps.

CHAPTER ELEVEN

$\mathcal{A}$methyst stuck to my side like glue the whole day after her possession. Although I understood her anxiety, I couldn't deny that having a shadow every time I used the restroom was getting annoying. I didn't know if she stayed beside me because she didn't trust me to keep her secret, or if she felt safer in my presence.

Either way, when the party rolled around and Amethyst opted to remain in the Green Tower, I wasn't disappointed. I needed to not worry about ghosts possessing people. To forget about Ishtar for a moment. To let my hair down and be a normal college kid.

As we walked through the woods to the King's Castle, the luxury dorm next to alumni housing, I was sure that my needs would soon be met. The revelry rang loud and clear halfway down the wooded path, electrifying me. And when we emerged from the woods to view the dorm, a smile bloomed on my face.

Made of glass, with the windows on the upper floors tinted for privacy, the King's Castle didn't really go with Spellcasters main building. Lanterns illuminated the walkway, their light reflecting off the glass. There was a porch where a few students lounged on outdoor furniture. Somehow, a massive trampoline had been brought on to Spellcasters' grounds, and a half-dozen third-years jumped, or rather, floated around, above it. My mouth dropped open as one guy began floating off the trampoline and over the tops of some smaller trees. He'd clearly perfected the levitation charm, a spell we'd learned at the end of last year. I still hadn't mastered it.

Hunter, however, excelled at levitation, and upon seeing so many people goofing around with his favorite charm, his eyes lit up.

"Anyone wanna go play?" A familiar mischievous expression flashed across his face.

Eva giggled. "I'm in as long as you catch me."

"Always, sugar. Always."

Alex and I declined, and our friends ran off to go have fun.

"Where to first, sweets?" Alex asked.

I looked around, unsure where to begin. Besides the trampoline, there was corn hole, a massive Twister board, and giant Jenga too.

"It all looks awesome," I admitted. "How about we get a drink first and then decide?"

Alex grabbed my hand, and together, we walked through the fun and games into the King's Castle.

Inside, the building was as polished and striking as I remembered. The foosball and pool tables stuck out as centers of rousing competition. Predictably, the bar, complete with a keg, was packed. Music thumped so loud that it vibrated the tables we passed. When it quieted for a moment sounds of a loud car crash filled my ears. I assumed a few people were watching a movie in the theater room down the hall.

Coming from Beverly Hills, I remembered feeling at home when I walked into the King's Castle last year. Yet, now it felt odd. Like it was all too much. I'd grown used to our small tower rooms, which were still nice, but older and less amenity-rich.

I guess you really can get used to anything.

Alex and I stopped by the bar. He grabbed a beer while I opted for a glass of white wine. We were about to mingle when I noticed Sam waving frantically at me from fireside seats that looked out over the front yard. I waved back, and she motioned for me to join her. When I saw who she was with, I understood why.

Sam sat in a chair across from Andre and Diana, who were next to each other on a loveseat. They were a *touch* closer than friends would sit. The way Diana's cheeks had reddened at the mention of Andre last night came rushing back, and I grinned. I'd bet a whole lot of money that Diana and Andre were into each other. Sam probably wanted backup—and of course to talk about the Games.

"Hey," I squeezed Alex's hand, "the other champions want to chat. Do you wanna join?"

He shook his head. "Nah. I'm good. There are a few people here I want to talk to. Catch you later, sweets?" He dimpled at me.

We kissed and split off. Alex headed straight toward two Crucible students who were in his Healing tutoring session.

My lips curled up. Alex was so driven to excel in the subject that he enjoyed. Even if I teased him, it was truly one of the things I liked most about him.

When I neared the other champions, Sam rose and pulled me into an awkward half-hug.

"Thank God you're here," she whispered. "If I had to put up with the covert flirting without backup, or Diana's ex-boyfriend sending death looks for a moment longer, I was going to throw someone across the room. Probably Diana, because Andre's too heavy."

My ears perked up. Diana's ex-boyfriend? She had been single during our Culling-year. It must have been a guy from before she was enrolled at Spellcasters. How scandalous!

Unable to help myself, I scanned the room. My gaze landed on a guy with shoulder-length blond hair, full lips, and a scowl directed straight at Diana. He looked like a young Brad Pitt, and for some reason, I found it hard to believe that he and Diana had been an item.

"That guy?" I whispered and aimed a finger behind my other hand.

Sam followed the direction that I pointed and nodded. "Jackson Hall. They dated during our Culling-year. He broke up with her right before she took her entry exams and dated someone else during the Grind. When she earned spymaster for your class at the end of last year, it pissed him off something fierce. Jealous, I think. He's never even gotten a rank of sorcerer spy. But now that she and Andre are . . . whatever . . . Jackson's been a *nightmare*. Clearly, he's not over her, even though he was the one who dumped her. Avoid him at all costs."

Damn. Memo to self: Ask Diana about her ex later.

Sam and I joined the other two, and right away, the topic turned to the Spy Games.

"The first event will be at Nightdwellers," Sam said. "Does anyone know anything about that school, other than that it's full of vampires?"

Andre and I shrugged. Hell, I'd known basically nothing about Spellcasters before I enrolled. The other schools were complete mysteries.

"The students do three terms at the school, but they're more like semesters rather than years," Diana offered. "After that, they transfer to work under a real spy for a year."

Sam nodded. "Because vampires have natural stealth, strength, and keen senses, the PIA accelerates their training. That makes sense. But I meant information about the academy's location, what they study, and what's nearby?"

Diana shook her head. "Sorry. Mother has never talked about that stuff. She's more the type to let me learn by experience."

"If you asked, would she tell you?" Andre asked.

"Ha! No way. Now that I'm a champion, she'd see it as cheating." Diana rolled her eyes. "Which is annoying because I bet Headmaster Ezra is telling his champions everything he can about Spellcasters. Mother is way too by the book."

"That's okay. I'm assuming most schools will choose challenges more suited to their students' strengths," I said, trying to bring the conversation into a more positive light. "We don't need to know where Nightdwellers is to brainstorm a challenge that would benefit a vampire. I think that's a good place to start."

"Great idea, Dane," Sam agreed. "Let me get something to write with."

Sam went to the bar to grab a notepad, and I used the time to take a bathroom break. On my way back, I spotted Alex clear across the living room in a rousing discussion with his fellow tutoring students. I smiled and waved, and he returned the gesture.

Sam had already jotted down two options when I arrived back at my seat.

I leaned over the arm of the chair and gasped. "No! Those would be awful!"

"That's a vampire for you," Andre said.

"What else?" Sam asked.

"What about an obstacle course of sorts?" Diana offered. "One that would require super strength and speed?"

Sam squished her lips to the side. "Maybe. It sounds a little too simple, but depending on the environment, I could see it. I'll put it dow—" She paused, and a look of fear flashed over her face. "Does anyone else hear that?"

The music inside was blaring and difficult to hear over, but Sam's reaction pushed me to try. I tuned out the music, and after a few moments, the sounds of growls and screams hit my ear. I hoped they were emanating from the theater room, but my senses informed me they were coming from the opposite direction—outside.

A sickening sense of déjà vu came over me, and I shot out of my seat. Spinning toward the window, I let out a yelp as a massive, black beast soared over the front lawn. I watched, mouth agape, as it flew over the trampoline and snatched someone straight out of the air with a vicious roar.

"What was that?" Diana appeared at my side.

It had moved so fast that I wasn't sure, but the answer came a moment later when a skinny third-year burst through the front door. A spell, obvious by the amber magic that spewed from his hands, flew up around him.

"The fae are here!" The guy's voice boomed over the music, magically amplified. "And they brought a dragon! Help!"

A dragon? What the actual shit?!

All of us champions dashed toward the door, my heart hammering harder with each step. I had no idea how we were going to fight the fae. The only other time I'd tried to fight one, he had gotten away. And a dragon?

My stomach sank.

Magicals had banished dragons to Faerie centuries ago. Occasionally, they emerged into our world, as they had when my parents were assigned to wrangle a wayward mated pair in their spy days. But mostly, the royal fae courts kept their dragons on a tight, metaphorical leash. Which meant few people outside of Faerie knew how to subdue the beasts.

But just because I'm ignorant doesn't mean others are, I reasoned, trying to calm my raging mind.

Someone here had to know something about taming a dragon. Right?

My rational thinking lasted until I exited the front door and came face-to-face with what we were *really* up against.

CHAPTER TWELVE

At least fifty fae ran across the lawn and through the woods, cackling with glee and lighting fires with magic. Ropes made of vines bound my peers' legs and arms, while gusts of air tossed people around like leaves in the wind.

But what caught my attention most were the two students trapped in separate spheres of water. Their fists slammed against the aqueous walls, and desperation lined their faces as bubbles escaped their screaming mouths.

I sprinted toward the water spheres. Somehow, although chaos was all around me, everything else fell away as I worked out how to save the drowning students.

I wonder if I could—

My head snapped to the side as a body came hurtling my direction and tackled me to the ground.

"Not so fast, pretty," a deep voice growled as someone pressed me into the dirt. A nail raked down my neck, burning the skin there, as the creature tried to pull my hair back.

"Get off of me!" I screamed. Magic flew from my hands, but since the fae had me stomach-down, my aim was poor, and I didn't hit my target.

"Perhaps after I send you into slumber. We're always looking for pretty and docile slaves in Dark Court. You might need help with the latter attribute, but it's nothing a little fae wine can't handle."

My blood froze. Send me into slumber? Docile slaves? Oh *hell* no.

I kicked and tried to yell for help, but my throat felt tight. After a few more attempts, I could barely breathe, let alone scream. For a moment I thought it was due to the fae's prodigious weight, but when my lungs began to burn, the truth hit me.

The fae was siphoning the air straight from my lungs.

My heart rate sped up, burning the little oxygen left in my system. I bucked, but the movement was weak. All my senses dulled. My hand flailed, a last-ditch effort to draw someone's attention.

Suddenly, hot liquid splattered onto my back, and air, precious air, flooded my lungs once again. I gasped as the fae's weight fell off of me.

"Holy shit, Odie!" Eva yanked me up off the ground.

I swayed, disoriented.

"What did he do to you?" my friend asked as she held me up.

I cringed, noting the blood dripping off her face. Then, I stiffened. Dripping. Like *water.*

I gasped. "Eva! Those people in the water." I spun to find they were still trapped, passed out. A trio was trying to save the girl, while Andre and Diana were working to free the guy. "We have to help them!"

We dashed over to help Diana and Andre. Sweat poured off them as they used spells and battle magic against the sphere.

"Any luck?" Eva yelled.

My eyes darted to the guy in the water globe. His skin was blue and his eyes closed as he floated lifelessly in the sphere.

"None!" Andre grunted. "We've tried dozens of spells, but we're either not powerful enough, or they aren't effective against elemental magic."

"Or both!" Diana yelled as she hurled a ball of glaring purple light at the water sphere. I watched it fly right out the other side.

"Your magic can go through there, though?" I asked, making sure that hadn't been a one-time thing.

Diana nodded. "Our magic can, but when we touch it, the damn thing is solid. Otherwise, I'd yank him out."

I had an idea.

"Andre, I'm going to make a warphole into the bubble. If I can't get out on my own, pull me back through. You might even have to keep it open if something happens to me in there."

Andre's eyes grew round. "Yeah, okay—I got you, Dane."

I felt a little bad. He was still so new to warping. Even so, he was the most qualified witch around, and we were running out of time.

I didn't need to go far, and I could see my destination, so setting up the warphole was easy. Just a visualization, a calling and redirecting of energy, and the hole appeared before me. Inside the bubble of water, a black dot lined with fuchsia opened. As it expanded, the water cage expanded too. I watched as it doubled in size, then tripled. So the warphole wouldn't pop the globe, but the bubble wouldn't expel my warphole either.

There was a chance this would work.

I seized the opportunity and stepped into the warphole. The familiar sensation of heat then cold enveloped me, but it was only momentary before water splashed in my face. My eyes snapped shut on instinct, but I forced them back open.

The drowning student was three or four feet away, but when I extended my hand past the safety of the warphole, I discovered that the current in the ball of water was crazy strong. Thankfully, I was a California girl and a good swimmer.

I took a huge breath and plunged. It should have only taken a few strong strokes to reach him, but because of the current, it took more. When my hands wrapped around his arm, he was ice cold.

My sense of urgency amplified.

Pulling him back to the warphole was ten times more difficult than reaching him had been. He was heavy, and my lungs started to burn. We were a foot away from reaching the safety of my magic, when something inside the globe shifted.

The current became a whirlpool, and I gripped the guy I'd saved tighter only seconds before we began spinning around. Stupidly, I let out a scream, releasing all my air. Outside the globe, I heard Eva yell my name, but I couldn't respond. Stars already dotted my vision. Flailing, I tried to expand the warphole toward me, but panic filled me, and manipulating warpholes required a clear mind.

This was it. I was about to meet my end. Ishtar would be so pissed that she never got to best me.

And Alex . . . I didn't even get to say goodbye.

Darkness descended—my grip on the guy loosened, but I used all my remaining energy to hold tight. I didn't want to die alone.

The blackness had almost taken me over, when two strong hands grabbed onto me and yanked.

I tumbled through hot air, then cold—warphole energy —and landed on something hard. I sputtered. Someone began pounding on my back, and I sputtered more. It felt like an ocean full of water was exiting me.

"Move over! I know CPR!" Diana's voice cut through me, and I forced myself back to the moment.

I couldn't slip off into unconsciousness. Fae and witches still battled all around me, and the guy I'd pulled from the globe might be dead.

"Odie! Are you okay?" Eva squatted in front of me, while Diana and Andre tended to the guy I'd saved.

"Hey! Help us!" another voice called out.

"She can barely breathe!" Eva clutched me and screamed back.

Shit. The other water sphere.

"Eva, I have to help. I'm the only one who can," I said as I worked myself out of her grasp.

"Dammit! Of course you are." Eva's voice cracked as she helped me to my feet.

"Make sure Andre watches my back," I said, sparing her a smile before turning and jogging toward the other sphere.

This time, I created a warphole on the fly, and dove back in.

As soon as my body hit the water in the second globe, I gasped. The current here was much stronger than that of the first water sphere. It felt like a riptide, and tore me away from the drowning girl after a single stroke. I glanced around in panic and noticed that this globe was larger too, its size comparable to that of a backyard shed.

It wasn't that big seconds ago . . . Oh, that little shit. Fury rushed through me as the truth of my situation became clear.

The fae who controlled this sphere was manipulating it to screw with me.

Using all my strength, I kicked and paddled. The effort gained me a few inches, but the girl's body was still much too far away. My heart began to beat dangerously fast. I still hadn't recovered from saving the guy, and I'd already lost more oxygen than the first time. I had seconds, maybe less, to save the girl and get out of the globe alive.

I gnashed my teeth together, determined to give it one more go before backing out.

And then, three goddamned piranhas appeared in the water and zoomed straight at me.

I flipped around and swam the opposite way. I'd almost made it to the warphole, when one of the little assholes bit my leg. I let out a scream, releasing the rest of my precious air.

Another bite, another drowned scream. Within seconds, my entire leg was on fire. My vision clouded, and my body began shutting down, giving up.

God, I'd been so stupid. Why had I tried to save her when I hadn't even recovered? Now we would both die in this damn bubble.

A piranha moved up my leg to my hip, but I could no longer find the energy to fight it. I was through. The fae controlling this sphere would drown me. Then the piranhas would eat my body.

Or at least that was what I thought until I caught a flash of crimson light. It streaked across the lawn, straight toward me, and pierced the water bubble. My eyes popped open as the red light connected with my totem, and a sphere of air surrounded my head.

Alex. I didn't know where he was, or how he'd given me oxygen, but he'd saved me. Him and his totem.

Gratefully, I breathed in the fresh air, and my strength

returned. The fish were no longer an issue, Alex's magic had killed them on impact.

That gave me an idea.

Just as I had done the night we faced Ishtar, I grabbed my totem and asked for help. Immediately, the necklace created a bubble around me. Thanks to Alex, I already had air, so I figured the bubble must serve another purpose. I pressed the side, and ever so slightly, it moved in the direction of my applied pressure. My heart leapt, and I pressed my hand toward the girl. The bubble responded, moving closer to her. The harder I pressed, the faster it rolled, like I was a hamster in a wheel. I reached the girl in no time and pulled her inside my protective sphere. Then I directed the bubble back to the warphole.

Finally, when I was right next to the warphole, a hand reached through. Dark fingers waved at me—Andre's. I extended my hand to grasp his, and he wrenched us out of the sphere.

This time, when I emerged from the water sphere, I shoved the girl into Andre's arms, instructed the others to perform CPR, and scanned the lawn. A flash of crimson helped me find who I was looking for, and when I laid eyes on my boyfriend, my heart stopped.

Alex was battling the freaking dragon.

The beast's razor-sharp teeth snapped at him in between streams of fire that Alex narrowly dodged.

Oh hell no, you're not messing with my man.

I sprinted toward Alex, intent on being with him, on helping him. I was almost there too, only a dozen yards away, when a blast of magical energy flew across the yard.

I blinked and saw the headmistress and a dozen Spellcasters professors rushing out of the woods, their magic knocking out at least twenty fae in one go. Another blast swooped in, and terrified and elated in equal measure, I hit the floor.

Their magic overwhelmed the space. Shades of gray, blue, navy, violet, and scarlet soared toward the fae, and otherworldly screams filled the air. Professors spread out and became warriors, but one instructor was even more awe-inspiring than the rest.

Ms. Seeley twirled and struck as she raced through the onslaught of fae toward the giant lizard. Every target she attacked fell, and when she had a clear shot, our Faeology professor went for the big guy.

I watched as a blast of violet magic ten times as large as any I'd seen from her streamed savagely toward the dragon. It struck the beast right where his head and neck met, and the creature let out a pitiable roar as it fell to the ground with a violent thud. Its eyelids fluttered closed as the last wisps of flames died in its mouth.

But the professor didn't stop moving. She dashed right up to the dragon, conjured a massive sword, and sliced through the creature's neck, finishing the job.

I choked out a sob, only then noticing that the dragon's head had landed a mere two feet from Alex.

I leapt up from my crouch and sprinted toward Alex. He met me halfway and wrapped his arms tightly around me.

"It's okay, Odie. We're all safe." Alex stroked my hair as my tears fell fast and free. He smelled like smoke and burnt hair, confirming that he'd had too many close calls.

"Somehow. I almost lost you. To a freaking *dragon*! And that bubble!" I sounded a little hysterical, but holy universe, both calls had been far too close.

"I know, babe. But we're okay now. The professors, they did something to the fae," Alex said. "They all look asleep —or . . ."

Dead. The word sprang to my mind, vicious and cutting.

Although the reasonable side of me knew it would be smarter to leave some of the fae alive, I couldn't help but hope they were dead.

When I pulled my head from Alex's chest and saw the carnage, the bodies of my peers lying on the ground, I didn't regret the violent thought.

CHAPTER THIRTEEN

The following day classes were canceled, and representatives from the Paranormal Intelligence Agency descended upon Spellcasters.

After they took in the scene at the King's Castle, analyzed the academy's wards, and closed the open faerie holes, the PIA agents interviewed students who had been present during the attack. I was one of the first called upon. When I arrived at the interview room I'd been summoned to, I found David Chena waiting for me.

"Odette Dane," David said with a grim smile. "You always seem to be in the middle of all the trouble, don't you?"

As a top spymaster for the United States government, David knew what had happened during the last Beltane Trial and my internship in Portland. In fact, he knew *almost* everything we'd been up against. Everything except Alex's and my relationships to M&M, and Amethyst's possession.

"Seems like it," I said, returning a smile as I sat down. "How have you been?"

David shook his head, and I took in the dark circles beneath his eyes.

Being a PIA spymaster was taxing work. I could imagine that with all the strange demon and faerie stuff happening, it had become even more draining. Especially for a human with no inherent way of defending himself against the creatures that kept popping up. The poor guy probably didn't sleep.

"Things have been hectic for a few weeks. And then this . . . massacre." David's voice broke, and he hung his head.

I gulped down the lump threatening to rise up my throat.

Massacre. That was exactly what it had been. The professors and the headmistress had arrived only ten minutes after the dragon, but those ten minutes felt like a lifetime of blood and terror.

There were countless injuries. What was worse, five Crucible students and two of my classmates from Grind-year were dead. Their parents were arriving later in the day to collect their bodies, and a quiet service was to be held for them that evening. The girl I'd tried to save from the water sphere was among those who had perished. Although I'd done what I could, a veil of responsibility for her death hung over me.

If I'd been faster, would she still be alive?

Andre felt even worse, although unjustly so. He was a brand new warper, unable to even create a true warphole on his own. But me, I'd been doing this for months. I should've been able to save them both in time.

"So, Miss Dane, do you mind if I ask you a few questions about last night?" David asked, his tone soothing.

I nodded. "Fire away. Although you should know that I might not be too helpful. I was focused on a single task for a lot of it."

He nodded. "I heard what you did. That boy owes you his life." My gut twisted at his omission of the girl. "Still, we like to interview everybody about their personal experience. You never know who might have witnessed the one key piece that brings a case together."

He began questioning me. Most of his inquiries were expected. Who infiltrated the school? Had I seen them actually get onto the grounds? Had anybody from the academy been acting suspicious at the party?

I answered everything to the best of my abilities, although none of my answers felt fully sufficient. Why hadn't I paid more attention? It was like I'd forgotten all of my training when it counted most.

After David finished his questions, he leaned back in his chair and rubbed his temples. "Thank you, Miss Dane. You are dismissed. When you leave, would you please tell my assistant to send for," he looked at the sheet in front of him, "Evanora Proctor."

I nodded. "She's my best friend, so I can send her myself, if you'd like?"

"Oh, that's right. Proctor was with you in Portland."

David sounded as if just thinking about Portland exhausted him.

"She was. She's still sensitive about it," I said protectively. "I'll send her in."

I walked across the room and placed my hand on the doorknob. I was about to let myself out when something I hadn't considered in a while, but had obsessed over constantly after it happened filtered into my conscious.

"David? Do you remember when last year's Culling class came to the PIA for a field trip?"

His lips quirked up. "How could I forget? Your group is a small but *very* curious bunch."

I laughed. That was a kind way of saying that a few members in our class had asked him a billion questions.

"You're right about that. I was wondering, can I ask you a question about that day? If you can't answer I understand, but I'm curious."

"Of course." David placed his elbows on the desk and leaned forward.

"Do you remember the witch I ran into in the hallway outside the cafeteria? The one being brought in by agents for questioning?"

David's face went blank, and his eyebrows knitted together. "I don't believe I remember."

"The one who yelled at me not to trust anyone."

I hadn't wanted to say the last part, since she'd been referring to the PIA, but I supposed there was no sense in keeping that from the spymaster. He'd probably been in on the case in some way or another.

David's confusion cleared, and something else flashed across his face. Anxiety? "Oh, yes. I remember the witch you're talking about. Why do you bring her up?"

"I was actually wondering what happened to her. Sometimes she shows up in my dreams."

I didn't add that when I dreamt about her, I often awoke to my totem flashing like crazy on my nightstand. The connection between the dream and my totem made me question if the witch was a demon sympathizer or something of that nature.

David squirmed a little in his seat. "I'm sorry to say that witch died after being brought to the PIA. She refused nourishment while under questioning. As you might recall, she was already quite ill when she arrived."

"Oh. Yes, I remember." A pang of remorse for the woman cut through my heart. "I'm sorry to hear that she passed. So sad."

"Yes. It was quite sad, but nothing could be done to save her."

My hand landed on the doorknob again, and I twisted it. "Thanks for answering my question. I'll see you around, David."

CHAPTER FOURTEEN

For the next five days, all the students could talk about was the fae infiltration and how the PIA had questioned everyone at the party: the professors, staff, and even Headmistress Wake.

The Culling students were the most skittish about everything that had happened, which made sense. It was only early September, and the poor newbies hadn't even undergone their Samhain Trial yet. The scariest thing they'd seen was probably Professor de Spina's demon conjurings.

To be fair, those still made me shudder, and I'd seen some *real* shit.

"So, hear any interesting theories about who they suspect?" Eva asked, taking a seat at my table for our final class of the day—Intermediate Potions and Poisons.

I shrugged. The PIA had detained Ms. Seeley for two whole days because she was half-fae, which prompted a lot of ignorant people to believe that she had something to do with the fae invasion. I thought all those people were idiots. There was no way Ms. Seeley would allow those monsters onto academy grounds. I remembered all too well how distraught she'd been when one little redcap had opened a faerie hole and tried to take first Mina, and then Amethyst back to Faerie with him.

"Nothing?" Eva looked disappointed that I didn't have new gossip

"To be honest, I can't imagine anyone here would do such a thing."

Of course, I had a personal theory. Because Ishtar could possess a ghost and gain access to Spellcasters, it didn't seem too far-fetched that somehow, she could get the Dark Court fae here too. But I couldn't tell anyone that, because I needed to provide proof. And proving it meant putting Amethyst at risk.

"Miss Dane?" Professor Bane, a younger woman who wore round, green glasses, stopped at my table.

A Crucible student who I'd often seen trailing Headmistress Wake and taking notes stood at the professor's side.

"Yes, Professor Bane?"

"The headmistress would like to see you."

I cocked my head. "Okay. Right now?"

Professor Bane nodded. "Leave your things. You may return to class after your meeting."

Eva placed a hand on my shoulder, questions plain in her eyes.

"I don't know," I whispered. "Guess I'd better go find out."

The Crucible student introduced himself as Tim and led me to Headmistress Wake's offices. I could have gotten there by myself, but this was part of his job, so I rolled with it.

When he knocked on her door, the headmistress answered right away.

"Enter!"

Tim poked his head in. "Headmistress Wake, Odette Dane is here to see you."

"Send her in."

Tim gestured for me to enter, and shut the door behind me once I'd walked into the office.

"Welcome, Miss Dane," the headmistress said without looking up from a pile of paperwork. "Please have a seat."

I obliged and crossed my legs. "You wanted to see me, Headmistress Wake?"

She nodded, and after a moment, shoved the pile aside and gave me her full attention. "Yes. It's about your schedule this month."

My schedule? Like how it was so full to bursting that I rarely got even six hours of sleep, and thought I might fall over from exhaustion any minute? Something told me that wasn't what Headmistress Wake was referring to.

"As you know, the first Spy Games event is at the end of September, during Mabon." She looked pleased that the game organizers decided to hold the challenge on one of the four sabbaths that many witches celebrated. "All Grind students must complete one of their three missions before Samhain. Since I do not want to risk you being injured for the Games, I've scheduled your mission to be the first in your class."

"As in, I'm going soon?" My mouth dried up. "With a partner, right?" I hoped that it was Eva or Hunter.

She nodded. "A very suitable mission arrived from the PIA. And yes, in the Grind, you will always work with a partner during your missions. Yours will be Phoebe. She passed her make-up Beltane Trial the other day."

"Alright," I sighed, but tried to contain my disappointment. At least it wasn't one of the people who had been snubbing me for four months. In fact, now that Diana and I had made up, Phoebe had been civil too. "Do we get any hints as to what we'll be doing?"

During our Culling-year, we'd gotten hints about what we'd encounter prior to the Samhain and Beltane challenges.

"None," Headmistress Wake said. "You and Phoebe will be on your own in almost every sense of the word." She opened a drawer and rifled through it, before producing an object that looked like a pin. "This will be your single life-line. If you find yourselves in a position requiring immediate extraction, all you must do is press down on the center of these pins. Professor Tittelbaum will wear a pin linked to yours. He will open a warphole to your location, and a team will bring you here. Phoebe has already taken one. This one is yours."

I took the circular pin. It didn't look like anything

special, just a small gold daisy-like flower, but I guessed that was the point.

"Is that all, Headmistress?" I asked and prepared to rise.

"Actually, Miss Dane, I have one more question.

My stomach clenched. "Yes?"

"You were at the Crucible party, correct?

I nodded.

"Rumor has it, you saved a student. Thank you for your bravery. Spellcasters is indebted to you for that."

"Thank you, but if they'd been able to, others would have done the same."

"Perhaps," she said and pressed her lips together briefly. "Other students mentioned that the Dark Court of Faerie took responsibility for those actions. Did you hear such rumors?"

"I did. A fae who attacked me said the same thing, so I believe it."

The headmistress nodded, and her gaze dipped to my ankle.

Suddenly, I knew what was coming. I couldn't believe that I didn't expect it sooner.

"Considering all the strange portals and otherworldly interference that have been prevalent lately, I must ask, did your demon-touched scar hurt when the fae were present?"

"No. And to be honest, I don't understand that."

The headmistress tilted her head. "Hmm. It does seem like they should be linked, doesn't it?" She paused and exhaled a soft sigh. "And there is nothing else, about that night or any other, that you wish to inform me of?"

The ghost possessing Amethyst was the obvious choice, but I couldn't tell the headmistress that, it would put Amethyst's life in danger.

I shook my head. "Nothing."

Headmistress Wake studied me as if I was an interesting specimen she'd never seen before, then nodded and waved her hand toward the door. "Thank you for your time, Miss Dane. I'll send instructions pertaining to your departure very soon."

After dinner that night, Headmistress Wake summoned me to the foyer of Spellcasters. Knowing I had little time, I found Eva, Hunter, and Alex in the spymaster's study area, and said my goodbyes.

"She said that this year our missions might last up to four days, so I'm not sure when I'll be back." I hugged first Eva and then Hunter. "Take good notes for me, okay?"

"You know the notes are all on Alex," Eva waved her hand dismissively and pointed to her temple. "I keep my knowledge locked up tight. No need for a bajillion notes."

I laughed. "Hear that, babe?" I wrapped my arms around Alex's trim, muscular waist.

"You can count on me, sweets," Alex said. Our lips met in a kiss. When we broke apart, Alex grinned. "Come back safe to us, okay?"

I nodded and descended the stairwell.

I didn't see Phoebe in the common area, so I assumed

she was already in the entryway. My hunch was proven right a few minutes later when I entered the academy foyer and found the headmistress, Phoebe, and oddly enough, Professor de Spina waiting for us.

I eyed the handsome, young Demonology professor. "Any last tips?"

He chuckled. "Unfortunately not. But Headmistress Wake requested that I look at your mark before you leave. She would like me to make sure it hasn't changed since the last time we examined it."

Inwardly, I groaned.

Professor de Spina or a healer from the infirmary had been checking on my scar every two weeks since the beginning of term. It was routine and often over quickly, so I didn't think much of it, but for some reason, Professor de Spina's presence here bugged me. It made me think that Headmistress Wake didn't believe I was telling the truth about the night at the King's Castle. Plus, Phoebe was looking at me all weird now.

It was pretty common knowledge that Ishtar had touched me, although few people knew what it meant because it had happened so rarely in history. I doubted Phoebe would ask me about it, but she'd probably grill Diana when we returned.

Way to alienate me even more, guys, I thought as I pulled up the leg of my pants and placed my foot on the step.

De Spina bent down and inspected the mark. He never touched me, although sometimes the intensity in which he stared made it feel as if his fingers were probing my skin, searching for irregularities or remnants of evil within me.

After a minute or so, Professor de Spina stood. "Miss Dane appears to be fine."

Headmistress Wake nodded. "Thank you, Professor. You may leave."

De Spina turned and strode down the hallway toward his classroom. When he was out of earshot, the headmistress turned to Phoebe and me and handed us each an envelope.

"These are your mission instructions. A car is waiting out front, and there are credit cards and plenty of cash in the denominations you need to complete your mission."

Phoebe shot me a wary glance. "We're not going to warp there?" she asked, disbelief dripping from her tone.

"No, Miss Pudeator. Unless Miss Dane is now capable of warping across state lines to an unseen destination?" She looked at me.

I shook my head, and Headmistress Wake nodded.

"I thought not. Except for the emergency pin I provided, you two are on your own this time around. Every year we will treat you more and more like regular spies of the Paranormal Intelligence Agency. As they have not had a warper on staff for thirty years, regular spies do not get warped from one assignment to the next."

I stared down at the envelope, a sense of unease washing over me. No wonder these missions took longer. Who knew where in the world we would have to travel before we started our mission?

"If there are no other questions," the headmistress said, "I will leave you two to it."

Phoebe and I exchanged glances and shook our heads.

"Best of luck, girls," Headmistress Wake said and walked away, leaving us to our own devices.

CHAPTER FIFTEEN

My lungs strained as we drove deeper into the Colorado Rockies. Phoebe had offered to drive, so I was relegated to the role of navigator for the duration of our journey from Denver to Crescent Springs, the old mining town turned resort mecca.

As far as I could tell, we were due to arrive at our destination at noon, and I couldn't wait to get there. Hour by hour, the reason they gave Grind-year students four days to complete a single mission became more clear. Without Professor Tittelbaum to warp us wherever we needed to go, missions took way longer.

I might soon warp myself vast distances to sites unseen, but without a vivid photograph as a guide or a prior visit, my confidence wasn't there yet.

"Are we close?" Phoebe asked.

I leaned over the old-school map the car rental agency had provided. Traveling without cell phones was a pain in the ass, but I'd have to get used to it. Spellcasters confiscated our phones at the beginning of each year. And even if I had a phone, I wasn't sure it would work this deep in the woods. The map was our only option.

"I think it's five more miles and to the right." My finger followed the line representing the desolate mountain road we were driving down.

Crescent Springs was at least an hour off a major highway, with no nearby towns. When we'd asked about it at the car rental agency, only two people had even heard of the place. And their reactions weren't promising.

Our checkout agent had wrinkled her pert nose and claimed that Crescent Springs used to be a dump where only biker gangs lived. Apparently, about five years ago, some rich family had bought up most of the property in the town and built a spa near the natural hot springs. Nowadays, it was a pricey boutique mountain village where tourists spent beaucoup money to relax in nature.

And that wasn't all . . .

Another agent overheard our conversation and added that if we planned on hiking, we needed to be careful. Lately, unidentified animals had been attacking visitors in the area. They had killed six people in the last month.

Phoebe and I soaked up all the information, knowing that anything and everything might prove useful in completing our mission. And we needed all the help we could get, because the objective the PIA and Spellcasters had given us was vague at best. We were to find an object, supernatural in nature, and extract it from Crescent Springs for the PIA.

"I feel like I should say something before we really get started on this mission," Phoebe said, ripping me out of my musings.

I turned from staring out of the window to face her. Her arms were unnaturally stiff as they gripped the wheel. "What's that?"

"I want to apologize for how I treated you last year."

I blinked. That was unexpected.

Phoebe darted a glance at me, clearly gauging my reaction. "Obviously, you hold no ill will toward me, and Diana said that you accepted her apology, so I don't know why it took me so long, but still . . . I wanted to throw it out there." She inhaled a big breath. "So I'm sorry, Odette. I was a jerk last year. I hope that you can forgive that. It was uncalled for, and I don't want my past actions to interfere with our ability to carry out this mission. Or any future relationship we might have."

Like her bestie, Phoebe didn't give half-assed apologies. And even though I hadn't actively been holding a grudge, the energy in the car shifted, telling me she'd given me what I needed to hear.

"Thank you, Phoebe. I appreciate that, and there are no hard feelings."

My mission partner let out a massive exhale. "No, thank *you*. I've wanted to clear the air for a while, but didn't know how to bring it up." She gave me a sheepish look. "Sometimes the simplest things are the hardest, I guess. At least that's what my mom says."

"Wise woman."

Phoebe nodded and then leaned forward over the steering wheel and pointed up ahead. "Is that the turn?"

I directed my attention to where she was pointing and nodded. "That's got to be it."

A minute later, she turned onto the road, and smooth cement became jostling gravel, occasionally broken up by potholes the size of roasting pans. It would be slow going the rest of the way.

My finger followed the line on the map. "Looks like we have about two more miles, and then this road becomes the main street of Crescent Springs. There are no turns or anything until we get into town, so we can't miss it."

"And they *definitely* won't miss us," Phoebe added.

She was right. Outsiders would be obvious in a town this small and secluded.

Gradually, the trees thinned, and a town emerged. My lips parted in shock. I'd expected Crescent Springs would be a sweet little resort town filled with tiny but chic boutique establishments.

I was so, so wrong.

Every single building on the main street was either a classy looking restaurant, a large hotel, or a legit mansion—some that rivaled those back in Beverly Hills. I peered down a side street and saw more of the same.

The overt lavishness seemed weird. Not because it was unexpected for wealthy people to enjoy rustic places. I knew better than that. But all my parents' friends preferred their fancy vacation homes in places they could fly directly to. Crescent Springs had taken us five hours to get to from Denver. I couldn't see many of my parents' friends committing to that sort of travel regularly.

And who in the world would have trucked supplies this far out? The construction costs of transporting and building this place must have been astronomical.

Phoebe found a parking spot right in front of a little French bistro. When we got out of the car, the tantalizing aroma of baked bread filled my nostrils.

"You hungry?" I asked, my mouth already watering. "Maybe we can grab a croissant and coffee, and walk around to get the feel of the town?"

Phoebe nodded, and we veered into the bakery. It was empty except for a girl our age behind the register who wore a name-tag proclaiming that she was Leslie.

"Hi, what can I get for you?"

"I'd like a coffee with cream, no sugar, and a pan au chocolat, please," I said.

Leslie nodded, got what I ordered, and rang me up. I tipped her generously. First impressions in a town like this were extremely important.

For the first time, she broke a smile. "Thanks so much," she said and then took Phoebe's order.

My partner wasn't as prepared as I had been, so it took her a few minutes to decide, which suited our purposes well. It gave me a moment to look around.

My eyes roved over the bistro. It was tastefully decorated with black and gold fleur de lis. Photographs of people in muted, natural surroundings lined the walls closest to the register.

"Are those the owners of the bistro?" I asked, gesturing to the nearest photo.

Leslie's eyes shot to the pictures, and she nodded. "Yup and some of their friends are in the others. If you guys are staying at the Crescent Springs Hotel and Spa, you'll probably see those two." She pointed to a picture of a handsome couple, both brunettes and in their mid-forties. Even though the picture was taken from far away, something about it caught my attention. The couple's eyes were a strange shade of amber and seemed to glow back at me.

My spine stiffened as I realized what type of supernatural we might find in Crescent Springs.

Shifters typically had amber or silver eyes, depending on their animal aspect. The brighter the color, the more powerful they were. The ones in this photo must be very strong, if the shade of their eyes was any indication.

"We haven't booked for the night," Phoebe said. "Should we have done that in advance? We heard it was the slow season."

Leslie shook her head and handed over Phoebe's latte and a pastry. "Nah, you're good. In two weeks, no one will get in without booking. But you two came at the perfect time. It seems like right now everyone is staying away."

"Staying away?" I asked, intrigued by how she'd phrased her explanation. "Why?"

"Animal attacks. When tourists come and stay here,

they like to visit the spa and hike. As half of those activities are off the menu, it's less appealing for them to come here." She shrugged. "You know, it's a long drive and all."

A bell tinkled behind us, and I turned to see a man dressed in slim-cut jeans, a nordic sweater, and rich brown leather loafers. He was an extremely good looking man of around thirty-five, confident in his gait and body.

When I turned back around to see that all the blood had left Leslie's face, my brows furrowed. Any guy who looked like that was someone I'd flirt with—if I were single. Why did she look so scared of him?

"Hi, Taylor," Leslie said, her tone shaky. "What can I get for you today?"

The closer Taylor drew, the more obvious it became that he was a shifter. If his silver eyes didn't give it away, the pulse of shifter magic as he leaned over the counter toward Leslie did.

"Leslie, honey. Be a doll and get me a cappuccino and one of those lemon muffins I like so much?"

Leslie nodded and shot away from the counter to get his order. She seemed so uncomfortable, there was no way I could leave her with the guy. I motioned for Phoebe to grab a table a few spots away from the counter.

Leslie returned with Taylor's order and handed it to him. I watched as his hand grabbed hers instead of the coffee, and he pulled her slowly but firmly across the counter and licked her cheek.

The girl gasped and reared back, spilling coffee everywhere, including down the front of the man's pants.

"Oh, dollface—you'd better help me clean up before you make me another coffee. Grab a rag and get to wiping." His voice had lowered to a level that I was sure he thought we couldn't hear. Truthfully, if I hadn't been paying such close attention, I probably wouldn't have noticed. But tough luck for Taylor because I heard every word and saw how Leslie's eyes dropped nervously to the counter.

"Maybe if you're feeling shy, we should go to the back and get me taken care of," Taylor growled suggestively.

Leslie's jaw tightened, and her hand darted to grab a towel that she tossed at him. "There you go. That's clean. While you're doing that, I'll grab you another coffee. On the house, of course."

"Honey, I insist that we go to the back. You know how I like to spend time with you."

"I've already told you, Taylor," Leslie's voice cracked. "I'm not interested in a relationship. Or anything really."

"Too bad, you owe me dollface."

My gaze shot to Phoebe's, and we stood.

"Get away from her," Phoebe commanded.

"Yeah. She said no." I crossed my arms over my chest as Taylor turned to face us. "You should leave."

"I don't see what all the fuss is about, ladies. I'm waiting for my coffee."

"No, you weren't," Phoebe snarled. "You propositioned her, and she's not interested. We might be visitors in this town, but you can bet your ass we'll be able to find the police station easily enough." She pointed to the door. "Leave."

Taylor's eyes narrowed. "Fine," he spat and snatched up the muffin. "But I'm not paying for this. You owe me, doll, and you can bet that I'll collect . . . later." He pushed past us and stormed out the door.

As soon as he disappeared, Leslie burst into tears. "Thank you so much. He's been pushy lately, and I don't know how much longer I can hold him off."

"You should go to the police," Phoebe said.

Leslie sniffled. "I know, but—"

"But what?" I pressed. "Did he threaten your life? If so, let us help."

"No!" Fear rippled across her face. "No . . . I'll do it. I'll do it—today. I close up soon. I'll go then."

"I hope you do." I sighed and grabbed my coffee off the table. "Do you need us to stay with you?"

Leslie shook her head. "You've done enough already. Thank you so much."

"Don't worry about it," Phoebe smiled at her. "But *please*, go to the cops."

We left the bistro and had made it halfway down the street when Phoebe inched closer to me. "That messed-up situation aside, did you sense the energies coming off of those two?"

Two? "Not Leslie. But that asshole was definitely a shifter."

"Leslie's a shifter of some type too," she said. "Weak blood, though—much weaker than that douche. When Leslie gave me my change, her skin brushed mine, and I recognized it."

I hummed, trying to calm myself and collect my thoughts. "And in the photo she pointed out, there was a shifter couple too—probably strong blood, considering the glowing amber eyes."

We walked another half a block in silence, both considering what this meant. Finally, Phoebe spoke up.

"So it seems like whatever we're here to do, we'll be up against shifters."

"Hopefully they're not all assholes like Taylor." I wrinkled my nose and shook my head. "I've never really dealt with them, but I know that their behavior depends on their animal aspect. The more aggressive the animal, the more aggressive the shifter, even in human aspect. So finding that out is paramount."

Phoebe nodded and bit her lip. "I agree that we need to find out what subspecies live here." Her gaze darted right and then left before she leaned close to me. "What do you think about the shifters having something to do with the so-called animal attacks happening in the area?"

I hadn't even considered connecting the two. Most shifters never attacked humans. They were more likely to fight or attack competing packs or prides than humans.

"What? You don't think so?" Phoebe asked, taking my silence as skepticism.

"No. It's not that. Actually, I think you might be right on the money. I wonder if the attacks are related to the object we're supposed to find?" I shook my head. "I wish Spellcasters had given us a little more info."

Phoebe snorted out a laugh. "They always want to make things a challenge."

There was no doubt about that.

After a couple hours of walking around the tiny town and seeing mansion after mansion, we discovered the area where people of more modest means lived. The neighborhood was a ways away from the main strip, and rundown. Although I understood why the town would want to put its best face forward, it still struck me as very odd that finding a single normal home outside that neighborhood seemed impossible. It reminded me of a slum, which was strange. Shifters usually took better care of their own kind.

After Phoebe and I received a few shifty looks walking through the ghetto, we made our way back into the town center and checked into the hotel. There were plenty of rooms, and the desk clerk, yet another young, weak-blooded shifter, mentioned that the hot springs were in the far back of the hotel, and that we should take advantage of them.

"We have a large group of guests arriving tomorrow, but tonight, there are only a few, so they should be nice and private," the teenager said as he handed us our room key.

Phoebe and I figured that hot springs were as good a place as any to talk, so we went to our rooms and changed. Ten minutes later, clad in shorts and tank tops—because neither of us had thought to bring swimsuits on a mission —we slipped into the mineral pools.

Phoebe sank deep into the pool. "So far, I've only met shifters, and they all seem weak, especially the young ones."

"Do you think it's that their species' blood has weakened over time?" I asked. "Like they mated with humans or something?"

"It's a possibility," Phoebe said. "But since we arrived, have you seen a single person you would say is straight up human?"

I thought back. Every single person I'd passed had radiated magical energies. "No, you're right. I didn't sense a single human."

Phoebe opened her mouth to say something, but the door to the spa flew open, and two raucous couples glided in.

"Hi, there." Phoebe waved good-naturedly. "Enjoying your vacation?"

The woman in the group's forefront stopped laughing and turned to face us.

I sucked in a breath, immediately aware that we had misjudged them as tourists. The woman in the front was the shifter from the picture in the bistro. Her amber eyes glowed even brighter in real life.

"We're not tourists, darling. I'm Rita Hayes, and this is my husband Bob," the woman said. "We live in town. Henry and Judith here," she gestured to the other couple, "are the proprietors of this hotel, and I own half of main street." Her nose tilted up in the air.

I pressed my lips together, trying to hold in my mirth. I'd led a charmed life, and money no longer impressed me, but there were always people whom it impressed a hell of a lot. More often than not, those people were new money and loved to flaunt it.

"This is Odette, and I'm Phoebe." My partner gestured to each of us in turn. "We've visited a lot of places on the main street today. As a matter of fact, we seemed to have covered most of the town already." She lifted herself out of the pool to rest her arms on the stone side. "Since you're locals, maybe you can suggest a few hidden gems we might not have noticed that we can try tomorrow? Or a safe trail? Or even . . . a place to commune with the magical elements around here?"

At the mention of magic, the couples exchanged glances. Henry's nose twitched, telling that he had the best sense of smell out of the four.

"Witches?" he asked tentatively.

We nodded.

"We go to UC Boulder," I said and gave them a conspiratorial grin. "We just needed to get away from campus for the weekend. The mountains were calling, as they say."

The foursome exchanged glances again. It was almost as if they were conferring with each other. I wondered if one was the alpha and could speak mind-to-mind with the others.

After their conference ended, the group moved toward

us in unison. Their movements reminded me of prowling wolves, and the strong shifter vibe intensified. I shot Phoebe a glance and noticed that she looked a little wary.

"As a matter of fact," Rita's lips curled into a smile as the group paused next to our pool. "I do have suggestions. There are a few trails close to the town that are safe. We'll leave a map of those at the front desk. But . . ." She pursed her lips playfully. "As college girls, you might have fun at our party tomorrow night. A lot of the town leaders are getting together for drinks and a good time."

Her friends nodded, and Rita wiggled her eyebrows. "If you two are looking for the real Crescent Springs experience, we'd love to have you. There will be a lot of shifters there, romping under the full moon. Some of them young like you, and very handsome."

"We'd love to come," I said, hiding my shock at the invitation.

It wasn't unheard of for magical species to mix, but being invited to a pack gathering when we'd *just* met was odd. But since we were spies-in-training, oddities were welcome opportunities to investigate.

"Can we bring anything?" I asked.

"Oh no, girls. We'll supply everything. You'll be our honored guests. We want to show you a good time." Rita pulled a tiny notepad out of the bag she carried, and jotted something down. "Here's my address. The party starts at nine."

I smiled and took the scrap of paper, praying to the universe that it was a lead.

CHAPTER SIXTEEN

*A*fter a day of searching fruitlessly for clues, we returned to the hotel to change into party attire. It was strange to be looking forward to a party in a strictly professional capacity, but as we hadn't come across a single lead all day, I was beginning to see the get-together as our last shot.

More than anything, I wanted to find the item Spell-casters had sent us to Crescent Springs for, and return to the academy pronto. My fingers sought my protective talisman, and I rubbed the pendant for comfort.

"I take it that's more than the emblem they gave us when we were inducted into the Society of Spies?" Phoebe asked.

I knitted my brows together. "What makes you think that?"

"You've been wearing it almost all year, even when it

didn't go with your outfit. And I might not know you well, Odette, but I know you like to look *good*."

Phoebe gave me a pointed look as she shimmied into tight leggings that she'd paired with a long, torso-hugging sweater. On the hem of the sweater, as if it were merely the emblem of the brand, was the pin Headmistress Wake had given us to use in case of an emergency. Phoebe looked put together, but not like she was trying too hard, and most important of all, not like a spy.

I nodded at her astute observation about the talisman. "Alex and I charmed it so that we'd know that the other is safe."

Phoebe smiled. "I know Di hated seeing you guys together last year, but now that everything is cool between you two, I have to admit, you're a cute couple. There's something about you. It's like you belong together."

"Thanks."

If Phoebe only knew the half of what was between Alex and me—an unexplainable connection that seemed to span centuries—she'd be gobsmacked.

Not wanting to think about M&M at that moment, I turned to pick out my outfit for the party.

Like Phoebe, I chose leggings and a loose tunic top that complemented my emergency pin. I almost went for a pair of ballet flats, but reconsidered and pulled out a pair of floral patterned slip-on sneakers that looked nice but were also comfortable. It was important for spies to be able to run.

"Ready?" Phoebe asked.

I nodded. "Let's hit the town."

Rita's home was located a block away from the main street and buzzed like a million bees swarmed inside.

Phoebe leaned close as we approached the door. "So after we get the lay of the land, we call for a bathroom break, and then you'll warp us into other rooms so we can inspect them, right?"

"Yup. We can't stay in the bathroom forever, but it's a good place to start."

Phoebe nodded. Flying under the radar for as long as possible was a necessity. There was no way either of us could outrun or outfight a pack of shifters without some sort of advantage.

"If we find what we're looking for and can't leave nonchalantly, we'll return to the bathroom, and I'll warp us to the car." We'd already packed up all our stuff and moved the car to a side street in the crappier neighborhood in case shit hit the fan.

"Perfect," Phoebe whispered as we climbed the front steps.

I rang the bell, and the door flew open immediately, making me jump.

"Girls!" Rita crooned. "So glad you could make it!" She motioned for us to come in, and we obliged, taking a few steps into a foyer that looked like it was straight out of Versailles.

Phoebe took the front position and began engaging Rita in small talk. This enabled me to take in my surroundings, which I'd need a thorough understanding of to warp us effectively. Already, my witch senses were tingling harder than they had all day. I was almost positive that our intuition about the party had been right.

We need to find whatever we're looking for in this huge-ass house, and leave fast.

Suddenly, Rita took a hard right into a shallow alcove and pushed open a set of double doors. Phoebe let out a little squeak and stepped backward, right into me.

I peered around her, and my eyes popped open. *Holy shit.*

"As you can see, this is our coupling room." Rita threw her arms wide, as if she was showing off a priceless piece of art and not a bunch of shifters ripping each other's clothes off.

"I wasn't sure if joining in on the full moon festivities would interest you girls, but thought I should inform you of them sooner rather than later." Her eyebrows wiggled. She looked delighted by the scene. "If you want to join, walk on in—with or without a partner. As the night wears on, this room will become more popular. There are also rooms upstairs, if you prefer more intimacy."

"Umm, thanks," Phoebe choked out. "We'll pass, but it's good to know our . . . *ahem* . . . options."

Rita's grin grew. "Do as you wish! I realize that witches are more prudish than shifters, but there's no judgment here." She shut the door. "Follow me, ladies."

Note to self: Do not warp into that room.

Rita continued the tour, showing us rooms with pool tables, an offshoot into an actual pool, and finally, to the main party space, where people huddled around a bar.

"You're free to explore, although I daresay most of the fun will be had in this very ballroom. We even have dueling pianos, scheduled to start in an hour!" Rita's grin grew as she twirled around in ecstasy.

I scanned the ballroom. There had to be at least eighty people in here, way more than Rita had led us to believe would be at the party. I was about to ask if she'd had a few last-minute RSVPs, when my eyes latched on to a familiar face.

Leslie stared back at me from behind the bar, a bottle of vodka raised as if she'd been about to pour a shot.

I waved, and her eyes grew as wide as saucers.

Interesting . . . "This is fabulous. Thanks for inviting us, Rita. Your friends look like a fun bunch," I said as I latched arms with my partner. "Wanna get a drink?"

"Sure?" Phoebe said, looking confused.

Her reaction wasn't unwarranted. Spellcasters allowed us alcohol during our missions, especially in situations in which it would look odd not to indulge. But one of the first rules of espionage was to get a lay of the land *before* ingesting any substance that may hinder your mental capabilities.

Rita clapped her hands together. "Go get liquored up! Our bartenders make mean martinis."

"We'll take you up on that," I said and pulled Phoebe away.

"I thought we planned to scout a little first?" she whispered as soon as we separated from Rita. She looked left then right and scooted closer to me. "Also, do you notice that the staring is super intense?"

I nodded. We were probably the only witches here, and outsiders to boot, so it made sense that people were interested. But something else lingered in their gazes too. Something that sent chills up my spine.

They looked . . . hungry.

"Recognize the girl behind the bar?" I asked.

Phoebe's attention shifted. "Leslie. She looks . . ."

"Shocked to see us? Frightened?"

"Like someone we should question."

There were two other bartenders, but we strode over to Leslie's third of the bar. Thankfully, fewer people crowded her side, so we weren't crushed by people or at risk of being overheard.

Leslie finished serving a man, and hustled over to us. "What are you two doing here?"

I arched an eyebrow. "Rita invited us to the party. I take it that's uncommon?"

Leslie bit her lip. "Less so than you'd think. I just didn't know that they'd invited any outsiders tonight. This party was supposed to be . . ."

I leaned over the bartop. "Pack-only?"

She sucked in a breath. "How did you know?"

"We're witches," Phoebe said, looking shocked that

Leslie couldn't figure it out. I suspected that it had something to do with her being such a weak shifter.

"Ohhhh." Leslie seemed to grow more tense. "That explains things."

A guest called to her from down the bar, and she assured him she'd be right there. "Do you girls want anything? Ricardo will only take drinks from me. And he gets stupid pushy if I'm not quick." She rolled her eyes.

We both ordered champagne, and Leslie poured the drinks.

When she handed them over, she held the glass for a second too long and leaned closer. "Be careful tonight," she whispered and then rushed off to help Ricardo.

"That was . . . odd," Phoebe said.

I nodded. "Something is totally up around here. It's time we give ourselves a tour."

We moved to the side of the room and slipped down a hallway where a few people mingled. Phoebe asked where the restroom was to deflect attention. Luckily, it was almost all the way down the passage, so we got to peer inside room after room as we went.

Most were empty, although people were engaged in quieter conversations in a few spaces. One room looked to be the home base of the old-boys club, with bountiful cigar smoke pluming in the air and whiskey in every glass. We were nearly to the bathroom when a slight shift in energy raised the hairs on my arms. And then, to my astonishment, my demon-touched scar began to burn.

My blood ran cold, and I stopped suddenly. "Did you feel that?"

Phoebe nodded. "The strange vibration? It's further down the hall, I think."

"Yup."

Darting a glance backward, I caught sight of a group of shifters at the end of the corridor staring at us. I beamed at them, and for good measure, leaned into Phoebe, locking arms with her sloppily.

The shifters must have thought I couldn't hold my drink, because they grinned and turned back around.

Suspicion averted, at least for now. "We should hurry, before others notice that we're nosing around—particularly Rita or her husband."

We walked further down the hall. Aware that people were probably still watching, I added a few stumbles and exaggerated sways to my gait.

None of the doors this far down were open, which had my witchy-senses pinging. Most of the vibrations were coming from the right side of the hall, and everything inside me screamed that we needed to open the last door. Something down there was putting off the wrong energies. I suspected that wasn't a coincidence. Rita had put it far away from the ballroom for a reason. But it would look too suspicious if we just went for it.

We needed to warp inside that room and discover what it was.

I loosened my grip on Phoebe and swayed to the side. "Oopsie!" I cried as my shoulder slammed into the closest door. I expertly twisted the handle as if to save myself, and for effect, I sloshed half the champagne out of my flute. "Dang! This stuff is *strong*!"

Phoebe's eyes darted to the end of the hall. "You're such a lightweight!" she scolded loudly for the benefit of those watching.

"Need another drink?" someone called.

I giggled and held up my nearly empty glass. "She won't let me." Then darting a glance into the room I'd opened, I gestured inside. "We found the library. I think I need to sit down until the spins stop."

The shifters nodded, and Phoebe and I shut the library door behind us.

She bit her lip. "They're watching us like hawks."

"Yup," I said. "Lock the door."

She arched an eyebrow. "What if they come to check—or Rita does?"

"Hopefully we won't be here still," I said, setting my empty glass down and facing toward the hallway.

Phoebe set her glass down too. "Can you warp in there, site unseen?"

"It helps that it's not far and I know exactly where the door is located. I need a moment to visualize the area."

Phoebe didn't respond, so I hopped to it, closing my eyes and visualizing the hallway. Mentally, I moved toward the end, and then opened the final door on the right. I had no idea what was inside, but the strange energies still vibrated within me, and my demon mark burned dully.

"Okay, when the warphole is open, let me go through first. When I say the word, you follow."

"Got it."

I wasted no time altering the surrounding energies, pushing and reshaping them so they formed a tunnel through space.

When the warphole was complete, a rush of heat washed over me. I opened my eyes. It was getting much easier, even if it still took loads of concentration. My lessons with Tittelbaum were paying off.

"Let's do this," I said and stepped through the warphole.

The moment I emerged on the other side, my heart stopped.

"We hit the jackpot."

CHAPTER SEVENTEEN

"What's going on in here?" Phoebe breathed as she scanned the space on the other side of my warphole.

"I'm not sure, but that thing must be what we came here for." A circle lined with bones and lit votive candles was in the center of the room. A glowing gem that I couldn't take my eyes off of rested in the middle. On one wall, an altar of sorts held various golden goblets, and although it was possible one of those was the item we'd been sent here for, every bone in my body screamed that the stone was our quarry.

"Let's grab it and get out of here. Something in this room feels very, very wrong." Phoebe glanced at the banners that hung along each wall, all of which portrayed wolves in violent acts, and shuddered.

I couldn't agree more. My demon mark burned like the dickens, and the very air in this space seemed to vibrate with malice. I wanted nothing more than to leave, and we would, as soon as I got that glowing stone.

I walked carefully toward the circle, trying to suss out any wards or harmful spells before I entered. It was unlike shifters to interact with magic other than the kind that allowed them to shift—but something was different about this pack. The fact that they were making circles meant that magic was not out of the question. They were dangerous too; the burn of my demon mark assured me of that much.

Phoebe stayed back, her hands directed at the door in case something happened, so I crossed the bone-and-candle threshold alone. The moment I did, the creeptastic factor intensified.

My scar seared, as if I had set my ankle on a stovetop. An image of Ishtar flashed in my mind, and the ruby red gemstone in the center of the circle glowed even brighter.

My heart began to thunder, and my pace quickened. I'd reached the center of the circle when the doorknob jiggled.

"Girls! Are you in there? This room is off limits." On the other side of the door, Rita's voice was high and falsely cheery.

"Odette . . ." Phoebe shot me a glance.

"I know, I have to make su—"

Before I could even bend down to pick up the massive hunk of ruby, a key clicked in the lock, and the door swung open. I whipped around to find Rita, her nose transforming as she took on wolf shape. There were other shifters at her back, already in their snarling wolf aspects.

"Well, well," Rita sneered. "I see you two aren't what

you seem either." Her eyes changed color to match the otherworldly glow of the red stone.

My mouth went dry. *Oh shit.* We were in major trouble.

I lowered into a squat to scoop up the gem.

"Stay away from my demon stone!" Rita screamed.

The ruby lifted off the ground, floating into the air, and a yelp escaped me as I fell backward onto my butt.

"Stupid witch. Not many of our sacrifices like to *expedite* their demise and give their life force to my stone." Rita shook her head as if we were the biggest idiots ever. "You didn't even indulge. A pity, as this will be your last night on this earth." She raised her hands.

The candles flared, and the bones began to glow an eerie red that matched the stone.

I gulped as what was happening—what had likely happened to all those tourists who disappeared—crashed over me.

"You've been siphoning life-force from visitors." My voice came out in a terrified croak.

Rita cackled. "Yes, yes. We started with the omegas of our pack, but had to put an end to that. The children kept growing weaker. It wasn't sustainable. But visitors, especially other magicals, are the *perfect* target."

"Why?" Phoebe asked, her hands still extended defensively.

"Have you ever been destitute?" Rita snapped. "This town was *nothing*. A decrepit mining town that survived on social services. I was sick to death of being the joke of the entire state. So I made a deal to change my fate, and soon realized I could elevate the status of my home too."

I shuddered at the implication. Rita had made a deal with a demon for power. And now all she had to do was spill a bit of blood to maintain it.

"The government knows," I said. "Give us the stone, and maybe they'll go easy on you."

"Spellcasters." Rita's eyes narrowed, and as if the shock of discovering who we were was too much, she reverted to a woman. "I always thought they'd send other shifters . . ." She threw her head back and laughed. "The Furies were right! We're the most powerful of our kind! I love it!"

The shifter extended her hand and squeezed her fingers inward. The demon stone, which had been hovering in front of me, soared toward her.

I jumped forward to stop it, my hands reaching outward. Fuchsia magic burst from them, and the stone stopped in mid-air as my magic fought Rita's power for control.

Rita gasped, and her magic—the power she'd gotten from the stone—faltered momentarily as the shifter thrust a finger at me.

"Fuchsia . . . It's you!"

My stomach dropped as I realized my mistake.

The leaders of this pack had made a deal with the Furies, a three-in-one aspect of a royal Princess of Hell. Which meant they knew about me, and that the royals wanted me for their own purposes.

"By order of our masters, capture them!" Rita screamed, confirming my worst fear.

The wolves burst into the room.

I moved to grab Phoebe and get us out of there, but the crazy girl leapt away from me, toward the jaws of ten wolves.

My blood skittered in my veins, and a shield flew from my hands, weaving together as it traveled, and wrapped itself around Phoebe with only seconds to spare.

Two of the wolves rammed straight into the protection and fell to the ground.

"Hurry!" I screamed as I manipulated a second shield around myself and prepared to open a warphole.

Phoebe was there in a second, snatching the stone out of the air and running back toward me. I pictured where we parked the car, and a warphole opened up between us. I dropped our shields, which were protections that warpholes did not allow for, and dove through.

Heat and then chilling cold engulfed us, reassuring me. No matter where we ended up, we'd no longer be in Rita's mansion. That was—

I released a scream as teeth snapped down on my foot seconds before I crashed onto cement.

"Close it, Odette! A wolf is coming through!"

I squeezed my eyes shut in pain, and following Phoebe's instructions, released the warphole. The sickening sound of ripping flesh and liquid dripping onto the ground hit my ears. The sensation of teeth piercing my skin disappeared.

"Oh my God," Phoebe said, and even though I knew the horrors I would see, I couldn't stop myself from looking.

A hand flew to my mouth as vomit climbed up my throat. Half a wolf lay in the middle of the road, glassy-eyed, with its intestines smeared on the ground. I'd closed the warphole around him and sliced his body in half. My stomach heaved, and I wanted to fall apart right then and there.

But I couldn't, because at that very moment an eerie howl broke through the night, sending chills down my spine as it snapped me to attention.

I sat up and scanned our surroundings. Even though we'd gotten away, we weren't safe yet. I hadn't landed us precisely where I wanted. We were still about a half a block from the car.

"Help me up," I said. "We have to get to the car."

Phoebe hauled me to my feet and slithered a shoulder under mine. We'd made it almost halfway when the howls grew louder.

I twisted to look behind us, and all the breath flew from my lungs. At least a dozen wolves were sprinting straight for us.

"Faster!" I screamed.

Despite my foot throbbing each time it contacted cement, we picked up the pace and actually reached the car, where I saw something that made my stomach drop to my knees. Someone had put a goddamned boot on it.

"Make another warphole!" Phoebe urged.

I closed my eyes, but the terrifying howls made it difficult to focus, and when I tried to create a portal, my magic didn't respond.

"Hurry!" Phoebe urged.

"I—I can't! Let's use the pin—*argh*!"

Someone grabbed my arm roughly and pulled.

"Come with me!" Leslie screamed, and using strength that she certainly didn't look like she possessed, she took half my weight and yanked me to a Jeep in front of our rental. "Get in!"

We did as she said, and Leslie hurled herself into the driver's seat and started the engine. Then she stepped on the gas, and we hauled ass to the main drag and then out of town, leaving a pack of wolves howling and snarling in our wake.

CHAPTER EIGHTEEN

"Holy crap, you had one crazy mission!" Eva squealed so loudly that an elderly patron of Potions and Pastries Café shot her a disapproving look. She lowered her voice. "I feel so bad for that girl—Leslie?"

I nodded. "I know, right? How much would it suck for members of your own pack to be siphoning off your magic all your life?" I shook my head, unable to believe what the girl had told Phoebe and me as we booked it out of Crescent Springs and back to Denver.

"But it worked out. Phoebe and I got the demon stone, which I guess gave the pack leaders immense power that no one was brave enough to challenge. Leslie escaped that hell hole and gets to start her life over. And the government apprehended Rita and the other pack leaders."

Eva grinned at me. "Damn, girl. You guys did good!"

I couldn't help but smile back. "We did, didn't we? And

I have to admit, it felt amazing to do something on our own."

Eva sighed. "I can't wait for my mission."

"I can *definitely* wait for the next one." I gestured down at my wrapped foot.

After Phoebe, Leslie, and I arrived back at Spellcasters, I'd stayed under quarantine in the infirmary for two nights. The head healer had released me only a couple hours before. After I was free, I'd met up with Alex for a few minutes before his tutoring session. Once he was gone Eva insisted that we venture to Wandstown for some girl time.

"I bet. What kind of special potion did they give you to heal?"

I huffed out a breath. "They didn't. After they were assured that I wasn't infected with a shifter disease, the healers decided that the wound should close naturally. They said it would be best for my body to do the work so my immune system will be in top form for the Spy Games."

"Oh my God, girl, you are on the move! I can't believe that's in a week!" Eva took a sip of her Earl Grey tea.

"You and me both." A wave of exhaustion rolled over me, and I changed the subject. "Anything happen while I was away? Alex said it was business as usual—lots of classes and physical conditioning—but you know how he is."

Eva shrugged. "Not much. No quizzes or tests. The classes were hell, but that's par for the course. I had a rune-reading session with Professor Adyto, which was interesting . . ." Eva trailed off for a moment before her eyes lit up. "Oh! Diana and Andre are a legit item now. I saw them kissing in the halls."

"About time."

"Yeah, they were *all* over each other."

"Any other juicy gossip?"

She leaned close to me. "It's not so much gossip, but I have noticed Amethyst is acting strange. She kept asking about you—almost obsessively. As if I would know what was going on with your mission. Alex mentioned it, too. Have you talked to her since returning?"

I nodded and bit my lip. Amethyst had found me right after I was released from the infirmary. After assuring her that I hadn't mentioned the possession, she'd backed off, but her persistence was a little unnerving. It made me wonder if *she* wasn't telling *me* something.

Had the ghost possessed her again while I was gone? I wanted to bring it up, but was worried that it would freak her out even more.

"Hey, you've gone all . . . serious. What's going on? I thought Amethyst was worried about your mission, but now I feel like it's something else."

I gulped. "It's nothing."

"Don't lie to me, Odie. I can tell that something is up." Eva studied me, her eyes narrowed. "Why won't you tell me?"

Something in me broke, and a wall—an admittedly flimsy one that I hadn't really wanted to hold up in the first place—came crashing down. "It's not that I don't want to. It's that I *can't*, or someone will get hurt."

"Amethyst?"

I nodded, but clammed up again as the owner of Potions and Pastries, Miss Iris, appeared at the table and asked if we needed any more tea. We declined, and Miss Iris bustled off, content to let us chat as she took care of her other customers.

I cleared my throat, desperate for someone else to know what had happened. "The same things that will hurt us, will hurt her."

Eva's eyes popped open wide. "This demon?" She touched her face.

I shook my head.

"So it's gotta be that one." She gestured toward my ankle, and I nodded. "The queen spoke to her?"

I bit my lip. But even as the hesitation rose, I knew there was no backing out now. Eva knew the most important part, and honestly, if I was going to free Amethyst from this threat, I needed help. Lots and lots of help.

"Spoke *through* her, in a special Rhines way."

Eva's hand flew to her mouth. "Spirit talking? Through a freaking ghost?" Her arm dropped to her lap, and a look of awe spread across her face. "Well, damn. That sucks. Impressive as hell, but still—sucks."

"And Amethyst has been freaking out about it. I'm not supposed to say anything, or the queen will return. Any ideas on how to keep her safe and prevent it from happening again?"

Eva was quiet for a moment. "Have you thought about asking Amethyst if she can confer with other ghosts about this? Perhaps they'll have answers."

My mouth dropped at the obvious and genius idea. "I haven't, but you can bet your butt I will now. And I'll want your help when I do."

I had a lot to catch up on after my mission, and didn't particularly want to confront Amethyst without thoroughly considering what to say, and all the possible scenarios.

Plus, that girl was damn busy. Of course, everyone in the Grind-year was busy, but Amethyst seemed extraordinarily so.

In the end, it took the rest of the week for Eva and me to find Amethyst alone in a library study pod. The pods were basically rooms for those who needed a small group space or extra quiet. I generally avoided them because they smelled of old books, which wasn't a scent that I loved, but Amethyst spent a lot of time in the pods because the Green Tower could get noisy.

"At least we have an out if Amethyst gets too upset," Eva said. "Dinner starts soon, and you need to be there right when they open the cafeteria. I plan on making you eat all the food, because who the heck knows if that vampire school will have normal food?! What if they only serve you liquid?"

I chuckled. "I highly doubt that. There'll be at least

twelve of us there who eat normal food and they wanted us to come a day early. Headmistress Wake wouldn't agree to that if they weren't providing regular food."

"Fine then, carb loading. I'll load your plate up with your faves! All the Hawaiian pizza you can eat." An envious expression crossed Eva's face. "Damn, when I think of carb loading, I kinda wish I was the Spellcasters champion."

Although I appreciated her attempt to remain light-hearted, her mention of the Spy Games tied my already testy stomach into deeper knots.

The champions were scheduled to leave early the next day for Nightdwellers Academy, the first host of the games. It was exciting, but also a lot to take in. I felt like I was just getting my feet beneath me after my mission, and now I had to leave again.

That's the Grind, I reminded myself for the millionth time, as we knocked on the door to the study pod.

Amethyst looked up from the text that she was scrutinizing, and a smile blossomed on her face. She waved us in.

I shut the door behind us. "Hey, girl. Can we talk?"

Amethyst's eyebrows furrowed together, but she shut her book. "Sure. What's on your mind?"

"First, I want to know . . . are there any ghosts around right now?"

Amethyst's gaze darted around the air for a few moments before she shook her head. "Nope. Just us."

"Good, because it's about that day in Tarot and Divination," I said, and the poor girl's eyes practically bugged out of her head as they shot from Eva to me and back again. "I know I'm not supposed to tell anyone what happened," I added quickly so Amethyst wouldn't keel over. "And I haven't, but Eva guessed that something was up."

Sort of—with some help.

"When," Amethyst demanded, her jaw set in a hard line.

"Earlier this week." Eva kept her tone measured and her face neutral as she sat across from Amethyst. I followed her lead, hoping that if we stayed calm, Amethyst would too. "And you're still here. Probably because Odie and I were careful not to mention any names or specifics."

Amethyst shook her head and stood, her shoulders trembled with anger. "I can't believe you put my life on the line. I *trusted* you—"

"We might have a way to get you out of this," I interrupted before she could work herself into a furious frenzy.

Her eyes narrowed. "What do you mean a way out? How can *we* outsmart a royal of Hell?"

I arched an eyebrow, somewhat offended. "You act as if *I* haven't already done that. Don't you remember who I fought during the Beltane Trial?"

Amethyst colored slightly. "I—that's not what I meant. This is different."

"She knows," Eva said. "And this is not the time to get all butt-hurt, Odie. Let's stay on track and see if what we came up with could even work."

My cheeks heated. Eva was right. I'd just grown so used

to having to defend myself against haters that sometimes a little attitude slipped out.

"Go ahead, then," I said. "It was your idea."

Eva turned her attention to Amethyst. "Have you considered asking other ghosts about the possession?"

Amethyst's spine straightened. "What do you mean?"

"I assume that there are lots of other ghosts here." Eva gestured around. "A school like this is a perfect place for them."

Amethyst nodded. "Spellcasters has about fifty in residence. Some pop in and out. I'd say half of those live here full-time."

Holy crap, fifty ghosts were floating around me all the time? I shivered, suddenly glad that I didn't seem gifted in spirit walking and taking.

"Do you talk to them often?" Eva pressed.

"Two or three like to chat, but most I can't reach yet. I'm not a fully trained spirit-talker, and I haven't even started spirit walking yet . . . except for that time in Divination."

"Which doesn't count, because you weren't in control," Eva said as if she knew everything on the subject.

"No . . ." Amethyst lowered herself into her chair and placed her hands flat on the table as if they would help ground her to one spot.

"Well, since you can access a couple of ghosts," Eva's voice dropped, and I inched toward her as if I didn't know what was coming. "Do you think they could tell you something about the ghost that inhabited you?" She reached across the table to lay a hand on Amethyst's. "Are you willing to ask around and get the information? If you do and want to share it with us, maybe we can help you banish the ghost or something."

"You may have noticed Eva and I are pretty good at evading powerful beings," I added, hoping to ease the lingering tension in Amethyst's shoulders.

It worked, and her lips twisted up in a small smile.

"I would have to be blind not to see that." She sucked in a huge breath and released it slowly, clearly processing the idea. "I'll admit, it's a decent plan. I'll start asking around tonight, and hope someone has an answer." Amethyst's eyes turned on me. "Thanks for looking out for me and trying to prevent another possession. Sorry I lashed out."

"No worries, girl. We'll do everything we can to help," I said, hopeful that together, we could find a solution that wouldn't put her life in danger.

CHAPTER NINETEEN

Later that night, as I perched on my bed, I groaned and grabbed my stomach. "Eva wasn't joking when she said she'd make me eat all the food. I totally overdid it with the Hawaiian pizza. I have a food baby."

Alex shut the door behind us and came to sit next to me. We were finally getting a rare moment alone since I'd returned from my mission, and already, I knew it would be too brief. I'd asked him to stay the night, but he'd declined. He didn't want to keep me up too late, because less sleep could affect my performance during the Spy Games.

I'd wanted to argue that him not being at my side the night before the start of a massive tournament might cause me to lose sleep too, but the excuse didn't work.

This is what I get for dating a healer. He's always looking out for my health.

"Eva is making sure you're prepared for the games in

the best way she knows how," Alex said. "Just like I'm about to do."

My ears perked up, and my hands went to the buttons on his shirt. They were there for only a second before he gently grabbed them and set them back in my lap.

"Not like that, sweets."

I pouted. "Tease."

"At least not yet." He winked.

Hope surged like fire in my blood, and giving in to whatever he had planned, I leaned back and propped myself up on my elbows. "So how are you going to help the Spellcasters team win against the other schools—if not by allowing me a much needed reprieve from stress?" I waggled my eyebrows, and Alex laughed.

The sound warmed my heart. Outside of classes, I hadn't seen as much of him—or anyone, really—as I would have liked.

Alex reached into his pocket and pulled out a small, golden vial.

My eyebrows knitted together. "What's that?"

"Part of how I'll keep you safe," he said as he pulled off the top. "Hunter and I made this potion. We had to sneak into the potion room to get some of the rarer ingredients, but I think it will be worth it for the peace of mind. It's supposed to repel vampires."

"Oh . . ." I trailed off.

"I'd appreciate it if you took it with you to the first Spy Games event. Assess the situation, and the vamps at Night-dwellers. If you trust them and think it's all friendly competition, don't drink it. But it's better safe than sorry. If any of them seem off—"

I plucked the vial from his hands. "I'll take it." I kissed him on the cheek. "Although, I hope I don't have to use it."

"Me too, sweets. Me too," Alex said. His gaze dropped to the talisman on my wrist.

I raised my hand. "I'm not going to use this, you know that, right? This is for *real* danger, not fabricated games."

He shook his head. "I know, but still wear it. None of the other schools will be as warded as Spellcasters. I'll want to know if the demons show up and you're in trouble."

I nodded. "I wish you were going with me. Having someone there who knows everything that's happening would be so nice." I pushed the fact that Alex didn't know about Amethyst from my mind. He worried enough as it was, he didn't need to hear about that. At least, not until we had a solution.

"Me too," he said. "Honestly, I kinda wish I'd entered the damn Spy Games. You and I had top choice, and I blew my chance to be at your side. I even considered going to the headmistress and demanding that I join the champions at the other academies, but that would raise too many questions. I figure I'll wait until the first game is over to become the overprotective boyfriend."

As much as I loved Alex, I so did not want him becoming that. "And I want the chance to prove myself."

"As if you haven't done that a hundred times already," Alex whispered and leaned in. He wrapped his arms around me and pulled me close.

The next thing I knew, we were kissing. Alex's hands roamed my back, sending a thrill up my spine. I wanted him close to me, as close as we could be, so I pulled back slightly and peeled off my shirt.

An appreciative look that never got old washed over his face.

"I've been saving it for a special occasion," I said, trailing a finger over the black lace of my new bra. "And the undies to match."

Alex's lips parted. "You've been hiding that all day, and you let me go on about vampire-repelling potions and how I feel like a lame boyfriend for not joining the Games?" His blue eyes bore through me. "You're a cruel woman."

I batted my eyelashes. "How can I make it up to you, Mr. Wardwell?"

Alex's eyes drifted to my chest. "There are ways."

"Ways? Like—"

Alex's hands gripped my shoulder as he laid me down on the bed and straddled me. His lips found mine, and I arched up to meet him.

If this was how I'd serve my penance, so be it.

CHAPTER TWENTY

My stomach jumped and twisted. The Spellcasters champions would soon travel to Nightdwellers for the opening of the Spy Games. Headmistress Wake had instructed us to pack an overnight bag, but I'd packed for a week because I liked to be prepared.

I loaded my duffel up with clothes, makeup, and some snacks that Eva had procured from the cafeteria at breakfast and insisted that I take with me. When the bag was almost full, I added the vampire-repelling potion, nestling it between a pair of jeans and my socks so it wouldn't break. Finally, I placed the name tag Headmistress Wake had given me around the handle.

Once I felt ready, I exited my room to find Diana waiting for me at the top of the stairs. Alex, Hunter, and Eva stood with her.

"Didn't know you guys were out here," I said, walking up to meet the crew.

"We'd never let you leave without saying goodbye." Hunter strode forward first and wrapped his arms around me. "Knock their socks off, Odie."

Eva sidled up to hug me next. "You got this girl. Kick their asses."

Alex was last, and his eyes went straight to the talisman on my wrist. "Good. You didn't forget to put it on this morning."

"As if I could. You only reminded me fifty-two times last night," I teased. "I packed the potion too."

"Just want to keep you safe, babe," He squeezed me tight. "I love you."

"Love you too." I returned his embrace. When we broke apart, I gave them all one last smile. "See you guys when we get back. Shouldn't be later than tomorrow night."

Alex's lips tightened. "Maybe a little later for me." He pulled a scrap of paper from the pocket of his pants. "I found this taped to my door after breakfast. I'll be leaving soon too. It seems that Headmistress Wake wants to take no chance that we might try to be together during missions."

I shook my head. That woman was so damn thorough. "Any idea where you're going?"

"Nope. Ms. Seeley will meet Mina and me with the details at two. But that doesn't matter. We'll handle whatever they throw at us, so don't worry. I'll be rooting for you and missing you."

"Same, babe."

We kissed one more time, before I broke off from my friends, who waved Diana and me down the stairs.

When we were at the bottom, I turned to the head-mistress' daughter. "I didn't expect you to wait for me."

Diana shrugged. "I figured we might as well go together. You know, start bonding early so we can kick the competition's ass."

A small smile broke on my face. Diana had sucked during our Culling-year. I appreciated that she was attempting to be a better person—maybe even a friend.

Only time will tell.

We made our way to Alice Kyteler Hall, where Professor Tittelbaum preferred to open warpholes. Despite being five minutes early, Sam, Andre, and Headmistress Wake were already there waiting.

"Ready, everyone?" The headmistress wasted no time as we joined the group.

Everyone confirmed that they were, and Professor Tittelbaum opened a warphole. One by one, we stepped through, and when I emerged onto a grassy downslope on the other side, I gasped with delight.

The school was a castle, black as night and gleaming in the morning sunlight that just managed to fend off the chill in the air. Hundreds of onyx spires twisted toward the sky, and a dozen towers rushed up between them, all vying for the status of tallest. To top it all off, the school was smack dab in the center of a ring of mountains so majestic they made my heart skip a beat.

"Holy crap," Sam said, inching up toward me.

"Took the words right out of my mouth," I said, unable to rip my eyes from the gothic wonderland down the hill.

"How do they protect themselves?" Diana, ever the practical one, asked. "I don't sense any wards."

"Just because they're not right in front of you, doesn't mean they don't exist." The headmistress pointed upward.

We followed her finger, squinting up into the sun. It took a few moments, but I caught the telltale signs of a shield shimmering and slightly pulsating in the sunlight.

"Only in the sky?" Diana's gaze dropped to meet her mother's eyes. "Like, to hide the school from planes?"

"The sky and all the way down to the tops of the surrounding mountains. When Nightdwellers was founded, witches created the shield and spelled the castle so that humans felt disinclined to climb these mountains."

That sounded like a lot of work. I wondered if the fae academy had to take even further precautions, as fae looked otherworldly without their glamour.

"The Spellcasters delegation has arrived!" a boisterous voice called from behind us, startling me out of my admiration.

I whirled around to find the tall, gangly form of Headmaster Ezra rushing down the mountainside. My eyes widened, taking in the incredible speed at which he ran, and the cohort of vampire students at his back.

It was the first time I'd seen the headmaster up close and without a black hood. It surprised me to see he was younger than I'd imagined—no older than forty. His dark brown hair showed no trace of gray, his eyes gleamed with youth, and there wasn't a wrinkle on his pale skin. While many people would opt to remain in their twenties if given the chance to turn into a vampire, looking at Headmaster Ezra, I disagreed. The headmaster had been changed in the prime of his life.

"I apologize that I was not at the door to welcome you," the headmaster said. "We were finishing up our exercise for the morning, and I saw you *pop* into existence." He held up a fist and flung his fingers open to demonstrate our sudden appearance.

"No matter," Headmistress Wake said. "You're here now. Shall we proceed inside?"

Headmaster Ezra motioned to his students. "Inform the kitchens we have guests who will require solid nourishment. Mathias and Jules, take the champions' bags and place them inside their rooms. Ensure that everyone knows that wing of the castle is off limits. If the champions' privacy is breached, the offender will suffer time in the dungeons."

My stomach tightened. *The dungeons? What the hell kind of school is this?!*

"When should lunch be ready for them?" Jules, the girl, asked.

"Three hours should be long enough. It will be served in the solarium so they might enjoy our mountain views," the headmaster replied after a moment's musing.

Three hours? That seemed like an exorbitant amount of time to prepare lunch. But then again, as Eva had pointed out to me before I left, people in Nightdwellers probably didn't cook often.

Take all the time you need, I thought, hoping we wouldn't

get served up a bowl of blood stew, or some other revolting dish.

We followed Headmaster Ezra inside the castle. As soon as the thirty-foot high doors shut behind us with a *thud*, a chill washed over me.

While Spellcasters was dark inside from its rich wood walls and decor, Nightdwellers was unlit to the point of verging on gloomy. I glanced up and saw that the chandeliers were forged of cold silver and had the bare minimum of candles lit to provide light. The walls were pitch black, and the few portraits that eased the starkness were of disturbingly pale or ashen people. Every single one seemed to be competing for the Most Dour Expression award.

And then there was the *other* art.

It was as if, between vampire portraits and cold, black walls, the only other suitable adornment at Nightdwellers was something that Goya might have created in his darkest period. Paintings rivaling the depravity of *Saturn Devouring His Son* stared down at us, making me cringe.

"That's not creepy at all," Andre whispered at my side. "And the government allows vampires to spy for them?"

"They don't merely *allow* it, my boy, they wish to employ *more* of us." Headmaster Ezra twisted to look at Andre, who blushed at being overheard. "Something to do with our keen senses, immense strength, and incredible speed."

At that, everyone fell quiet, and Headmaster Ezra began to lead us around the school.

I'd expected a short tour, followed by time to rest and

get acclimatized. As it turned out, however, my expectations were not met. The headmaster spent the next two hours and forty-five minutes playing tour guide. He particularly seemed to delight in regaling us with the creepy history behind the decorations of Nightdwellers.

Finally, lunch was pronounced ready, and Headmaster Ezra led us to a long, dark hallway. He pointed to the door at the end. "That is my suite. The Spellcasters students will stay in rooms sharing my hallway the evening before the games. The rooms are labeled, and your bags are already inside."

"Why are we not rooming near the students we're supposed to be getting to know?" Sam asked. "I thought this event was for making friends with other magicals as much as friendly competition."

"Of course, you will have time to meet them at the feast this evening. And if you wish, I can arrange new accommodations afterwards. However, be aware that my students have a competitive streak. I would not put it past them to . . . sabotage your chances," Headmaster Ezra commented. "If you were to sleep near me, there would be less chance of such tomfoolery."

"Where are the fae and shifter champions staying?" Sam asked, quickly picking up on the fact that the hall didn't have enough doors to house all the visiting champions and their chaperones.

"The fae will stay one hallway down this corridor, where my most trusted staff lives. The shifters, however . . ." The vampire shook his head, as if he were amused. "Well, let's just say the shifters and my students have a bit of a healthy rivalry. They declined to room under my protection. I suspect that after the Inaugural Feast this evening, much mischief will be had."

"Alpha Conon always had an *interesting* leadership style," Headmistress Wake said, clearly unimpressed by the shifter headmaster. "I thank you for placing my students here. Now why don't you four go wash up for lunch? Afterward, we shall have some downtime."

We all nodded, and happy for a moment alone, I slipped through the door to my room and shut it behind me.

CHAPTER TWENTY-ONE

*C*hatter and laughter rang in my ears as we approached the dining hall of Nightdwellers Academy for the first Spy Games Feast. I inhaled softly to quell my rising nerves, and squared my shoulders, preparing to be in the spotlight.

"You two ready for this?" Sam slid up between Diana and me.

"I think so." Mentally, I ran through the last-minute etiquette tips that Headmistress Wake had given us about interacting with vampires, fae, and shifters. I didn't want to embarrass my academy.

"If you're at a loss, let Andre and me lead," Sam suggested. "We've had more diplomatic training and experience with other creatures."

My lips pulled up in a smile. Although I was sure that Sam was as nervous as the rest of us, I appreciated the offer.

There had to be a leader of our little foursome, and it was nice to lean on someone else when my nerves were jangled.

"Done and done," I agreed.

Diana nodded her agreement too. We slowed down to let the third-years pass us to walk in front.

A vampire gripping a steel staff that was taller than me stood at the entrance to the dining hall. When we approached, he motioned for us to stop and banged the rod on the ground. Voices in the chamber fell to a hush, and a wave of respect rolled over me. Nightdwellers totally creeped me out, but it was obviously regimented, and the students seemed to honor the headmaster and those above them.

"The final champions have arrived," the staff-wielding vampire announced. "Please allow me to introduce the witches of Spellcasters." He stepped aside, giving us a view of the room.

I gasped. Headmaster Ezra had referred to the space where the feast would take place as the dining hall. But the name didn't do the luxurious gothic hall justice.

As with the rest of the castle, darkness prevailed, but strategic applications of light highlighted the room beautifully. Twisted metal centerpieces on every table held at least a dozen flaming red candles. Above, silver chandeliers dripped a stream of black crystals so long that they hovered only a few feet above the candle flames. The firelight made the crystals glow beautifully. Around the circular tables sat high-backed, black velvet chairs studded with steel. The entire room was striking and unlike anything I'd seen before, but four tables in the middle of the room—the champions' tables—stood out the most.

At the far left of the line sat the vampire champions, all in suits and gowns, looking elegant and poised. As my gaze scanned the table, I locked eyes with a female champion with hair so black it appeared almost blue. Her eye contact was hard, unyielding in a way that sent shivers down my spine. Uncomfortable holding her gaze, my eyes flitted to the chalice before her.

Bad choice. The glass brimmed with blood, and my stomach heaved so I had to place a hand in front of my mouth.

The girl caught the gesture, smirked, and brought her goblet to her lips. Instead of sipping it, however, she bared her fangs and poured the red liquid on her lips. It cascaded down her front, coloring the pale skin of her décolletage crimson.

Her classmates burst out laughing, and even Headmaster Ezra looked amused by the girl's antics.

Aware that the raven-haired vampire wanted to intimidate me, I arched what I hoped looked like an unimpressed eyebrow and turned toward the fae.

The fae delegates and their chaperones retained their glamour, but a strong, otherworldly energy vibrated off them. I'd felt a similar sensation before, wafting off of Ms. Seeley. Standing before five full fae, however, made it clear that Ms. Seeley's witch side was more dominant.

The shifter participants sat sandwiched between the fae and vampires. It was impossible to tell what sort of animal they shifted into, but their amber and silver eyes glowed in the dark, hinting at their power.

Our table waited on the far right, and as soon as we settled in, Headmaster Ezra stood and moved to an empty space in front of the four champion tables. "Now that everyone is present, it is time to meet the champions of the first annual Spy Games!"

I withheld a groan. Why couldn't we eat and *then* do all the rah-rah crap? We'd spent the hours since our surprisingly tasty lunch in the solarium studying the magical races of our opponents, and working out so that our muscles would be ready for the start of the Games the next day. As a result I was freaking starving.

"In this corner, for Nightdwellers," Headmaster Ezra swept back over to the vampire table. His exaggerated motions and obvious excitement reminded me of an announcer on a wrestling program. "Are the vampires!"

The room roared on cue. Students pounded their fists on the tables and a few leapt on to the table tops and released a proud hiss. I sighed and reluctantly settled in for what was sure to be a drawn-out spectacle.

When the cheering died down, Headmaster Ezra held a hand over a vampire with albino-white skin and vibrant blue eyes.

"First up for the host academy is Francis!"

Francis stood and began blowing kisses and waving to the crowd, who voiced their pleasure loudly.

Headmaster Ezra moved on to introduce the other three champions with equal fanfare.

Magdalena was a short, Hispanic-looking girl who seemed like she'd been about my age when she was turned. Compared to the headmaster and Francis, she was meek—merely waving and smiling at the crowd as she received her applause.

Anton sat next to Magdalena. He was a stack of pure muscle who might have hailed from the snowy plains of Russia.

And then there was the final vampire, Simone, the girl who had poured blood down her front. When the head-master introduced her, she jumped onto the table, raised her arms to the sky, and released a chilling vampiric hiss in the direction of her competitors.

I exchanged a glance with Sam, who looked about ready to burst into laughter, and rolled my eyes.

Headmaster Ezra, however, seemed delighted with Simone's theatrics. He patted first her and then Francis on the back, but ignored the other two. I took this to mean that the flashier champions were the headmaster's pets, which meant they were, most likely, the strongest of our four vampiric opponents.

After the vampires were done putting on their show, Alpha Conon stood to introduce the champions for the Shifter Academy of Spies. He did so perfunctorily, requesting that his students stand and move to the space in front of the champions' tables.

Only one shifter champion was female, Dasha, and it seemed to me that the three males, Heath, Howley, and Gregor, were all a touch infatuated with her. She was beautiful, with glowing, golden eyes and golden tresses that grazed her booty, so I couldn't blame them. And yet, it felt like something more drew them to her than her beauty. Perhaps she possessed alpha blood? I made a note to ask later.

The Fae Academy of Elemental and Arcane Arts was next. Headmistress Cristala swept toward the front of the room, her blue silk dress fluttering behind her like butterfly wings.

"My students are pleased to be here, competing for the honor of our academy." The fae headmistress smiled, and the effect was almost blinding, her teeth were so white. "It is with great pride that I call up Ayla Torna and Sana Torna."

Two female fae stood and glided to the center of the room. My eyes darted from one to the other, searching for differences I couldn't find. They had to be sisters—probably twins.

Although the Tornas hid their true fae nature beneath a glamour, it was easy to see they were not fully of this world. Their red locks were a little too bright, their green eyes too vibrant, and their skin glowed even more than the vampires'. The girls joined their headmistress and beamed at the crowd.

Something in the air shifted, and a few of the vampires sitting in the sea of tables stood up. Their eyes glowed red, and their mouths opened to reveal extended fangs.

Oh shit.

My heartbeat sped up as I remembered that the blood of

magicals appealed to vampires even more than human blood. And they generally considered fae blood the most delicious. A lot of times, a fae's glamour dimmed this effect, but clearly, the Torna twins were too tasty-smelling for their own good.

"*Girls*," Headmistress Cristala admonished while the vampire headmaster signaled for the affected vampires to leave.

"Apologies," Cristala said. "As we do not want to reveal our true nature until the first game, the girls were trying to give a mere taste of their power. However, they don't know their own strength."

Oh snap. My gaze shot to the Nightdwellers table. Simone and Francis were frowning. They'd caught the indirect jab, the suggestion that the fae champions' power could affect how vampires acted, and they didn't like it one bit.

"And now to introduce our male champions. Luvon Iarro and Volwin Valar, won't you join me?"

The male fae joined the females. Although their size and build brought to mind gladiators, they didn't quite hold the same aura that the girls did. I suspected that while the men might have been chosen for physical strength, the females were the ones with the magical skill.

Note to self, watch out for the Tornas.

Once everyone had gotten a good look at the fae, the champions returned to their seats, and Headmistress Wake stood.

A shiver rolled up my spine. It was our turn. Immediately, trusty mantras began rolling through my mind.

I've got this. I'm here because I've proven myself capable.

With enthusiasm and charm somewhere between the shifter and fae leaders', Headmistress Wake introduced us, starting with the Crucible students.

She hadn't requested that we move to center stage, so Sam and Andre simply mimicked the headmistress and stood from their chairs. Diana followed suit, her face stoney compared to the other two. If I hadn't been so nervous, it would have made me giggle. But then again, maybe it shouldn't. Diana was obviously trying to put up a tough front so no one would underestimate us.

"And finally," Headmistress Wake's words snapped me back into the moment. I was next.

Prematurely, I began to rise.

"The other Grind-year student participating in the Spy Games for Spellcasters is Odette Dane."

My stomach twisted as a collective gasp filled the room, and every single eye in the place shot to me. Even those at the champions' tables perked up, and a few began studying me like I was some sort of mythological creature.

My face warmed at the intensity of it all. I doubted that my own reputation would garner such a reaction. Clearly, people in the crowd had heard of my parents and all their exploits.

Oh joy.

Thankfully, Headmistress Wake requested that we sit quickly, which I did, and Headmaster Ezra took the reins once again.

"Wonderful! Wonderful!" The headmaster rubbed his

hands together. "We're so pleased to meet all of you, and we look forward to the Games starting bright and early tomorrow! For now, let us get to know one another, as friendly competitors should."

He clapped, and a deluge of servers darted into the room carrying trays weighed down with food.

The headmaster threw his arms up and tossed his head back. "Let the Spy Games Feast begin!"

I waddled sleepily to my room after the feast, alongside the other witch champions. It had been a long three hours of small talk with other magicals who had been either attempting to suss out our weaknesses or intimidate us. I'd met both tactics with the same response. Eating more. Now my belly was so full, I regretted stuffing myself; although, truth be told, I wouldn't have been able to stop.

Any fears I had about vampires not being able to cook were very misguided. All the food I'd been served at Night-dwellers was on par with Michelin-starred restaurants.

"Oh my God, I hope all that cake doesn't weigh me down tomorrow," Sam moaned as we reached our rooms.

"Same," I agreed. "Why couldn't I have stopped at two slices?"

"What time is everyone getting up tomorrow?" Diana asked, ever the business-oriented witch, as she leaned against the door to her room expectantly.

"The games start at ten, so eight?" I suggested. "To eat and prepare?"

"Don't even talk about eating," Sam quipped.

A few minutes later, we decided that we'd all wake at eight and breakfast together. Putting on a united front was important, and that would give us time to discuss last-minute strategy.

We said our goodnights, and I locked myself in my room, put on my pjs, and brushed my teeth. I was about to wash my face and crash when a knock came on the door.

Turning off the tap, I went to check who it was and found no one was there.

A moment later, Sam poked her head out of her room, then Andre, and lastly, Diana. Everyone looked as confused as I felt.

"Did someone knock on your doors too?" I asked.

They all nodded, and then Sam gasped. "Look! Under the rug!" She pointed to her feet.

I glanced down, and my lips parted in surprise. Tucked beneath the hallway runner, almost out of sight, was an envelope bearing my name.

CHAPTER TWENTY-TWO

"I don't think this is a good idea," Diana said as we tiptoed through the halls of Nightdwellers Academy. "What if it's a trap?"

"Or what if it's a party, like the invitation said?" Sam retorted.

I wasn't sure what to think. Diana could be right, but then again, the vampire champions might actually have invited us to a party. All I knew was that it would look chickenshit not to go.

"I hear voices up ahead," Andre said.

I tilted my head. I heard them too.

When we reached a T in the hallway, we discovered that the voices belonged to the fae champions. They'd obviously received the invite too, and even more apparent was the fact that they were walking the wrong way.

"Hey! Guys!" Sam waved her arms as if the fae weren't twenty-feet away.

The champions spun around, and the twins beamed.

"Did you guys get invited to a party too?" One twin asked as their group jogged over to meet us.

I nodded and upon taking in her outfit, I wished that I'd brought something cuter to wear. The sisters were decked out in short navy dresses and tall brown boots that hit mid-thigh. They looked hot as hell, and even though I'd felt confident in my shiny black leggings and tight-cut sweater before, now I felt frumpy.

"I'm surprised that you guys are going," Diana commented. "Didn't those vamps want a taste of you earlier?"

Luvon, the larger male, stepped forward and grunted, but a twin pulled him back.

"She didn't mean it that way, Luvon," she said, her tone smoky. "Sorry, he's protective. And don't worry about our fae essence. Our headmistress helped strengthen our glamour so we shouldn't affect even the most sensitive vamps anymore."

Huh. That was interesting. I hadn't known that a fae could manipulate other fae's glamours, but I supposed it made sense. Only aether-blessed fae could create glamours and they were rare. Judging by the stunned looks on my team's faces, I hadn't been alone in my ignorance.

There was an awkward silence, which the smoky-voiced twin broke. "Since you probably can't remember which one of us is which, I'm Ayla. You can tell by the gold jewelry." She lifted her arm to reveal a stack of gold bangles, and pointed to a gold necklace around her neck. "Sana is wearing silver. That way, people who meet us can remember."

Sana gestured to the guys. "They're easy to remember. The dark-haired one is Luvon, and Volwin is the blond with the beard." Both guys looked tense, not at all as if they wished to be going to a party.

"Umm, hi," I said, and Volwin scowled.

Sana batted his shoulder. "Seriously, stop it. They're trying to be nice. You can chill on the guard duty."

"Guard duty?" My eyebrows pulled together.

They had introduced the guys as champions, not guards. And why would Sana and Ayla need guards anyway?

Sana looked like she wished she hadn't said anything, but Ayla waved her hand dismissively. "It was bound to get out anyway, sister." She focused her attention on us. "Sana and I are of the Riverlands royal line, so we travel with a guard."

I gaped. They were royalty? Why were they here and not in Faerie?

Ayla rushed to explain. "Not like *real* royals. I'm sixth in line for the crown, and Sana is seventh. Even if all our relatives died off, it's unlikely the Riverlands Court would crown one of us, as we've only been to Faerie once. But our parents don't see the difference." She rolled her eyes. "They're so protective, they wouldn't let us attend spy school without escorts. We're hoping that if we do well in the Spy Games, they'll loosen the reins a bit."

"Or at least stop commenting that we should leave

school because it's too dangerous," Sana added.

Oh my God, it's like they're me from last year.

When no one said anything, Sana bit the inside of her cheek. "It might sound dumb to you guys, but—"

"No," I blurted. "It doesn't. I can relate." I smiled, and she beamed back. "Why don't we all walk to the party together, and you can tell us all about your situation?"

The twins moved to either side of me, and their guards winged them. As we walked, I learned about the twins and a bit about the Fae Academy of Elemental and Arcane Arts. There were many similarities to Spellcasters, but many differences too—like how in their final year, the Academy of Elemental and Arcane Arts expected the fae to spend a month at court in Faerie.

When we reached the Dark Tower, where the party was being held, I was disappointed to have arrived so quickly. I really wanted to find a quiet spot and keep chatting with the twins. But showing our faces was what we'd come to do. So instead of asking the twins to hang out with me in the corridor, I followed the group into the party.

Unsurprisingly, the tower was dark, although the strobe lights that pulsed from every nook and cranny alleviated that effect somewhat. Music blared, but even so, most of the people in the tower had very sensitive hearing. They turned to study us as soon as we walked in.

"Excellent! The witch and fae champions have arrived!" Francis, the albino vampire champion, swept over to meet us, somehow not spilling a drop of blood from his shallow cocktail glass as he moved. "We worried that the fae wouldn't show due to the newbloods revolting manners earlier."

My mouth fell open. "Newbloods?" I croaked.

Newblood vampires were freshly turned and possessed *terrible* impulse control. It took months just for them to stifle the urge to jump on someone and drain them dry.

Why would Nightdwellers allow them at the academy?

"Not *real* newbloods." Magdalena, the Hispanic champion, joined Francis. "It's just what we call first-years here."

A wave of relief washed over me, and apparently it was obvious, because both vampires chuckled. Not wanting my opponents to think me nervous and naïve, I straightened my spine. "So, what's the party for?"

Francis smiled a sly smile. "If it were up to our headmasters and headmistresses, we'd only interact at proper dinners and the Games. But we wanted to have a little fun and get to know everyone in a lighter manner."

"That's half the reason for the games, right?" Magdalena supplied. "We'll all be working for the PIA one day. It would be nice to see familiar faces when we get there."

At Magdalena's reassurances, my shoulders relaxed. Although they were both my competitors, I trusted her way more than flashy Francis.

"Great point," Sam said and cast a glance around. "So, where are the drinks?"

Francis wrapped his arm around her shoulders, and shockingly, Sam didn't balk at the attention. He then proceeded to lead our group to a bar on the far side of the circular tower.

On the bartop, all the usual drink stared back at me, and since we were at a vampire school, bottles of dark red blood were present too. In fact, the bartender had placed them front and center, which I found a little strange. That is until a vampire approached and gave Diana a hearty sniff as he reached for a bottle. I shot Francis an accusatory glance.

He held up both hands. "I *swear* he's not a true newblood. The swine merely has poor manners. They don't even allow newbloods into Nightdwellers. You have to have been a vampire for a decade to apply."

I pursed my lips. "Good to know."

We ordered drinks, and I began making a loop around the tower. Almost right away, I found the shifter champions. They were huddled near the fireplace, nursing beers, and looking as if they were ready to bolt.

I steered that way, curious about the group and intent on getting some answers.

"Hey. Crazy party, huh?" I said as I approached them. "It's like a gothic rave in here." I gestured to the wider room with my soda and lime.

Dasha, the female, grinned at me. "It's interesting. Not quite my taste. Still, I figured it would be worth it to check out the competition."

"But you're all alone," I teased.

The burliest male grunted. "Finally."

Dasha rolled her eyes and ran her hands through the man's long, red hair. "Please excuse Gregor. We just broke away from Simone. She claimed that she needed to go . . .

nourish herself. She was quite intense, and the guys don't like people trying to dominate me."

I tilted my head. "Can I ask what might be a dumb question about shifters?"

"We're here to learn about each other, aren't we?" One of the males held out his hand. He wore glasses and had a slender, muscular frame beneath his tight black t-shirt. He wouldn't have looked out of place in a tech company. "I'm Howley, by the way. If I recall, you're a Dane?"

I nodded, but not wanting to get into my family history before I figured out the dynamic, I caught Dasha's eye and blurted out my question. "Are you an alpha? I sense something between you four, but I can't place it—probably because I haven't been around a lot of shifters. And those I have been around were . . . unusual." Memories of Colorado flooded my mind and, unable to help myself, I cringed.

Dasha's eyes widened, catching the gesture. "To answer your question, yes, I'm alpha blood—but that's probably not what you sense."

Slowly, she moved to stand between the guys, and their attention followed. She caressed Howley's arm and batted her eyelashes at the one who hadn't spoken yet—Heath.

"I'm not technically an alpha yet. I won't be until my mom dies. In the meantime, I wanted to spy for my country. But the magic in my blood is already working to make sure my reign is powerful. It's chosen a mate for me—actually, three."

I gulped. Holy crap. I'd heard of fated mates among

shifters, but never of anyone having more than one. My gaze swept Howley, Heath, and Gregor. All three were super hot and clearly infatuated with Dasha.

As long as they didn't tear each other to bits, she was one lucky lady.

"It's unusual," Dasha admitted, "But then, you're unique too, aren't you, Dane?" She sat in an armchair in front of the hearth and patted the one next to her. "I've heard about your parents. But most recently, word of your latest mission reached our academy."

I joined her by the fire. "How?"

Dasha's lips curled up in a smile. "Leslie is now enrolled full-time at the Shifter Academy of Spies. She had a lot of valuable information on the Crescent Springs pack. The PIA asked how they could reward her for divulging it. She chose a career in espionage. I'm mentoring her."

"I didn't realize that. Good for her. I hope she's doing well."

"She is. I bet once I tell her we met, she'll be excited to see you when we host the Games."

A smile broke on my face. "Tell her I'm looking forward to seeing her again. I—"

The music cut, and the sound of cymbals crashed through the room.

I sat straight up in my armchair. "What the hell?"

"Oh for shit's sake," Gregor muttered. "She's back."

I twisted to face the room, and my eyes went straight to Simone, sitting in a chair raised up over the crowd by four other vampires, like she was a queen.

"Quiet! Quiet peons! Champions of the Spy Games, may I have your attention? It is time for the festivities to truly begin!"

I rolled my eyes. *This girl is seriously into herself.*

"If my fellow champions will join me at the bar, we at Nightdwellers have a special treat for you. A hosting surprise that you've surely never experienced before," Simone's perfect red lips formed a dazzling smile.

I glanced at the shifters. They looked as resigned to the situation as I felt, and also like they were having a mental conversation.

"We should go. We're trying to make friends, not enemies," Howley said out loud, probably for my benefit.

A low growl emanated from Gregor, lifting the hair on the back of my neck.

"He's right, Gregor," Dasha said with a sigh. The future alpha stood. "You coming, Dane?"

I noticed that Diana, Sam, and Andre were making their way to the bar. The Torna sisters and their guards were already there. "Guess so. I wouldn't want to be the odd one out and put a target on my back."

"It would be a poor strategy to begin the Spy Games with," Dasha agreed.

We approached the bar. All around us, vampires watched Simone, eager to see what she had in store.

"Thank you for joining us at our prestigious academy." Simone leapt gracefully from her throne to the floor and sashayed toward the other champions. "As most of you know, vampires are creatures who honor tradition."

She extended her hand toward the bartop, and with long, slender fingers, plucked a bottle out of the offerings. "Did you know that in Victorian times, vampires ruled most of London?"

The Torna sisters frowned, and Simone, having caught the expression, chuckled. "Other magicals had their say, but humans *especially* loved vampires." She shook the bottle. "And this little drink was partially to blame."

Francis, the showboater, slung his arm around Simone's shoulder. She snuggled into him, and I realized that the pair weren't just champions and headmaster's pets—they were an item.

"This bottled delight is crème de violette. Victorians were *obsessed* with violets, and as you can tell, its dark color resembles blood. The taste is potent, much more so than wine. It can cover up many sins and even a bit of blood poured into a glass. This allowed vampires to take part in society like they never had before. And our kind took advantage of it."

Simone tossed the bottle in the air and caught it with the opposite hand. "This brand of crème de violette was the favorite of Queen Victoria herself. A treat worthy of royalty . . . or champions. It's basically impossible to find in the modern world." She arched her eyebrows. "Tonight, we'd like to share it with you, fellow champions."

My shoulders loosened. *Shots? They want to take shots?*

A trill of laughter flew from my lips. Shots weren't really my thing, but if it meant tossing one back for camaraderie's sake, I would do it.

"Well, what are you waiting for?" Andre spoke up first. "Pour the damn shots."

The bartender obliged. All champions toasted one another, and on three, we slung the drink back.

I was surprised by the taste. Obviously, it was floral. It was also a little medicinal, and way more appealing than I thought it would be. I could see how blood could hide within the drink and allow for vampires to move through society without attracting attention.

"Another!" Anton exclaimed.

Magdalena giggled and motioned for the bartender to pour everyone one more. The second one went down just as smoothly, and I sighed as crème de violette flowed through my body, warming me and erasing my anxiety. A cloying laugh hit my ear. I twisted to see Dasha pressing her lips to Gregor and then turning to kiss Heath.

Jealousy that Alex couldn't be here and then worry over his mission filled me. My party vibe plunged, and I set down my shot glass. Not wanting to be a total downer, I stepped away from the bar. Right away, Diana was at my side.

"Are you trying to make a graceful exit too?" she asked.

I hadn't been, but now that she mentioned it, I did want to leave. After all, the Games would start tomorrow, and I wanted to be well-rested.

I shrugged. "Yeah, let's get out of here."

Although a few people protested that we were being party-poopers, Diana and I left the Dark Tower together to prepare for the start of the Spy Games the following day.

CHAPTER TWENTY-THREE

The moment my alarm woke me the next morning, I knew something was wrong.

My stomach rolled, and nausea swept through me like a wave. Moaning, I grabbed my gut and sat up slowly. Despite my precautions, the world spun from the pain. I blinked, unable to see straight.

Am I sick? After a brief self-assessment, I realized that only my stomach hurt. The rest of me felt completely fine. I shook my head, unable to understand.

Diana and I had left the party before ten. I'd had two shots and drank water when I got back to my room. I'd felt good then, too, tired and lightly buzzed, but not drunk . . .

My eyes popped open wide. *Did the vampires rufie that drink?*

Taking care to stand, I left my room to find Diana. When she opened her door, the sweat that glistened on her face told me I wasn't the only one feeling ill.

"Is your stomach killing you?"

Diana nodded.

"Those bastards." I clenched my fists. "I think the vamps drugged us."

Diana's blue eyes grew as large as saucers. "Oh my God. I think you're right. I thought Simone was *way* too happy when the fae took another shot."

My jaw tightened. "All I know is that neither of us should feel this sick with how little we drank. And I chugged some water before I went to bed. I'm sure you did, too . . . right?" Diana seemed to be the type who would avoid dehydration, which could cost her the edge in . . . whatever she was doing.

"Absolutely. Hydration is key for any physical competition," she said, confirming my beliefs. "And since we're going up against vamps, I figure that a physical challenge is the most likely scenario."

I groaned. She was right, and at the moment any sort of physical activity sounded horrible. Then a terrible thought struck me, sinking my aching gut.

"We need to wake up Sam and Andre," I said. "They stayed behind. What if they—"

As if he knew I was talking about him, Andre's door opened, and he stuck his head out to vomit on the hallway runner.

"Shit!" Diana screamed as Andre continued to cough and sputter.

"I'm gonna go check on Sam!" My fury at the vampire

champions somehow dulled my pain, and I raced to Sam's room.

I knocked, and when she didn't answer, I knocked again. The minutes ticked by and still nothing, so I threw courtesy to the wind and opened the door.

My eyes just about bugged out of my head when I saw Sam lying facedown with a pillow over her head, still in the clothes she'd worn last night.

"Sam! We have to debrief. The Games start soon!"

A muffled groan came from beneath the pillow.

I bit my lip. "You feel like shit, don't you?"

Another groan, this one even more pathetic, met my ears.

Crap, crap, crap! We so did not have time for this. I needed to do all that I could to get my team feeling better fast. I pulled the pillow off Sam and flipped her over. Her face was red and swollen, and there were huge bags under her eyes, but at least she hadn't been laying in a pool of her own vomit.

"Get up." I rushed to the adjoining bathroom and filled a glass with water. "Drink this."

Sam brought her hand to her mouth, her gaze tentative.

"You have to flush whatever poison the vampires gave us out of your system. Water will help."

With trembling hands, Sam took the glass and sipped. I gave her an encouraging nod, and she sipped again.

As Sam drank, I was filled with hope that she could turn her condition around. I encouraged her, and she managed to finish half the glass.

My tension had just started to dissipate when suddenly, she lurched forward and threw up, barely missing my sock-clad feet.

I swore under my breath and fetched another glass of water.

Miraculously, Diana and I patched up our teammates well enough that they could walk to breakfast on their own. The only thing they could stomach was water, and they occasionally broke out in sweat from just looking at the food, but I told myself that was good. It meant they were sweating out the toxins.

I was thankful that the vampire champions were notably absent, and that Headmistress Wake sat at a table with the other heads of school. It gave us time to regroup in peace. When, at the end of the meal, the headmistress approached us and motioned for us to join her in the hall, we put on our bravest faces and followed.

"I've gathered information that the first challenge will be held outside," Headmistress Wake said in a low voice. "We must make sure you are properly attired. Go to your rooms and put on warm clothes. Then meet at the front door."

I was still considering possible scenarios for outdoor events when we rejoined Headmistress Wake at the door to Nightdwellers.

All the other champions were already there, but my

gaze latched on to Simone, Anton, Francis, and Magdalena. I gritted my teeth, and my fingers itched to strangle the cheating little shits.

So much for inter-school relationship-building.

"Rise and shine, witches," Simone chirped. "How are you feeling this morning?"

My fists clenched, and I prayed to the universe that Sam and Andre wouldn't vomit again. At least if they did it during the event, we could claim it was from exertion. Here, it would be too obvious that the vamps' plan had worked.

"We're doing well. How about you?" Diana played it cool as ice. "I hope nothing befell your health last night?"

Simone arched an eyebrow, and her gaze roved over us. She paused longest on Andre and Sam, who puffed up their chests and beamed as if they weren't dying inside. Simone seemed to deflate a little.

Done with the vampires' shit for the moment, my attention moved to the shifters and fae. Both looked healthy. My eyebrows furrowed.

"Shifters have high metabolisms," Sam whispered. "They probably quickly burned through whatever poison we drank. Plus, they stopped drinking after those two shots, and left ten minutes after you and Diana."

"And the fae?" I asked.

"I don't get why the girls aren't falling over. They took at least two more shots than me, and they're teeny-tiny. I think the guys only took the first one because of guard duty."

Before I could respond, Headmaster Ezra swept down a staircase and clapped his hands. "Good morning, champions! Today is the big day!" He made a show of cupping his ear and gestured to the door. "It seems that others are as excited about the start of the first Spy Games as we are."

I realized that there was a low humming noise—the drone of voices—coming from outside the main door. Probably half of Nightdwellers was waiting out there, and I'd been too busy being pissed at Simone to notice. That wasn't a good sign.

Get your head in the game, Dane.

I straightened my shoulders and tilted my chin up. Even if I felt like shit and was worried about my team, I didn't need to look like it.

"Today's event will take place outside," Headmaster Ezra beamed. "Why don't I lead the way and reveal what it is?"

Everyone nodded, and the vampire headmaster practically skipped to the front door. He was clearly having such a great time that it was kinda cute. It almost made me forget about my aching stomach.

Almost.

We gathered behind the headmaster, and he opened the massive castle doors with a flourish.

"Thank God. I thought I would die from the stench of vomit," someone whispered.

I twisted my neck to see Simone smirking knowingly at me. A snide retort was on the tip of my tongue, but the crowd outside began to cheer, and a cold wind swept over me, stealing the words from my mouth. I looked outside, and my heart dropped.

It had snowed overnight and at least a foot of the white stuff covered the ground. I'd been so busy that morning trying to get myself and my team in order that I hadn't even noticed.

Snow? In September? What the hell?!

Whatever we were about to do, I was sure that snow would only make it more difficult.

Someone had cleared a path leading to where a red ribbon had been strung between two metal poles. We followed the path, and when we reached our destination, the sound of humming generators filled my ears. Two large-screen televisions played footage of a tranquil mountain scene on either side of the metal poles.

"The event is an obstacle course." Headmaster Ezra pointed to the red ribbon. "The course will begin and end here."

"Are there markers along the way to keep us on track?" Andre asked as he glanced at the snow. His voice was raspy and he sounded exhausted.

Out of the corner of my eye, I noticed Simone and Francis smirk.

So help me, I would punch them both in their faces.

"There are red flags to guide your way, and another positioned at each obstacle. Those at the obstacles should be plain, just as the obstacles themselves will be." The head-master's arms swept up the mountain.

My gaze followed the motion, and once I caught sight of what he was referring to, my mouth dropped open.

About halfway up the tall mountainside stood a pole with a massive red flag. Next to the flag were four towering trapeze apparatuses that made my heart skip a few beats. The headmaster continued to point to the right, and against my better judgment, I followed with my eyes. My heart sank to my knees.

Miles and miles of snow-covered mountainside spanned the space in between each obstacle.

We're at such a disadvantage.

Hell, even if half of my team wasn't sick, that would be the case. Vampires and shifters were both super fast. The fae were still glamoured, but I thought it was likely that at least one of them had wings.

"The rules are as follows," Headmaster Ezra clapped to ensure he had the crowd's attention. "Everyone on your team must complete each obstacle. Impartial representatives from each magical race are present at the obstacles to ensure that no one skips a step. They have been instructed to remain invisible, so just because you don't see them, do not assume they are not there." A sly smile crossed the vampire's face. "First place gets ten points, and every team after gets two fewer. That scoring will be standard throughout the tournament. Understood?"

I nodded because my throat was too dry to speak.

"Splendid. Now if the champions would line up behind the red ribbon, we'll begin on my mark."

CHAPTER TWENTY-FOUR

The starting pistol went off, and the Nightdwellers' champions shot out of the gate, their legs moving so fast that they seemed to hover above the snow. Within seconds they'd disappeared into the trees. Just behind the vamps, the shifters transformed. My mouth dropped open when they revealed their animal aspect for the first time.

White wolves. Of course they would be wolves acclimated to snow. I grunted as the wolves entered the forest while my team ran laboriously through the powder.

The fae remained only slightly ahead of us, but the moment their glamours began to fade, I knew we were in for trouble. My fists clenched as Luvon and Volwin sprouted wings, grabbed Ayla and Sana, and soared after the shifters and vamps.

"Dammit!" Diana swore.

I knew how she felt. We hadn't even gone one hundred

yards, and already Andre had fallen, and Sam clutched her stomach like she would die any second.

Oh my God, what if we don't even finish the first challenge?

"This can't be happening." Diana shook her head as she helped Andre haul himself up. "Why would they even bother poisoning us? It's obvious we're at a disadvantage."

I huffed out a breath of air. "Yeah it's not like we have super strength or super speed or wings. All we have is—" My mouth snapped shut, and I whirled to face my team. "Warping. We have warping."

Diana's eyes grew round. "Can you do it even though you haven't seen the obstacles yet?"

"It will be hard, but being able to see those flags should help. I won't have enough juice to get us through all the obstacles and back to the finish, though."

My eyes shifted to Andre, whose dark brown skin had taken on an off-putting gray tone. He looked awful. Under normal circumstances, I wouldn't ask him to expend his energy, but he was the only one who could help.

"If you waited until the very end and saved your strength, do you think you can get us from the third obstacle to the finish line?"

Andre looked doubtful, and I didn't blame him. Besides being sick, he'd only created two warpholes in the few lessons that we'd had so far.

"You can do it," I encouraged because he looked like he needed it. "I'll talk you through it, and if I have any energy left over, I'll help. We might be able to morph our energies together." Alex and I had used our totems to create a warphole once. Andre didn't have a totem that connected to mine, but it might still work.

"I'll try my best," he said and shot Diana a look. "I might need help getting through the obstacles, though. You know, to save my energy for warping." His dusky cheeks grew red at the admission.

I felt a little bad for the guy. Diana was a formidable woman, and to have to admit he needed her help in physical challenges when he was supposed to be the stronger, older guy . . . well, it would suck. To Diana's credit, however, she merely placed Andre's arm around her shoulder.

"I'm here for you," she said. "I have a bit of experience helping people through trials. Just like Odette, here." Diana gave me a small smile.

Not wanting to waste any more time, I thrust my hands out and called on the energies all around me. "Then it looks like I should get a warphole started."

It took two tries, but I got us to the first obstacle. When I looked down the mountainside, I was astonished to see how far we'd come. The Nightdwellers students standing at the starting line looked like insects.

When we arrived, the shifters and vampires were already flying through the air on their academy-specific trapeze apparatuses. Unsurprisingly, the vampire champions were almost done with the obstacle, and yet, seeing the outraged looks on Simone's and Francis' faces when we popped into existence made their clear lead less annoying.

Plus, now that we had a plan, I was sure that if we could complete the obstacles within a decent time frame, we wouldn't come in last. After all, we hadn't regularly experienced the hell of physical conditioning since our first week at Spellcasters for nothing.

I sucked in a breath to amp myself up. We were strong, even if half of us were severely poisoned. We could do this.

I looped my arm through Sam's and helped her shuffle to the trapeze station designated for our school. "I'll climb first. Diana, you're good at levitation spells, right?"

She nodded.

"Then you go last, and levitate Sam and Andre if they need help. I'll assist from the top."

"Sounds good."

The climb was hard and taxing, which made me worry about Sam and Andre. But when I got to the top, I saw that Sam was already halfway up the ladder. She grimaced with every rung she conquered, and she looked super sweaty even from where I stood, but the determination etched on her face gave me hope.

Since she was still a ways away, I scanned the area.

A camera was positioned on our platform, and judging by the blinking red light on the other platform the end one too. The televisions down by the starting line sprang to mind, and I realized that the students were all watching us —and would be the whole time.

Wonderful, I thought, my gaze trailing down the line of trapeze apparatuses.

The vampire champions were long gone. And the fae, who had arrived just after us, were already finishing up the task. As it turned out, trapeze was cake when you had wings.

The shifters, however, were a different story. Although they were athletic-looking in their human aspects, both Howley and Heath had already fallen into the safety net below. Only Dasha had made it across. She was now trying hard to coax Gregor off the ledge so she could swing out and get him.

Even from a distance of thirty feet away, I could see Gregor tremble. I felt bad for the guy, but also a little bolstered by his reluctance to make the leap. It gave us a fighting chance in the competition.

In the time it took for my team to make it to the top of the platform, I watched both Howley and Heath swing across the expanse once more. Heath succeeded, but Howley fell again. Now that I'd seen an example of the right and wrong techniques, I had a plan.

"Unfortunately, warping is no good here. The bar moves too fast for accuracy. But what do you guys think about a magnetism or sticking spell?" Although I didn't know how to do those spells, I hoped that the Crucibles would have learned something along those lines.

"Genius," Sam said, and her tired eyes brightened a bit. "I can do that. Let's try the sticking one first."

I held out my hands, and Sam cast the spell on them and

the bar. When I wrapped my fingers around the bar, my grip felt strong—like I could hold on for a really long time and not slip.

A smile broke on my face. "Perfect. I'll cross first. If I give you the thumbs-up, that means this solution worked well, and you should enchant the others' hands too."

"You got it," Sam said.

I turned and faced the vast expanse between platforms. My hands stuck to the bar, but that didn't stop my anxiety from rising. There was a shitload of open air below me. I wasn't sure of the exact distance that we had to swing, but the second platform was *really* far away. Even with the safety net, the idea of falling terrified me.

But I didn't have a choice. We had to move.

Taking a massive breath, I stepped off the platform.

Cold air whistled in my ears, and my stomach dropped to my knees as I plummeted down. Suddenly, the line pulled tight, and with a terrifying *snap*, I swung forward. Although I wanted to close my eyes, I kept them wide open. The bar on the other side was clearly magically enchanted, because it soared toward me at the same pace that I was approaching it. I just needed to grab it in midair.

My stomach twisted as the bar came closer. I hoped that spelling my hands to be sticky wouldn't work against me. I hoped that I could continue to hold on with one hand as I reached for the other. I hoped I was dexterous enough for the transition. I hoped—

Nope. The bar was almost to me. I was all outta hopes.

With trembling arms, I released one hand off the bar. To

my surprise, the stickiness of Sam's spell was a little difficult to overcome, but not really that bad. I'd have to ask
Sam exactly how it worked later.

My heart thundered as my fingers stretched. Suddenly,
they hit something hard—the bar!—and I clung to it.

"Oh crap!" I squealed. Caught between two bars and
carrying a crapload of momentum, my body twisted wildly.
Instinctively, I let go of the first bar to grip the second for
dear life.

Cheering rose from behind me, but I didn't dare twist
my neck around. The second platform was approaching
fast, and there was no way in hell I would miss my landing.

When my feet hit the platform with a *thunk*, I let out a
massive sigh of relief and released the bar. Amazingly, it
stilled, waiting in midair for the next champion to traverse
the expanse. Now that I wasn't moving, the deluge of sweat
running down my spine became apparent.

Thank the universe that's over. I twisted to face the Spellcasters' starting platform and gave my team a thumbs up so
they knew it was safe to proceed.

"Nice work!" a voice called. From one platform over, I
saw Dasha waving at me. Back at the starting line, I'd been
a little annoyed at the shifters and fae, thinking maybe
they'd known what the vampires had done. But Dasha's
genuine smile said otherwise.

"Thanks! I hope the others make it too," I called back.

"Yeah. Same. If Gregor would ever freaking jump, that
is."

I turned to face the starting platform and saw that she

was right. Howley was on his third swing, but Gregor remained planted on the platform.

Andre leapt next. The bar next to me swung into action the moment his feet left the platform.

It should have been beautiful, the way the bars soared toward each other at the same speed, but Andre kind of ruined it by barfing his guts out a quarter of the way across.

"Keep it together!" I screamed, my eyes glued to him as he flew closer and closer. He was almost to the middle, and I wanted to close my eyes so as not to witness the tragedy of Andre missing the bar.

And then, to my everlasting glee, he released the first bar before I ever would have had the guts to, and flew toward the other bar like a legit acrobat. There was a *whack* when his hands met the wood, and unable to help myself, I let out a whoop.

"Hell yeah, baby!" Diana screamed.

Andre flew toward me, and I reached out to grab him.

"Thanks, Odette," he managed to mumble before hurling his guts out over the side of the platform.

Vomiting aside, this trial was turning out better than I could have imagined. We were keeping up with the shifters!

When Sam stepped off the platform, my hopes had already started to rise. Which was why it crushed me hard when Sam missed her transfer.

"No!" I whisper-screamed.

To make matters worse, Howley had finally gotten the timing right, and landed on the final platform. The shifters yelped and jumped with glee as my stomach sank.

Sam swung back to the first platform, and Diana caught her. The third-year appeared to be swaying violently, and I realized that while she wasn't puking, Sam was as bad off as Andre.

I needed to help her, or she'd never make it.

At my side, the trapeze bar hovered, waiting for Sam to leap again. Following my instinct, I placed a hand on it. "Diana! Sam!" I waved to get their attention.

The ladies had been discussing something, but their necks twisted at the sound of my voice.

"I'll meet her in the middle!"

Sam gave me a thumbs-up.

It was go time.

Once again, when Sam leapt off the other platform, the bar hovering on mine soared toward the middle. The only difference was that this time, I clung to it.

"Let go on my call!" I screamed as Sam and I flew toward one another.

"Got it!" she yelled back.

Closer and closer we came until only a few feet separated us.

"Release!" I screamed.

Sam complied and she barreled toward me, arms outstretched. Throwing caution to the wind, I unlatched one hand and reached for her. Her fingers grazed mine, and I closed my hand.

And we missed.

Sam plummeted, and reflexively, I kicked my leg out at her. "Grab on!"

"*Oomph*!" she grunted as my leg smacked her in the face and torso.

But I'll be damned if she didn't latch on like a baby monkey.

Correction, a desperate baby monkey. Her nails dug deeply into my skin as she tried to climb my leg. I winced and grasped for any part of her to hold on to. Unfortunately for Sam, the first thing I grabbed was her hair. She released a yelp of pain as we soared backward toward the second platform.

Hold on. Hold on. Hold on, I chanted as if it was one of my tried-and-true mantras.

She held steady and when we reached the other platform, Andre caught us.

"That was so amazing!" he said as soon as we were stable. "Quick thinking, Odette."

"Thanks," I said, glad I'd taken the risk even though my legs ached.

Sam said nothing, merely crawled over to the edge of the platform and vomited.

Andre watched her, pity in his eyes. "It sucks, but I think it's better she gets it out of her system. I've puked four times now, and I actually feel a lot better. I think I can rally for the rest of this course."

Examining his face, I noticed that he was no longer sweating, and his cheeks seemed to have a healthier glow. Maybe he was right, and Sam needed to purge.

I didn't have much time to dwell on the idea, though, because a few seconds later, Diana joined us on the final platform.

"Let's get moving." She gestured to the ladder.

"Hold on." I held out a hand to stop her. "I can see the second flag, so I'm going to warp us from up here to save some time."

"*Excellent* idea," Diana said.

"Everyone stand behind me," I ordered.

They complied, and I focused on the flag and pushed my magic out. A warphole appeared in front of us, and throwing up a prayer that it would lead us directly to the second obstacle, I led the way through.

Hot air, then cold enveloped me. No longer did I find the contrast striking. It was simply a part of making a warphole.

When I stepped out of the warphole, frigid, thin mountain air caressed my arms. I shuddered as I took in my surroundings. My mouth fell open with relief.

By some miracle of the universe, we'd exited only about twenty feet from the flagpole.

"I can't believe it!" I shouted and began jumping up and down.

My team piled out after me, and Diana was so pumped that she actually wrapped her arms around me. "Thank God you're on this team! We'd be so screwed otherwise."

I blinked. Having her like me was still so odd, but it was way better than the alternative, so I rolled with it. "Let's figure out this next challenge."

We approached the flagpole, which was pressed up against the side of a cliff. Four holes barely large enough for a person to fit through dotted the mountainside, each with a little sign over it indicating which species should enter which tunnel.

I moved closer to the hole bearing the sign of a witch and peered inside. It was black as night. My skin began to crawl as flashbacks of walking through the underground of Portland hit me hard.

Well, shit. This sucks.

"We have to go in there?" Sam croaked.

"It appears so," Diana sighed. "I can go first this time, if you want, Odette? I cast a good illumination spell. I'll spread it on the walls too, so everyone else can see."

Sounded fan-freaking-tastic to me. My nerves already tingled at the idea of army-crawling through a dark tunnel, and visions of demons were popping up left and right in my brain. I was in no position to lead this time.

I nodded, and Diana wasted no time climbing in the hole and disappearing into the mountainside.

$\mathcal{I}$ wasn't sure how far I army-crawled into the tunnel before my breathing became labored and I started shaking with fear, but it definitely didn't seem far enough. Instead of giving in to the sense of the walls closing in around me, I tried to zero in on Sam's feet jostling and kicking in front of me as we progressed.

With each inch, the jagged rock we squeezed through soaked my clothing a little more, leaving me cold and wet. The ceiling mirrored the ground, dripping cold water onto my backside. With each tiny drip, terrifying visions of the mountain collapsing on us ran through my mind. I shuddered.

You'll get through this. You're strong enough. You're brave.

I chanted a few mantras, although they didn't have the effect that they usually did. What was worse, the appearance of multiple tiny red dots in the tunnel, the recording lights of cameras, assured me that hundreds of people were watching me break down. This was a shitty time to discover that I had a fear of caves.

Somewhere up ahead, a rock fell. I screeched and tensed.

"It was just a pebble!" Sam called back.

But I was already too far gone down the rabbit hole. My eyes were squeezed shut and my body trembled. Strange sounds were coming out of my mouth, reminding me of a caged animal. I couldn't move another inch. *If I don't make it out of here—oh my God, I need to stop thinking that—we'll fail. We'll—*

"Hey! I found a cavern!" Diana's voice echoed down the tunnel.

My eyes popped open wide, and for a moment, my trembling ceased. A cavern was still a cave, but at least it was bigger. The train of witches in front of me sped up noticeably, and somehow, I found the strength to follow.

"Thank the universe we're out of there." I breathed my first full inhalation in what felt like forever as I emerged from the tunnel after Sam, who had her eyes closed and was taking long, slow breaths.

"Agreed." Andre rubbed his arms with his hands, presumably to stop them from shaking.

Diana was the only one who didn't seem fazed. In fact, she was already walking around the cave, examining it and looking for how to proceed.

Aware that the sooner we found the exit, the sooner we'd be out of there, I turned to explore in the opposite direction. Right away, I noticed that the four holes designated for the magicals to enter had all exited next to each other.

Noises came from one, the tunnel I thought belonged to the fae. I leaned close to it, cupping my hand around my ear.

"I'm stuck!" a gruff voice—Luvon's—grunted.

"I'll help push you!" Ayla said, her smoky tone worried.

"Why not just use earth magic and clear the way?" another male voice, Volwin's, asked.

"No!" Sana cried out. "We need to try every possible avenue before trying earth magic. I can't guarantee that it won't collapse our tunnel—or the others. It's a last resort only."

My eyes popped open wide. "Diana! The fae are considering using earth magic. We need to get out of here!"

"So stop standing around and look for an exit on that side," Diana said right before disappearing behind a rock that jutted up out of the ground.

She'd been out of sight only ten seconds when a blood-curdling scream cut through the cavern.

My heart rate spiked. I rushed to her aid and turned the corner just in time to see Diana fall to the ground, and the ghost-white visage of Francis zoom away.

"Hey!" I chased after him, but he was a vampire with super speed who darted to the side of the cave and vanished. I approached where he'd disappeared and sighed. It was yet another godforsaken tiny tunnel. Pissed, I slammed my fist into the rock. "You won't get away with this!"

An evil laugh echoed back at me.

"Odette," Diana wheezed. "Help."

I whirled around and ran to her. "Andre! Sam get over here!" When I reached her side, I dropped to my knees. "What did he do to you?"

Diana's hand covered her arm, and when she pulled it aside, a cut glistened up at me. It was small, but pulsed and oozed a white, foamy substance. Where the foam touched her skin was slightly swollen.

I reared back, disgusted by how alien the wound looked. "What the hell?"

Diana shook her head. "I thought I heard something and *still* came over here alone. How stupid of me!"

My hand landed on her shoulder. "This is *not* your fault. That asshole attacked you. If anyone is to blame, it's him."

Our friends appeared, and Andre pulled Diana into his arms.

Diana released a long breath. "All I know is that we need to move. I'm almost positive that the blade he cut me with was dipped in a turgeo potion."

"Oh shit," Sam whispered.

"Yeah. 'Oh shit' is right," Diana agreed. "Especially considering where we are. If I don't get the antidote in an hour or so, my whole body will swell. I won't be able to fit through any exit holes if they're the same diameter as the entrance ones."

I didn't question how she identified the potion. Diana

excelled in Potions and Poisons, and had independent study with Professor Bane, who taught the subject at Spellcasters.

"We have to get going then," I said, all too aware that now three fourths of my team was injured or ill. "Can you crawl?"

"I'll try my damnedest," Diana replied.

"I saw Francis escape out of an exit hole. It's right over here." I pointed to where I'd seen the vamp dive into the rock wall just as a scream emanated from one of the entrance tunnels.

Someone was in trouble.

My stomach clenched. I liked the other teams, but this was a competition. Plus, if we didn't get Diana out of here fast, who knew what would become of her? I shivered, and not just from the persistent chill.

"Let's go," I said, making a choice. "Before anyone else catches up and clogs up the hole. I'll lead."

Andre pulled Diana to her feet and helped her to the exit.

I bent down, murmured an illumination spell, and peered inside. My insides chilled. *Sweet holy universe, is it my imagination, or is this tunnel even tinier and darker than the first?*

Another sound came from the opposite side of the cavern, and I gulped. Even if this was the smallest and blackest tunnel in existence, we didn't have a choice. This was the way out. It had to be, or else Francis wouldn't have taken it.

To bolster my willpower, I imagined that on the other side of this tunnel, light and fresh mountain air called to me. A spark of hope ignited within me, and using that as fuel, I crawled into the darkness.

The exit tunnel was largely identical to the entrance tunnel. Or at least, it was until about ten minutes in, when I encountered a freaking fork in the mountainside.

I did my best to hurl a ball of light down the fork to the right, but considering the cramped conditions, it didn't make it that far. All I could see was darkness and more darkness. Everyone on my team trailed behind me, and could see even less. In that moment, I would have given anything for a shifter's sense of smell, or a vampire's keen eyesight. I bet the damn vamps could see the outside light from inside the cavern.

I never thought I'd think this, but being a witch sucks right now.

I paused for so long that Sam, who had been bringing up the rear, asked what was going on. Her voice wobbled, like she was terrified too. Realizing that sticking in one place wasn't doing anyone a bit of good, I made an executive decision.

"Go left when you hit the fork! Pass it on!" I yelled, and was reassured to hear my words echoed down the line.

My hands and feet had long since gone numb from the cold, and my arms ached from all the scratches on them.

Needing to reaffirm my strength, I ducked my head to turn inward as I crawled and began reciting my mantras.

You can do it.

You can do it.

You can—

My head collided with hard rock. *"Ouch!"* Rubbing my head, I extended my hand and bid the light in my palm to flare.

A solid wall of rock stood in front of me.

I'd run right into a dead end.

Tears filled my eyes. "No, no, no."

Moving forward through the tiny-ass tunnel had been hard enough, but moving backward?

Another possibility, even more terrible, entered my mind. What if this wasn't the exit at all? What if Francis had hidden in here and exited while I checked out Diana's arm? He was a vampire and could move in perfect silence. I probably wouldn't have heard him.

I groaned and then yelped as someone rammed into me from behind, sending my skull into the rock wall a second time.

"Ow!" Andre yelped. "What's going on? Why are you stopped, Odette?"

"It's a dead end. We have to backtrack to the fork," I said, my voice small.

Andre spat out a curse, and I heard Diana moan.

"I'm so sorry." My voice came out in a defeated squeak. "I chose wrong. I should have—"

"Don't blame yourself," Andre interrupted. "You're the

only reason we've even made it this far, and there's no way you could have known which direction to take. We'll figure out how to back up and get out of here."

And that was exactly what we did. Painfully slowly, we inched our way backward. What seemed like an hour later, we got to the fork and, reversed the order of our witch train, and took the right tunnel.

When light began to pierce through the darkness, I nearly burst into tears of joy. Or maybe it was frustration. If I had just chosen correctly the first time, we would have been out of the mountainside forever ago.

Don't dwell on it. There's no going back. Just forward.

I was still telling myself that when I emerged into the brilliant sunlight. Air filled my lungs, and a sense of appreciation for how fresh it tasted rushed over me. I was about to close my eyes to savor it when a voice from the tunnel we'd just emerged out of cut through my serenity.

"I can smell the witches. The trail is fresher this way. Go right," Dasha instructed.

I loosed a sigh. The shifters were hot on our tails.

I raised a hand over my eyes to shield them, and spotted the third flag. "Everyone ready to warp?"

Andre had been trying to clean Diana's wound out with snow, but at my word, Diana shook him off. She stepped forward with a look of determination on her face. "Let's finish this."

"Alrighty. Here we go again." I conjured up the warphole.

The instant we stepped out of the warphole, a powerful, horrible stench hit me so strongly that I almost wished I was back in the tunnel.

We were in a large clearing. The pristine white snow was dotted with copious amounts of red blood. Horrifyingly enough, the source of the smell *and* the blood was a massive creature lying on the ground a few feet away. Blood poured from its neck, and a mouth full of rotten teeth was open wide in death.

My stomach heaved, and I clapped my hands over my eyes, wanting to block out what I could never unsee.

"Release the Spellcasters' troll!" a voice boomed from above.

My spine stiffened. The Spellcasters' troll? Was that what the thing on the ground was? Now we had to face one too?

In answer, the sound of lifting metal gates hit my ears, followed by a groan—Andre's.

"Don't tell me that is what I think it is?" I whispered, still unable to uncover my eyes.

"Okay, I won't tell you, but I'm guessing you know, seeing as some asshole just announced it," Sam muttered, her tone dark.

Somewhere in the woods, a creature roared, deep and furious. My stomach tightened.

Fine. We had to defeat a mountain troll. I opened my eyes once again. Hesitantly, they flitted to the dead creature on the ground. Someone—the vampires, I suspected—had already completed their task. No doubt they would finish the event at any minute.

Confirming my beliefs, cheering arose from down the mountainside. A whistle pierced the air, and celebratory music began to play. Yep. The vampires had just finished the first event of the Spy Games.

I didn't have time to dwell on that annoyance for much longer, because the next second, our troll made an appearance through the trees. He was bounding toward us, knocking over full-grown pines with a sweep of his arm as he went.

The creature was at least twenty-five feet tall, with a forehead like a Neanderthal's, and lips that were puffy and red and covered in blood. I didn't want to think about what the troll had been eating before they'd released him, although I was glad that he'd eaten *something*. Surely a troll that had just been fed would be less likely to want to chew on us, right? I hoped so, but truth be told, I didn't know the slightest thing about trolls. They weren't something that spies had to deal with—at least, I hadn't thought they were.

Clearly, whoever designed the Spy Games believed differently.

"Anyone know of a spell to knock out a troll?" I hoped unconsciousness would be sufficient. As gross as the creature was, the idea of killing it for sport made my stomach roll.

"Coming up blank," Sam said, her teeth chattering.

"Same," Andre agreed.

Oh my God, what's the use of having third-years with us if they don't know everything?!

I turned to Diana, who had remained oddly silent, and saw she was gritting her teeth so hard that the blood vessels in the side of her face were popping. My eyes shot to her arm, and I gasped. The gash there had widened and become puffy. Now her arm was the size of her thigh.

"Everyone circle up around Diana," I said. "Diana, if you get a good shot, take it. Otherwise, do what you can to protect us."

She jerked a nod, and we formed a ring of protection around her.

Since no one knew what they were doing, I prepared to take the first shot. Using techniques I'd learned in Battle Magic, I harnessed the prodigious fear and anger I was experiencing, and aimed it at the troll. Fuchsia magic burst from my hands, and slammed into his chest. The creature stopped dead in his tracks. He glanced down, and my gaze followed.

There was nothing there—not so much as a tiny cut. Apparently coming to the same conclusion, the troll released another roar and continued his charge.

"Crap," I muttered. "We can keep pummeling him with Battle Magic, but unless you guys have some serious pent-up issues, I don't know if that will work."

"I don't think it would, anyway," Sam said. For the first time since we started this stupid event, her voice sounded strong and sure. "But I actually might have an idea. Andre, conjure me a blade."

My eyebrows furrowed. As a Crucible student, she should be able to conjure a blade.

"I can do it," Sam assured me, reading my expression. "But I'll need every ounce of energy I possess to enact my plan."

"What do you need us to do?" Andre asked, handing her a dagger.

"A troll's skin is notoriously thick, which is why Odette's magic wasn't effective. I need you to distract him so I can latch on to his leg."

My heart began to thunder. The freaking ground was shaking with the troll's steps, and Sam wanted to ride its leg?

"Why?" I squeaked as I shot off another blast of magic, hoping to hold the beast off.

It slammed into his cheek, but didn't do jack.

"So I can carve a rune into his skin," Sam said. "It's the only way."

I decided to take her word for it, because the next moment, the troll was upon us, his stinky breath bearing down as he released a hair-raising roar. Andre and I flanked him and hurled beams of power one after the other to distract the beast. Diana remained just behind Sam, shooting magic at the creature when she could get a clear shot.

Sam, the crazy-ass girl, continued to inch closer to the troll. At one point, the troll lashed out at her, swinging his hand. By some miracle, she leapt out of the way and twirled to land behind his calf.

He noticed, but I spewed a blaze of fuchsia magic at him to distract him. It worked and the troll focused on me once again. He swiped at me. I darted backward just in time.

"Hurry, Sam!" Andre shouted, attacking the troll from the other side.

"I'm going! It's got to be just right, and he keeps moving!"

A massive hand swung by me again, reminding me that I should be paying attention to the grunting beast and not Sam. Retreating faster this time, I came up against the body of the dead troll before spinning and slamming the living troll's kneecap with another stream of magic. The troll roared and lurched at me.

My heart raced, and I turned to run, but like an idiot, I forgot where I was and tripped over the dead troll. My arm landed in its mouth, and when I tried to yank it back, it wouldn't budge.

Crap, crap, crap!

I twisted and caught a flash of our opponent flying toward me. But before I could figure out a way to save myself, he slammed into my body, and my world went black.

CHAPTER TWENTY-SIX

My eyelids fluttered open.

"I think she's waking up!" a familiar voice—Eva's—said.

A hand landed on my arm and someone came closer. A scent that reminded me of the Spellcasters Healing Sanctuary washed over me.

Alex.

But where was I? And why was it so hard to open my eyes?

I released a moan, and with great effort, forced my eyes to open the rest of the way. Bright lights assaulted me, making me whimper.

"Turn them off."

Someone moved to shut off the lights, and slowly, I opened my eyes again.

Alex, Hunter, Eva, and Sam hovered around my

bedside. Past them, the Spellcasters infirmary spread out before me.

At this rate, I should ask if they have a punchcard or something.

"Hey sweets," Alex said, his voice soothing. "How you feeling?"

"Awful. What happened?"

I wiggled my jaw. My words had come out garbled, which was just as distressing as how terrible my body felt— like a dozen trucks had run me over.

"You came back from the Spy Games yesterday afternoon. Headmistress Wake brought you straight here," Eva said. "You got knocked out, although no one has told us how yet." She glared at Sam, but the third-year didn't seem bothered by it.

"I told Headmistress Wake," Sam said. "She was the only person who needed to know what happened before Odette woke up. But if Odette wants, I'm more than happy to fill the rest of you in."

"They can hear," I said.

"See?" Eva crossed her arms over her chest, eliciting a chuckle from Hunter.

"Sugar, she just did what she thought was right." Hunter kissed Eva's cheek. "Calm down. We won't be in the dark anymore."

"Whatever," Eva said. "Just spill it."

Sam arched her eyebrows. "Keep that attitude. It'll serve you well in your Crucible year." She turned to me and leaned closer so I wouldn't have trouble hearing her.

"Remember the troll?"

"Yeah."

"Troll?! What the actual hell!" Eva looked gobsmacked, and if laughing wasn't such a painful prospect, I would have done so.

"Oh, girl, you don't know the *half* of what we did," Sam gave a dismissive wave of her hand. "The troll was gross, but the least difficult task. That much has to be true, because we beat him even with Odette passed the eff out."

My lips curled up, and Sam patted me on the shoulder. "You know it's true. We would never have made it through the other challenges without you—particularly Andre and me. Thanks for keeping the team together. And for being an amazing warper."

"Oh my God, will you just tell the whole story already?!" Eva looked about ready to burst.

"So we went through this three-part challenge, which was *hell on a stick,* mind you, only to have to beat a mountain troll for the final task." Sam turned to my friends. "The vampire champions had poisoned us the night before, so Andre and I were barely hanging on. If we'd had to run the many miles from task to task, we *never* would have made it. But because Odette is a warper, we got to skip the mileage and just perform the tasks."

"Andre still can't warp yet?" Hunter asked.

"Let me finish!" Sam said. "Anyway, I was clinging to the troll's calf and had carved half a rune meant to petrify him when the asshole went after Odette. She was too close to the corpse of another troll that the vampires had killed, and she tripped over it. That's where things got sticky—literally." Sam stuck out her tongue.

Alex sucked in a breath. "Troll saliva is sticky. Did you touch it, Odie?"

My eyebrows furrowed. "Maybe?"

"She sure did," Sam said. "Her arm fell right in his mouth, so she couldn't move. The other troll was going after her fast. I only finished carving the rune right before he got to her." Sam gave me a look of pure repentance. "I had no way of knowing that the momentum from his run would pitch him forward—right on top of you."

My eyes popped open. "That *massive* thing landed on me?" *How am I still alive?*

Sam winced. "Well, kinda. He extended his fist, and it hit you. You kinda rolled to the side a little so only half of him landed on you. But then again, the thing was enormous, so . . ."

"I got knocked out, and now I'm here." I tried to shake my head but stopped when a burst of pain shot up my neck. "Did we lose the first round?" Andre wasn't a skilled warper yet, and if they had to drag my unconscious body to the finish line, that would have slowed them down a lot.

But instead of confirming my fears, Sam grinned. "Nope. By some miracle of miracles, we got *second* place! Andre actually warped us to the finish line! The vampires nearly exploded with anger, I wish you'd seen it."

"No way," I breathed, excitement rising within me. "Who took third and fourth?"

"The shifters got third, and the fae last. The fae dudes

were too beefy, they apparently got caught in those mountain tunnels."

"Wow." I couldn't believe it. The day had started out so dire, and we'd still earned second place. Right after the . . .

"Goddamned vampires," I muttered.

Alex caressed my arm. "Did you use the potion?"

"No. I didn't think I needed to. They didn't try anything obvious on us. And I didn't drink that much the night before the event. Not like . . ." I gave Sam an apologetic look.

"Not like our dumbasses," she said. "Believe me, neither Andre nor I will make that mistake twice."

"Thank the universe," I muttered. "I can't go through a trial like that again."

The conversation veered off to fill Sam and me in on what we had missed around Spellcasters. Eventually, I remembered to ask Alex about his mission, and was unsurprised when he said he passed it with flying colors. We chatted for a few minutes more before the healer in the infirmary informed everyone that visiting hours were over —two hours ago.

It was just as well. The interaction had worn me out. I needed my rest so I could get discharged from the infirmary quickly. Homework was piling up, and if I fell behind during my Grind-year, I might never catch up.

CHAPTER TWENTY-SEVEN

The infirmary released me two days later, but I couldn't simply return to business as usual. The troll had not only knocked me unconscious when his fist slammed into me, he'd fractured one of my ribs when he landed on me too. Thankfully, the head healer at Spellcasters kept bone regeneration elixir on hand at all times. It accelerated the mending process greatly, but I still had to take it easy for a week.

To be honest, I relished the downtime. Eva, Hunter, and Alex were extra attentive to my needs, and I got to skip Physical Conditioning—a major win.

But of course, Headmistress Wake didn't just let me lie around when I should be at Physical Conditioning. However, since her alternative suggestion played into an interest of mine, I didn't mind. And I even had company.

Diana's arm still hadn't healed from Francis' turgeo potion—a potion which, to my great annoyance, he had not received a penalty for using. Diana and I were to study and write a ten-page paper on one notable witch in history; the more obscure their accomplishments, the better. Unlike me, Diana didn't have a particular witch in mind, so I suggested one.

"What period of Merlin's life are you going to focus on today?" I asked as Diana and I walked into the library on our second day of research.

Her eyes narrowed. She'd gone along with my suggestion that she study Merlin, although seeing as my interest in her research rivaled my own, she was suspicious.

"I'm not sure, Dane. Why don't you tell me what I should look up?"

I pretended to be deep in thought. "What about his relationship to his protégés? He had a lot of them, I think. You could focus on their combined accomplishments?"

Alex had studied the same thing last year, but seeing as Diana had grown up frequenting this very library, she might find additional information.

Diana snorted. "Sure. Whatever you want."

After gathering the books we'd requested from the rare book stacks—a spymaster privilege—we settled down at a table and spread out.

I cherry-picked a tome I'd started the day before that detailed the life of Morgan Le Fay better than most others. I'd only read a few pages when a soft hum came across the table.

I glanced up to see Diana's brows knitted together.

"What's up?"

She pointed to an illustration made by a woodcarving. "You're studying Morgan Le Fay, right?"

My heart rate kicked up. Had Diana already found something amazing? "Yeah, why?" I looked at the book in front of her. "Weren't you reading that one yesterday too?"

Diana nodded. "Yup. It has a lot of info, so I just picked up where I left off—right before the section on Morgan. Apparently, she was a disciple of Merlin. Closer than a disciple, actually. This text insinuates that they might have been lovers, which is racy for a book written in the 19th century."

My face fell, but I recovered quickly, not wanting Diana to become suspicious and start asking questions.

"But that's not the oddest part," Diana continued, catching my interest again.

"Oh?" My pitch went up. "What did you find?"

Diana looked up from her book. "For a spy-in-training, you're not very smooth. It's obvious that you want me to study this for . . . Well, I'm not sure why yet. I'm going along with it because I was a jerk last year and I really don't care who I write this paper about. But if you chose Merlin for an important reason, you should tell me. You know I'm capable, and if I can help you, I will."

My mouth dried up. *Should I tell her?*

Having Diana as an ally would be powerful, and I certainly *wanted* to tell her. But no . . . I couldn't, not without talking to Alex first. It wasn't only my secret to keep. Plus, it was a dangerous. The fewer people who knew it, the better.

"Maybe one day, I can tell you," I said carefully. "For now, would you accept that I'm suggesting you study Merlin for an important reason? One that might change the world."

Diana's eyes narrowed. "Change the world? Are you serious?"

I gulped. "Or save it."

"From the demons popping up everywhere?"

I nodded.

Her face blanched. We remained staring at each other for God-knew-how-long. I was just beginning to wonder if this would be too much for her, and if she would bail on helping, when she exhaled a long breath of air.

"Jesus, Dane. You're a magnet for trouble." She shook her head. "I'll help, but if something goes down—like, *really* goes down—you'd better fill me in."

"I will," I whispered. "So, what did you find?"

She bent her head over the book. "According to this text, Morgan and Merlin were together during a few events that the ancient world would have described as cataclysmic. Floods, fires, plagues, you get the idea. They're glossed over, which makes sense because a lot of this is based on oral history. But there is one that this author details well. They must have had a lot of sources to get this much information."

Diana flipped the book and pressed it toward me.

"An earthquake? In England?" My lips pressed together in a line. "Isn't that unusual?"

"Yes, particularly of this magnitude. A witch in the area

described it as being so strong that her neighbor's home toppled. But the writing goes on to say that no one outside of what would now be considered central London felt it. That's an isolated shaker." Diana arched an eyebrow. "And that's not the only odd thing. The book claims that the skies grew black as night and swarmed with screaming bugs during the earthquake. According to a handful of magical witnesses, the earthquake was so strong, it created a crack in a river. Fire sprang up from the water and the river turned red, like it was full of blood. Even more crazy, after this whole catastrophe happened, only a few remembered it."

What the hell? "But how could they forget *that*?"

"It's suggested here that Morgan and Merlin didn't want to traumatize people, so they altered their memories." She paused and read a little more before continuing. "It says here that the affected river flows through the center of present-day London. Lucky for them, the population was smaller back then. It would be easier for them to modify memories." Diana shook her head. "Although, since this document is written well after Merlin's lifetime, I'd venture to say that the few people who knew the truth—if this *is* the truth—passed it on. Probably they were magicals. Maybe Morgan and Merlin were unable to modify the memories of the magicals present. Or they didn't want to—but why wouldn't they?"

While Diana spoke, dread descended over me. Now I was encased in it, my breath tight and thin.

They modified hundreds of memories so people wouldn't

remember that a river had cracked open to spew out fire and run red with blood. A river in the middle of London. It has to be the Thames.

As far as I could figure, there was only one reason someone would go to such great lengths to erase history, but strategically allow others to remember.

They *wanted* some people to remember. Those who might make a difference if another cataclysmic event occurred—magicals. From this information, I made a terrifying deduction.

The River Thames was the entrance to the Hellgate.

CHAPTER TWENTY-EIGHT

My revelation about the location of the Hellgate was monumental, but also a little anticlimactic. I told Alex, Hunter, and Eva, and all three responded to the discovery with the appropriate amount of awe and horror.

But then, it just sort of *was* . . .

We knew where the Hellgate was located. So what? Until the demons tried to break through, there wasn't much we could do about it. And although Ishtar had insisted that she didn't need Alex or me for such a chore, I wasn't sure I believed her.

After all, she was a demon and untrustworthy by nature.

Still, I chose to believe that as long as we remained vigilant about protecting ourselves, and used every advantage we had, everything would be fine.

At least, that's what we told ourselves.

The denial method usually worked, and time passed like it was any other school year. Actually, considering that we were in our Grind-year, it passed *way* freaking faster. Samhain, and with it, the Culling-year Samhain Trials, were approaching with astonishing rapidity. The traumatic flashbacks of that day, and wondering if the Culling students might repeat the horrors my class experienced, stressed me the heck out.

My anxiety might have also had something to do with the fact that the next Spy Games event was slated for shortly after Samhain.

Whatever the case, I was one hundred percent thankful for a Sunday in Wandstown with my friends. I needed a break from the books, my spymaster duties, and training for the Spy Games, if only for a few hours.

"Who's up for Potions and Pastries Café?" Hunter rubbed his hands together, presumably at the thought of the café's éclairs, his favorite dessert.

"Yes please," I said.

We made our way to the café, which was open late to accommodate socializing before the Samhain Trial festivities took place the next day. Trial day was a rare freebie for most Grind and Crucible students, so we took advantage of it.

And we weren't the only ones. Many people from the PIA were in town to view or work the trials. Almost all of the PIA agents stayed at the Wandstown Inn and supported the local economy heartily for the duration of their trip. After all, supernatural spies and spymasters, rarely got a night off. It was even more unusual that the humans who worked for the PIA were allowed into a place like Wandstown. They had to live it up while they could.

The moment we entered Potions and Pastries, a wave of cheer and the aromas of beer and wine floated over to greet us.

I grinned and caught Eva's eye. *Watch your guy,* I mouthed, to which Eva rolled her eyes and looped her arm through Hunter's.

There had to be at least twenty PIA employees here, and if she wasn't careful, Hunter would try to schmooze every single one.

We snagged a table, and Miss Iris, the café owner, bustled over.

"Good to see you four out and about. It's always a relief to know that students are surviving their Grind-year." Miss Iris winked. "What can I get you?" Her cheeks were flushed with excitement, and a smile played on her lips. She thrived on the hustle and bustle. Or maybe she was thrilled for the influx of cash the weekend would bring.

We ordered a pitcher of beer and a couple of desserts to share. Miss Iris delivered the pitcher within minutes. Once we'd served ourselves, a bout of inspiration hit me, and I held out my glass. "To not having to take part in the Samhain Trials."

"Oh my God, preach," Eva said, toasting me vigorously. Everyone drank, and then, as if we finally realized that we could relax, we leaned back in our chairs.

"Holy shit, sitting here is the most amazing thing."

Hunter tilted his head back over the flower-patterned chair. "How have the last four months been the most difficult months of my life?"

"Not everyone is born with a silver spoon in their mouth," Alex quipped.

Hunter's head snapped up, but when he saw that Alex was grinning, he shook his finger at his cousin. "You—"

The guys began to banter, but I ignored it and twisted to Eva. "You holding up okay? Tomorrow's the anniversary of . . ." My fingers traced the spot on my face where her scars were.

She released a heavy sigh. "Yeah. I'm okay. Taking it one day at a time. To be honest, so much has happened since then, it seems like . . ." She trailed off, at a loss for words.

"A different lifetime?" I suggested.

"Pretty much," Eva held out her pint, and we saluted each other once more.

We'd just set our beers down when someone appeared at our table.

"Spellcasters students, am I right?" The man, who looked very familiar, stared down at me.

"Yup," Eva replied. "Are you PIA?"

A smile broke on the man's lips. "Here for the trials. We," he hitched his thumb to indicate a table near the back, "knew Miss Iris' father, and wanted to catch up with his daughter while in town. As usual, catch-up led to a beer and then another and another." The man shook his head sheepishly. "You know how these things go."

I smiled, still trying to place him. Hunter invited the

guy, who introduced himself as Andrew, to sit. He obliged and ordered another pitcher of beer for the table. Miss Iris was just depositing the second pitcher and our desserts on the table when I snapped my fingers.

"I remember how I know you!"

Andrew brought his hand to his chest. "I should hope so, I just introduced myself."

"No. I recognized you from before, but couldn't put my finger on it. Do you remember when last year's Culling class came in for a field trip?"

Andrew narrowed his eyes. "Kind of. I was off site for some of it."

"Yes! I saw you arrive!"

My eyes narrowed as I tried to recall the scene better. There had been two guards. One wore a newsboys cap, and was more violent than his partner. I was sure that Andrew was the quieter agent.

"I'm almost positive that you were one of the guys I ran into who were bringing a dangerous witch in for questioning. Your partner wore a newsboy cap and clocked her over the head to quiet her. Do you remember the witch?"

The memory of the witch screaming and flailing in the agents' arms would never leave me, but I couldn't assume the same for two seasoned PIA officials. They'd probably seen it all.

"She was older and very sick," I pressed when Andrew continued to look confused. "She screamed for me not to trust anyone. It was right by the cafeteria in the PIA."

Now that I'd latched on to the memory, I could hear the

woman's screams and smell the coffee I'd been holding as if it were yesterday, not almost a year ago.

"I think so . . ." Andrew trailed off, and a horrified look crossed his face. I was about to react, when he seemed to catch himself and smiled conspiratorially. "But I could easily be mistaken. We get all sorts of wackos coming into the PIA. You'll see when you work there." He took a hearty slug of beer.

While the agent was occupied with his drink, I shot a glance at my friends. I'd told them what the witch had said, and I was sure that they remembered. She hadn't seemed crazy to me. And David Chena had told me she was sick. But if she had been sick, why would Andrew have looked so alarmed that I remembered her? My friends looked as confused as I felt.

"I guess so," I said once Andrew set his beer down. "But she didn't strike me as crazy. Frantic, yes, but not crazy. Although when I asked David Chena about her, he did mention that something had been wrong with her health. That she'd needed help."

Andrew snapped his fingers. "Ahhhh, I remember it all now! Yes, we had to keep her under quarantine for a very long time. She left earlier this year."

My spine straightened. David had told me she was dead.

"Left?" I asked. Maybe I'd misunderstood. "Got to go free?"

"Yup. Walked out on her own two feet," Andrew said with a grin.

Realizing that I was on to something, I leaned closer to Andrew. Hunter set down a half-eaten éclair, and each of my friends mimicked me, placing their hands on the table—ready to protect me should I need help.

Andrew seemed to have realized that he'd said something wrong, because his grip on his beer mug tightened, and he pushed back from the table. "You know what? I think I should get back to the inn. The beer has caught up with me, and as you might recall, we need to prepare for anything and everything during the Samhain Trials tomorrow."

"You're not leaving yet." I placed a hand on Andrew's forearm.

The PIA agent looked down at it and sneered. "Girl, if you think your little hand will stop me, you're wrong. I—"

"Not her hand," Hunter cut him off. "But the shield I put around us might."

All the blood left Andrew's face, and he whirled around to look at his table of colleagues in the back.

No one so much as glanced his way.

"Hey!" Andrew yelled. "Guys!"

Still no one paid him any attention.

Hunter laughed. "You can call for backup all you want. They won't hear you. No one will until I want them to."

Andrew whipped back around, and anger blazed in his eyes. "You're a Grind-year?"

Hunter winked and flipped his shaggy blond mop back like he was a surfing god. "Yup. But I'm already kickass at shields. I can even make them colorless and soundproof, if I wish." He arched an eyebrow. "You should know that everyone at this table excels in one aspect of magic or another. And we're even better at learning things we shouldn't know."

"And something is up with your story," I said, drawing Andrew's attention back to me.

"How would you know?" he spat. His jovial nature had vanished. He was terrified that we would uncover something we shouldn't. "You saw that woman once, and you're not PIA. You have no clearance."

"That's true," I said simply. "But I'm acquainted with a lot of powerful witches. If I tell them that the PIA is lying about the fate of their kind, they might feel threatened. These witches are legends, and if they moved against the agency, others *would* follow."

"What makes you think I'm lying?" Andrew's hard eyes locked with mine.

"Because you said the witch left the PIA on her own two feet. But David Chena told me that she died."

For a millisecond, I thought Andrew would try to defend himself, to claim that he was wrong, or try to burst through Hunter's shield. So when he slammed his hands on the table and leaned back in his chair, it shocked the hell out of me.

"She's as good as dead," he muttered.

"Like she's still ill?" I asked. "Not out of quarantine?"

Andrew twisted his neck to glance at his colleagues' table. Still no one watched us, and when he turned to face us, Andrew looked relieved.

"Like she's gone somewhere, and she's not coming back. That witch was a top agent once, but times are changing at the agency. A few of our most skilled agents went rogue last year. We've found them all, and now they're . . . somewhere."

"Somewhere?" Hunter sounded incredulous. "Come on, man, if you're gonna spill, be more specific."

"I can't tell you where because I don't have that information. All I can say is they're locked up. Probably for the better, if you ask me. Shit's getting dark."

I sucked in a breath, and my friends turned to me. "Remember during our internship how my parents mentioned some of their friends were missing?"

Eva's blue eyes popped. "Oh my God. Do you think . . . ?"

I nodded. "Yup."

"Why are they disappearing spies?" Alex asked Andrew. "Did they break the law?"

Andrew shook his head. "Not to my knowledge. It's more like they went against the PIA. I don't know their motives and I don't intend to find out." He perched his elbows on the table. "I'm telling you this not only because you're four smart little shits, but because you should think twice before joining the agency. Leave the academy. Do something else—*anything* else. They won't come after you then. Not like they will me." A shadow fell over his eyes, and he took another swig of beer.

"Are you going to desert?" I whispered.

Andrew nodded. "As soon as the Samhain Trial is over. I

felt like I owed it to the school to attend, seeing as how they opened my eyes to how the world really is. I told myself I wanted to do more to keep students like you safe. Maybe, though, I was really hoping someone would question me and allow me to pass on some info." Andrew locked eyes with me. "Seriously, get out while you still can. Something dark is happening at the PIA. Good kids like yourselves don't want anything to do with it."

"Thanks. We'll consider it," I said, even though I knew we'd do the exact opposite.

My friends and I were already in too deep. Our only option was to attempt to understand the turmoil spinning around us. And once we figured out what was going on, we would move mountains to make it out alive.

We left Potions and Pastries shortly after Andrew. He'd made it clear that we should keep the information we'd learned secret. While that was sound advice, I had no intention of following it.

"Who do you think will let us use their phone?" I asked my friends as we strolled down an empty Wandstown street. "I would have asked Miss Iris, but the chances of the other agents overhearing was too great. Still, my parents need to be informed."

"Mine too," Alex agreed. "Let's try the Wandstown Tavern. I've been there before with my parents, and the owner, Jamal, seems like a good guy." He led the way, and after entering the Tavern, waved at someone right away. "He's over there. Let's go talk to him."

As soon as we approached, Jamal embraced Alex like a son. After that, it was only a matter of a little small talk before I felt comfortable asking to use the phone to call my parents. My request made Jamal clutch his heart.

"I find it so cruel that Spellcasters doesn't allow students to speak with their families." He shook his head as he gestured for us to follow him to the back.

"So many kids come in here, nearly broken by the academy, and needing a slice of home. A poor Culling-year girl was in here earlier today and positively frantic over the Samhain Trials." Jamal's lips pressed together. "I can't imagine that I'm the only shop in town letting kids break the rules."

Asking a Wandstown business if I could use their phone had never crossed my mind before tonight. Apparently, I was in the minority.

"Well, thanks for letting us use it," Alex said as Jamal funneled us into this office. "We'll be quick."

Jamal threw a dismissive wave. "Take all the time you need."

He left us, and my friends made themselves comfortable while I dialed.

Mom picked up on the second ring. "Hello?"

"Hey, Mom, it's me. I'm calling from the Wandstown Tavern," I explained, realizing that the strange number showing up on her cell had probably confused her.

"Odie! Is something wrong?" Fear laced Mom's voice.

"I'm fine, Mom. Safe, and hanging in Wandstown with the gang. But yeah, something is up. Something you and Dad should be aware of."

I relayed all that Andrew told us. Once I was done, the other end of the line remained silent.

"Mom? You okay?"

She cleared her throat. "I'm fine, honey. A little anxious that you interrogated a PIA officer, but—"

"He's deserting, Mom. He won't say anything."

"Let's hope so." She released a heavy sigh. "Thank you for telling me. I knew something was amiss. I'll spread the word to trusted sources. I'll also call Priscilla Wake and insist that she strengthen the wards around the school. After this—"

An idea popped into my mind at that moment. "Mom . . . she sends students to the PIA. What if she's involved somehow?"

It felt wrong to ask, but better safe than sorry.

"No, honey. I doubt that. Headmistress Wake is devoted to the PIA and her country, but she would *never* endanger her students like this. This is different from the trials or missions that have been vetted. This is unconnected to Spellcasters. I can feel it."

"You and Dad will get to the bottom of it?"

"We will, honey." Mom said, her tone strong and reassuring. "That's what Danes do, isn't it?"

CHAPTER TWENTY-NINE

The Samhain Trials were far less momentous than last year's, and absolutely nothing out of the ordinary occurred. This was welcome, and as the students exited Merlin Amphitheater, it was like everyone released a collective sigh of relief.

Eva's was the loudest and largest of all.

I noticed the tense lines of my friend's shoulders slope downward as we walked inside the main building of Spellcasters.

"A nice long bath would be amazing right now." I sidled up to Eva and wrapped an arm around her shoulders.

"Hell yeah, it would," she murmured. "I feel like I can breathe again."

"I know. It's hard to revisit trauma, but something tells me that the first-years are totally safe."

Eva snorted. "Yeah, only *we* aren't. Way to sugarcoat it, Dane."

I cringed. "Sorry. I didn't mean—"

She placed a hand on my wrist. "No. Stop. My response was sarcasm, and inappropriate considering all we've been through. Don't feel bad."

A lump rose in my throat, and as a swell of appreciation for my bestie telling it like it was washed over me, I pulled Eva into a tight hug. She squeezed me back, and we stayed like that for a while. When we finally pulled apart, two figures stood off to our side.

"We didn't mean to interrupt," Holly said, worry lining her tanned face.

I smiled at her and Heidi. "No worries. Congratulations on finishing your first trial. Feels good, doesn't it?"

They both exhaled loudly. "*So* good," Heidi said. "Actually, our class is having a little pow-wow tonight in the initiate tower to celebrate. We were wondering if you two would want to come? You've been so sweet and helpful to us, and we'd love to show you a good time. You can bring your boyfriends too."

My heart warmed a little. During our first-year, the Grind students had ignored us until February because that's how it had always been done. I hated the idea, and was proud to rebel against that Spellcasters tradition.

And yet, the party did *not* sound appealing. My whole body ached from holding in tension all day. And because we'd spent hours watching the trials with bated breath instead of studying, I was even more behind on homework than usual.

"Thank you guys, but I'll pass," I said.

"Yeah, me too. I'm just . . . so tired," Eva said.

Heidi bit her lip, her blue eyes scanning Eva. "Oh, right. I didn't consider the emotional toll today would have on you. Sorry."

"Don't be sorry," Eva said. "Why would you consider that? You were worried about passing your own trial." She smiled to show that she meant it.

"Seriously, you two have a blast," I egged them on. "Drink a beer for each of us."

"Dude," Eva said after we parted ways with the girls and trudged up the stairs. "We passed up a party because we're tired? We're old AF."

I slapped her shoulder playfully. "Speak for yourself, granny! I'm not—" I stopped walking and leaned over the third-floor railing to peer into the entryway below.

"Odie? You okay?" Eva asked.

I nodded and waved her over.

"What are you looking at?"

"Look straight down and to the left, right where the hallway begins. See that little alcove?" I pointed.

My friend followed my directions, and a frown spread across her face. "Is that David Chena talking to Holly? Like *really* close?"

"Too close for comfort," I confirmed, taking in David's stance and how he was whispering in Holly's ear.

Eva turned to me. "What are you thinking?"

Andrew's words from last night and David Chena's lie that the witch had died swirled in my mind.

I loosed a sigh. "I'm thinking I might have changed my

mind about going to the party tonight. And although I know it's the last thing you want to do, I'm hoping you'll go with me."

Because Eva was a trooper and the best friend any girl could have asked for, she accompanied me to the initiate dorm.

"How are you going to bring David up to Holly?" Eva asked for the tenth time.

"Just gonna wing it," I said as we stopped in front of the tower and knocked.

"Waiting to be let in feels *weird*, doesn't it?" Eva asked as she readjusted her dress.

"Totally," I agreed.

A young man who I'd never met opened the door a second later. When he saw that two Grind-year spymasters were waiting outside the tower, his eyes bulged. "Uh, hi. Are you here for the party?"

"Yup. Heidi and Holly invited us," Eva said, her tone light and her smile bright.

"Wow . . . I mean . . . Okay. Come on in." The door opened wide, and the familiar scent of the initiate tower and sour-smelling beer filled my nose.

As we walked through the common space, people stared, and a hush fell in a wave. It was strange, but I should have expected it. Other than Eva and me talking to Heidi and Holly, the upperclassmen ignored the initiates, so this was a first for most of them. That I was a school champion probably didn't hurt either.

Eva and I approached the keg, and a guy who still hadn't grown out of his acne phase leapt up to help us.

"Here you go," he said, handing two plastic cups over with trembling hands.

"Thanks," I responded and looked around. "Have you seen Heidi or Holly?"

"They're getting ready in their rooms!" a voice called from the crowd.

"Oh, okay. I guess we'll just wait."

The pimply guy shook his head. "I'll show you where they are."

He climbed the stairs, and we followed. When he exited onto the floor that Eva and I had lived on the previous year, I gave her a wide-eyed look. One that grew even more incredulous as our guide stopped right in front of our old, adjoining rooms.

"No way," Eva whispered with a grin. "Looks like we get to go down memory lane."

"Looks like it," I said. "Thanks for escorting us," I told the guy, who gave us a quick smile and scampered off.

Eva and I stood there, soaking in being so close to our old home. Since we were so quiet, I noticed voices escalating from the other side of the door. I tilted my head. I couldn't make out actual words, but it sounded as if one person was mad at another.

Were we visiting at a bad time? Or the perfect time?

Following a hunch, I knocked. "Hey, Heidi and Holly. It's Odette. We came by to say hi."

The voices ceased. There was a loud scuffling, and then Heidi flung the door open.

"Hey!" She beamed at me. "Sorry about that! I was just finishing getting ready."

She wore a dress, but her hair was about half done, so I could believe it.

"Is this your room? Where's Holly? I thought I heard her too."

For a moment, Heidi's expression faltered, but like a good spy-in-training, she brightened almost instantly. "We were just talking, but she was in a towel and didn't want to be embarrassed. She'll be over in a sec." Heidi gestured for us to enter. "Come on in."

I glided over the threshold of my old room, and smiled as I went to the window that looked out over the lake. "You probably have no idea, but this is my old room."

"What?!" Heidi's hand flew to her mouth. "No way!"

Eva laughed. "And if Holly is your roomie, then she's in my old room."

"Oh my God, that's so cool!" Heidi exclaimed. "It's like we were meant to be friends. I *have* to tell her. She needs to hurry anyway." She gave me a sly look. "Make yourselves at home! Ha!" She laughed at herself before dashing off through the bathroom.

More talking hit my ear, and sooner than I expected, both girls reappeared through the bathroom door.

"Hey, Holly," I said, trying to pretend like nothing was

amiss, which was hard, because her red eyes made it obvious that she'd been crying.

"Hey," she replied, her voice only the slightest bit raspy. "Heidi told me about the rooms. That's crazy."

"Yeah, it is," Eva replied. An awkward moment passed before she reached out to Holly. "Are you okay?"

Holly sniffed. "Yeah, I am. Sorry, I didn't want anyone to see me like this. It's why we're not at the party yet—but I should be."

"And why's that?" I asked.

"To show her asshole ex that he can't get to her," Heidi responded for her friend.

Asshole ex? I hadn't been aware that Holly was dating anyone.

"Who?"

"Caleb," Heidi said. "You probably saw him down there. He's super tall and loud."

I hadn't. "Did he break up with you?"

Once again, Heidi took the lead. "Hell no! She broke up with him after her trial. But he was super mean about it. Said some shit that broke her heart—you know, just hurtful stuff because he was feeling wounded."

"Well, you know what that means, right?" Eva said, stepping forward and wrapping Holly in a hug.

"What?" Holly's voice was muffled by Eva's shoulder.

"You have to go downstairs and show him he didn't get to you. Good thing you have Odie and me to help."

～

The night had become way more complicated than I could have imagined. I was trying to get Holly alone to talk to her, a feat that proved difficult, as Heidi kept trying to show her roomie the time of her life. But I was also trying to be a supportive pal.

One thing was for sure, this whole evening made me grateful that Alex and I had a relatively drama-free relationship.

It was well past midnight when the break I'd been waiting for presented itself. Holly proclaimed that she had to go to the bathroom, and I hopped up from the chair I'd been lounging in and said I would join.

We chit-chatted up the stairs, all the way to her room. When Holly closed the bathroom door, I sat on her bed, my knee jumping up and down as I waited for her. I needed answers, but considering her breakup, I also wanted to be delicate about it.

The toilet flushed, and the faucet ran. A moment later, Holly flung the bathroom door open with a flourish, a grin on her face. "I think we're getting to Caleb. Honestly, I can't thank you and Eva enough for coming. I've had so much fun—"

"Holly," I blurted out, unable to hold it in for a second longer. "Why were you whispering with Spymaster Chena today?"

Holly took a step backward. "Wh—what are you talking about?"

I sighed. "I saw you today, after the Samhain Trial. You two hovered in an alcove off the school entryway—hidden from most people, but not me. I was climbing the stairs, and from my vantage, I saw that you and Spymaster Chena were close. *Very* close." I bit my lip. "Did he ask you to do something? You're not in the Society of Spies yet, and you don't have to do it. Or did he . . . hit on you?"

I couldn't picture either scenario. The spymaster had always been someone I respected. But the way they'd been talking, like people sharing an intimate secret or like lovers, had left only two options in my mind.

"Is he forcing you—"

"David would never do that!" Holly shouted, and then catching herself, flung her hands over her mouth.

David? As far as I knew, I was the only other Spellcasters student who called Spymaster Chena by his first name. That was only because he respected my parents a lot and had insisted upon it.

"What do you mean?" I stood from the bed. "What's going on between you two?"

Tears formed in Holly's eyes.

"Holly, you and I are friends. You can tell me. Are you doing something you shouldn't be? Is he making you?"

She covered her face with her hands. "David and I are together! We've been having an affair since my PIA orientation. It's why I needed to break up with Caleb. Please don't think I'm a whore!"

CHAPTER THIRTY

Six days later, I still felt guilty for thinking that Holly might be up to something foul. Even though I thought her relationship with David was inappropriate—the power imbalance alone made it sketchy—she was eighteen, a consenting adult. What she did in her spare time was none of my business.

I'd quickly apologized after she told me about the affair, but Holly definitely had not forgiven me for thinking the worst. The week had been filled with her tossing hurt glances and scowls my way every time we passed in the halls.

I was reminding myself that she probably just needed time, after yet *another* uncomfortable run-in, when Amethyst sprinted up to me.

"Odette! I need you to come with me! *Now!*"

"What?! Is someone hurt?" *Geez, why is that always the*

first thing out of my mouth? Shows what kind of life I'm leading . . .

"I can't say here. Just come on!"

Amethyst led me down a series of hallways and into a room that I hadn't been inside since our initiate orientation night. Despite the months that had passed, the Marie Laveau Room was just like I remembered it, dark and den-like. A fire was lit and beating the fall chill from the room. The rack of antlers above the hearth looked as impressive as ever, and a scent of sage, as if someone had just cleansed the area, hung in the air. To my great surprise, Eva was already there, sitting in an armchair by the fire.

"That was fast," Eva said and then patted the seat next to her. "I expected her to take longer than two minutes to find you."

"I had help this time."

My eyebrows shot up, but I took a seat. Once Amethyst locked the door, she whipped around, her brown eyes sweeping the room.

I shot Eva a glance. "Is she—?"

"No freaking idea," Eva whispered.

"You can reveal yourself," Amethyst said.

"We're right—oh shit!" My heart rate spiked, and I gripped the armrests of my chair as a ghost appeared in the wing-backed seat across from me.

Eva's gaze followed mine, and she released a loud yip.

Amethyst, however, didn't look surprised at all. She simply dashed over and took the seat next to the ghost.

"Thank you for meeting us here. And for making yourself visible. It will help them." She gestured to Eva and me.

I cleared my throat. "So, who's your friend?"

Amethyst crossed her legs, and the one on top began bouncing up and down. "This is Ronald Percy, intermittent ghost of Spellcasters. He just returned from a little vacation to . . . Where did you go again, Ron?"

"Scotland. I like the autumn months there."

"Right. The highlands. Ronald here, unlike the more permanent ghost residents of the academy, is a talker. And he's not afraid to talk about the ghost that you-know-whated me."

Amethyst gave us a pointed look. "Anyway, he's been back for a week and heard that I'd been trying to connect with a spirit. The ghosts here are a little cliquey with each other, and he wanted someone to talk to, so he found me. Which was lucky, because Ron has a lot of superb information. Would you mind telling them what you told me?" She grinned at the ghost next to her.

Ronald tipped his pageboy hat at Amethyst. "Of course, my dear friend." The ghost turned to Eva and me. His pale white eyes, which were even whiter around his irises, bore through us.

I gulped. I'd never imagined what it would be like to be a spiritwalker or talker before, but sitting in front of Ronald made me glad that I didn't seem to have that gift. It was too eerie, and I didn't like to think that they could pop into whatever room I was in for a word.

"You're the one the malevolent ghost is preying upon," Ronald pointed a thin finger at me.

I sighed. "If you're talking about the one that Amethyst is well acquainted with, then, yeah, probably. Actually, knowing my luck, *all* the bad ghosts at the school are preying on me."

Eva snorted. "Or me. We're magnets for evil juju."

"What else have you learned about him, Ronald?" Amethyst ignored our dramatics.

"He has the backing of a queen and seems to have found a home at Spellcasters."

Eva leaned forward. "What do you mean 'found a home'?"

Ronald turned to look at Amethyst, his white bushy brows pulled together.

Amethyst sighed. "He means that someone, a witch, is helping the ghost and giving him a place to stay. But you don't know who it is, right Ronald?"

The ghost shook his head. "When ghosts find a home, they keep quiet about it. No one wants another specter trying to move in on their person. After all, few people are open to having us around whenever we wish."

"Does he possess him or her?" I asked, my mind reeling.

"I would assume yes—but with permission, of course— so it's not a true possession." Ronald shrugged.

I turned to Amethyst. "And he hasn't been back for you?"

She shook her head. "I haven't picked up on any ill will,

which I felt in spades that day." She pulled a chain out from under her shirt, and her expression turned a little sheepish. "Part of that might be because of this necklace. I went to Wandstown and used a phone to contact my parents. I didn't tell them anything specific, but they've been around spirits long enough to guess that I needed protection. Apparently, trickster ghosts sometimes like to take budding spirit walkers and talkers for a spin. Mostly, it's harmless, but not always. My parents packed a ghost-specific protection talisman for me should it ever become an issue."

"And you never found it before?" Eva asked.

Amethyst chuckled. "Mom hollowed out an old Battle Magic book that she knew I'd never open and stuck the necklace in there. I'd wondered why she'd insisted that I bring the thing to school for two years. Now I understand."

"Smart woman." I focused on Ronald again. "So we know this ghost likes to deliver his queen's messages. Am I in any danger of being possessed by him?"

Amethyst had assured me that ghosts only possessed people receptive to ghostly spirits, but still—another opinion never hurt.

Ronald gave me a long look. "It seems not. But you," he turned to Eva. "You are at risk—albeit a small one, as you don't seem extremely receptive to specter possession."

"Thank God for that," she muttered.

Ronald nodded. "However, if he cannot possess either of you, he will continue to work with the person he's found and wreak havoc at the school."

"Havoc?" My eyebrows knitted together. "Aside from

the fae invasion, things have been quiet since the start of term. Do you think he has plans?"

"Ghosts like him always have plans. It's just a matter of time until he enacts them." Ronald paused and brought a finger to his lips. "Unless . . ." He trailed off and fell into silence.

"Unless what?" I prodded, annoyed. "You can't just go all silent like that on us. If there's a way to stop him, we have to try."

"Apologies. I was mulling over if it's worth it to try. After reading your energies, I believe it will be difficult, but not impossible." Ronald pointed to my ankle. "With the marks you bear, you might exert some control over this ghost."

"How?"

"The ghost is a creature of Hell. As Hell's essence runs in your veins, you might be able to call and banish him. Much like someone might with a ghost who has bonded with them."

"Can they do it alone?" Amethyst sounded very skeptical.

Ronald gave her a soft smile. "No, my friend. They are not in tune with ghostly energies. You will need to teach them the correct ways of calling a ghost, and then pass along the banishing incantation. But with your guidance, it might work. Once he leaves, theoretically, everyone should be safe."

～

Amethyst remained in the Marie Laveau Room with Ronald to discuss matters of banishing a ghost, while Eva and I walked to the Green Tower.

Our footsteps reverberated through the empty corridors. It seemed like most students had returned to their dorms, or were in the library studying—which was exactly what I should be doing, although I wasn't sure I could manage it now.

"Do you think we can do this?" I asked Eva, hoping that talking about it would help ease my anxiety.

"We don't have a choice," she shot me an apologetic glance. "If her talisman works, Amethyst isn't in danger anymore, but there's at least one other person at the academy susceptible to ghostly energies. The ghost's home. That bastard ghost will just work through them."

"But won't Ishtar just send another ghost?" I asked. "Hell is probably full of evil spirits wanting a second chance in our realm."

Eva shrugged. "Who the hell knows? Not me, that's for sure."

We entered the Grind-year Tower and climbed the stairs. As soon as we set foot onto the spymasters level, Hunter and Alex poked their heads out of the private study.

"Waiting for someone?" I teased as I went to meet my boyfriend.

"Why wouldn't we be waiting up for our hot ladies?" Hunter replied as he wrapped his arms around Eva and laid one on her.

"What he said," Alex murmured, pulling me close and

pressing his lips to mine in greeting. "Where were you girls?"

"With Amethyst, talking to a ghost."

Alex's eyebrows rose. "Okay . . . Why?"

I took his hand. "Eva and I have a few things to tell you guys. Is the library free?"

"Diana's not in there, if that's what you mean."

It was. I couldn't risk her telling her mother about our plans.

"Perfect. Let's go chat."

A half hour later, we'd debriefed the guys and left them looking shell-shocked.

"Sorry for keeping this from you. I didn't even tell Eva, she *guessed*—well, mostly."

Alex nodded. "I get why you did. If you're telling us now, I'm assuming it's because you want our help with the banishing?"

"Absolutely," Eva answered. "We'll have to ask Amethyst how to best use your powers, but just having you there would make me feel way better."

"We'll do anything you need." Alex turned to me. "And I don't think those warping lessons can wait any longer, babe. Things are getting weird around here. Obviously, I won't be great at it right away, but after we take care of the ghost, can you give me a lesson before you go to the Fae Academy?"

I gulped. The next Spy Games event was in four days. I had a mountain of course work and a ghost to banish before I left. But looking at Alex's earnest face, I couldn't say no.

And if it eased his anxiety about me being away, why would I?

It was unlikely that he'd take to warping quickly—if at all—but we'd give it a try.

"Tonight, I *seriously* have to get some homework done. We're banishing the ghost tomorrow." I wrapped my hand in his. "The next night, you'll have your first lesson."

CHAPTER THIRTY-ONE

"*I*n the Riverland Court, the royals rule in a more democratic fashion than in the Snowcap Court." Ms. Seeley pointed out the adjacent kingdoms on the map of Faerie tacked to the wall.

While I found the various court workings of Faerie to be interesting, I fought to keep my eyes open. After meeting Ronald the night before, staying up half the night to finish homework, and then worrying about Alex's first warping session, I was running on two hours of sleep. While some blessed people, like Hunter, could be charming and energetic on a ten-minute power nap, I'd never been one of them. Exhaustion had sunk into my bones, and the only thing that would alleviate it was a good snooze.

Maybe I can sneak in a nap before dinner. Or I'll just skip dinner and sleep . . .

I darted a glance at the clock and groaned. We'd only

been in class fifteen minutes. This was officially the longest day ever.

I'll just rest my eyes for a few minutes. My eyelids fluttered closed, and relief washed over me.

"Miss Dane? Miss Dane? Are you okay?"

I jerked up and nearly toppled out of my desk.

"Wha—what?" My face grew hot as I cast a confused glance around.

A few of my classmates who were gathering their belongings laughed. I set my hand on my desk, right in a wet spot, and groaned.

Oh my hell. I'd slept through class. I bit my lip as Kira Johnston walked past me, her dark brown eyes narrow and judging.

After we'd returned from the first Spy Game event and word got around that I'd helped the group tremendously, a few Grind-year students had warmed to me again. Kira was not one of them. Unfortunately, a whopping quarter of my year was still in the 'Odie sucks' club, and sleeping through class probably didn't help my rep.

I flung my head into my hands.

A moment later, Alex was there, his hand resting on my shoulder. "You okay babe?"

I nodded, still not daring to remove my hands from my eyes as I listened to the sounds of the class emptying.

Alex stayed silent, rubbing my back and allowing me to collect myself. Soon, the only sound in the room was the clacking of footsteps approaching, heels.

"Mr. Wardwell," Ms. Seeley's musical tone hit my ear. "I'd like a moment with Miss Dane, please."

"Oh, umm—"

I lifted my head from my hands to meet my boyfriend's eyes. "It's fine, Alex. I'll meet you in Potions and Poisons."

Once he left, I turned to the professor.

"I'm so sorry, Ms. Seeley. I didn't mean to fall asleep and disrespect you like that. The topic is super interesting, I'm just so—"

"Exhausted. I know, Miss Dane." Ms. Seeley patted my hand, and her violet eyes sparkled. "It happens to everyone during the Grind. Even those who are not also acting as school champions. Don't be so hard on yourself."

I gave her a weak smile. "Thanks. I'll try not to let it happen again. I need to learn as much about the fae as possible," I said, referencing the fact that the fae were set to host the next Spy Games at the Fae Academy of Elemental and Arcane Arts.

"About that," Ms. Seeley turned and moved back to her desk. "You probably don't need anything else to study, but let's just say I have a feeling about your event. This might come in handy." She pulled a scroll out of a drawer and handed it to me.

The paper was thick, with a silver ribbon tied around it. "Thank you. I—"

The owl hooted, indicating that the next class had already started. I began picking up my things. "Looks like I'd better run." I held up the scroll. "But thank you."

"You're welcome, Miss Dane," Ms. Seeley said before waving me from her classroom.

The last class of the day was sheer torture, but I managed to sneak in an hour nap during dinnertime, before Eva collected me to banish the evil ghost.

We met Amethyst in the woods behind the academy. She'd chosen the spot to avoid tripping any of the new wards inside the school. It had the added advantage of being out of sight of all the towers, and far from the King's Castle.

Secrecy was of the utmost importance, and not just from other witches. We couldn't be sure that Ishtar didn't have other ghosts working for her in the academy. Until Ronald verified that information, a task he'd already begun, keeping quiet would keep Amethyst safe.

A late fall chill had settled permanently over Maine, and I wrapped my large scarf around myself as I surveyed the area. We were in a small clearing, barely large enough to fit the circle of salt Amethyst had drawn on the ground. A silver bowl sat lonely in the center, and at what I assumed were each of the four cardinal points, a single crystal rested between three burning candles. The gems were all different colors. I had a hunch that we might have covered why in Divination and Tarot, but I couldn't recall the reason for such stones. It didn't matter anyway. Amethyst knew what she was doing, and except for the part Eva and I would play in calling and banishing the ghost, the spirit talker was running the show.

"Where do you want us?" I asked, not trying to waste time when it was freezing out. "And what should we be doing?"

Amethyst pointed to two opposing spots on the circle, and instructed Eva and me to each stand at one. She then pulled two small daggers out of a bag and handed a hilt to each of us.

"What are these for?" Eva asked, her voice squeaky.

"Since you two are not practiced at calling specters, but have a bond with this ghost, you will need to spill a little blood to get him to come. Just make a small cut on your finger and drip it on the crystal in front of you."

I gulped. This reminded me of the blood-covered runes that had brought the demons over in Oregon. Across from me, Eva's face was tight. I would bet all the breath in my lungs that she was thinking the same thing. Neither of us had a chance to talk about our anxiety before Alex and Hunter appeared through the trees. As I knew he would when we'd requested his help, Alex had brought a bag chock-full of emergency healing supplies.

"Perfect timing," Amethyst said and ushered the guys into the circle. "Do *not* move an inch from this spot. Got it?"

They nodded, and Amethyst went about finishing her preparations.

Alex gestured to the knife in my hand. "What's that for?"

"Blood sacrifice. I have to put a little on the crystal." I pointed to the stone at my feet.

"Greaaaat. That isn't reminiscent of anything creepy at all." Hunter echoed my previous concerns.

Amethyst shot him a strange look, but no one expounded, and she continued working.

I watched her, feeling bad that she only had half the information. Amethyst knew that I was demon-touched. And since I felt like her possession was my fault, I'd even revealed that being demon-touched meant I could sense demons. She'd learned about Eva's mark after Ronald blabbed that Eva was connected to the ghost. Amethyst was more informed than most other students at Spellcasters, but that didn't mean I'd told her everything—like about Portland.

A few minutes later, she finished preparing the circle and took up the lead position in the middle.

"Here's how this will go. Odette and Eva must be the ones to actually call and banish the ghost. Since none of you are specter-sensitive, I'll set the energies for the circle and invoke the incantation too. That way, the magic can pass the veil. Once it's on the other side, your blood will do most of the work. So place a drop on the crystal and speak the incantation '*crucilarva*'. The lure of a blood sacrifice in combination with the spell will bring him here."

She turned to Alex and Hunter. "The second the ghost is in this circle—he'll come for the blood—you two throw up a shield and trap him. That's all I want you doing. *No* heroics. If you involve yourself in any other way, you're risking us all, and I won't have you in my circle. Got it?"

"Got it," Hunter nodded once.

Alex took a second longer, but at my nod, he sighed. "I understand."

"And the banishing incantation?" Eva asked.

"I'm getting there," Amethyst assured her. "Once we trap the ghost, he'll be *pissed*. He'll probably start trying to break out of the shield, which ghosts can do, although it takes some time. Most importantly, he will *not* want to drink the blood you offered anymore. He'll see it as deceit." Amethyst cast a wary glance at me. "But he must ingest the essence of his *master* in order for us to banish him."

My eyebrows knitted together. Why did she look so worried? "Yeah, and I thought Ronald said that was all we needed?"

Amethyst bit her bottom lip so hard that it turned white. "That's true. Your blood is connected to Ishtar and what we need. In fact, it's the most important aspect of this circle."

She bent down to pick up the bowl in the center of the circle and brought it to me.

"What Ronald didn't mention is that the lure for him to drink must be *irresistible*. Cut deep and fill this as much as you can. The more blood there is in one spot, the less he'll be able to resist. Once he drinks it, and he'll probably need to drink a lot, you can speak the banishment incantation '*protero*'."

A strangled sound came from Alex. Clearly when he asked if he should bring healing supplies, Amethyst had not told him that I'd be giving so much blood. But it didn't matter. What was required, was required, so I held up a hand, stopping his protest.

"How will I know when he's had enough to drink?"

"I'll let you know the second I think he's had enough," Amethyst assured me.

I inhaled and gulped. "Then let's do this."

CHAPTER THIRTY-TWO

_T_he air shimmered around us as dusk fell in earnest.

In the center of the circle, Amethyst raised her hands to the sky and murmured an incantation I'd never heard before.

A chill swept over the clearing, and all around the circle, my friends' eyes widened. The shift in energies and vibrations resonating around us was unlike any I'd ever experienced. I suspected that it was something only Amethyst could tap into, but the rest of us could sense to some extent or another.

"On this eve, we ask that the veil thin," Amethyst began. "All those who have passed before us, hear our plea and put us in touch with the one we seek." Her hands twirled through the air in a predictable pattern, and once again, Amethyst began murmuring words in another language.

The cold penetrated all the way to my bones, and a shiver dashed down my spine. Any moment now, my time to call the ghost would come.

It happened faster than I expected, with a snap of the air and a crackle of lights blooming from Amethyst's hands. The tiny flames of the candles surged up to hip-height, and then shrank back down to nothing but a whisper of flame.

Amethyst dropped her hands to her side and her gaze shifted between Eva and me. She nodded, and I raised the silver blade to my palm.

"With this offering, I call the spirit of Hell's blood. The spirit of my blood. *Crucilarva.*"

Eva murmured the same words and the incantation. Together, we sliced the blade across our palms and knelt so that droplets of crimson would soak into the stones.

The guys tensed and stood at the ready. Eva and I locked eyes, unable to tell if what we had done had worked or not. Amethyst seemed half in this world and half not as she gazed at the stars just beginning to pop in the darkening sky.

The seconds ticked on. The cold grew more persistent until my bones seemed to vibrate with it. When I couldn't take it a second longer, I opened my mouth to ask if we had done something wrong.

Amethyst lifted a finger to her lips, her eyes still firmly on the sky. I closed my mouth, confused.

Then I heard it. A low keening ringing through the forest outside Spellcasters, lifting the hairs on the back of my neck.

My eyes shot to Amethyst. Her lips were curled up, and when she caught my gaze, she gave a single nod.

A thrill ran through me. One immediately tempered by the shackles of fear.

The ghost was coming.

The guys stood motionless, their eyes searching and hands limp at their sides as if they were only bodies to fill the circle. Eva and I dropped our blades to the ground, and a heartbeat later a flash of white appeared over the evergreen pines. It soared from the direction of the school and drew closer and closer with every passing second. My breath caught in my chest, and before I knew it, the ghost was there, hovering around the edges of the salt circle. I hadn't seen him when he'd possessed Amethyst, but I recognized his energy. The same malevolent vibrations I felt that day rolled off of him now in terrible waves of hate, fear, and malice. I shuddered. This was no regular ghost. His rightful home was in Hell and his time here was, hopefully, short.

"Someone called?" the ghost's eyes, white as frost bore through me.

"I called you," I replied. "And as your master's essence runs through me, I insist that you join us in the circle."

The ghost laughed, but it was a front. My words had affected him because the way he floated right outside the salt barrier had changed. Before my command, he'd hovered stock-still. Now he seemed to be vibrating. He was fighting the effect of my words and Ishtar's essence running through me.

This might just work.

"So this is what happens when one who *thinks* she knows the ghosts, tries to call one?" His tone was snide, meant to wound Amethyst. "It is not enough for you to *want* me to join you. Your call is not strong enough. Your power is not alluring enough." The ghost laughed, low and evil. "I might fly away at any moment."

Shit. I darted a glance Amethyst. Unlike me, she didn't look worried. No, Amethyst met my gaze with a hardened expression and nodded down to where I had dropped the blade.

"We'll see about that." I scooped up the dagger and dug the blade deeper into my skin. My blood welled, red and bright in the candle's flame. I tilted my hand, and a few ruby drops poured over the crystal.

A sound between a moan and a cry of indignation rang from the ghost's mouth. "You're no match for—"

I squeezed my hand and another trickle of crimson ran over the stone.

The ghost gurgled, and unwillingly, he jerked into the confines of the circle.

"Now!" Amethyst screamed.

The guys flew into motion, and shields of crimson and dark green wove together overhead to create an impenetrable dome.

The ghost wailed. "How dare you trap me?! No shield can hold me forever! Nothing can!"

To prove his point, he slammed upward.

Hunter fell to the ground with a groan.

I tensed as a momentary hole appeared in the shield before Alex's crimson magic stopped it up. But as fast as Alex worked, and Hunter hauled himself back up, the ghost worked even faster, hurling his body into the dome again and again.

My stomach dropped to my knees as I watched the guys do damage control. The truth crashed down over me. There would be no second chances. If he broke out of the circle, he would bring Ishtar back. If that happened, we were all screwed.

I glanced at the blade in my hand. Right below the hilt, my veins pulsed. Only my blood would entice him to stay.

I brought the blade to my wrist and sliced, first one, and then the other.

"Odie!" Eva dropped her blade as her hands flew to her mouth. She took half a step toward me.

"*Stop!*" Amethyst roared, her hands shooting out to stop Eva. "Only I can move, or he escapes! Don't make her sacrifice for nothing!" Amethyst darted my way and set the silver bowl right beneath where blood poured from my wrists.

Sweat dripped off Alex's jaw, and Hunter grunted as they worked to keep their shields up. I watched as Eva tossed her power into the mix, and the shield now boasted swirls of sunshine yellow in addition to crimson and green. Her face twisted in pain and concentration.

Even with their combined powers, the ghost still screamed and wailed and flung himself from one side of the circle to the other time and time again. His attacks never lessened. His eyes, now glowing red with rage, never dimmed. He was determined to escape, and since he was a ghost with limitless energy, eventually, he would win.

Unless I stopped him.

Gritting my teeth, I clenched and unclenched my fists, pulling blood up and out of my wrists. Amethyst's hands began to shake, and the reason was frighteningly obvious.

The bowl was filling fast.

But my dangerous sacrifice was also working. With every additional drop poured into the bowl, the ghost slowed his assaults. His moans deepened, more telling of distress than anger. His eyes dimmed from red to white.

And then, finally, he stopped and drifted down to hover in front of me. The ghost's eyes looked pained and hungry as he stared into mine. "Your sacrifice was brave, but stupid. She'll just find another, you realize that, don't you?"

I gulped because no doubt he was right that Ishtar would try. But until that happened, my path was clear.

He caught the gesture, saw that I understood the truth in his words, and a low laugh rumbled through him. "In that case, witch, I'll see you in Hell." Then the ghost dipped his head into the bowl and drank.

My vision blurred. I only had moments until I would pass out, but there was no way I was pulling my wrists away. What if he needed more for my incantation to work? Plus, only Eva and I could banish the ghost. I had to stay awake for Amethyst's word.

The ghost drank deep, relishing each glug with a drawn-out moan.

Nearly all the blood in the bowl was gone, but I didn't dare move my wrists unless the ghost needed more for my spell to work. When my knees buckled, Amethyst ripped her gaze from the bowl to land on me.

Her eyes bulged. "Say it now! *Say it!*" She looked like she was screaming, but to me, it sounded as quiet as a whisper.

I heard Eva say the incantation, saw the ghost stiffen a bit, but because I had yet to do my part, he continued to drink. My mouth opened to follow—to speak the banishing spell. My lips felt dry, the saliva in my mouth sticky. The incantation worked its way up my throat, thick and clumsy.

"*P—pro—protero,*" I forced out.

The ghost's head shot up from the bowl. I blinked, taking in the strange sight of his blood-red mouth as a bone-shaking scream rang from his lips. A heartbeat later, he shot up toward the heavens. His ghostly body smashed through our shield, and he soared over the forest and away from Spellcasters, wailing the entire way.

The great, white streak of his body was the last thing I saw before I collapsed.

CHAPTER THIRTY-THREE

I awoke with a gasp. Sensing that I was laying on the cold, hard ground, I pushed myself up. I seemed to be in a sterile, long, and rectangular white room. From the opposite end of the space a bright light blazed toward me, warming me, welcoming me. Nothing else stood between me and the light that beckoned me forward. Not even my own will. The light was too beautiful. Just seeing it made my body radiate peace and wholeness. It felt like nothing would ever hurt me again.

In the air, strange strands of every color and length spun around my head, teasing and urging me to touch them. One soared near my ear, and the soft laughter of a child rang out.

What are these things?

I reached out to pluck the nearest tendril, itching to see if it felt as silky as they looked. My fingers grazed it, and it vibrated like a guitar string. Suddenly, a memory of my

Dad and me skiing in junior high played out before my eyes, as vibrant as a film.

"What is this?" I whispered, watching in awe.

The vibrations slowed, and the moment the thread stilled, the memory halted, as if someone had turned off the T.V.

Intrigued, I touched another thread, this one further away, and watched as a younger version of my mom and dad zoomed around a roller rink holding hands.

The realization as to what these strands were crashed over me, and I smiled.

Time. Threads of time surrounded me. And here, in this strange, bright, welcoming place, it seemed I could touch time, bend it, and—I stuck out my tongue, savoring the salty sweetness of the air—even taste it.

The white light that I'd seen when I first entered the room pulsed, recapturing my attention and giving me another option. I could walk right past time, toward the lovely light that beckoned me.

After a year of fear and toil, the light was too beautiful to ignore. I began to walk toward it.

"Odie! Odie! Come back!" a familiar voice called out.

I stopped where I stood. I recognized the importance of the voice, but couldn't quite place it. It seemed like the person lived in a different plane of existence.

I looked around and immediately, the voice lessened because I was here. Glorious, lovely *here*.

I took another step forward, down the white tunnel,

embracing wherever the beauty would take me. Everything was light and smelled wonderful and—

Something gripped my shoulder, and I jerked backward with a gasp. It felt like fingers had caught on my shirt. I wriggled and tried to smack them away, but instead of leaving, the fingers pulled me back, away from the beautiful light.

A cry of desperation left my throat as the light got smaller. I grasped for it as whatever had attached to me pulled me away from all that was beautiful and good.

"Odie, sweets. Come back."

"Please, Odie, please!" A sob choked up someone's throat. "I need you, girl!"

"Come on, Odie. You got this."

My heart gave a single hard thump. Those voices. I recognized them now. With every inch the fingers pulled me backward, their faces solidified in my mind. The love in their voices became more real.

Alex.

Eva.

Hunter.

Where were they? I glanced around. The shine of the room had dulled. Just a second ago, this place had seemed so beautiful—but without them, it was nothing.

"I have her! Alex, keep working!" Another voice, one I couldn't recognize as clearly, spoke.

"I'm trying!" Alex said, his tone frantic. "Her pulse is weak, but still there."

"I'll pull her back harder," the voice without a name said.

Another hard tug yanked me backward. This time when it touched me, the bones in the fingers and the warmth of a hand were discernible.

I gasped as everything became clear. Amethyst—that's who the fourth voice was. She was trying to reach me.

Trying to pull me back from . . .

Holy universe. I'm dead.

I blinked at my surroundings even as Amethyst pulled and pulled, moving me away from the white light.

Or was I? Whatever Amethyst was doing seemed to keep me away from the tunnel of light. And as enamored with it as I'd been just moments before, the luster was gone.

I wanted to go home. I wanted to see my love and my friends.

So I stopped moving forward and allowed the fingers grazing my back to yank me into the darkness.

"Her pulse! It's getting stronger. I'm going to sink more energy into her."

I heard the words, knew they were Alex's, but as air slammed into my lungs like waves ravaging a rock on the coast, I could only focus on one thing.

Breathing. Air—precious air.

Nothing else mattered.

I gasped and gasped and gasped, until finally, what felt like years later, the sucking of air slowed.

A sob sounded from nearby, and I heard a man assure a woman. "It's okay, sugar. She's back. She's alive."

Hunter. Eva. Alex.

The three who had changed my mind.

"Her spirit is in her body now," Amethyst said, and I recalled her place too. She'd pulled my spirit back, saved me. "Give her everything you've got, Alex. Her wrists already look better."

My wrists? With a massive effort, my eyelids fluttered open. The world was blurry, but I recognized my loved ones—standing around me. In the woods?

The last part made little sense, but that was hardly important. What was important was my friends' presence. And . . .

I blinked, confused. My totem blazed red. The exact same color as Alex's magic. I sucked in another breath as understanding and memory surged up through the cloudy confusion of death.

Amethyst had brought me back, but Alex was healing me. Healing the cuts I'd inflicted to banish the ghost, and probably regenerating my blood too. He was doing what only the most advanced healers could. He was sending his own life-force into me—gifting a part of his own life. And my totem was helping.

The thought was so overwhelming, so miraculous, that my eyes slammed shut and I passed out once more.

I awoke the next morning to Alex's arms wrapped tightly around me, and an insistent knock on my bedroom door.

"What the hell?" I rolled out of bed and found not only Alex in my room, but Eva and Hunter too. They were spooning on a mattress on the floor. Mascara stained the pillowcase beneath Eva's head, as if she'd cried herself to sleep.

But why?

My eyebrows furrowed, and I reached for my robe on the back hook of the bathroom door. The sunlight streamed in from the window. It caught my wrist, and I gasped.

Marks were present on my skin, thin white slices that stood out against my normal olive complexion.

Scenes from the night before came rushing back, and I had to grip the bathroom doorknob to keep from falling.

I'd cut myself to banish the ghost. The bleeding hadn't stopped. I'd died, and my friends—Alex and Amethyst, in particular—had brought me back.

"Holy shit," I whispered, recalling how Alex had poured his own glowing life-force into me.

I glanced at my boyfriend on the bed. No wonder the knock on the door hadn't woken him up. He'd spent so much energy saving me that he was probably dead to the world.

Another knock came at the door. "Miss Dane? Are you in there?"

Why is the headmistress here?

I grabbed my robe off the hook, sidestepped my friends sleeping on the floor, and opened the door.

Headmistress Wake stood in the hall, her face set in hard, frustrated lines.

I closed the door just enough so she couldn't see Alex shirtless in my bed, or my friends on the floor.

The headmistress gave a soft, unamused laugh. "Please, Miss Dane. It's not as if I don't realize what happens in these towers. Although I do find it strange that the four of you insist on being together so much. But that is your prerogative. Why don't you shut the door and join me so as not to wake them?" She turned and placed her arms on the banister to look out over the quiet common space below.

A hard pit formed in my stomach as I slid my feet into slippers. Why was she here? Headmistress Wake rarely intruded on our dorms, and she'd never sought me out in my room. The pit deepened as two options stuck out to me. Either she knew about last night and wanted to confront me about it, which, considering the precautions we'd taken, seemed far-fetched.

I gulped at the second, more likely option. I'd just told my parents that there was something strange happening at the PIA. Did someone find out, and now Mom and Dad were among the disappeared?

My heart rate broke out into a gallop. "Did something happen to my mom and dad?" I blurted.

The headmistress turned to face me. "Pardon me, Miss Dane?"

"My parents. Are they okay?" I gulped. "Are you here to tell me they've disappeared?"

Headmistress Wake's eyebrows pulled together. "You're more informed than I believed about the strange events in our world."

My hand flew to my mouth. "No! Are you serious?"

"That is not what I meant, Miss Dane. To my knowledge, your parents are well in California. However, seeing as they've had no connection to the espionage world, save you, for years, I'm interested to know why you would think they may have disappeared?"

My mouth snapped shut. Well, shit. I'd just gotten myself into a dilemma.

Under the guise of pulling myself together, I wiped my eyes.

"Miss Dane," Headmistress Wake pressed. "Is there something you wish to share with me?"

With my eyes on the floor, I pulled in a shaky breath. "No, Headmistress Wake. To be honest, I've been worried about them since they mentioned that a few of their friends had gone missing. As you said, things have been strange lately." Hoping she wouldn't be able to tell I was hiding something, I wrenched my gaze from the ground. "Plus, you've never come to my room. That made me think something serious happened."

The headmistress studied me with her intense, chocolate gaze for what felt like forever before shaking her head. "You are not wrong in anything that you've said. And unfortunately, the reason I have come here this morning is serious." She released an annoyed huff. "The fae have altered the timing of the next Spy Games event. We leave today. As you did when we went to Nightdwellers, pack a bag. This event might take multiple days, so please be sure to have all that you need."

My eyes bulged. "Wait? Can they do that? I had plans!"

Alex was going to flip if we skipped his warping lessons. Hell, after last night, I doubted that he would ever let me out of his sight again.

"As it is their event to host and their . . . atmosphere . . . they may do as they wish. Meet our delegation in Alice Kyteler Hall in precisely two hours."

With that, Headmistress Wake made her way to Diana's door.

My lips tightened, but there was no use in fighting it. At Spellcasters, what Headmistress Wake said was law. And as far as I could tell, she wasn't too happy with the new arrangements either.

Exhaling a long breath, I turned to my door and twisted the knob.

Despite my attempts to let them sleep, Alex was already wide awake and sitting up in bed.

"Hey, babe," he whispered. "Where did you go?"

I bit my lip and went to sit next to him. "Headmistress Wake came to talk to me," I whispered, not wanting to wake Hunter and Eva. "The fae academy has moved up the day of their event. I leave in two hours, and according to Headmistress Wake, I might be gone for multiple days."

As predicted, Alex stiffened. "No! But we—"

"Shhh, I know." I grabbed his hand. "I'm so sorry, but there's nothing I can do."

Alex grabbed my hand. "It's just . . . sweets, you might not remember, but we almost lost you last night."

My throat tightened. "I remember, most of it—the important parts. What you and Amethyst did was amazing. I can never repay you." Tears leapt into my eyes. "I don't want to leave, but if I don't, we'll have a lot of explaining to do. Explaining that neither of us are ready for yet."

Alex's lips pressed together until they became white. "No. Not yet. After last night, I think we only have more to consider. I planned on having a long talk with Amethyst about last night. Make sure nothing we did could have changed or harmed you."

I nodded. "That's smart. Actually, I'd like it if you told her *everything*. She's earned our trust, don't you think?"

"Absolutely."

On the mattress below, Hunter stirred, and we fell quiet until it became obvious that he wouldn't wake.

I placed a hand over Alex's. "I'm sorry, but I don't see a way out of this. We'll just have to make your warping lesson our first priority when I get back. I promise. Nothing will be more important."

"Goddamn flighty fae," Alex muttered.

I didn't know a lot of fae, but I was inclined to agree. Why had it been so important to move their date up? Were they just trying to throw us off our game?

I huffed out a breath. "I'd better get packing."

CHAPTER THIRTY-FOUR

A warphole deposited us mere paces from the gate of the Academy of Elemental and Arcane Arts. Like Nightdwellers, when I laid eyes on the fae academy, I lost my breath. The fae attended school in a gorgeous castle just like the vamps, but there were more differences than similarities.

Whereas the vampires' castle was dark, brooding, and gothic, the fae's castle gleamed brilliant white. Its blue-topped turrets rose above the gate, as did stone work featuring the elements. My ears told me that a river ran somewhere nearby, enhancing the feel that we were in an enchanted forest. Everything around the castle sparkled, and a floral scent laced the air despite the winter month. Come to think of it, it didn't feel like winter here at all. A warm breeze fluttered by, and the sun shone bright above, as if we were back in California.

"Where are we?" I asked.

"All I can tell you is that the fae academy is on the west coast of the U.S. Only the warpers are privy to exactly where the opposing schools are located."

In a way, that made sense, but it also seemed to go against the Spy Games' goal of camaraderie.

"Who cares where we are?" Sam said, spinning on the spot and taking in all the ethereal beauty around us. "What we should be asking is, are we the only academy *without* a castle? If so, that's messed up!"

Headmistress Wake chuckled. "No, Miss Pines. The Shifter Academy is merely a *massive* estate as well. Now, what do you say we meet our hosts?"

The headmistress indicated the white wall of stone in front of us. She parted our group and made her way to the pale wood door. Massive, white stone knockers crafted in the face of a beautiful woman were positioned in the middle of each door.

Headmistress Wake grasped a knocker, lifted it with both hands, and let it fall on the castle gate.

The resounding *boom* sent a thrill up my spine, and the next second, as if it had been waiting for us, the gate burst open. A flood of winged people flew over us. Sparkling confetti rained down, along with flowers, and the fae clapped and sang a song in a different tongue.

"Wow. Talk about a warm welcome," Diana breathed, her blue eyes shining with wonder as multi-colored confetti fluttered to land on her head.

"That was the idea," a clear voice rang out, and we

looked down to find Headmistress Cristala and the four fae champions waltzing toward us. "Please, come in."

Headmistress Wake led the way, and we fell in line, gawking and gazing at our surroundings.

"This place makes Spellcasters look like a hot mess," Andre whispered.

I laughed. He wasn't wrong. The fae school, with its ivy and flowers cascading down impeccable white stone, and the lush gardens that lined the walk to the castle, was probably the prettiest place I'd ever seen.

Headmistress Cristala and the fae champions led us to a courtyard brimming with flowers. A gigantic water fountain featuring stonework of the four elements stood at the heart of the courtyard, providing a peaceful ambiance. Harp music played from somewhere, and when I licked my lips, I caught the taste of cotton candy on the air.

The shifter champions stood off to the side of the elemental fountain that featured a tree spouting water from its branches. They looked as dazed by their surroundings as I felt. Alpha Conon moved to speak with our headmistresses, so the rest of us went to greet the other champions.

"Hey!" I said, latching on to Dasha first. "Fancy seeing you here."

She surprised me when she gave me a wide smile and held her arm out for a hug. Since I was the hugging type, I moved in. Our bodies pressed together, hers much harder and more muscled than mine, and her apple-scented shampoo enveloped me.

"I'm so sorry about the Nightdwellers games," Dasha whispered. "I had no idea they drugged those drinks. I should have scented it, but I think they used something undetectable. I was oblivious to the fact that your team was so sick until I saw Andre vomit on the trapeze. Please don't think we condone that kind of poor behavior?"

I broke our embrace to pull back and look her in the eye. "I never thought that."

Relief washed over Dasha's face. "Thank goodness. I didn't get a chance to tell you because they rushed you back to Spellcasters. Alpha Conon told us what happened later, and he was *furious* on your behalf."

My eyebrows knitted together. I'd never said a word to the alpha headmaster. And yet, he had been upset for me?

Dasha gave me a small smile. "Alpha Conon has a strong sense of justice. Congratulations, by the way. Despite half your team nearly dying of poisoning you guys killed it. Something that I heard was because of your skill?"

My cheeks warmed. "Andre helped. He's a warper too. We would have never stood a chance against the other teams' strength or speed otherwise."

I looked around. Everyone else was chatting, but the vampires were still missing.

"Where are the Nightdwellers champions?"

No sooner had I asked than the vampires marched into the courtyard. Simone was in the front, sneering, and Francis looked nearly as pissed off. Anton and Magdalena followed their more showy teammates, their gazes downcast. But it was Headmaster Ezra's expression that shocked me the most. The joviality that I expected from him was gone. His face was a mess of hard lines and rigid planes.

Dasha leaned close. "Headmistress Cristala heard what happened too. She wouldn't let the vampires into the castle without a *thorough* body check."

A laugh snorted out of me. "No way."

"Yes way. They searched us too, but just a quick pat-down. Alpha and Headmistress Cristala are sort of friends, so there's some trust there."

"No one searched us. I wonder why?"

Dasha rolled her eyes. "I don't. Your headmistress is *terrifying*. The other heads of the schools know that she'll keep you guys in line much better than they ever could."

"Touché," I said just as Headmistress Cristala clapped to get everyone's attention.

"Once again, I'd like to welcome the participants of the Spy Games to the Academy of Elemental and Arcane Arts." Her eyes twinkled, reminding me of Ms. Seeley. "We are honored to host the second round of the Games and introduce the champions to more of our kind. However, I have a surprise."

My spine straightened.

"As you all know, the participating spy academies seek to make the challenges they host unique and memorable. Well, I can think of no better way to do so than what I have planned for you." Headmistress Cristala glided toward the water fountain. When she got there, she stepped up onto the edge and grabbed a stone branch of the tree that was spouting off water. She yanked it down, and the branch bent in half. There was a loud *click,* and the sound of moving gears tore through the enchanting harp music.

"There was a reason we asked you to come earlier than expected," the fae headmistress beamed. "You will probably need a day and a night to fully acclimate to the environment of the next event."

"And that would be?" Simone spat out, clearly over the fae's presentation—or maybe she was still pissed about being searched like a criminal.

Headmistress Cristala's lips pulled up in a brilliant smile, and she pulled the stone branch down just a little more.

The trunk of the tree in the fountain opened, and a gate appeared over the water. A blast of light emanated from inside the tree, and a strange, otherworldly aura that made me feel lightheaded seeped into the courtyard.

Shockingly, Diana gripped my hand with a gasp.

"Whoa," I breathed, as Headmistress Cristala's implication became clear.

We were heading to Faerie.

CHAPTER THIRTY-FIVE

The moment we stepped into Faerie, I understood why Headmistress Cristala deemed it necessary that we arrive early. Right away, my head spun as if I were drunk, and the skin on my arms tingled strangely.

"What some of you are no doubt feeling are the effects of Faerie magic," Headmistress Cristala said after Howley face-planted upon crossing into the other realm. "Move slowly and breathe. A nap is advisable during your first few hours here. The calmer you are, the faster the effects of Faerie will wear off."

A hand grabbed my shoulder to keep from falling, and I turned to find Diana clinging to me.

"This is wild," she said, blinking hard. "I mean, a little freaky too, because I can't see straight, but as long as it gets better soon, who cares?"

I had to agree. The fae rarely allowed witches, shifters, and vampires into Faerie. We had to be the first since . . . I frowned. I couldn't recall the last time I'd heard about a delegation of mixed magicals being permitted into Faerie.

Seeking an answer, I twisted to find Headmistress Wake, and gawked. Her spine was still ramrod straight as she chatted with the other heads of the academies. Faerie's magic wasn't affecting her at all.

"Headmistress Wake?" I called, and cringed at how loud my voice had come out.

The headmistress excused herself from her discussion and strode toward me. "Yes, Miss Dane?" Her eyes strayed to her daughter, who had taken to spinning in place. "Are you two okay?"

"I don't know. Things are fuzzy and getting fuzzier," I blinked a few times to refocus. "But I was wondering . . . when was the last time a witch got invited into Faerie? And why do you not look—drunk?" The word popped out, and I clapped my hands over my mouth in horror. "I mean! Faerie drunk! Not—" My arms began to tingle harder, and the sensation was almost unbearable, so I started to rub them vigorously.

"It is all right, Miss Dane. I understand what you meant." Her lips were curled up slightly at the corners. "I suspect that the last time a witch came to Faerie was when I arrived at this very court to approve this challenge. And I do not look drunk because I have been here before, and my body has already acclimated to fae magic."

Diana stopped spinning, and her mouth fell open in an uncharacteristically dramatic manner. "You came here and didn't tell me?! Why do you never tell me *anything*, Mother?"

I patted her on the back and swayed with the motion of my arm. "My parents don't tell me anything either."

This time, Headmistress Wake actually did chuckle. "If I told you, then you'd know about the challenge wouldn't you, Diana? That wouldn't be fair."

"Fair schmair, Mother! How could you go to Faerie and not say a thing!" Diana almost toppled to the floor—how, I wasn't sure, maybe she tripped over her own foot?—but Headmistress Wake caught her and righted her.

"Yes, Diana, it happened. I'll tell you about it later. For now, I think it's best if you and everyone else take Head-mistress Cristala's suggestion and go lie down. Come with me, I'll show you to our rooms."

We tried to oppose her, but as Headmistress Wake had her wits about her and we didn't, the fight was short-lived. Before I knew it, Diana, Sam, Andre, and I were being escorted by four armed fae guards. They moved so fast that I could barely keep up, let alone absorb my surroundings without running into someone or something. Everything, from the fae we passed to the castle itself, seemed like one big, loud blur.

"The Spellcasters champions will stay here for the dura-tion of their challenge," a guard said as he turned down an empty hallway.

I squinted, trying to see his face more clearly, and became mesmerized by his pointed ears. Without thinking,

I reached out to touch them, but Headmistress Wake stopped me.

"Miss Dane. It is inadvisable to touch a fae's ears, or any part of anyone who does not give you their express permission. Am I clear?"

"But . . . they're so . . . pointy." My voice was breathy and high, and I grabbed at my throat, startled by the strange sound.

The guard chuckled. "It's no problem, Headmistress. We understand that getting used to Faerie's magic takes time. They should be fine in a few hours."

"Thank you, gentlemen," Headmistress Wake said. "And you'll be just outside their doors?"

"A force will be positioned here until the last champion awakens," the guard confirmed.

"Very well, then let's get this lot into their rooms."

When I awoke later, I shot up, my heart hammering as I absorbed my unfamiliar surroundings. I lay in a bed covered by a mountain of blankets. Someone moved behind me, and I twisted to find Diana, her mouth hanging open wide as she snored softly.

"What the hell?" I whispered, pulling the covers aside.

Immediately, I missed the warmth of the bed as I walked to the window. As soon as I looked outside and saw that I was in a castle in a snow-covered mountain range where winged unicorns flew through the air, all thoughts of the chill vanished, and my memories returned.

"We're in freaking Faerie!"

"Holy shit!" A beam of purple magic shot past my shoulder, and I spun, hands extended defensively, to find Diana gaping at me. "I'm so sorry, Odette. I woke up and didn't know where I was, and then I sensed you by the window."

I dropped my hands. "Thank God your aim sucked. Remember where we are now?"

Diana nodded, but her eyebrows remained furrowed. "Faerie, for the Spy Games. But why are we in the same room?"

I shrugged. "Let's go see if someone can tell us."

We found two fur-lined jackets that someone had set inside the room for us, and pulled them on. After a quick once-over in the mirror, we peeked into the hallway to discover that we were being guarded by four handsome fae soldiers.

They hadn't seemed to notice that we'd awoken, so Diana and I stepped into the hall and closed the door loudly. Every single guard spun to face us.

"How was your rest, champions?" the shortest said, a wide and welcoming smile on his dusky face.

"Errr, good," I said. "Are all the champions sharing rooms?"

All four soldiers chuckled.

"What's so funny?" Diana said, her tone demanding like her mother's.

The short guard composed himself and stepped forward. "Apologies. You each have your own rooms. But when Headmistress Wake brought you here to sleep off the effects of Faerie's magic, you two refused to be separated from the other." He smiled at us kindly. "It was sweet to see such a strong friendship. I have twin girls. I hope they might have friends like you two one day."

I thanked the universe above that Diana and I were no longer mortal enemies and this was way less embarrassing than it could have been.

"Thanks. Where are the other champions?"

"We have taken them to the lounge to relax," the guard said. "Once everyone is awake, you will meet Queen Tially."

We would meet a queen?! My head swung toward Diana. She too looked stunned.

"Would you like to join the other champions now?" Another guard, this one with long, flowing, blond locks and pointed ears, stepped forward and gestured for us to follow.

"Please," I said.

Blondie guided us through a pure white castle. Along the way a few works of art dotted the halls. A lot of them featured a snowy owl, which I figured must be the royal house's emblem. Mostly, though, the castle was bare and pristine.

"If you don't mind me asking, where are we? And why is it so white?"

The guard turned vibrant violet eyes on me, and I

sucked in a breath. If I wasn't happily with Alex, this guy would interest me.

"I apologize that no one has told you yet," he said, his voice lyrical. "Often when people visit Faerie for the first time, we wait to fill them in. It can become a bit much for their mental faculties." The guard motioned us to the window. "All that you see within the mountain range belongs to the Snowcap Court. You are in Winter's Hall, the seat of House Frost."

Wow. That was a lot of snow and ice and frost. I was getting cold just thinking about it. "And because it's so snowy . . . the whole castle is white? Or close to it?" I gestured to his light silver uniform.

The guard beamed. "Almost everything. Some decor is colorful. Your rooms, for instance. And the royal family and those they invite to court often dress more colorfully. However, you're correct in thinking that servants honor the Snowcap Court by donning its colors."

I glanced out the window again. Just past the mountain range a verdant river valley spanned for miles, and then to the left, a swath of dark clouds. "What's the green kingdom down the mountainside? And that expanse of black fog?"

The guard gulped, and discomfort flashed across his face. "The greenery past the mountain foothills belongs to the lovely Riverlands Court."

"Oh! The Riverlands!"

The Torna sisters were close to their familial seat. I wondered if they knew that already.

"Yes. It is a beautiful place." The guard turned to continue on his way, but Diana stopped him.

"What about the black expanse she mentioned?" She pointed to the fog.

The guard shuddered, and when he pivoted back to face us, his mouth was set in a wary line. "That, dear champions, is the Dark Court. Foul happenings have been occurring there for many years. We in the Snowcap Court rarely speak of the place."

A pit in my stomach deepened, and feeling faint, I grabbed the edge of the window.

The Dark Court. We were next door to the demon's allies.

After I assured the guard and Diana that everything was fine and I would not collapse at any moment, the guard showed us to the lounge.

Most of the other champions had already arrived and were enjoying little plates of snacks. Only Howley and Gregor remained in their rooms, sleeping off the fae magic.

I was starving, so I veered toward the snack table before saying hello to anyone. Diana followed, and we filled our plates with food, some familiar, most fae.

The massive golden apples that seemed to shimmer, and plump, red berries stood out most. I recalled Ms. Seeley showing us photos of the Faerie Fruit once. If a human ate the fruit, they would be trapped in Faerie until a fae set them free. Since I was a witch, that magic didn't apply.

Thank the universe for that. It's too cold here to be trapped forever.

"They'll be so upset that I left our suite," Dasha sighed as Diana and I joined a group composed of champions from every academy except Nightdwellers. "But Heath was up too, and we wanted to explore." Her hand rubbed the shifter I'd secretly dubbed "the quiet one".

"Shifters have the hardest time adjusting to Faerie," Sana said as she offered both Diana and me something that looked and smelled like tea. "It will clear your mind. According to Queen Tially, our trial begins tomorrow, so they're trying to hurry the acclimatization process along."

The queen? "Have you already spoken to her?" I asked Sana. "Do you know what we're doing here?"

Across the room, I caught the vampires' heads swivel to stare at us. I returned their attention with a scowl, which at least made them turn back around. They could probably still hear us, but I didn't want their cheating eyes on me.

"Absolutely not. The queen only stopped by our rooms to greet us once we settled in. Our families are friends, after all," Ayla said, coming up to join us. She sat down and leaned in closer. "But I can guess what they will ask us to do."

I plopped myself onto the couch next to her. "Go on . . ."

"Ayla . . ." Sana warned, but her sister waved her off.

"It's just a guess. Don't be such a stickler, Sana."

The younger twin huffed and took up position on the other side of her sister.

"How familiar are you guys with Faerie?" Ayla asked.

"I'm well versed in the fae species and the courts we've studied so far," Diana said. "Which is about half of them."

Sam and Andre said they were both pretty knowledgeable.

I just shrugged and was relieved to see that the two shifters did too. Thankfully, I'd packed the sheet that Ms. Seeley had given me. I made a mental note to study it when I returned to my room.

Ayla nodded. "This is the Snowcap Court. It borders the Riverlands, where our family hails from, and the Dark Court." Her face grew serious. "I've heard that in recent years, the Dark Court has been growing stronger. I bet you anything that our challenge has something to do with them."

My heart sank. I'd wondered as much when the guard in the hall had pointed out the Dark Court's proximity, but to have Ayla say it out loud made it seem much more likely.

"Stronger?" Heath asked. Since he talked so little, the single word got everyone's attention. "How so?"

"They allow no one in or out of the kingdom. Only those who can fly incredibly fast through the Rift—that vast expanse of darkness that can suck out your soul, and separates the Dark Court from the other kingdoms—have even glimpsed that land in ten years. That isn't very many fae. But those who have succeeded say that the shadow fae, that's what we call their people, are building an army."

Holy shit. Did Headmistress Wake know this? Did anyone in our world? Something told me they had to. But why hadn't they mentioned it?

A million questions bubbled through me. "What are they going to—"

The doors to the lounge burst open, and Howley and Gregor stormed in with ferocious looks on their faces.

"Dasha! How could you just leave the room like that!" Gregor roared.

A line of fae guards rushed forward to stand between Dasha and her mates.

"Here we go," Dasha rolled her eyes and stood. "You two were zonked out hard. Heath and I shook you and you didn't wake. What did you want us to do? Stay in the suite until you regained consciousness?"

"Yes!" Gregor and Howley growled in unison.

The line of fae guards brandished their swords.

"It's okay," Dasha said, coming up behind the guards. "They're my mates. They're upset, but they won't hurt me. I'm their alpha, and they must obey. So when I tell them to *calm down* they will."

The fae looked confused by the whole multiple-mate situation, but they backed off so the last two shifter champions could join us. Heath moved seats, allowing the other two guys to claim spots by Dasha. The second they were next to her, they calmed. And when Dasha gave each a soft kiss, all the anger in their expressions vanished.

The multiple mates thing was interesting, but definitely too much testosterone for me.

A guard near the door banged his staff on the stone floor. "Champions. Now that everyone has arrived, I am pleased to announce Queen Tially Frost of the Snowcap Court."

He opened the door, and a beautiful woman with long, blonde hair and piercing, ice-blue eyes glided through. She wore a dress of pale gold that fluttered around her like fine silk. A stole of white fur wrapped around her shoulders, and a delicate crown of gold and diamonds perched atop her head.

The Torna twins stood and fell into elegant, deep curtseys. I couldn't pull off their grace, but I followed suit alongside everyone else, standing and bowing for the queen.

"Welcome, champions." Queen Tially's voice was musical and light. "The Snowcap Court is delighted that you are here. Please, continue eating and sit. I'm aware that traveling to Faerie is a feat for those of your world."

Everyone obliged. Only once I settled in did I notice that the heads of the spy academies had followed Queen Tially into the room.

The queen sat in front of us on a plain wooden chair, although the way she perched on it made it seem like a grand throne. "I'm thankful that you've joined us, and delighted that you will perform the second event of the Spy Games here. I believe that we have set a suitable challenge for spies of your caliber."

Behind the queen, Headmistress Wake gave a small nod of her head. She looked pleased, which told me the challenge was not only suitable, it would be very difficult.

"Many of you may not be intimately familiar with our courts or customs, but that is unnecessary. You will meet those who matter tonight at a state dinner. And tomorrow, you will deduce which of those fae is the traitor whom I seek."

A coughing fit overcame Ayla, which prompted Queen Tially to place a tender hand on her own chest.

"I'm sorry for the interruption, Queen Tially," Ayla said once her coughing stopped.

"Not at all, dear young Torna. I'm sorry to have startled you so." The queen smiled kindly. "You see, champions, my middle son is to marry tomorrow. There is no better event than a royal wedding for those who seek to wreak havoc upon a kingdom. In fact, we have already uncovered some unpleasantness." She wrinkled her nose.

Sam raised her hand.

An amused look crossed the queen's face at the gesture, but she nodded. "Yes, Spellcasters champion?"

"If you have a traitor in your midst, why don't you just question everyone?" Sam asked, her tone laden with confusion. "Or am I misinformed that full-blooded fae can't lie?"

I arched my eyebrows. She was right. The fae in our land were more often than not demi-fae. Their mixed blood allowed them to lie, although they weren't usually the most apt at it. But the fae of Faerie were almost always pure-blooded, and the magic of their kind prevented them from outright lying.

The queen gave Sam a grim smile. "You are correct. The fae of Faerie cannot lie, but as I'm sure you're aware, many of us can twist the truth quite skillfully." Queen Tially released a frustrated sigh. "Everyone in the castle was questioned after the first incident, but we were unable to find anything unusual."

The way she said *incident* sent a shudder down my spine.

"And we are quite good at ensuring that no one is twisting the truth. However," the queen shook her head, as if she could not believe what she was saying, "atrocities are occurring. That much is undeniable. Due to this, we believe that someone has acquired the means to lie—somehow."

The Torna twins looked aghast, which made me wonder what a fae would have to do to be able to lie. Something horrendous, clearly.

The queen rose as gracefully as a ballerina. "That is all I can tell you for certain. I will leave it to my guards and your lovely headmasters and headmistresses to fill you in on the gruesome details of prior occurrences. Just know, tomorrow must be executed perfectly. And we are counting on you to discern the identity of the traitor in our midst."

CHAPTER THIRTY-SIX

Headmistress Wake was less delicate regarding the "unpleasantness" that Queen Tially did not wish to speak about. She gave it to us straight and in detail.

Once I learned that three prominent fae visiting from Prince Elran's bride-to-be's court had been found beaten and ripped open, I understood the haste in getting us here. Someone did not approve of the new alliance being formed between houses, and the royal family was concerned that the next body to show up dead would be the future princess'. They wished for us to find the killer before the wedding that afternoon.

To say I was thankful that I'd packed the sheet Ms. Seeley had given me was an understatement. Despite having met the royals and those closest to them the night prior at dinner, the sheet documenting Faerie's royal courts acted like a security blanket. I'd studied it all morning and now felt like I had a good grasp of the Snowcap Court.

That Ms. Seeley had given it to me was such a coincidence that I wondered if she'd known about this challenge. Did she know more about the Dark Court and the happenings there too?

But those questions would have to wait. Today was Prince Elran's wedding day. I had to be on point if I wanted to find the killer and bring victory to Spellcasters. Thankfully, the haze I'd succumbed to when I'd entered Faerie had cleared, and I was ready.

The queen told us to play the part of distant part-fae relatives. Or, in the case of Ayla and Sana, who bore distinct characteristics of the Riverlands Court, visiting diplomats. As undercover guests, we were to eat, drink, and mingle while sussing out the traitor.

Taking Her Majesty's instructions to heart, I made my second trip to the buffet in Snowflake Hall. House Frost had laid out a veritable cornucopia of food, so that guests could graze and socialize before the main event. I appreciated this fae custom of gluttony because something about Faerie made me ravenous. I'd just finished examining a plate of hand pies, decorated with snowflakes and roses for the groom and bride respectively, when the first remarkable thing of the day happened.

I walked right into the very blond and regal Prince Elran.

"I'm so sorry, Prince Elran! Please excuse me!" I bent to clean up the fruit I'd dropped on the stark white floor.

Before I could do so, however, the prince grasped my hand and pulled me back up.

"Please. Don't bother yourself with that mess," he said, his tone low, and his ice blue eyes earnest. He straightened his silver cloak and the owl pin that had gone off-kilter when I ran into him. "The servants will tend to it. To hear my mother speak, your time is better spent elsewhere. I believe that I have a lead for you."

I blinked. "Oh? Have you told anyone else?"

A smile tugged at lips so perfect, a master sculpture could have carved them from marble. "Not yet. You are the first I saw when I arrived here, and I will not bother with the vamps." His mouth twisted into a look of disgust. "Our kinds don't usually mix. However, I will tell the fae and shifters, so use your advantage wisely, clever witch."

The prince skirted me around the edges of the room. "See that group of men over there? One is dressed in the sea blue of the Cove Court, two others in Riverlands green, while the rest are in my house colors." He nodded to a collective of diplomats chatting at the edge of the room beneath gold-framed archways that overlooked the vast mountain landscape outside.

I took in the shades and different styles of dress, and committed them to memory as fashions of differing courts. "Yes, I see them."

"Three of them live at the Snowcap Court, but the others are visitors who arrived a week ago. Since then, I have noticed a difference in how our residing diplomats have been acting. One even attempted to seduce my future queen." He frowned. "But when asked, he swore he did not mean to do it. Fae cannot lie, and the behavior was very unlike him anyhow. Which is why I believe someone manipulated him into it. The same person committing murder."

"Thank you, Prince Elran," I said. "We'll investigate."

He honored me with a shallow bow, which I returned.

"Thank you, witch. I hope that one of your teams apprehends the traitor before the ceremony this afternoon. I would hate to enter into my eternal union knowing that bad blood was in my midst."

Apparently done with me, the prince floated off toward his bride.

I sucked in a breath. *Right. No pressure. Except it's already almost noon. Better hurry.*

I scanned the crowds for my teammates and found Sam first. She was chatting with a gaggle of women dressed in gem-toned gowns dripping with crystals and beading and feathers. For the millionth time since breakfast, I wished that I was wearing one of those beautiful gowns, but it would have been impractical.

Instead, our heads of schools spread the word that everyone from where we lived wore military-inspired attire to weddings. It was a bummer, but being able to run would be imperative if we found the killer. So I brushed the annoyance aside as I made my way over to Sam and joined the group.

"Hello, ladies. Might I steal my friend, please?" I smiled and inclined my head in a manner that Headmistress Wake had assured us was an appropriate greeting for anyone but royalty and priestesses of the fae religion.

The fae, who I believed were courtesans, returned the gesture with a pleased titter and bid Sam a pleasant day.

Once we were alone, I relayed what the prince had told me.

Sam's eyes snapped over my shoulder to study the men. "Have you gotten close to them yet?"

I shook my head. "I wanted backup."

"Well, you moved too slow. The Torna twins are already staking a claim."

"What?!"

I whirled around and saw that Sam was right. The twins had joined the circle of diplomats. Not only that, but they'd gone for the divide-and-conquer route with each twin monopolizing the attention of three fae.

"Crap," I said, which earned me an offended look from a passing pixie. "What should we do?"

Sam shrugged. "Why not do what they're doing? Divide and conquer. The prince might be right, but he also might not. I don't think we should put all our eggs in one basket, or bring Diana or Andre with us." She gestured to a far corner, where our teammates chatted with a fae who wore the dark green and gold garb of a high priestess. "They can keep putting their feelers out. If we notice anything off, we'll notify them."

"Good call," I said. "Okay, let's split up. I'll take Ayla."

The elder Torna twin didn't even know I was coming until I slithered an arm around her delicate shoulders.

"Hey, Ayla, why don't you introduce me to your charming friends here?" I batted my eyelashes at the fae men, all of whom were young, attractive, and definitely interested in a little female attention.

"Hello, Odette," Ayla spoke. The lyrical quality of her voice sounded enhanced from when I'd heard it in our world. Was it being in Faerie that did that? Or was she working it to convince these guys she was one of them? "I thought I recalled that you didn't like elves much, otherwise I would have waved you over long ago."

The guys frowned, and seeing as they bore the distinct pointed ears and impossibly tall bearing of elves, I could understand why.

Ayla clearly hoped that her little remark would have me running off with my tail between my legs. The little shit was playing to win.

Unfortunately for her, so was I.

"What made you think that?" I asked Ayla. "I adore all types of fae, but I have a particular penchant for elves. The ears are so *hot*."

Two of the elves broke out into wide smiles.

"I'm Odette, a witch from the human realm, seventh cousin of Prince Elran, and happy attendee of the royal wedding."

The guys introduced themselves as Raya, San, and Orlando. They each wore silver-blue clothing and claimed to be permanent residents at the Snowcap Court.

Ayla and I continued to chat up the guys, peppering them with questions that would allow us to glean information. And while their answers interested me because the fae culture was fascinating, after ten minutes, I was sure they weren't our traitors. Perhaps Prince Elran could feel bad juju coming off them, but I couldn't. And judging by how Ayla's jaw had hardened progressively, she was coming up short too.

When an appropriate lull entered the conversation, I looped arms with the fae champion. "I'm so sorry, boys, but I think I must steal Ayla away. I've forgotten where the washrooms are, but I bet you remember, don't you, Ayla?"

She beamed. "Of course, I'll take you there."

Once Ayla and I were a good distance away, I turned to her. "Damn, girl, playing dirty."

She bit her lip. "Sorry! We're so far behind in points, and I can't bear to lose in Faerie of all places."

I chuckled. "You don't have to defend yourself. I want to win too. So may the best spies win."

To make our excuse look legitimate, we took a brief walk in the hallway. It was mostly empty, as everyone was in Snowflake Hall, or preparing the throne room for the wedding.

When I returned to Snowflake Hall, I spotted Sam. She was still talking to the trio of guys, but Sana had ditched. Curious to see what had kept Sam there, I joined her.

"Oh hey, Odette!" Sam welcomed me with open arms. "Meet the guys. This is Sirus and Tolan from the Riverlands." She gestured to an umber-skinned fae with vibrant blue eyes, and a blond dwarf who wore a shield at his side. "And this is Gian from . . . What was the other court?" Sam asked, her eyes locking on a red-haired fae with brilliant emerald eyes who wore dark blue.

"The Cove Court, by the Western Sea," the ginger replied. "To be honest, I have not been home for some time, but I still claim it as the land of my heart."

"Why haven't you visited?" I asked.

Immediately I realized that I'd said the wrong thing as the eyes of the Riverland fae fell, and an uncomfortable hush blanketed our small circle. "I'm sorry, if I've said something offensive. It's my first time in Faerie, and I'll admit, I'm not knowledgeable of all the courts and their intricacies."

Gian gave me an understanding smile. "I can relate. I felt much the same the first time I visited the Snowcap Court. I stop by so rarely, that I still feel like a unicorn in the wrong forest sometimes. Court life seems to change daily." He sucked in a long breath. "As for the Cove Court, I'm afraid I have not been there, because I cannot venture into my homeland without risk of death."

"That's terrible! What happened?"

Gian grew silent, and Sirus stepped forward to help. "Allow me, Gian. The truth is painful, I can see." His dark eyes turned on me. "Only the Western Sea and the Dark Court border the Cove Court. Since the Dark Court placed the Rift between its lands and all kingdoms east, the Cove Court has been isolated for years. Am I missing anything, Gian?"

The ginger-haired fae smiled sadly. "Only that the Rift

encompasses the sea line of my homeland, Sirus. They are truly trapped." He dropped his gaze to the floor.

My heart broke for the fae who had been displaced by the very same court looking to harm my world. "I'm sorry for the fate of your people, Gian. If there was something I could do, please know I would help," I said wholeheartedly.

Against Headmistress Wake's suggestion that we never touch a fae without permission, I reached out to comfort Gian as I would anyone in my world. My hand landed softly on his shoulder, and the moment my skin touched him, my demon-touched mark seared.

I sucked in a sharp breath.

Gian's head snapped up, his wild and frantic eyes locking with mine for a heartbeat, before suddenly, a wall of flame bloomed between us.

I yelped and jumped back. Tolan and Sirus sprang into action, water spewing from their hands to quench the flames.

When the fire died out, Gian was no longer there. I scanned Snowflake Hall to find him running out the door.

My heart began to thunder and the truth of what just happened crashed over me. Sucking in a breath, I barreled through Sirus and Tolan, and sprinted after the traitor.

CHAPTER THIRTY-SEVEN

Rapid footsteps followed me through the palace halls. I hoped that they belonged to Sam, or someone else on my team, but didn't dare look back. Gian was tossing too many fireballs over his shoulder for me to take my eyes off of him for even a second. And considering he wasn't checking where he hurled them, his aim was stellar—almost hitting me too many times for comfort.

As much as I wanted to fight back, I feared injuring the random innocent servants or wedding guests we encountered. Onlookers who Gian used for cover as he dodged and wove and tossed people to the ground in his wake.

To make things more difficult, Gian was fast. I was outright sprinting to keep up with him.

What if the vampires saw me leave? I gnashed my teeth together and despite the ache in my lungs, bore down. I had to give this my all because the vampires could catch up too easily and steal the win.

We took a sharp turn, and seeing that no one was around, I hurled a shield charm just over Gian's head. He darted out of the way right before he would have slammed into it.

I spat out a curse and shot another blast of magic. This time, he tripped trying to dodge it, slowing him slightly.

Taking advantage of his disarray, I chanced a glance behind me, and my heart leapt.

Hell yeah!

Sam, Diana, *and* Andre were in on the chase. Catching my eye, Sam motioned for me to move to the right. I did, and she shot a blazing spell past me that barely missed my shoulder. Right away, I piggybacked on her assault.

Our spells struck one after the other, and Gian let out a roar as he fell to the floor. Diana's purple magic flew over my head and created a shield around him.

My heart skipped a beat. *Holy shit. We got him.* I stopped running and turned to face my teammates. "Nice work, guys!"

"Thanks. Now are you going to tell us what the heck went on back there? When you touched him, everything changed, but I'm not sure how." Sam arched an eyebrow.

Oh crap.

Did I have to tell them about everything my mark could do? Some of them might not know about it at all, and I'd rather not change that . . .

A million stories ran through my mind, but before I could land on a believable one, footsteps sounded down the hall. At any moment, we'd have company.

"Can it wait?" I asked, happy to have bought some time. "I promise I'll tell you when we're alone."

Sam's lips pressed together, but Andre nodded. "It can wait. We owe you from the last event."

"Thanks," I said. "I'll explain everything later."

Hopefully I can come up with a good story in the meantime.

Together, we walked toward Gian, and were quickly joined by Prince Elran, a contingent of royal guards, and Headmistress Wake.

The headmistress rushed to my side, and while the prince barked orders, she leaned in close. "How did you know?" She glanced down at my ankle.

I nodded. "Exactly how you think."

"Say nothing to the court."

Relief that I hadn't told my teammates about the mark rolled through me. Keeping a secret was easier when fewer people held it.

"Release the shield," Prince Elran commanded as soon as soldiers had surrounded Gian.

Diana did as he said, and Gian, knowing he was beat, remained on the ground, a scowl on his face.

"Gian, my old friend. Our informants have singled you out for a reason, so if you have obtained the means to lie, please spare us your untrue words. Tell me, are you the traitor who has been leaving death in your wake?" The prince's face screwed up in pain.

My heart went out to him. He'd called Gian a friend. It would suck to learn that a friend had betrayed you.

Indecision flashed across Gian's beautiful features for a

moment before he threw back his shoulders to look as dignified as one could while sitting on the floor, surrounded by armed guards. "The Snowcap Court chose wrong all those years, old friend. Soon, the time will come when you will realize that. The Dark Court will bring unforeseen glory to Faerie, and I will be there, a sole envoy from the Cove—a new king."

Prince Elran's chin jutted out. "And what makes you think your people will welcome a king who allowed them to starve for years? Someone who isolated them from the rest of Faerie?"

Gian sneered. "It will not matter what they think in the beginning. Soon enough, they will see I was right and support the Dark Court." His eyes shifted to me and glinted green with malevolence. "The real question is how did *this* one discover my secret when no one else has for years? What dark magic do you know, witch?"

My spine stiffened as the fae turned their attention to me. Thankfully, Headmistress Wake saved me by stepping in front of Gian, her arms crossed firmly over her chest.

"My student knows nothing of dark magic," she scowled down at the culprit. "You may have kept your secret from those who trusted you for years, but Spellcasters instructs students not to trust anyone until they prove their worthiness. Odette clearly learned that lesson well." The headmistress extended a finger at the fae, and for a moment, I thought she might zap him on my behalf. "Not to mention, you seem to have gotten sloppy. Perhaps next time, you'll mend your pockets before intending to wreak havoc at a royal wedding? That thing is glowing so brightly, how could Odette miss it?"

My gaze shot to where the headmistress pointed, and I stifled a gasp.

Gian's pockets had ripped wide open, and a stone, one smaller than the one I'd discovered in Crescent Springs, glowed in its depths.

"A demon stone!" Elran darted backward. "Say it isn't so, Gian! Say the darkness is not in your bones."

Gian raised his hands, and black wisps of smoke began to trail from them. For a split-second, it looked like he might use the demonic magic to attack, but he obviously thought better of it, and the smoke dissipated. "Bones, blood, and heart, my friend."

Elran shook his head. "Guards, seize him. Use the iron shackles and iron-lined cell." The prince turned to us and approached Headmistress Wake. "Will you take the stone? We fae are superstitious, and—"

The headmistress approached Gian and scooped the demon stone out of his pocket. "Don't fret, Prince Elran. I will dispose of it when I return home."

Prince Elran exhaled. "Thank you. Who knows what chaos Gian might have brought upon my impending nuptials with such a horror in his possession? We are forever in your debt."

The prince and his soldiers carted Gian off. Only my team and Headmistress Wake remained in the empty hall, and a few seconds had passed before I realized that they were all staring at me.

"So, do you want to explain how you knew about the stone? Because his pocket wasn't ripped before my mother showed up." Diana broke the silence, her blue eyes hard.

Good grief, why were my teammates so on top of things?

I bit my lip, unsure what to say. The headmistress knew that my demon mark was sensitive to demons, but she was among the few. If I told Diana, Sam, and Andre the truth, it would increase the chances that other people at Spellcasters would find out. Would that help or harm me? What would others think?

Unsure how to handle the dilemma, I looked to Headmistress Wake.

"I believe," the headmistress began, her tone careful, "that it is time to let your team, and perhaps others whom you trust completely, in on the quirks of your demon mark, Miss Dane. If the demon stone is any indication, the time for secrets is drawing to a close." Her gaze leveled on me, and I wondered if she had a hunch that I kept other secrets too.

"However, it would not be ideal to discuss such matters here," Headmistress Wake added. "The halls of fae courts have ears, but I have taken the proper measures to secure our rooms. You can talk about your mark safely in my chambers." She held my gaze, waiting for my response.

Inwardly, I debated if this was really what I wanted to do. Was it time to let go a little? To trust that others wouldn't judge me for the events of the past? My eyes traveled over Andre, Sam, and Diana. Each wore interested and compassionate expressions on their faces.

That's when it hit me. They weren't just teammates. They were friends. People who had helped me as I'd helped them. If I couldn't trust someone like that, who could I trust? Perhaps Headmistress Wake was right and it was time that I became more open to discussing Ishtar and how thoroughly she'd changed my life.

And I would start with the people in front of me.

"Hold up!" Diana raised a hand. "So your demon-touched mark not only connects you to Ishtar, but you can sense *other* demons too?"

I nodded and crossed one of my legs over the other. We were in Headmistress Wake's chamber at the Snowcap Court, and I'd just revealed one of three major secrets.

"You discovered this during your internship?" Diana asked.

"Yup."

"Do Eva's act similarly?" Diana pressed.

I gulped, and shot a glance to the headmistress who gave a small nod of her head. It wasn't my secret to tell, but Headmistress Wake was right. The time for secrets was drawing to a close. I inhaled a long breath. "Yeah, Eva discovered that her mark works similarly. The succubus who scarred her was pregnant with Lucifer's child, so his essence was inside the succubus and now in Eva too. There are minor differences in how our marks react, but it might be down to the fact we're infected by the essence of different royals."

Sam's eyes were so wide, I worried that they might pop out of her head, and Andre's umber skin seemed to have whitened a few shades.

"I assume that is how you discovered the demon stone the fae carried so easily, Miss Dane?" Headmistress Wake prompted. "Because the fae had been using it, and hence taking a royal's power into himself to perform dark deeds?"

"I think so," I spoke slowly because I wasn't sure. "Actually, I have a question on that matter."

The headmistress nodded, so I went on.

"In my first Grind-year mission, I also found a demon stone. I can't remember if I touched anyone skin-to-skin, like I did Gian, but if those shifters had been using it for power, wouldn't I have sensed it?"

Headmistress Wake's lips curled up slightly. "That all depends on which royal demon enchanted it. If it was not Ishtar, you might not be as sensitive. Royal demon power can be more subtle and nefarious than other demons. They have the ability to smother their power if they wish, unlike greater or lesser demons. I suspect that a demon stone gives its keeper that same power so they can fly under the radar. But if someone like you, who is familiar with the energies of the royals, touches that person, there is no hiding."

My lips formed an O as a slice of understanding cut through me. "Rita, the shifter alpha who I brought down in my mission, mentioned the Furies. So her stone must have been from them."

"Then Gian's could have been from the Furies, Xaphan, or Lucifer," Diana mused. "Since you didn't sense it from afar but had to touch him, right?"

"Yup."

She leaned back in her chair and crossed her arms over her chest. "I've said it once, but I'll say it again. I misjudged you last year, Dane."

A knock on the door saved me from deciding how to respond. Headmistress Wake went to answer it.

"Greetings, Headmistress," Prince Elran's distinctive voice rang out over the chamber. "I only have a moment, but I wonder if I might speak with your team?"

My spine straightened. The prince was at the door? But his wedding would start at any minute!

"Of course, Prince Elran." Headmistress Wake stepped to the right, and the prince strode inside, his silver cape billowing behind him, and a white fur stole around his shoulders.

We stood and bowed.

"I heard a rumor that once the discrepancy between the other spy schools' points is resolved, you will leave Faerie immediately," Prince Elran said. "I did not want to get caught up in the revelry—fae weddings can last many days —and not thank you properly."

"But you've already thanked us," I said.

"Yes, but it is not enough. Gian has already confessed that he planned to kill my bride-to-be's father on this very night. You have saved my family, and for that, your reward should fit the deed."

"Oh . . ."

The prince was still looking at me, and I felt compelled to answer.

"Thank you."

He smiled a dazzling white smile that reminded me of the snowy mountaintops outside. "I do hope you'll accept my gift."

I hadn't noticed the small leather-wrapped package in his hand until he extended it to me.

I took it. "Should I open it now?"

"I'd be forever grateful if you did," the prince replied with an amused grin.

Okay, stop being awkward and entertaining the fae prince, Odie. Just unwrap the damn package.

I did so carefully, not knowing what to expect. And when the items were revealed, I was glad that I'd taken care.

Four sharp-looking daggers glinted up at me. As far as I could tell, they were plain and silver. Nothing like the etched and jeweled ones I'd noticed on the hips of the fae soldiers, or even in the cases at Spellcasters.

"Oh." I looked up at the prince, who was still regarding me with an amused look. "They're so . . . pointy. Thank you," I said somewhat lamely.

Andre appeared at my side and sucked in a breath. "Are those what I think they are?"

The prince grinned. "I'm glad someone recognizes

them." He winked at me, and my cheeks heated. "Yes. These are demon daggers, otherwise known as hell blades. One for each of you."

"Holy crap!" Andre snapped up a dagger from the pile and began to examine it with such reverence that I couldn't hold in my next question.

"What do hell blades do?"

The prince lifted a blade from my hand. "They are the only weapon in the universe known to be deadly to every level of demon." His finger ran over the sharp blade. "The metal used in these blades is incredibly rare, forged from the pits of Hell itself. Each blade is an item of extreme value. A great warrior of the Snowcap Court brought back enough metal to create ten blades over a century ago. Since then, no one else has made the journey." He extended the blade to me, hilt-first. "I thought it a proper gift for those who apprehended a demon-lover in my castle."

I took the dagger and was unsurprised when the mark on my ankle burned. Yes, these things held power. And while I wasn't an ace with a dagger yet, I would do well to learn to use this one.

"Thank you, Prince Elran."

"Thank you," the prince performed a shallow bow and gave another brilliant smile before leaving the room.

We left the Snowcap Court quietly. After all, the day should be about Prince Elran and his intended, not the team that discovered a traitor. Plus, according to Spy Game rules, we had to be in our world to call the points for an event. And apparently, since I'd apprehended Gian, the points had been the source of some angst.

To put it bluntly, the vampires were *pissed*. Scowls marred their beautiful faces as the four teams, and the heads of their respective academies, lined up and strode through the warphole.

I'd never been so happy to see someone—or in this case, four cheating someones—so angry.

We entered our world again right where we'd left it, in the courtyard of the Fae Academy of Elemental and Arcane Arts. The sound of trickling water filled my ears, and warm, *blessedly* warm air washed over me, erasing the persistent chill of the Snowcap Court.

I was a little sad to be leaving Faerie so quickly. It was unlikely that I'd ever go back. But if I did, I'd prefer to stay at a much warmer court next time.

"Ah! It is splendid to be in our realm again, is it not?" Headmistress Cristala twirled, making her silk dress shimmer and sway around her.

"Faerie is nice to visit, but I could not see myself living there," Alpha Conon commented, and the other heads of schools agreed.

"And now that we are back, we can finalize the ratings for the second event," Headmistress Wake noted practically.

"Indeed," Headmistress Cristala's eyes glinted.

I wasn't sure how the points had played out, because we

hadn't had a moment to catch up with the other champions before returning home. Although I did know that something unexpected had occurred.

The fae headmistress twirled her hands, and a stone bench that weighed more than she did shot from the side of the courtyard to halt in front of her. Delicately, the fae stepped up onto the bench.

I blinked. I'd expected there to be an audience present like at Nightdwellers, but it appeared that we were doing the points ceremony right here and now.

"The undisputed winners of the fae challenge," Headmistress Cristala waved a regal hand in our direction. "The witches of Spellcasters Spy Academy."

A smile bloomed on my face, and elation swept through me as the shifters, fae, and heads of the academies clapped. Only the vampire champions refrained from celebrating, but that was expected of those assholes, so I didn't let it bug me.

"Coming in second place . . . the Fae Academy of Elemental and Arcane Arts, for their capture of an accomplice to murder!"

I whipped around to face the fae, my eyes wide. They had captured a baddie too?! I caught Sana's eye and knitted my eyebrows together in question.

Tell you later, she mouthed, and I gave her the okay signal.

"The rankings of third and fourth place had to be decided upon by an impartial party, as none of the heads of houses could come to a fair decision," Headmistress

Cristala said, her tone dramatic as she pulled a small enve-lope out of nowhere, opened it, and pulled out a slip of paper.

"A tie! We have a tie! By order of Queen Tially Frost of the Snowcap Court, both Nightdwellers Academy and the Shifter Academy of Spies will receive six points!"

"We deserve nothing," I heard Dasha say.

"I'll agree to that," one of the vampires—Francis, I was pretty sure—sniped.

"Now, now, champions," Headmistress Cristala admon-ished them. "Just because neither school discovered a traitor does not mean that you weren't helpful. The queen has eyes everywhere. She took all that you did and your methods of espionage into account. It may not be where you wanted to land in the rankings, but claim the points with pride."

"And if you dislike it, perform better next time." Head-master Ezra glared at his students.

Yikes. I wouldn't want to be a Nightdwellers champion right now.

Thankfully, Headmistress Cristala broke the tension by sweeping off the bench and bidding us all to say goodbye.

I turned to the shifters and fae, competitors who I also considered friends, and did just that.

CHAPTER THIRTY-EIGHT

"For a human, Dante was extremely astute. He recognized that Hell consisted of circles. Unfortunately, nine is a woefully small number." Professor de Spina swooped around the Advanced Demonology classroom, his dark eyes narrowed in concentration. His hands flew through the air as he moved, releasing gray magic that transformed into a three-dimensional visual that hung in the center of the room for us to study.

And study it, we did. The hundreds of concentric circles of Hell were simply too horrible and intriguing to take our eyes off of.

"To be fair, not even magicals know the exact number of levels that Hell possesses." The young professor shrugged as he added a bit of flair to the middle circle and placed the royals on thrones made of bones. The Furies, a three-in-one aspect of a royal demon, barely fit, as they all had to share one throne. "Few wish to venture there to find out. And we rarely chat with demons about their home when they find their way to our realm."

My stomach twisted, as it so often did when I thought of demons surging into our world.

"But there are *some* magicals who speak to them," someone said from behind me.

I twisted in my chair to see Diana studying the conjuring of Hell intently.

"Absolutely," the professor agreed. "Black witches who make a deal with demons for additional powers are one example."

"Yes, but that wasn't what I meant," Diana said, not about to let the conversation move on until she'd said her piece. "While I find the circles of Hell interesting, Professor, I was wondering if we might detour into talking about demon stones for a moment? In the last Spy Games event, they charged us with finding a traitor. Odette discovered the person by the demon stone they had on them. We hunted down the fae who held it, but we never got a thorough explanation as to what they do. Or who distributes them."

A few of my classmates' eyes darted to me—most of them, people who had been standoffish all year. While I appreciated Diana asking the question, I sort of wished that she hadn't credited me.

Although I'd signed up for the Spy Games to show those same students that I deserved the rank of spymaster, I found that my motivation for the Games had changed. Now the camaraderie that the events brought drove me because I recognized that these relationships would be what helped us defeat the demons.

Of course, beating the pants off the vampires would be great too, but the validation of my classmates? Almost half an academic year had already flown by. They would either accept the fact that I earned head spymaster or not. I no longer had the energy to work on convincing them.

"Demon stones . . ." Professor de Spina trailed off. "Yes, I suppose considering recent events, that would be a worthy side topic." He twisted to face the visual of Hell again, and a gray pointer stick appeared in his hand.

"Demon stones, along with many other enchanted dark objects, are born in Hell. From what we know, they are fired in the flames of this circle for at least a millennium." His pointer moved to a circle about five away from the center. "And once savvy greater demons have found a person willing to do business with evil, they bring the stones to a royal demon for a blessing."

"Blessing?" Kira asked. "That sounds good, though."

De Spina arched his eyebrows. "Are we not always the hero of our own story, Miss Johnston? When the demons bring the royals stones to bless, they believe they are doing it for the good of their kind. So yes, they call it a blessing."

"What does the blessing entail?" Mina Köhler twisted her long, black hair thoughtfully.

De Spina's lips flattened for an instant. "That depends on what the human or magical wants most. Many desire power, money, or fame, but a blessing is not limited to any of those. As long as the bearer will fight for the demons and give their souls over once they perish, the royals of Hell will promise anything."

My mouth went dry. Despite having found two stones this year, I hadn't realized how truly powerful they were. That a stone could give the person who possessed it anything—and that they gave their soul to Hell for one— made it an object worth dying for.

An amazing bargaining chip.

For the first time, I dared to wonder just how many demon stones there were in our world.

The Physical Conditioning room was packed as always when Hunter, Eva, Alex, and I walked in. Although I was behind on my exercise requirement for the week, I didn't care. There were more important things to consider. Like making sure we knew how to use the dagger that Prince Elran had gifted me.

Bypassing the treadmills and weights, my friends and I went straight to the back room, an open space where magic and physical sparring was allowed.

Two third-years, one of them Diana's ex-boyfriend, sparred in the far corner, but that was fine. The target boards were on the other end of the room, in the opposite direction of the students.

"So this bad boy can kill any demon, huh?" Hunter asked, twirling my hell blade in his hand.

I smiled at his flagrant display of skill. Of the four of us,

Hunter was easily the best at wielding blades. His totem was an emerald encrusted dagger, and he practiced with it often. "Yup. Says Prince Elran of the Snowcap Court. As far as I can tell, it's not much different from any other dagger, but I still want you three to work with it. Just in case."

Diana had actually brought up the idea that our closest friends practice with the demon blades too. Even though there were only four blades, she had a good point. The more people who were familiar with the blades, the better. What if something happened to me during a fight? More than anything, I'd want my friends to scoop up the dagger and use it to the best of their ability.

"It's light—like it weighs nothing," Hunter commented. .

"Good thing you're practicing with it," I pointed toward the target, "because you're up first, Wardwell."

Hunter grinned and strutted over to face the target. Gripping the dagger in his hand, he pulled his arm back and hurled the blade toward the target.

It missed, hitting the wall with a deafening *clang.*

He groaned. "If that were my totem, I would have sunk it."

"But you didn't, babe," Eva said, not one to sugarcoat things. "Which is why we need to practice. Go again."

Hunter hurled the blade a dozen times more. By the end, he seemed to have gotten used to the weight, and actually sank a bullseye.

We rotated through with the demon blade after that, one person hurling it, while the others practiced sparring with blades of a similar size.

When it was my turn with the hell blade, I was the worst at throwing it, never hitting the target once. I wasn't terrible at fighting with daggers, but since I didn't relish the idea of getting too close to demons, I made a resolution right then and there to practice dagger-throwing daily.

One more thing to add to the list.

I was about to turn the hell blade back over to Hunter so everyone could get in another round, when I noticed a group of six students hovering by the door. They were watching us.

I signaled to my friends to stop sparring. "They look like they want to talk." I waved our peers over.

Kira and José, both people I thought of as friends last year, but who had been haters this year, led the group over and stopped in front of us.

"Hey," Kira said, and pulled her bundle of black braids over her shoulder.

"Hey," I said, dropping the dagger into the scabbard I wore at my hip for safer transport. I glanced to the other half of the room. Diana's jealous ex and the other Crucible student were still sparring, now with magic instead of fists. "Did you guys want to use this area? Because we'll finish in a half hour tops."

It was almost eight, and I still needed to squeeze in a warping lesson with Alex before homework and bed.

"That's not why we're here," José said. "Actually, we came to apologize to you, Odette."

My mouth dropped open. *Well, this is unexpected.*

Kira nodded. "We've been shitty all year." Her cheeks,

the color of light mocha, pinked slightly. "I'll be the first to admit that I was jealous. I only got emissary spy, and didn't think you deserved your rank." Her gaze dropped to the ground. "But I've heard stories from Andre and Diana, and am woman enough to admit that I was wrong."

"We don't know what's going on around you," Dakota Wily spoke up. He was a thin, very academic guy with horn-rimmed glasses who I'd rarely spoken to last year and not once this year. His inclusion in this group surprised me. "But we recognize that something is up. Something that might have to do with the curse of our year. We want to be allies, if you need us."

Curse of our year?

So much had happened since the end of last term, I hadn't even considered that others were still fretting over the curse. That was probably because I knew the truth. There was no curse on our year, only a prophecy relating to Alex and me. While I didn't know everything about it, I knew enough. The demons wanted us to open the Hellgate.

"That is, if you'll have us," Jasmine Shani added, clearly taking my silence to mean I was mulling over their offer of friendship. "We understand if you want nothing to do with us, but like Kira said, we heard about the games. You've been a key component to your team twice. Obviously, we were wrong to think that you weren't skilled enough."

Annie Thomas and Nian Zhen, who stood at the back of the group, both nodded their agreement.

My heart swelled. I'd given up on a quarter of my class liking me, but here they were, offering friendship.

An alliance. One I wanted and would most likely need in the future.

A smile broke on my face. "Thank you, all of you. I appreciate that very much. And yes, I'd love to be friends."

I was still riding high from the interactions in the Physical Conditioning room when Alex and I snuck into the woods to begin his first warping lesson.

Although it felt like bad juju, we opted to practice in the same clearing where we'd banished the ghost. It was open, quiet, and most of all, private.

I was under no illusion that the professors or staff would be happy to find me teaching Alex how to warp. With only six months of warping under my belt, I was considered too new to be teaching others the dangerous skill of warping.

"Are you sure you want to do this?" I asked as we walked through the woods. "I've heard that some people lose limbs or get fourth-degree burns from manipulating energy incorrectly."

"You won't scare me out of this, Odie. I'm well aware of the risks." He darted a glance to me. "Plus, not all students hurt themselves—you never have. You didn't even have a lesson before your first experience. And you warped us all the way from New York City to Maine."

I snorted. "Yeah, but I'd been accosted by Ishtar and had an army's amount of adrenaline running through my veins when I first warped." I squeezed his hand. "I also had your totem to help me out."

He shot me a sheepish grin. "Okay, okay, I get it. It's not an apples to apples comparison. Still, you can't blame me for wanting to try. And if you don't show me, I'll just do it myself."

Universe have mercy. Why was my boyfriend stubborn at the most inopportune times?

"Fine. But it's freezing out here, so an hour max. You probably won't be able to last that long anyway," I said, recalling Andre's first lesson.

He'd tapped out after a half hour of trying—and he'd shown ability beforehand. To my knowledge, Alex had never even attempted to create a warphole.

The minute we entered the clearing, I pointed Alex to the far side. If by some miracle he opened a warphole, I'd have him start by traversing short expanses. Being able to see the exit spot was best.

"Okay, so I'll teach you two ways. The first is how Professor Tittelbaum does it. He's more technical, and since you're . . . you, I think that might work."

I laid out the rules of warping as detailed by Professor Tittelbaum as best I could. Then I demonstrated using my mentor's method. The difference in my method and the professor's was enormous, and the resulting warphole was reminiscent of one of the first ones I'd ever created. It was more rigid, not as natural, and when I stepped through, it felt all wrong.

When it was Alex's turn, he closed his eyes to try his hand. I felt the energy shift around him. The air began to shimmer a light red, and as he extended his hands, a ball of crimson formed in front of him.

I sucked in a breath. Was Alex going to turn out to be a warper like me?

But the ball fizzled in the next instant, and Alex dropped his hands and began panting. Even though it was November and frigid, a bead of sweat dripped down his face.

"You okay? Feel anything . . . different?"

Alex's eyebrows knitted together. "Not so much *different*, but the sensation of running into a wall was intense. It was like my magic could flow, but only so far."

I nodded. "I experienced that when I first tried warping to sites I couldn't see."

"Does that mean I'm on the right track?"

I shrugged. "It could mean that, or it could mean your magic doesn't know what to do. Try again."

He did. Five times. Then he grudgingly had to take a seat on a nearby stump.

I squatted next to him, and noticed that his legs were trembling. "Here, eat this." I held out a protein bar that I'd snagged from the cafeteria for this exact reason.

Alex took it gratefully and inhaled the bar. "I'm not sure Tittelbaum's method will work. What do you say we try it your way?"

I had hoped that we wouldn't get to this point, because I knew that my method was so not going to jive with my analytical boyfriend's nature.

"Do you have enough energy to go again?" I asked.

"Come on, babe, I'm not that weak," Alex said, and I noticed the muscles in his legs stiffen as if he was contracting them so they'd stop shaking.

"Suit yourself," I sighed. "If you're going to try my method, you'd do best to erase Tittelbaum's teachings from your mind."

Alex snapped his fingers. "Done. Teach me your ways, Obi-Wan."

"Okay . . ." I drew in a breath. "I make a warphole by feeling it in my bones."

Alex laughed. "Nice try, sweets. Really, how do you do it?"

I'd known he'd have this reaction. "Seriously, that's it. I understand the other ways, but it always feels so forced. I sense the power, all the energy deep inside, and then I just . . . manipulate it."

Alex's jaw dropped open.

"That's not what you want to hear, or what resonates with you, but it's the truth."

His mouth snapped shut. "No, it's fine. I guess I didn't realize what a prodigy you were."

Heat rose in my cheeks. "I wouldn't say that—"

"I would. And since we're short on time, I think I should just get on trying your method." Alex stood. "Lead me back to the circle, Master."

"If we plan to do this weekly, I'm bringing Hunter next time," I said as I helped Alex climb the stairs to the third floor after a completely unsuccessful first warping lesson. "You're too heavy for me to shoulder all your weight."

"One," he held up a single finger. "Everyone says warping takes an enormous amount of physical energy, but I didn't think I'd be unable to make it up the stairs alone," Alex said, the exhaustion obvious in his voice as he held up a second digit. "Two, I don't weigh that much. And three." He sighed and dropped his hand. "I didn't realize you would pull that 'I feel it in my bones' voodoo crap. I'm going to ask Andre how he does it."

"I'm not sure that's such a good idea."

"Why? He still sucks at it?"

"No, but there are training regulations for warpers, and we're breaking all of them."

"Can *you* ask him then?"

I figured that couldn't hurt—Andre would probably just think I was curious. "Fine. We have our next session later this—"

A scream cut me off, and we stiffened.

"That came from the Green Tower," Alex said, and apparently finding a surge of energy, ripped himself from beneath my shoulder and sprinted toward the sound.

I dashed after him, and the moment we turned into the hallway that led to the tower, we both skidded to a stop.

The protective glass that housed the precious items

lining the corridor had been smashed to smithereens. Jasmine Sahni stood in front of the destruction, her hands over her mouth.

"Jasmine! Are you okay?" I asked, rushing up to her.

"Fine. I'm fine." She shook her head. Her brown eyes were large, but she didn't appear injured. "I was in the library and left to turn in early, and then I found . . . this."

"It looks like most of the items are still here," Alex said, striding down the hall and examining the cases.

Mentally, I ran through the list of items I walked past daily. Most were pretty and historical, but fairly useless. The only ones that had a purpose other than decoration were the weapons.

But we can get weapons easily enough by going down to the Battle Magic classroom. They'd be in better condition too. Why would someone take one from here?

I began to take inventory as well, and when Alex stopped to pick up a wand that had been tossed carelessly on the ground, I moved past him. I was almost to the door of the Green Tower when my blood ran cold.

I'd found which item was missing.

The Realm Slicer.

CHAPTER THIRTY-NINE

For the second time that academic year, the PIA descended upon Spellcasters to question people. This time around, they insisted on interviewing every single person in the academy.

Unsurprisingly, as one of the first three students on the scene after the Realm Slicer was discovered to be gone, the PIA called me in for questioning first. What *did* surprise me, however, was that I did not speak with David Chena. In fact, the few times I'd seen him in the corridors, he'd pretended not to notice me.

He seemed to be avoiding me. Maybe because I knew about him and Holly? Whatever the case, his avoidance stung—although I tried not to dwell on it. I had enough to worry about, and an embarrassed man-child who I was losing respect for was low on my list of priorities.

"When do you think they'll leave?" Eva asked as two PIA agents marched by us on our way to Battle Magic.

I shrugged. "The Realm Slicer is a massive deal, so probably never."

Headmistress Wake had called an assembly after the blade disappeared, and spelled out the severity of the matter. In the hands of a powerful enough magical, the Realm Slicer could open up holes between worlds. This included Faerie, the ghost plane of purgatory, Heaven, and most bone-chilling of all, Hell. As far as I was concerned, the PIA could stay for as long as they needed to find the weapon—which some people believed was still on academy grounds.

"Are you and Alex practicing warping again soon?"

"Are you crazy? No way." I shook my head as we began to descend the stairs into the basement. "With the PIA here, it's too risky. We're already breaking the rules, I don't need to get in trouble with the government for it."

Eva loosed a sigh. "It's so annoying. We can't do anything with them snooping around. I asked Headmistress Wake if going to Wandstown was an option, and she refused. I'm going stir-crazy." She dragged her hands down her face for emphasis.

"Would some dagger-throwing help ease the boredom?" I opened my bag to reveal that I'd brought my demon dagger with me.

Professor Thrax had been on a major weapons kick. I was hoping his enthusiasm would continue today.

Eva's eyes lit up. Although she wasn't amazing at dagger throwing like Hunter, she enjoyed doing it. "Better than studying."

I placed a hand over my mouth. "Who are you and what have you done with my bookish best friend?"

"The Grind is getting to me, girl." Eva glanced from side to side. "I've even dreamt about burning my textbooks! What if this distaste is permanent?" For a moment, she looked worried.

I laughed. "No way. We're all tired. It's normal." Pulling the blade out of my bag, I handed it to her. "If Thrax allows weapons today, you get first dibs on the demon blade."

"Yaaassss."

We entered the Battle Magic classroom and chatted for a few more minutes until Thrax marched in. A sword hung at his hip, and his kilt flapped around his knees.

"Once again, we'll focus on weaponry today, but this time you spar, two-on-two," the professor's Scottish brogue filled the cavernous classroom. "Unlike usual, we're workin' until we draw blood—nothin' vi'al."

A low murmuring filled the class, and Dakota Wily raised his hand. "May I ask, why blood, sir?"

"Word has it yer second round of missions are just around the corner. You should receive the notices ri' after Yule. In yer second mission, yer given the option of bringin' a weapon, so we like to make sure yer familiar with them."

"Hot damn," Hunter breathed, and I could just see the gears spinning in his head. If he got to bring another weapon in addition to his totem, he'd be formidable.

"Today, there'll be three sessions with three different weapons. I'll call time when each session is up, and you'll switch. Pair up with someone you haven't worked with in the past week." Thrax clapped his massive hands. "And begin."

Since we worked together as often as possible, Alex, Hunter, Eva, and I went our separate ways. Kira approached me, and I partnered with her. Diana and Amethyst challenged us, and after choosing our weapons, we claimed a sparring circle.

Our daggers slashed and whined through the air, and twice, Diana came close to slicing my shoulder. All four of us danced, parried, and jabbed like pros, and before I knew it, Thrax was calling time to change out our weapons.

Everyone ran over to the wall of weapons, and as much as I didn't want to, I set down the dagger I'd been practicing with.

I glanced at Kira. "What do you think? Broadsword?"

The broadsword was my worst weapon, and it was unlikely I'd ever use it in the modern world, but what if, one day, I had to? Spies had been forced to fight with far stranger tools, which was why we trained with so many different items at the academy.

"Hell yeah," Kira beamed and hoisted a sword most people would have considered too long for her.

Those people didn't know Kira.

She winked. "I'll protect you this round, Dane."

Once Amethyst and Diana had chosen their weapons—a whip for Diana, and a mace for Amethyst—we reclaimed our training circle. Our second round of sparring was just about to begin when the door to the Battle Magic classroom opened.

Headmistress Wake entered, and Spymaster Chena followed close behind.

"Pardon my interruption, Professor Thrax," the headmistress said as she marched toward the instructor. "But Spymaster Chena would like a word with Miss Dane and it cannot wait. Can you spare her?"

"Absolutely," Thrax boomed. "Dane!"

"I'll hurry," I said to my group before dashing toward the weapon stash to set my sword down.

I'd just placed the sword in its spot when Eva's voice cut through the classroom.

"*Odie!*"

I whipped around and found Eva in a sparring circle close to where Spymaster Chena waited by the door. Her eyes were wide and frantic.

"Eva? What's—"

She held up the demon blade I'd let her use, and my mouth snapped shut.

It glowed a brilliant red. The hair on my arm raised. But why? What did that mean?

The headmistress was at my side in an instant, her hands gripping my shoulders tight. "Miss Dane, is that the blade I think it is?"

"Yes, but I've never—"

Before I finished my sentence, Headmistress Wake's head snapped toward the doorway. I followed her gaze and gasped.

David Chena was gone, and in the space where he'd just stood, only a cloud of black smoke remained.

CHAPTER FORTY

$\mathcal{A}$fter David's disappearance, our entire Battle Magic class aided Headmistress Wake and Professor Thrax in searching for him. When we came up short, the questions began.

Headmistress Wake explained that she believed Chena must have had a demon stone on his person. Otherwise the blade would not have lit up in his presence, and more importantly, he wouldn't have been able to disappear in a cloud of black smoke.

He was only human, after all.

Although I knew I had to, and even wanted to because it might help people find Chena, it took me three days after his disappearance to inform the headmistress about David's relationship with Holly. As a result, Holly underwent a week of questioning at the PIA. When she returned, I tried to talk to her, but she wanted nothing to do with me.

Even though I might have lost my friendship with Holly

—and by extension, Heidi—I didn't regret it. I wasn't sure what was up with David, but one thing was clear.

He'd deserted the PIA and allied with the demons. Which meant he was my adversary.

How long has he been playing me?

The thought ran through my head for the millionth time as I trudged through the woods to meet Alex, Hunter, and Eva for yet another warping lesson.

The weeks had flown by since David Chena's disappearance. A thin layer of snow lay on the forest ground and Yule was fast approaching.

The difference was only weeks, but so much had changed. The PIA was in an uproar, conducing investigations. Rumor had it that five more spies had been discovered to be traitors.

My whole world had flipped, but one thing remained constant. Alex had had zero luck in warping since our first lesson. Despite this fact, he remained undeterred in his wish to continue trying. In fact, since Chena had been exposed, Alex became more militant about our lessons, and insisted that Hunter and Eva join us.

Not one of them seemed to have the knack for warping, but there were some side benefits to practicing. Since they'd begun trying to warp, each of them had tested and strengthened their magic. Eva could now easily perform many spells that had caused her issue three weeks ago, and the guys noticed similar results.

"There you are!" Eva said as I stepped into the clearing where we'd banished the ghost. "Who goes first today?"

I scanned my friends, gauging their exhaustion. "Alex," I said after assessing Hunter's dark circles, and the massive bags beneath Eva's eyes. "But this time, we're trying something different."

My friends' eyes narrowed, but I brushed off their skepticism. They hadn't had any luck with Professor Tittelbaum's, Andre's, or my methods. It was time for us to get innovative.

"Alex, start here. I'll move about thirty feet into the woods. Aim for me."

Alex's brows furrowed. "What's the point of this?"

"I want to make sure I'm not hogging all the warping energies in this area. I'll also be working magic over there to make warping more accessible. You'll only have to create half a warphole."

He looked skeptical.

"Humor me, okay?"

He released a huff. "Sure. It's not like anything else is working." His tone sounded sour.

I suspected that the upcoming Yule holiday worried him. We would be separated for part of it, to spend time with our families. Plus, the next Spy Games challenge had been moved up a month to throw off the rogue agents who knew the original date, and that frustrated Alex.

I placed a hand on his shoulder. "This might change everything."

He gave me a grim smile.

"Okay, I'll flash a ball of light once when the energies are ready. Try to warp to me."

With that, I broke away from my friends and ran the short distance into the woods. Once there, I began to manipulate the surrounding energies into what I would use for a warphole. I pushed them to the point that it would require only a smidge more magic before a warphole would appear.

It felt weird to nearly make a warphole but stop myself —it wasn't something I'd ever done before.

The air shimmered with the act, and thin, colorless lines appeared in my vision.

Weird, but cool, I thought, lifting my other hand and calling a ball of light. Fuchsia flashed bright in the darkening sky, the signal for Alex to proceed.

From Alex's stance, I could tell that he'd started working magic. His hands moved through the air, twirling in a graceful manner that, so far, seemed ineffectual. My breath stopped in my lungs, and I hoped more than ever that this would work. If it didn't, my boyfriend would be a train wreck while I was at the Shifter Academy for Spies.

Seconds passed, and Alex's shoulders inched closer to his ears. Even though I was far away, I could feel the tension coursing through him.

Calm down. Clear your mind. I squinted into the night, willing him to hear my thoughts, and pictured Alex next to me, victorious. The image was so vivid, so real, that I could almost smell him and feel the heat of his skin as he stood by me. *Come on, babe. You got this.*

Then, something in the air shifted.

On Alex's hand, a flash of light—fuchsia—bloomed, while at the same moment, my necklace pulsed red.

My heart skipped a beat, and an alien tingle rippled across the nape of my neck.

What the—?

My hands flew over my mouth, and I released all my power as Alex disappeared and reappeared five feet from me.

His eyes were wide and terrified, but when they caught me, he smiled. "Holy shit! I did it, didn't I?!"

I blinked. Had he? I didn't see a warphole and didn't feel my power respond to it. I hadn't even felt the powerful bloom of heat and cold that always occurred in warpholes.

My gaze veered down to Alex's totem on his hand, and then to my necklace. Both still glowed, as if they were telling me something.

"Odie? Are you okay?" Alex rushed forward to stand in front of me. "Did my warphole hurt you somehow?"

"I—" I paused, knowing that what I was about to say might crush the pride I'd seen on his face. "I'm fine."

Alex's shoulders loosened, and he beamed. "Surprised, huh? To be honest, I kind of am too. I thought for sure—"

"Babe." I gripped his arm. "I'm sorry, but you didn't make a warphole."

Alex's eyebrows knitted together. "Yeah, I did. I'm here, aren't I?"

"Something happened—that much is for sure," I admitted. "But I promise that wasn't a warphole. That was something . . . I've never seen before. Magic neither of my mentors have mentioned." My fingers found my totem and rubbed it. His totem encircled his finger. Had it actually made that fuchsia ball of light? "Did you see your ring flash before you appeared here?"

"See my ring flash? What?"

Footsteps came closer through the trees, and Eva and Hunter appeared.

Hunter's handsome face split in a grin when he saw us. "Cuz! You did it! That—"

Alex held up his hand, stopping his cousin. "Odie says I didn't. But I don't understand how I got here if I didn't warp."

I gulped as my friends' attention pressed down on me. "I don't understand it either, but I watched your progress closely. Both our totems lit up, mine was red, and yours was fuchsia, and then you popped into existence over here."

"I saw fuchsia too," Eva said. "But I was so shocked that Alex moved, that I couldn't be sure if it was in my mind or real."

"Definitely real," I whispered, "and I'd bet everything I own that what Alex made wasn't a warphole. It was something else." I shook my head, trying to piece together the events of the night. "I just don't know what it means."

CHAPTER FORTY-ONE

*A*lex gripped my hand as we marched up the walkway to the fancy restaurant behind my parents. "Calm down, sweets. We're doing the right thing."

I gulped. Maybe, but holy universe was I uncomfortable. I'd always kept my romantic relationships fairly private. While my parents knew Alex and I were together, we'd only talked about my relationship superficially. I'd certainly never mentioned that Alex and I were fated to be together and what we were meant to do.

A soft groan left me. What would they say when I told them everything? It was so much.

My eyes flitted down to where our fingers intertwined, and caught on Alex's totem. After the strange warping session in the woods, we'd spent every possible second of the weeks before winter break trying to discover other totems that had acted like ours.

We'd come up with nothing—which I totally wasn't

buying. We couldn't be the *only* witches in history whose totems were so connected that they could share magic and make one totem owner appear before the other.

And if they were, what the actual hell?

"Dane, table for four. As I said when I made the reservation, we prefer a quieter area." My dad slipped the hostess a bill that made the young woman's eyes light up.

"We saved you the perfect table, sir," she said. "Right this way."

When she deposited us at a lone table in the far back, Dad's shoulders loosened. I cocked my head. It seemed like he was anxious too. Did it have to do with the disappearing spies? Although the PIA was under heavy investigation, no one seemed to know anything about those who had vanished. But maybe my parents had discovered information?

Everything proceeded fairly normally as the waiter took our drink order, brought bread and beverages, and jotted down our orders with astonishing speed and attentiveness. I had a feeling that the hostess might have bragged about the fifty Dad slipped her, and the waiter was hoping to impress him even more.

Finally, we were left alone.

"So, did you kids enjoy the Yule Ball?" Mom asked. "I thought it was a marvelous affair. Too short to see everyone I wanted to catch up with, but it was last year too."

"It was wonderful, Mrs. Dane," Alex said with a charming smile. "Even better than last year's ball."

"Uh huh," I agreed half-heartedly, squirming in my chair a little.

Despite the safe topic, the thought of what we really needed to talk about persisted in the back of my mind, and I felt my face warm.

Mom looked at me and her eyebrows furrowed. "You okay, honey? You've been acting a little strange today."

A little? She was being kind. I'd acted like a total spaz all day and I knew it. As much as I didn't want to have this discussion, I needed to get it over with so my heart could beat normally again.

"Err, I . . ." My eyes darted to Alex, begging him to take the lead.

He released a long exhale. "Actually, Mr. and Mrs. Dane, Odette and I have something to tell you. After we do, we're hoping you can enlighten us on the matter."

Dad leaned forward. "Is this about the disappearances? Because I've been thinking about that too. I wanted to wait until we got back to the hotel, but—"

My spine straightened. *I knew it! And yippee for a distraction!*

"Actually, it's not about that," I cut Dad off. "But I really want to hear about those spies, so why don't you go first?"

Beneath the table, a foot slammed into mine, and Alex shook his head.

I ignored him, my gaze set on Dad.

"Well, it seems that you stumbled onto something big, pea," Dad admitted as he tore a hunk of bread off of the loaf. "Things have been kept rather hush-hush at the agency, but we know the right people. Or at least, we did until recently. Before we received a call from Headmistress Wake informing us about Spymaster Chena's desertion, and how other spies deserted after, we were in contact with old friends at the agency. Our old colleagues told us that ten active spies have gone missing since the start of the year." Dad's hazel eyes darted from side to side. "Two were very good and old friends of your mother and me."

My stomach twisted. Ten spies? But where was the PIA, or whoever was responsible for their disappearances, taking them?

I stuffed a hunk of bread in my mouth, trying to shove down the well of emotions rising up.

"Of course, since the demon infiltration has become known, our sources have clammed up. Honestly, I don't think they really know anything about it besides the fact that people are missing, and now they are scared to talk because of the interrogations. But we won't just stand by idly," Mom said, her lips pursed. "Your dad and I are personally looking into it, alongside a couple of other retirees from the service."

"Be careful," I whispered.

"Of course, pea," Dad replied. "Apparently, there hasn't been a single disappearance since Chena deserted, so we're hoping that means he was involved and now people are safe. But either way, your mom and I know how to cover our tracks. We used to be damn good at it, in fact."

"That's an understatement." Alex chuckled, and the sound was so welcome that for the first time since we sat down, a teensy bit of tension between my shoulder blades dissolved.

I leaned back in my chair.

Mom smiled, noticing that I'd relaxed a smidge. "We're speaking to Headmistress Wake regularly about it too. If anything major happens while you're at the academy, we'll have her tell you."

"She didn't seem pleased that I knew about the disappearing spies when I asked about you guys before the last Spy Games."

Mom shrugged. "She doesn't like that you're so involved, but Priscilla will have to deal. Especially after what's been happening at the academy, I'd much rather my daughter know exactly what's going on than be in the dark." Mom took a sip of her white wine and sighed. "Speaking of being in the dark, why don't you tell us why you're so wound up, and what Alex is doing here? Judging by how you're sweating, I'm pretty sure it's not an engagement announcement, although I *am* holding out hope." She arched an eyebrow.

I coughed. "Err . . . umm."

Alex squeezed my hand and swooped in.

"Then we're of the same mind, Mrs. Dane." My heart stopped at his words, but Alex didn't seem to notice, and kept right on talking. "Although, what Odette and I want to talk about is much more pressing."

"We're all ears," Dad said, amused eyes sliding from my face—which was probably beet red by now—to Alex.

My boyfriend placed his hand on the table and nodded

to his totem. "Odie and I have discovered a connection between our totems."

"A . . . what?" Mom's eyes narrowed in confusion.

"They have a shared past," Alex explained. "One that, as it turns out, allows Odette and me to accomplish miraculous feats of magic together." Alex shot me an unsure glance. We'd decided to tell my parents everything because we needed help, although neither of us were *completely* sure it was the right thing to do.

Realizing that it wasn't fair for Alex to shoulder all of the burden, I cleared my throat. "Our totems once belonged to famous witches—ones who we're fairly certain are of our bloodlines."

"Do you mean Deliverance Dane, honey?" Mom asked.

"Even farther back than Salem. Someone indisputably powerful and more famous." My hand pressed against my totem, and I inhaled a shaky breath. "This used to be Morgan Le Fay's necklace, and Alex's ring belonged to Merlin."

Dad began coughing and pounded his fist on his chest.

"As in *the* Merlin?" Mom's eyes were locked on Alex's ring, and for some reason, Ishtar's taunt about people remembering Merlin and not Morgan rang in my ears before I batted it away.

"Yes, *the* Merlin," I said. "He was Morgan's teacher and lover and apparently, they accomplished great things together. Like sealing the Hellgate."

Dad regained control of himself and sat up straight in

his chair. "How do you know all of this, Odie? And why didn't you tell us sooner?"

I told them the truth. That we'd learned it piece by piece and until recently, it had felt too personal to share. I still didn't want any Joe Schmoe knowing, but as crazy events kept piling up, we knew we needed to tell someone. Plus, if I didn't survive the catastrophe that I was sure was coming, I wanted my parents to know why.

While I told the tale, the food arrived, and yet, no one moved to take a bite. Mom looked physically ill, and a line had formed between Dad's eyebrows.

When I was done, I set my hands in my lap, not sure how to proceed.

Mom broke the silence first.

"Obviously, you're right that your totems have a shared history. While I don't know a lot about Morgan and Merlin and why the totems reacted the way they did the night you saw Ishtar, I have an idea as to what happened during your last warping class," Mom said, her tone tight and emotional.

She glanced at Dad, who gave her a single nod.

Mom sighed. "When I was at the agency, I studied totems. Only a few are as powerful as yours, and even fewer are known to have done what I'm about to tell you." Her gaze shot from the stones on my necklace to Alex's ring. "Your totems were already bound by previous owners, but the night that Alex saved your life—" Her voice broke, and Dad placed a hand over hers.

Mom sniffled, and I felt terrible for telling her about the

ghost banishing and the extremes I'd gone to to save Amethyst.

She sniffled again and wiped her eyes before continuing. "That night, Alex poured his magic into you—a lot of it, if I'm not mistaken. And now some of it lives on inside of you. Your totems now recognize your need to be together. Their understanding of that need was what brought you physically together that night. Not true warping."

My lips parted. It was strange, but it did explain how Alex had simply appeared before me.

"Do you think it worked so easily because I'm a warper?"

Mom shrugged. "Possibly. The few other cases that I researched didn't involve warpers at all. In three of the cases, one person showed up to the other's aid when they needed it, but it was a traumatic experience." Her lips pursed. "Which clearly wasn't the case for Alex—new, perhaps, but not traumatic. You might be onto something, honey. I wonder if it would be easier for you to find Alex in a terrible situation, rather than vice versa?"

"As in, Odie can use the totem's power more easily because she can travel through space, whereas I might only feel the pull?" Alex frowned at the revelation.

I pressed my lips together, knowing exactly why that annoyed him. He was, after all, taking warping lessons so that *he* would be able to find *me* if I needed his help.

"It seems that way," Dad said. "But from what you two have told us about Morgan and Merlin and everything that connects you, who knows? You might be breaking all the rules."

"There seems to be a lot of that going on lately," Mom added. "I'll do more research on the totems and Morgan and Merlin when I get home. Thanks for telling us."

Alex continued to look dejected, and since my parents seemed to have told us all they knew in regards to our totems, I sought to change the subject.

"Speaking of upheaval, did you hear that the shifter Spy Games event has been moved up? I leave the day after we get back to Spellcasters."

Dad's brows furrowed. "Why would they do that, pea?"

"To ensure that the PIA agents who knew about the games before they deserted no longer know the date," I said. "It's a safety precaution."

Mom exhaled softly. "I have to say that makes me feel slightly better. Who knows what these agents are up to or how you two fit into their plans? Everything seems so scattershot, but my intuition is strong that all of this is related."

I felt exactly the same way.

CHAPTER FORTY-TWO

"Our quiz on the poisons discussed today, and their antidotes, will be given next Friday." Professor Bane pointed to the whiteboard, where a list of fifty poisons stared back at me. "I may also throw in a few bonus poisons later next week." The professor's lips twisted up in an evil grin that had half the class groaning.

The owl hooted, dismissing us from the last class of the day, and one by one, my peers stood.

"Until Monday!" Professor Bane threw a wave.

I closed my eyes, trying to squash my rising anxiety. I had two missions coming up, a seemingly never-ending mountain of coursework to complete, and two more Spy Game events—one of which I was leaving for in three hours. To say that I was starting to question my sanity over volunteering for the Spy Games was the understatement of my life.

Five more months, and this will be over. I'll be at an internship of my choosing. That can't possibly be worse than the Grind.

"Take a breath, Odie," Alex whispered as he joined me.

Geez, I must really look like a mess.

Not wanting to look as harried as I felt, I repeated a few calming mantras and took slow calming breaths. When my heart rate slowed, I focused on Alex.

"Trying. How is it that this is only our first day back, and I'm already stressed the hell out?"

"This year has been a lot," Alex rubbed my back. "What do you say we get a little snack, and then you can pack for the Games?"

"Sounds perfect," I said, gripping my stomach.

Our Battle Magic class, combined with a physically rigorous Advanced Demonology session that morning, had me burning through calories. I'd been starving all day, but was told not to eat dinner before we warped to the Shifter School of Spies. As usual, a pre-event feast would be served there.

We left the classroom and wove through the hallways. As we approached the Grind-year tower, people clapped me on the back and wished me luck in the event to come. Of course, not everything was hunky-dory, but overall, almost my entire class believed in me now.

I found it hard to care about the few who didn't, because the support and cheer of everyone else was so infectious. Everyone was getting really excited because after the shifter event, Spellcasters would get our turn to host the

Spy Games. As for me, I just wanted to do them proud and keep Spellcasters in the lead.

With Nightdwellers only two points behind us, it would be a tall order to fill.

After a flurry of squeezing in coursework and packing, I said goodbye to my besties and made my way to Alice Kyteler Hall to warp to the Shifter Academy of Spies. The other champions and our headmistress were already waiting. Andre and Sam chatted merrily, while Diana sat with her back to the wall, scribbling in a notebook.

Apparently, I wasn't the only champion feeling squished for time. My gaze shot to Andre and Sam, who didn't appear to have a care in the world.

I can't wait for Crucible year, when I can get rid of a couple classes.

Professor Tittelbaum created the warphole, and we stepped through. As soon as I emerged onto the other side of the warphole, I pulled my jacket tight to protect from the bitter cold in the air.

The Shifter Academy of Spies was definitely not as austere or beautiful as the fae and vampire academies. It was more like Spellcasters, an impressive manor house, but with fewer flourishes. Although, to account for the needs of the creatures who studied within its walls, the academy did possess an interesting quirk.

On one side of the academy, a massive cave nearly the

height of the school yawned opened wide. On the other side lay a forest heavy with evergreens covered in snow. The difference in environments was stark, but also fitting when one considered that many North American shifters thrived in those environments.

As if he'd smelled us, Alpha Conon stepped out of the woods and made his way to our group.

"Good afternoon," he said and held a hand out to Headmistress Wake. "I'm pleased to have you at my school. Allow me to show you to your rooms so that you might put your bags down."

My lips tugged up in a grin. Like his academy, Alpha Conon was the least flashy of all the heads of schools. Even Headmistress Wake had a flair for drama from time to time, but I'd never witnessed that tendency in the wolf-shifter.

"We'd appreciate that, Alpha," Headmistress Wake said. "Are we the first to arrive?"

He shook his head. "The vampires are already here. I believe the fae will arrive right before dinner. You know how their timelines differ from most magicals'."

It was true. Fae were generally creatures of the afternoon and night.

Alpha Conon led us through the front of the academy. It seemed that most of the shifter students were in their rooms, but the few we passed were definitely sizing us up. I wondered if Dasha and the guys had said anything about us.

While Alpha Conon and Headmistress Wake chatted, I took a moment to absorb my surroundings. In comparison to the other academies, the shifter school was barren of decoration, save for the trees and plants that lined the hallways. Although it was simple, the greenery was a nice touch. And considering that shifters needed time outdoors to maintain their health, it made a lot of sense too. I bet the vegetation saved the sanity of cold-blooded shifters who couldn't brave the frigid winters as easily as their long-furred cousins.

Suddenly, the alpha stopped and gestured us down a hallway. "I expect you will return to your respective academies tomorrow evening, although that depends on your performance during the challenge. Whatever the case, all of the champions will be staying here tonight."

My eyebrows shot up and I shared a glance with Diana.

"Yes. Even the vampires," Alpha Conon said, correctly interpreting our expressions. "One of the aims of the Games is to instill camaraderie. Therefore, you will be in close proximity—as will your heads of academies—*and* share a table at dinner."

Oh great. I adored the fae and shifter champions, but sharing a table with Simone and Francis, or even Magdalena and Anton? *No thank you.*

"I'm not gonna lie, I'm a little worried about sleeping next to the vamps after the Nightdwellers games." Sam voiced a valid concern. "Who knows what kind of shady shit they'll pull?"

Alpha Conon gave her an understanding smile. "I thought you might say that, but do not worry, I have everyone's best interests at heart. The rooms for the Spellcasters students are the first four on the right. Directly across from the shifters, who all have excellent hearing. What's more, each room is equipped with a strong lock, and of course you may ward them at your pleasure. In addition, there will be two shifters on guard all night long. They have pledged to protect each champion, should another try anything dishonorable in the name of competition."

That made me feel better, and assured me that Alpha Conon wasn't blind to what the vampires might do.

"Right then, we'd better prepare," Headmistress Wake said. "What time is dinner?"

"In an hour," Alpha Conon replied. "If you would like to rest or change beforehand, I will leave you to it."

"Thank you, Alpha," Headmistress Wake said, before ushering us to our rooms.

s the Spellcasters champions descended upon the dining hall, I hoped that I wouldn't have to sit next to any of the vampires.

As it turned out, I was fated for disappointment. The fae sat on one side of the table, and the shifters directly across from them. All the champions from those schools gabbed merrily, while the vampires sat in a line facing the crowds. Their eyes were narrowed, and their lips formed a thin line, as if they were trying to intimidate *everyone* in the room and not just the other champions.

And now we get to sit right across from them. Oh joy.

Headmistress Wake motioned for us to join the champions' table, and with Andre in the lead, we walked one by one through the cluster of tables decorated with lush plants and candles. I brought up the rear, and a few shifters smiled at me as I passed. I grinned back, pleased to be welcomed so warmly. When I reached the front, I took the only seat remaining—which of course was directly across from Simone.

Universe help me.

"Hello, witches," Simone said, her goblet of blood pinched between her fingers. "It's about time we had a little chat."

"Maybe. That depends on what you'd like to chat about," I said as I unfolded my napkin.

Unlike at Nightdwellers, there was already food on the table, and as soon as I sat down, people began to dig in. The Shifter Academy of Spies gave fanfare little weight, which considering that I was starving I was pretty stoked about. I slowly began picking out foods and placing them on my plate, my eyes drifting up to Simone for only a moment as I did so.

"But I won't be bullied into talking about anything I don't want to."

Simone's full lips flattened for a moment before she leaned forward. "I don't want to bully you, witch. I want to know how you discovered that fae in Faerie. I went to see him in the dungeons, you know. He was passed out from the iron they had wrapped around him, but nothing smelled or looked off about him. Did he perform dark magic in your presence?"

I could feel the eyes of the shifters and fae watching us, and on the other side of me, I heard Diana snigger.

I made a show of taking a few bites of my food before setting my fork and knife down. When I looked up again, I bit my lip to stop from laughing.

Both Simone's and Francis' faces were so red, it looked as if they might explode at any moment. Even Magdalena and Anton, the more chill of the vamps, appeared stony.

Okay, enough screwing with the vamps, Odie.

I leaned back in my chair. "No, I suppose you wouldn't smell or see the effects of a demon stone, but because I'm demon-touched, I felt it."

My fellow witch champions jerked backward, clearly shocked that I'd admit such a thing. A few gasps came from the fae and shifter end of the table. The vampires, however, seemed unaffected as they studied me—exactly how I thought they'd react.

Inspired by Alpha Conon's talk of camaraderie, I'd thought intensely about coming out as demon-touched while I prepared for the feast. After telling my fellow Spellcasters champions the truth of what being demon-touched meant, it no longer felt like a cloud hanging over my head. Right before leaving my room for the feast, I'd concluded that Alpha Conon was right. We needed each other. So this was a test. Depending on their reactions, I would tell them more, and maybe, in time, we'd become allies.

Finally, after ten seconds of silence that felt like far longer, Francis leaned over the table. "Demon-touched? As in, by a royal?"

I nodded. "Ishtar."

Simone's eyes widened for a heartbeat before she caught herself.

"And my best friend is demon-touched by Lucifer," I added. "Outside the safe walls of our academies, evil is building like never before. The demons want to invade our realm. And because I have a connection to them, I can feel their presence—and that of demon stones."

Anton shook his head. "Why are you telling us this, though?"

I turned to the massive blond. "We're supposed to be building camaraderie here. Obviously, it's also a competition, and I expect that tomorrow, you guys will be all cutthroat as usual. But what I'm talking about is *real* life. You might be affected too. And you should know the truth so that you can save those you love when things start happening." I twisted to make sure that none of the heads of schools were approaching. "These past few months PIA agents have gone missing. I only know of the witches, but perhaps you've learned of others?"

Each champion looked shocked, and then, surprisingly Volwin, Sana's bearded guard who had barely said a word during the Games, spoke.

"Actually, yes. I've heard of fae agents disappearing. My older brother is one of them."

Sana gasped, and her hand gripped Volwin's forearm. "You didn't tell me that!"

Pink bloomed on his pale cheeks as he glanced down at Sana's hand. "Apologies, Lady Torna, but I don't like to burden you with my personal issues."

Hurt flashed across Sana's face. "You could *never* burden me with your problems. We're friends . . . family, really. I don't want you to hide anything from me."

I cleared my throat, not wanting to lose momentum

when I was learning new information. "When did your brother disappear?"

"Two months ago," the fae replied.

My gaze ran across the shifters and vamps. "No one else has heard anything?"

They shook their heads.

"Alpha Conon runs a tight ship," Dasha spoke up for the shifters. "No news gets in or out. We don't even have a cute little town nearby to get news from, like I hear Spellcasters does."

"Neither do we," Magdalena piped up.

"Interesting. We—"

A howl rang from behind me, making me whip around. When I saw what had made the sound, my mouth fell open.

Alpha Conon had shifted into a midnight black wolf the size of a 4-wheeler, and was prowling the dining hall, waiting for everyone to quiet down. Apparently, the Alpha did have a theatrical flair.

"Holy crap," I breathed, then shot a look to Dasha. "Are you that big?" I didn't remember her being so large when she'd transformed at Nightdwellers, but I'd also been pretty preoccupied, and she'd been far away.

She shook her head. "Less than half his size, but I'll fill out. Conon is what wolves like to call an alpha's alpha. He's one of the biggest to have ever lived."

And if the intimidating way he prowled and growled for attention was any indication, one of the most fearsome too. In a matter of seconds, a chattering room full of shifters had quieted. When Alpha Conon shifted back into his human aspect, any residual noise halted with a clap of his hands.

"Tonight, we break bread with the champions from our sister spy schools. Everyone, please join me in welcoming them to the Shifter Academy of Spies."

Polite clapping filled the hall, and everyone at the champions' table waved.

Once he'd decided that we'd been properly respected, Alpha Conon lifted a fist, and the sounds stopped. "Tomorrow, these sixteen students will participate in a challenge at this very school. One that will test their abilities to seek and find, and also determine how well they work as a team. Because as my kind knows, lone shifters often die, but teams—or packs and prides—survive."

"Teams survive," the shifters in the crowd murmured as if they'd done it a million times before.

The alpha turned to face our table, and a wide grin spread across his face. "And tomorrow, your pack will need to work together even more efficiently than usual, for one member will be missing."

My spine straightened. *What?*

"Tonight, after you retire to your chambers, the heads of house will collect one member of each team at four in the morning. That member will be tasked with leaving three, and *only* three, clues for the rest of their team as to their whereabouts. The other team members shall have to find them. Whoever finds their lost team member the fastest wins."

I groaned. This event totally favored the shifters. I bet

they didn't even need to use clues. Especially if Dasha was taken, the guys would be able to sniff her out, no problem.

"The task begins at 5:00 a.m.," Alpha Conon continued. "Due to this, I ask that you finish your meals if you have not already, and retire early. Everyone will want to be up to watch the event." And with that, he retook his seat.

"What the actual fuck. Five in the morning?" Francis flung his head into his hands. "What is wrong with shifters?"

I couldn't help but agree. Seeing as we began dinner later than usual to accommodate the fae, it was already almost nine.

While we wolfed down our meals, the other champions continued to pepper me with questions about demons and demon stones. Since none of it was too personal, and was good information for anyone to know, I did my best to answer while eating.

When the Alpha dismissed the room, everyone rose together. My team and I fell into a discussion about who we hoped would be taken, and how best they could benefit the team. Sam thought Diana was the best choice, but everyone else considered her an optimal pick.

My eyelids were drooping when we turned down the hallway where our rooms were located, and I caught sight of a familiar face.

"Odette!" Leslie ran toward me, smiling brightly. She about barreled me over with a hug, and immediately, I recognized that she was stronger than before.

"Hey, Leslie," I grinned at the girl who'd helped me

escape Crescent Springs. "It's so good to see you here. Dasha told me that you were enrolled. Are you liking it?"

Leslie beamed so brightly, it was like she was a different person from the girl I'd met in Colorado. "Absolutely. I'm never going back to that hellhole."

"Understandable. So, were you waiting to say hello?" I gestured to the door to my room.

Leslie laughed. "No, silly. I'm on first rotation for your guard. I volunteered, and even though I'm still not quite as strong as the other students, Alpha Conon let me. He knows I'd protect you—and the other champions—to my dying breath."

Yeesh, talk about dramatic. "Thanks," I said, "But hopefully that won't be necessary." My mouth opened, and I accidentally released a yawn.

"Oh moons! I'm in your way, and you're probably exhausted!" Leslie stood to the side, allowing us to pass. "Have a good rest, Odette. If the shifter school can't win, I hope your team does."

I locked myself in my room and took a second to relish in the blissful quiet. Then I went about preparing for bed, thankful that Alpha Conon had insisted the feast end quickly, because I was dead on my feet.

At half past nine, I slipped between the sheets and released a happy sigh. My body relaxed, and my muscles softened into the mattress like jello. I could feel that the blissful oblivion of sleep was only a few heartbeats away, so I closed my eyes and willed it to pull me under.

The blackness had almost completely taken me when a

searing pain wrapped around my wrist and radiated up my arm. I sat up with a gasp, and looked at the talisman Alex and I had made. It glowed red and hot in the pitch black of my room. Seconds later, the realization of what that meant crashed over me.

Alex was in danger.

CHAPTER FORTY-FOUR

I burst out of my bedroom door, barefoot and clad in my pajamas. Leslie and the other shifter on guard whirled around to face me.

"Odette! What's wrong?" Leslie scanned the hallway behind me.

"Where's Headmistress Wake staying?" I yelled, not caring if I woke anyone else up.

Alex was in danger, and I needed to find him.

"I can take you to her," Leslie's eyebrows furrowed. "Why don't you put on some shoes, though? The manor is cold."

"I don't need shoes, dammit!" My voice rose. "Take me to her now!"

"I—"

"*Now!*" I roared, and Leslie leapt back.

Doors opened behind me.

"What's happening?" Sam's voice rang out. "Odette?

Are you okay?"

"No. Something's happened to Alex. I need to get to him." I held up my talisman and whirled around.

A soft gasp left me. Every single champion was standing in the hallway in various states of dress and disarray. I gulped, realizing that I was about to spill some more secrets—ones I wasn't sure I was ready to tell everyone. But the alternative of wasting time in saving Alex was too much to bear.

"This burns if he's in danger. I need to find Head-mistress Wake *now*."

"Who do you think took Alex?" Simone asked.

Although she was dressed in a short, *very* sexy silky nightgown, she didn't seem to be embarrassed. If anything, she appeared genuinely curious and even a little worried. It seemed that our dinner discussion had sunk in.

My talisman burned again, hotter and more urgent this time. *Screw it. If I'm in, I'm going all-in.*

"Ishtar. Lucifer. The Furies. Xaphan." I spat out the names with vehemence. With each one, the expressions on the other champions' faces transformed from looks of surprise to fear.

"Wait a minute. You only said you were demon-touched and could find demons and those stones because of it." Francis the Flashy waved his hands in front of his face. "Now you're telling me that the royal demons are after you?"

"Yes. They think that we have the power to open the Hellgate—even before I was demon-touched, they thought that." I turned back to Leslie. "Now can you please tell me where my headmistress is staying? I need to tell her that something is wrong at Spellcasters."

"Follow me," Leslie said, her face about ten shades paler than when I'd busted out of my bedroom. She started speedwalking, and I fell into step behind her.

Footsteps followed, and I twisted to find the champions trailing behind us. I wasn't surprised to see the witches, but the rest . . .

"You guys don't have to—"

"No way," Sana said. "We might not know everything that's happening, but if there's a royal demon threat, I want to be in on stopping it."

"Absolutely. No one messes with my friends," Dasha growled so strongly that I sensed her wolf aspect was simmering just below the surface.

My eyes shot to the vampires. Simone smiled a sly smile. "I too am interested in this royal demon threat. Tell us more."

And so, as we wound down the hallways, I did. I told them about everything except Amethyst's possession. I talked so much that by the time we stopped before a door that I was fairly sure ended in a tower, I was out of breath.

"Holy crap," Howley, the nerdy shifter, breathed.

"No shit." Anton ran a massive hand through his blond hair. "I've lived a century and have not heard a story that wild."

"Well, now you have." I directed my attention to Leslie. "Is this her room?"

Leslie nodded. "This tower is divided into suites, and each head of house has one. They wanted to be close to discuss business, I guess."

I sidestepped her and pounded on the door. Footsteps came from the other side, and an older woman dressed in a dark blue uniform of sorts and holding a used tea set answered.

"May I help you?" Her eyes darted behind me to latch onto Dasha.

"Tins, this is an emergency." Dasha came to stand next to me. Her solid presence was welcome when it felt like everything was crashing down around me. "Can you wake the Spellcasters headmistress—and Alpha Conon too, while you're at it?"

Tins' eyebrows pulled together, and she shook her head. "I wish I could Dasha, but none of the headmasters or head-mistresses are in right now."

"What?" Gregor stepped up next to his mate. "Where did they go?"

Tins shrugged, and the simple gesture stopped my heart. "To do something related to the event tomorrow. I believe half are in the woods, and the other half in the cave system. We can—"

"No. Nevermind. I'll figure it out myself," I cut her off, unwilling to wait a second longer to find Alex.

Pulling away from the group, I began to call my magic, and within seconds, a warphole to Spellcasters—specifi-cally, the Grind-year tower—opened up in front of me. Without hesitating for a moment, I stepped through.

When I entered the Green Tower, I gasped. Hunter and Holly were fighting in the common space.

What the—?

A blast of Hunter's green magic slammed the Culling-year student in the center of her chest. Holly toppled to the floor with a groan, and to my great surprise, Hunter followed a second later.

My heart stopped.

I ran to him, and other footsteps followed. One quick glance behind me told me that every single champion had walked through the warphole after me. It was shocking, but I didn't really have time to dwell on it. I fell to my knees and after I turned Hunter so that he was face-up, my hands flew to my mouth.

A gash at least six inches long tore through his abdomen.

My first thought was to get Alex, but of course he wasn't there. My eyes snapped to Holly, a few feet away.

Her chest was moving up and down, but she was clearly out. I wasn't sure why she'd attacked Hunter, but I had a hunch that it was related to Alex.

I whipped around and my eyes sought Diana's. "Get Eva and Amethyst. And check Alex's room. Fast."

She took off and dashed up the stairs to the spymaster level, while I did my best to close the wound with my hands. "Hunter? Hunter? Can you hear me?"

"This is not Alex?" Anton's cold voice asked from behind me.

"No," Andre replied. "It's his cousin, Hunter. Odette is

friends with him."

"It appears that he's rapidly dying," Simone quipped. "Move aside, witch." She bit into her wrist and suddenly, I understood what she meant to do.

Vampires were generally strict about sharing blood, and for good reason. It had many desirable properties—one of them being miraculous healing abilities. Simone was going to save Hunter.

"Andre! Help us," I said and gestured to Hunter's mouth.

The Crucible student pried Hunter's lips apart just enough so that the vampire could pour a few drops of blood between his lips. Then she moved her wrist down-wards and dripped blood on the wound that I held closed with my hands. Immediately, the gash began to heal, and Hunter's eyes fluttered open.

"Odie?" Hunter asked, his voice cracking as he took in first my face, and then my hands on his body. "How—"

"Shhh, we'll talk about that later. What happened? Why did Holly attack you, and where's Alex?"

As if just remembering what had happened to him, Hunter's eyes grew as wide as saucers and he struggled to get up.

"Whoa, slow down there, pretty boy," Simone said. "My blood is strong, but you still need a few minutes to allow it to work."

"Blood . . ." Hunter's gaze roved over Simone, and she helped him out by exposing her fangs. "Holy shit! Am I vampire?!"

"She just healed you, I promise. Now answer my questions," I snapped, impatiently. "Holly and Alex."

Once again, Hunter's eyes grew wide. "Shit! Alex!" He looked around as if his cousin should be right next to him, and then, fearfully, his eyes found mine. "I don't know where he is. Eva turned in early and I was coming down here to study when Alex and Holly burst through the door. It looked like he was running from her. Some weird shit happened—I think I saw a flash of white and then Alex just . . . disappeared." Hunter shook his head.

"But what about Holly?"

"She seemed happy about it," Hunter said slowly. "And then she attacked me. But I don't know why."

I had a hunch, but was saved from responding, because at that moment, Amethyst, Eva, and Diana showed up. Eva dropped down beside me and began tending to Hunter.

"Alex didn't answer his door, and I didn't hear a sound. I don't think he's in there," Diana panted, out of breath from running up and down six flights of stairs at top speed.

"I know," I replied as I stood and turned to Amethyst.

"I think Holly's possessed by a royal demon's ghost, and the ghost sent Alex somewhere against his will. Can you tell me if she's possessed or has been?"

Amethyst wasted no time running over to Holly. I followed, and together we dropped to our knees and flipped Holly onto her back. Amethyst's hands began traveling the length of the girl's body, and despite being right next to her, I couldn't hear the incantations she quietly murmured.

But when she gasped and jerked backward, I sure as hell heard that.

"What happened?" I asked, my heart thumping hard.

Amethyst's brown eyes latched onto mine, frantic. "You were right. A possessed ghost—I can't tell which of the royals possessed it—was living inside her. It's done a lot of damage. Honestly, it's a miracle she's still breathing. She must have an aptitude for spirit walking and talking." Amethyst's gaze dropped to the girl sadly, and even though Holly had just sent Alex to God only knew where, I felt a little bad for the girl too. I doubted that she knew what she'd gotten herself into.

"She'll be okay, though?" I asked Amethyst. "Is the ghost gone?"

My friend nodded. "Yes on both accounts. If Alex is gone too, I bet the ghost transported him through the spirit realm. It's kind of like warping, but only ghosts and their passengers can do it." Amethyst gulped. "We should get her to the infirmary quickly so the healer can assess her health."

"Right," I said. "Do you think she'd be able to tell us where she sent Alex?"

Amethyst shook her head. "I doubt it. It will probably take hours or days for her to even wake up."

I bit my lip. There was no way I was sticking around for hours until Holly regained consciousness. I needed to act now.

"Odette," someone spoke up behind me, and I turned to find Diana watching me.

"Yeah?" I asked, my mind still on the issue of getting out of the tower to wherever Alex was and saving him.

"I told you once that if shit went down, you needed to ask me for help. Is now that time? Because if it is," Diana gestured back to the champions, some of whom were huddled over Hunter, and some whom were watching me.

My eyebrows furrowed when I noticed that Sam and Andre seemed to be missing, but I didn't have a second to question it because Diana kept talking.

"You have a squad behind you. The fae, shifters, . . . shit, even the *vampires* want to help."

"Try not to sound so surprised," Simone said coldly.

Diana rolled her eyes. "We're all behind you. Sam and Andre have already gone to get their hell blades. I grabbed mine upstairs. We're ready. What do we need to do?"

I stared into her serious blue eyes as the seconds ticked on. Things were coming to a head, I could feel it. But most of these people had just learned what was going on. Did they truly realize how dangerous helping me would be?

"Seriously," Diana urged. "Let us help."

As if her final words broke the spell, I nodded and gestured to Holly. "Someone help Amethyst get Holly to the infirmary. I'm going to grab some shoes and clothes I can fight in. I'll get stuff for the others too." My eyes flitted to Simone in her silk nighty. It would not do for what I suspected was about to go down. "Once everyone returns, we're going to find Alex."

CHAPTER FORTY-FIVE

*B*y the time the vampires and Amethyst returned from taking Holly to the infirmary, I had a plan.

And holy universe, I hoped that it worked.

"If you want to come, get behind me," I instructed.

I waited and was shocked to find that every single champion and Amethyst moved to stand at my back.

Tears threatened to cloud my vision. After I spilled the truth of what was happening, I thought that it would only be only a matter of time before the others ditched and only Eva and Hunter remained. They would have been enough, but to know that others believed me meant a lot. Although I still wasn't sure they understood just how dangerous it would be—which was something I needed to rectify immediately.

"You know you don't have to. I won't judge—"

"No way, witch," Simone cut me off. "You aren't getting

rid of any of us, so stop trying. Amethyst expanded on your story. She told us all about the first ghost. It seems like this is the real deal. The calm before the storm, if you will." The black-haired vampire looked to her teammates. "This is what we've all trained to do, and we're coming too."

"The shifters second that," Dasha stepped forward.

"The fae are in too," Ayla piped up for her crew.

My gaze trailed over the witches.

"We're all in," Diana said firmly. "Every single one of us has been affected by the demons trying to cross over in one way or another. We want to help."

"Then I'm going to call a warphole," I said not about to beg them to rethink it. I respected them too much to do that. "It will be unlike any I've done before."

"How so?" Andre stepped up to stand next to me, presumably to help, although in this instance, he wouldn't be able to.

I pulled my totem out from under the long-sleeved shirt I wore. "I'm going to use this to guide me to Alex. We did it once, when I was trying to teach him to warp."

Andre's eyes bugged out at that admission, but I didn't have time to explain so I kept talking.

"Just let me go through first. I'll call back if it's safe. If you don't hear me . . ." I trailed off, unsure what to say, because I had no clue what would happen if I screwed up.

"We're with you," Amethyst said.

I turned my back to them and gripped the totem with one hand. Never having asked Alex exactly how his totem had deposited him next to me during our lessons, I wasn't sure what had happened, but I could make an educated guess. Our totems seemed to give us what we needed to survive, when we needed it. All we had to do was ask.

And if I could help it along, all the better.

Extending my other hand, I began manipulating the energies around me to create a warphole. Once I felt the shift, the mixture of heat and cold that signified I was making a portal, I requested assistance.

Please, take me to Alex. Wherever he is, I need to go there and save him.

The change was instantaneous. A flash of mixed fuchsia and crimson light blasted through the tower. I closed my eyes, and my friends cried out. The light didn't let up. I was just about to open my eyes and see what was happening when I felt the energy of my warphole ripple across my skin, hot then cold, and darkness washed over me.

Seconds later, everyone in the Green Tower was deposited into a dirty cobblestone alley.

"I thought you said we'd have to walk through the warphole," a voice—Anton's, I think—asked.

"I did. Apparently, I was wrong." I twisted to look at the group. "Seems like we're all fine, though."

Francis chuckled. "Good to know you're so concerned with our well-being."

"I am," I said. "But out of everyone here, you four can definitely take care of yourselves."

Vampires were practically indestructible and excellent fighters. And even though I wasn't exactly sure where we stood on the friends-to-enemies scale, having them behind me was quelling my nerves.

"So where are we?" Sana asked as she glanced around and rubbed her arms with her hands to warm them.

I followed her gaze, taking in the buildings that climbed to the sky on either side of us. Two cars drove by at the end of the alley. A faint scent of fried food was in the air, and wherever we were, it was definitely nighttime.

"If the voices I hear a few streets over are any indication, we're in the UK," Magdalena offered and tilted her head. "Most likely London, judging by the regional accents."

The passage Diana had pointed out to me earlier that year ran through my mind. My jaw tightened momentarily.

London. Of freaking course we're in London.

"If that's where we are, I have a hunch where we need to go. Anyone here know London like the back of their hand?"

Anton stepped forward. "I lived here for half a century. Only moved about five years ago."

"Perfect," I said.

Having the vampires in my corner was proving to be more beneficial than I ever could have imagined. I was happy that I'd followed my intuition and told them the truth.

I pointed to the end of the alley. "Let's get onto that street. From there, we need to find the Thames."

We emerged onto the main street and upon seeing a red phone booth, confirmed that we were indeed in London. After that Anton zipped through the side streets so fast that all the non-vampires struggled to keep up. We'd been sprinting for about five minutes straight when I begged him to stop for a moment so I could catch my breath.

And that's when I saw it, illuminated by a pub's single outdoor light.

A wisp of black smoke trailing around a corner.

Someone in the group gasped, and I whirled about to see Eva's hand fly to her scar. My attention dropped to my ankle and through the cold, damp winter chill of the London night, I could feel a slight burning of my demon mark.

Demons were nearby.

"If you have a weapon get it out," I hissed.

The others, particularly the fae and shifters, looked concerned.

"Here?" Sana squeaked. "In the middle of the city?"

"Yes, I—Oh *shit!*" I reared back as glimmering black smoke on the wind flew by my face.

A growl quickly followed, and I spun to see a race of demon I didn't recognize prowling around the corner. He bared twenty sharp rows of teeth, and vicious claws snapped out of his hands.

Ayla, the closest to it, noticed the beast right after me and screeched.

"Spread out and surround it!" I yelled, but as it turned out, I didn't really need to take the lead.

Luvon, Ayla's sworn guard, was already in motion to protect the royal fae. His wings snapped out of the jacket he wore, and he soared toward the demon and ripped its head clean off. The second the head and body separated, the demon went up in smoke, leaving not a trace behind.

Bile climbed up my throat, and I twisted away, trying to stop the reaction. Behind me, I heard puke splatter on the ground and gagged.

"Thank you, Luvon," Ayla said, and a few others echoed her gratitude.

I wiped my mouth, and decided that I needed to toughen up. Decapitation was extreme, but clearly, it got the job done.

Finally composed, I turned back to face the fae guardian. "Yes, thank you. Now does anyone know what the hell that thing was?"

Blank stares met my eyes, and my stomach sank. I'd been holding out hope that someone would be able to identify the race of the demon. That they couldn't was ominous.

I couldn't help but think that we might have just encountered a new breed of demon—perhaps offspring of the royals. But since I didn't know for sure, I didn't mention it. There was no need to scare anyone. I had a feeling that there would be enough fear and terror tonight without me adding to it.

"Let's keep moving toward the river." I nodded at Anton, who once again led the way.

Less than five minutes later, I caught a glimmer of water through the densely-packed buildings, and stopped the team. "We're almost there. Be careful, and when we get to the waterway, look for a guy with black hair and glasses—

that's Alex." My heart squeezed hard at the thought of finding him.

Everyone nodded, and we crept closer to the riverwalk. When we reached it, I inched my way to the edge of a building and peeked around the corner.

All the breath flew from my lungs.

We were in so much trouble.

CHAPTER FORTY-SIX

"Get your weapons out," I whispered, taking in the wall of magicals that stood about one hundred yards away.

Even at that distance, I could sense a strong shifter vibe wafting off of the line. The effect was reinforced by their tough-guy stances, arms crossed and scowls on their faces. Not one of them spoke or glanced at the person next to them. It was as if they were on guard.

Or waiting for someone.

I turned to my group. "There's twenty-plus magicals out there. Judging by the magical energy radiating from them, most are shifters. They're guarding something on the river-walk. If anyone wants to back out now, there's no shame in leaving."

"Is Alex there?" Hunter craned his neck as if he could see through the brick building.

"I can't see him, but I'm fairly certain that they're

waiting for me. If that's true, they know I'm coming for Alex." My gaze scanned the crowd. No one had moved so much as an inch. They were still in.

Their loyalty made my throat tighten, but I did my best to push the emotion aside. I needed to save all my feelings so I could perform some freaking amazing battle magic.

"I don't know what's past the line of shifters. It could be more adversaries. Be prepared for that."

"Yeah, yeah, yeah." Simone cracked her knuckles. "Let's just do the damn thing."

"Shifters should be cake," Francis added and shot a sly glance at our shifters, who wisely chose not to react to his taunt.

For the first time, I was thankful for the vampires' huge egos. At least someone thought this would be easy.

"We're ready, Odie," Eva pressed.

I gave a single nod. "Okay. The witches will go first and put up a shield. We'll try to protect everyone with it for as long as we can."

Shields bloomed from the hands of my peers, and as soon as the other magicals were behind us, we broke around the corner and sprinted for the shifters.

The moment our opponents noticed us, their eyes flashed crimson, making my stomach drop. *They have demon stones on them.* Right away, half shifted, and tigers, bears, wolves, and even a wolverine appeared.

"Careful! They have demon stones! We should attack them first," I yelled. Fighting off a bear-shifter whose hide was imbued with protective magic and bolstered by a demon stone's power would be a major feat. We needed the advantage of first move.

Hunter took a shot and hit a shifter who was mid-transformation. The limbo state made him vulnerable, and the lion-shifter collapsed to the ground.

Magic flew from all the witches' hands as our opponents charged toward us. Four other shifters went down fast. But those still in human form remained still, too far away for us to attack, while the others in animal aspect were coming ever closer as they dodged our attacks.

We were within twenty feet of the beasts, and I was preparing to blast them with battle magic, when the vampires flew by our front line.

What the hell?

My breath hitched as each vampire, moving so fast they were a blur, flung themselves onto an animal and sank their fangs into their necks.

The bitten shifters let out a piercing wail, and then, to my surprise, exploded in a cloud of black smoke.

Well, I'll be damned. I—

My heart lodged into my throat, and I nearly stopped running. The next round of shifters transformed and rushed forward to fight, leaving a large gap in the center of their line. The person they'd been protecting was now visible.

My breath hitched as I saw Alex lying prone on the ground. David Chena stood over him, watching the fight with the Realm Slicer in his hand.

The shield in front of me faltered and then dropped altogether as fear and fury took over. My vision tunneled, and I sprinted forward, attacking and defending myself on autopilot. I fought my way through the shifters, punching, hurling magic, and stabbing them with my demon dagger —all with one common goal.

To get to Alex.

Bam!

A huge body slammed into me from the side, and a screech ripped up my throat as I fell to the ground. A second later a bear appeared above me, his paws on both sides of my arms and his stinky breath flowing straight into my nostrils. The bear swiped a massive paw.

I rolled out of the way just in time to hear the scrape of claws on cobblestone. Reacting quickly, I hurled my power at him. With only inches between us, it should have at least stunned the beast, but he didn't even blink.

Shit, shit, shit!

I rolled to the other side and tried to shimmy out from under his chest, but the bear's massive paw slapped me so that I was forced squarely beneath him again. His teeth were inches from my face.

I'm a goner, I—

Suddenly, where the bear had been, there was only a massive cloud of black smoke.

I coughed, trying to clear my lungs.

When the smoke cleared, Andre stood over me, a hell blade in one hand while the other one was extended to me. "You okay?"

"Yeah, thanks," I said, accepting his help to stand. As soon as I was up, my gaze searched for Alex.

Chena was squatting over him, pulling the Realm Slicer, now dripping blood, from Alex's arm.

Oh crap. I need to get to him, and fast.

I called all the surrounding magical energies to me, and was two seconds away from making a warphole, when Chena slammed the blade into the ground. I watched, wide-eyed as the area beneath Alex began to shimmer, and he sank through the riverwalk.

"Nooooooo!" I screamed and thrust my hands toward Chena. A veritable blaze of power soared across the space between us.

The traitor spymaster barely had time to look up before my magic hit him, and he crumpled to the floor.

"Odie! Where'd Alex go?" Eva asked, running up to me.

Her presence snapped me out of my trance, and I cast a wild, defensive, glance around. We were kicking our opponents' asses. The demon blades and the vampires had made a bigger difference than I ever could have imagined. Only three shifters remained fighting in animal aspect, and the fae and our shifters were tag-teaming them.

Eva gripped my arm. "I saw Alex, and now he's gone!"

"I saw him too," Magdalena came up behind me. "But I can no longer see or smell him. It's like he vanished into thin air."

I shook my head, and a lump rose in my throat, alongside the words I never thought I'd say.

"No. Not thin air. Alex is in Hell, and I'm going after him."

"What?!" Hunter yelped, and I jumped because I hadn't realized that he was behind me. "How?"

I pointed to Chena, lying motionless on the ground, the Realm Slicer at his side. "If he can use the Realm Slicer, I can too. If it doesn't work for me, I'll figure out how to warp there. I have to."

"Well you're not going alone," Eva said.

"No, Eva, . . . I am. No one is going with me." I twisted to face Hunter. "Here, take my demon blade. When I come back with him, I bet there will be more demons."

Hunter shook his head. "No way, Odie. I'm going too."

I fought their ludicrous wishes, but in the end, no one would let me get close to the Realm Slicer unless I allowed them to join me. All the witches except for Sam and Andre would join me in Hell. As would Simone and Francis. Magdalena and Anton wanted to come too, but the other vampires pulled rank. They insisted that we would need them here when we reemerged, which was probably true. I had a feeling that when we returned, we'd probably have a demonic tail following us.

"Why do you guys even want to go?" I asked Simone and Francis as I bent to pick up the Realm Slicer.

"Demons are disgusting, and we don't want them in this world either, but their blood is good. I want first dibs," Simone admitted with a shrug. "Plus, we're lethal and practically indestructible. Who better to fight them?"

Touché.

I faced those who would stay behind. "The rest of you, be ready to fight. In fact," my eyes found Andre. "We'll need backup. Can you warp to Spellcasters and wake the professors? Tittelbaum first, so he can send people as you alert them."

Andre looked unsure, but nodded.

"Go then," I said. "But first, give the others your demon blade, in case you don't make it back in time."

Diana and I were leaving ours with the fae. They would do us no good in Hell. On the contrary, if they glowed red like they did in Chena's presence, they'd give us away. There was a *tiny* chance that we could pass as cambions—half-human, half demonic offspring—in the underworld, but not if we traveled with blades meant to kill demons. When the moment came to fight we would have to rely on vampire strength and the incantations we'd learned to protect ourselves.

"Have the professors notify the other heads of schools too," Dasha said. "Everyone needs to know."

Ayla stepped forward. For the first time, I noticed that she was absolutely covered in blood. "We can help too," the fae said and gestured for her sister to join her.

I shook my head. "I already told you, I can't risk anyone else coming. The group is already larger than I'd like."

"We understand. We'll remain here and fight, but Sana and I can still help you in Hell." She lifted her hand, and it began to glow.

I'd only ever seen fae use elemental powers. "What are you doing?"

"Using aether to create a glamour for you guys. Hoping that someone will think you're cambions just isn't going to work. Now stay still. It's hard to make these so fast. We'll have to tag-team it."

Light poured from the Torna sisters as they worked. The blaze they directed at me made me squirm. It was uncomfortable, mainly because it reminded me of the day I'd almost died and the tunnel of light. Still, I allowed them to create the glamours. Even though every cell in my body wanted to barrel forward and save Alex, we had to be smart. Who knew how many thousands of demons were in Hell? If spending a couple extra minutes on a disguise meant the difference between success and death, I'd bear it. We needed all the help we could get.

I knew the exact moment the magic settled over me. It felt like I'd slipped a glove over my body. "Will this hinder our magic in any way?" I asked as the sisters moved on to glamour Eva.

"No," Luvon answered because the girls were sweating with how much energy they were exerting. "Your magic will work as it always has. The only difference is you no longer look like yourself."

"What do I look like?"

Volwin offered the demon blade I'd given him, and I angled it at a street lamp. The lighting was low, but I didn't need much to see the changes.

A seductive succubus with red eyes, crimson lips, moon white skin, and raven-black hair stared back at me. "I look like a demonic Snow White."

"Yeah, well, check me out," Eva quipped.

I looked up to find that my best friend had grown at least six inches and was now the most buxom of blondes.

"Like a playboy bunny," I said, almost laughing despite the direness of the hour as Eva suggestively swung her new, wider hips.

The twins learned to work faster with each glamour they applied. Once they finished, our group was comprised of two succubi and five lesser demons.

"We weren't able to make you all beautiful," Sana said, throwing an apologetic glance at Diana and Amethyst. "It would be too suspicious if a bunch of greater demons were together. Even two succubi might be pushing it, but—"

"It's better than five witches and two vamps," I cut her off, not about to let them apologize for disguising us.

"True, and we made sure to differentiate the wraiths." Ayla pointed out that Diana had black hair while Amethyst's was more gray.

Hunter was a daeva, which generally looked human-like but had a distinct gray tinge to their skin. While at first glance, his glamour seemed to have been simpler, it wasn't. Actually, the twins' magic was even more astounding where Hunter was concerned because when he opened his mouth wide green gas floated out of it to mimic the noxious fumes daevas produced.

Simone and Francis were also easy to identify because the twins had transformed them into imps that looked like small, ugly versions of the vampires.

"You guys did great. Thanks for giving us a leg up. In fact, thank you all for coming with us." I gave the fae, shifters, remaining vampires, and Crucible-years a grateful smile—a smile that I hoped was not my last. "It's time for us to go."

I turned to my team. "Those who are going to Hell, place a hand somewhere on me. Everyone else, stay way back. I don't want to bring you on accident."

Everyone did as I said, and once we were in position, I gripped my totem. I hoped that between it and the Realm Slicer, I'd get where I needed to go.

My eyes closed as I thought back to de Spina's conjuring of Hell. In my mind's eye, I zeroed in on the center circle—and the ominous thrones of bones. When it was cemented in my mind, I took the Realm Slicer and sliced open my shoulder. Alex's blood was already on the blade, and I added mine to the mix. Only once the blade was absolutely covered with blood, I knelt. Gripping my totem tight, I begged for help, for it to take me to the throne room—to Alex.

And then, I placed the blade's bloodied tip to the ground, and everything around me vanished.

CHAPTER FORTY-SEVEN

The moment we reappeared, the stench of sulfur made me gasp. I coughed as greenish steam infiltrated my lungs, and heat pummeled my skin. And yet, despite all the distractions, everyone in my crew fell back on their training and went on alert.

The vampires crouched and bared their fangs, while the witches thrust their hands out in front of them, prepared to strike. If anyone had been around, the reflexive actions would surely have given away our true natures.

But no one was there.

No one, that is, except for Alex.

I dropped the Realm Slicer and the sound of metal hitting stone reverberated through the room as a sob wrenched out of my throat. Alex was sprawled out on the black stone floor in front of the thrones of bones. A thin moat of lava ran around the thrones just inches from his body. Even from where I stood at the entrance to the throne room, I could see the deep gash on his chest and how blood pooled around him. His beautiful blue eyes were closed.

Was he already dead?

No. Surely not. I would feel that, I thought as I rushed toward him, jumped over the lava barrier that separated the thrones from the larger chamber, and fell to my knees. The gash was deep, making me wonder if they'd been trying to reach his heart. He still breathed, but shallowly.

"This is Alex?" someone behind me asked.

All I could do was nod my head. My heart was breaking into a million little pieces seeing him like this—not knowing if I could save him.

My crew approached and Eva, Hunter, and Amethyst joined me on the floor. Eva wrapped her arm around me, while Amethyst placed her hand on Alex's chest.

"His soul is still there," Amethyst whispered after a moment. "He's alive."

"He'll be okay, Odie," Eva assured me. "We'll get him out of here and fix him up."

"Not unless you plan on acting quickly." Francis moved to stand opposite me. "His heartbeat is weak—too weak to move him. I can give him blood to help his healing. If he's as important to the fate of our world as you say, it would be an honor."

I looked up at Francis and then at the horrific room we found ourselves in. Fire and black stones that jutted out of the ground littered the vast space. The brightest objects were the bones upon which the monarchs sat, and the acrid stench of blood and sulfur and death and fear infiltrated my nostrils, making my heart race. We were in the very center of Hell, and everything about this place was terrifying. We needed to leave as quickly as possible.

"Please. Please do it, I—"

"You'll die down here!" A waterfall of cackles rang out, sending chills down my spine.

Francis' head snapped up, and he took a step back. "Oh shit."

I tensed. Anyone that made a vampire recoil like that couldn't be good. I desperately wanted to be a coward and just sit with Alex until he healed, but I knew that couldn't be. So I gathered all my courage, and twisted to see who had discovered us.

Three women, all as blonde and beautiful as they were horrible, strutted around at the entrance to the throne room. Metal glinted in a burst of flames that shot out of the ground, and my heart stopped. One of them held the Realm Slicer.

Mentally, I cursed myself for being so stupid as to drop the thing. On the outside, however, I kept my cool as I stood and placed my body in front of Alex.

"You think you can save him, pretty?" the woman holding the blade waved it in the air.

I pressed my lips together in defiance.

The woman snorted and pointed the tip of the Realm Slicer at me. "You're brave, that's for sure, but you won't be saving that boy. Not if the Princesses of Hell have anything to say about it."

The realization of just who these women were slammed into me, making my breath hitch.

The Furies.

The story went that the Furies—the ancient goddesses of retribution and vengeance—had once been obsessed with stamping out sins and violent acts against the gods. But the less their followers believed in them, the more vengeful the Furies became. Then, in a massive screw-you to the humans who abandoned them, the ex-goddesses joined up with Lucifer and Xaphan, a fallen angel, to live in the underworld. In the pits of Hell, the Furies were all-powerful once again as the three-in-one demon figurehead and princesses of the underworld.

Involuntarily, I began to tremble. Things were bad —*very* bad.

"That's better," cooed another one of the Furies as she eyed my trembling form. "Proper respect, that is." She smiled, and something dark in nature and oily slithered over my skin.

"Not only are they intruders who brought exactly what we needed," the third Fury purred. "They're also not who they seem." She brought her hands out in front of her, palms out, and then flung them away from each other, toward the side walls.

The fae glamour ripped off of me in one quick stroke, leaving me breathless.

"Thought they could fool us!" A Fury screamed. "Maybe a stupid wraith but not princesses of darkness!"

She cackled and the other two princesses burst into laughter too.

I took advantage of their distraction, whipping around and gesturing to Francis and Simone, who like everyone else, had been de-glamoured. "Heal Alex," I hissed.

When I twisted to face the Furies once again, the one holding the Realm Slicer was watching me with narrowed eyes. "I *know* you. Now that you're uncovered, I can *feel* your mark. You're the one dear Ishy is looking for, aren't you?"

"No," I lied.

Another Fury flicked a finger down at my ankle. My mark burned as if I'd stepped into a barrel of flames and a scream flew up my throat as I collapsed.

"Yes, yes you are, little witchy," the first Fury said, as an evil grin spread across her face. "We should probably tell sweet Queen Ishy that you're here. Or perhaps we just take you to her?"

Suddenly, black tendrils of magic flew from each of the demons. Hunter and Amethyst went on the attack as my heart leapt into my throat. Knowing we had to leave before this got out of hand, I scampered backward until I nudged Alex.

"Francis! How much time?"

Francis was watching the tendrils too, his eyes wide with horror as blood dripped from his wrist into Alex's mouth. "He needs more blood to regain consciousness quickly. The chest wound needs to close more too, or else he might die in transit." He gestured down to where Simone was applying drops of her blood to Alex's wound.

"Our blood is strong, but we need at least a minute," she said, not even bothering to look up from Alex's chest.

Shit, I thought as I shot up from the ground and thrust my hands out so I could help my friends. A blaze of fuchsia flew from my fingertips to deflect a stream of encroaching tendrils. Sunshine yellow and purple magic followed as Eva and Diana vanquished two tendrils that had been creeping toward us from the sides of the room.

My eyes snapped away from where the magic had been advancing, back to the Furies, and all the hair on my arms lifted. Only two stood at the entrance of the room.

Where did the third one go?

The answer presented itself as the ground beneath my feet began to rumble. My throat closed up, and sweat dripped down my face.

The blade had my and Alex's blood on it. She left to use the Realm Slicer. We have to get out of here and help those above! Over the sound of rock grinding on rock, I shouted, "Francis! Can we move him now?"

The Furies were pointing and laughing. They recognized the fear in my eyes and they loved it.

"Almost! He—"

"It doesn't matter where you meet our sweet Ishy, girl! She'll find you, and when she does . . ." One of the Furies' perfect lips spread in a horrible smile. "Ishy is ready to have some fun in your world—starting with *you.*"

My heart leapt into my throat. "Everyone to Alex!"

Diana, Eva, and Hunter blasted off a few more spells and retreated to join us. I shoved Simone to the side when I reached Alex.

"We're out of time," I said.

"I don't think he's ready yet," she said, and glanced down at the wound that her blood had been slowly closing.

I shook my head. "He has to be. They have the Realm Slicer."

"The what?"

"It creates holes between worlds that people . . . creatures . . . can travel through. They've already opened a portal to our world."

Somehow, Simone's ivory skin paled even more. "Well, what are you waiting for, witch?"

I began manipulating a warphole. Doubt that I could make one here, in a different realm, rushed through me, but I had to try. And perhaps because Hell and my world were merging, I was met with less resistance than I thought possible. In fact, while the energies of Hell felt different, they almost felt right—*familiar*.

My eyes darted down to my still-burning demon scar, the likely culprit for these disturbing thoughts. In response, it seared even hotter, and a thrill of pleasure ran through me.

Eva gasped, and her eyes caught mine. "Did you just feel something?"

I gulped. "Lucifer and Ishtar. They know we're here." I didn't know how I knew that. I just did. The understanding only added to my desire to get the eff out of there. I pushed my magic hard, and in response a warphole whooshed open.

"*Go!*" I screamed.

My allies didn't waste a second, and began jumping through. Before Francis could disappear, I stopped him.

"Help me lift Alex?"

"Help? We don't have time to be gentle." Francis gestured to where the Princesses of Hell stood.

A stream of profanity left my mouth. A wall of flame was barreling toward us. Just in front of it, hundreds of smoke-black demons with fire blossoming from their mouths—ifrits—charged.

"Come on," Francis said, yanking me from my horror as he darted past me, Alex hanging lifelessly in his arms.

I rushed to follow, leaping through the warphole and closing the portal behind me. A dim sense of relief shone through the fear. I'd done it. We were out of Hell—safe. I exited the warphole and stepped onto cobblestone, breathing in the cold of London as it washed over me once more.

Hands gripped me protectively—Eva's. I was about to turn and tell Francis where to set Alex when a boom rang out and a stone's throw away the Thames split open.

CHAPTER FORTY-EIGHT

The roar of demons spewing out of the Hellgate was so loud that my knees began to quake. Tears pricked in my eyes as winged beasts zoomed out one after the other.

The fae and shifters stood a ways away, their mouths hanging open, and bodies stiff with horror.

Andre wasn't there. Perhaps he'd never made it all the way to Spellcasters. At this point, it hardly mattered.

We could never fight and conquer this many demons.

A groan sounded behind me, followed closely by Alex murmuring my name. My heart leapt, and I spun to face him.

Still cradled in Francis' arms, his eyes were fluttering open. He was waking. *Thank the universe, I'll get to say goodbye.*

"Put him down," I said, not wanting a vampire hovering over us during such a private moment.

Francis complied, his gaze locked on the swarm of demons circling the night sky. They swooped above the Thames, waiting for someone—or multiple someones—to join them.

"Everyone should leave," I said, kneeling and taking Alex's hand in mine to assure him that I was there. "Vampires, take the witches on your backs, if you can. Alert all the magicals you know about what happened." I gestured to the cloud of devils growing ever larger. "We can't beat this."

Simone's gaze snapped to me. "And what of you? I thought you two were supposed to save the world?" Her eyes were narrowed, as if I'd tricked her into coming here.

"*I'm* staying here to try to do just that," I retorted.

"You're *not* staying, Odie," Hunter interceded, his brows pulled tightly together.

A roar cut through the air, and my demon scar burned, making me gnash my teeth together. Of course, I didn't *want* to stay here, but I knew my role in all this. The time had come for me to fulfill a destiny started by Morgan and Merlin, and I had to face it. I kissed Alex's forehead before standing and turning to face the river.

Small stone platforms were rising from the churning waters. Demons who couldn't fly were positioned on them, snarling and growling and howling excitedly. In the center, on the largest stone platform circled by fire, six devils rose. Three were the Furies. On the other side of the dais, another figure hyped up the demons around him. His black wings were spread and glimmered in the moonlight. That had to be Xaphan, Prince of Hell.

Lucifer and Ishtar stood in the middle, their hands twined together, and smiles on their faces. Ishtar wasn't as large as she had been when I met her in New York. But with curled horns, black-blue wings, and blue skin, she was just as terrifying as I remembered. Lucifer looked much like Ishtar, except red and larger.

"Everyone, *go*," I choked out. "There's no fighting this."

The demons hadn't seemed to notice us yet, which meant the others could still escape. But Alex and I never would—perhaps not Eva, either. She would always be bound to Lucifer.

My heart clenched for my friend, and I hoped that for tonight, at least, she could remain free.

Only Alex and I had to stay. We . . . or I, seeing as he still wasn't completely conscious yet, had to try and finish the job meant for us. I hoped I was strong enough.

Francis eyed me thoughtfully before giving a single nod. "Good luck to you, witch. And believe me, we won't stop fighting the devils."

"Never," Simone added.

"Take them with you," I gestured to Amethyst, Diana, Hunter, and Eva.

Francis reached for Eva, but she batted his hand away.

"I'm sticking with Odie. Take Amethyst." She pointed to the spirit talker, who was trembling so hard that I doubted she'd even heard Eva.

This time, the vampire didn't hesitate. Francis scooped up the spirit talker before she could protest and dashed off.

"I'm staying, too," Hunter said before either vampire could move toward him.

Simone took a step in Diana's direction, but the head-mistress' daughter shook her head.

"Get Sam."

Simone gave Diana a long look before complying, darting over to the other group, and snapping up Sam as if she weighed no more than a baby. I watched as Sam thrashed in Simone's arms, but the vampire didn't acknowledge it, as she and Francis spoke to the other champions.

Immediately, the shifters shifted, and the fae's glamours disappeared to reveal wings. The wolves sprinted away, the fae flew to hide in the city, and the vampires retreated so fast, they were nothing but a blur. They were safe—for now.

I turned to Diana, Hunter, and Eva. "Go. Seriously. There's nothing—"

"You're going to try to close the Hellgate, aren't you?" Diana interrupted me. "With him? Because he's of Merlin's blood?" She gestured to Alex, who groaned again.

I nodded, aware of how stupid it sounded.

Alex's eyes weren't even fully open. How was he going to help me do what we were meant to do?

"It's not going to work," Diana spoke my fears out loud. "Put a shield over him. I'll help you."

"Me too," Hunter and Eva said in unison.

No . . . This wasn't how I wanted this to end. "Guys, I—"

"*Stop*, Odie," Eva commanded. She lifted a finger to tell me off, but a *crack* sounded, and a roar filled the night air, swallowing her words. Eva's jaw hardened at the interruption. "You're not getting rid of us. Now help us make a shield over Alex before they stop grandstanding."

There wasn't time to argue, so I yielded, and fuchsia magic mixed with yellow, purple, and green. Our power wove together to create a shield around Alex.

"That will not keep us out," a voice boomed the second the shield was in place. "You realize that, mortal?"

I sucked in a breath, and my eyes roved over my brave friends. "Distract them while I work," I whispered before turning to face my nightmare.

Immediately, I jerked back. Ishtar and Lucifer were much closer than I'd thought, only twenty or so yards away. The Prince and Princesses of Hell stood flanking them, and the swarm of demons that had flown out of the Hellgate hovered over the riverwalk. In the center of the Thames, more devils poured out of Hell by the second, adding to the army of at least one hundred. Over one hundred to five. Those odds were not good.

But at least one thing was in our favor.

With the royals intensely focused on us, the Hellgate was practically wide open.

"Oh, she knows a little shield can't stop us, Lucifer. This one is simply obstinate," Ishtar said, her familiar voice lifting the hair on the nape of my neck. "But that stubborn pride will end tonight. I am here, and as I am her master, she *will* bow to me."

My mark began to burn hotter than ever before, and I gasped. Against my will, my torso bent toward the ground.

I tried to stop it, to force myself back up, but I couldn't. I wasn't strong enough. Not compared to the Queen of Hell.

Ishtar boomed out a laugh that went on and on and on.

I gnashed my teeth together. The center stone on my necklace flared bright fuchsia and taking the hint, I grabbed for my totem.

Help me fight her.

The change was instantaneous. My spine slammed up straight and my breath came easier. Once again, I was in control of my body.

Rumbling growls rose up from the demons, and Ishtar stopped laughing and scowled. At her side, Lucifer grinned a dangerous grin.

Ishtar held up her hand, and instantly, the sound of howling demons stopped.

"No one move. These little witchlings are *ours.*"

"I do love breaking the willful ones best." Lucifer took a step closer, and from the corner of my eye, I caught motion.

Diana's purple magic zinged across the expanse separating us from the demons, and slammed into Lucifer's chest.

He tripped backward, and once again, the demons growled and roared. As if playing off their minions' fury, Lucifer's and Ishtar's eyes began to glow a brilliant red.

My blood skittered in my veins. *They're going to possess us. We have to distract them.*

"Now!" I screamed, and sprang into action.

Magic flew, hitting demon after demon as my friends attacked. The queen and king's eyes dimmed, and they twisted, uncaring that we were injuring their peons, as they watched my magic stream over their heads and into the Thames.

The torrent of demons trying to exit Hell released horrible screeches. I held my breath, hoping that the hole would close and the sounds would stop. But the cries didn't cease. If anything, as the seconds ticked on they became more intense. But then I heard a *crack*, and a stream of crimson flew over us to join my power.

I gasped, and although it was idiotic to turn my back on the King and Queen of Hell, I whipped around.

The shield we'd placed around Alex was split in half, and he was sitting up. One hand clutched his chest, the one sporting his totem was spouting magic that mingled with Alex's own.

"Odie," he croaked. "Push harder. Now."

I spun, and bolstered by hope that we could do this together, magic burst from my hands like it never had before and soared toward the river. It slammed into the water, sending ten-foot-tall waves to each side.

Lucifer and Ishtar finally saw fit to retaliate. Flourishing their arms, they sent tendrils of black, glimmering magic straight for Alex and me. But our friends doubled down on their attacks, hurling power at the queen and king in addition to the peons at their back.

Knowing that we had to hurry; I pushed harder. The others could only hold the royals off for so long. Especially, if they changed their mind and sent their minions after us.

Close the Hellgate. Please close the Hellgate, I begged my totem—Morgan's magic—to aid us. She'd done it once, and she could do it again. I knew she could.

The seconds ticked on as I poured energy into the open Hellgate. Despite the winter cold, sweat ran down my face, and every muscle in my body trembled with exertion.

Then, things went from bad to worse. Ishtar, who had been fighting Hunter, flung a stream of power to the sky. It reached its apex and burst like a firework, producing shining tendrils of black power that fell in a massive dome, encompassing the Hellgate and ending just behind us.

We were trapped.

Ishtar began to cackle. "Give up!" the Queen of Hell screamed. "You're never going home or anywhere in this world ever again unless I command it! I am your *master*!" She flung her hands to the sky, and a chorus of screeches and guttural bellows sounded.

I shook my head. My friends were still fighting—even Alex, and he could barely sit up. There was no way I would let them down. I pulled from deep within me and begged my totem for help. If closing the gate took every ounce of magic I had, or every bit of power Morgan could give, I'd give it.

Stars began to swim in my vision, and suddenly, I saw threads of all different colors spinning around me. The colors grew more vibrant, the yellow, purple, and green sticking out the most.

I gasped. "Diana! Hunter! Eva! I need your magic in the Hellgate!"

My friends switched tack right away, and part of the power that had been killing demons and battling royals diverted to stream over the horde. As soon as their magic hit the water, I felt the shift, the change in the air. My magic surged, and a sizzle of electricity zapped all my nerves. Then a *whoosh* hit my ear, followed by a massive *boom* that shook the ground, knocking me over.

Ishtar released a blood-curdling scream, and my heart squeezed. I glanced up to find that demons no longer streamed from Hell.

"Holy shit," Hunter's exhausted voice breathed. "We did it."

A smile broke on my face, only to vanish a moment later when Ishtar spun around, her eyes blazing red and staring straight at me. Her wings snapped out.

My heart stopped. I had seconds to act.

I leapt up and summoned the energies around me, preparing to make a warphole. They came readily, naturally. I manipulated them and flung them out in front of me as my mouth opened to instruct my friends to rush through the portal.

But nothing happened.

No warphole appeared and the magical energy I'd just worked with fizzled on the spot. A pit formed in my stomach.

Ishtar's laughter boomed. "I told you witch! This world is cut off to you! There will be no warping to safety this time. You're *mine!*" She gestured to the shield, and I realized it was somehow nullifying my ability to make a warphole.

She knew I'd try this and came prepared to stop it. My jaw clenched, but not about to give up, I tried again. Sweat rolled off my face as I pushed myself and my magic to do as I wanted. Fuchsia poured into the air, and yet, it never coalesced into a perfectly circular warphole.

This cannot be happening! Help me Morgan!

The plea ignited my totem once again and light and color that was not mine poured from it, illuminating the pink and purple hues of my magic. And then, something I saw made me stop. The threads of color I'd noticed earlier popped in the fuchsia, but as I stared more joined them and spun around us. Every color of the rainbow was present in varying lengths, and I swore that I heard voices—children laughing, women talking, a couple conversing.

I'd seen this before. Time was presenting itself to me. I sucked in a breath and following a hunch that I knew was coming from Morgan, called on the strands of time.

My totem lit up brighter than ever, the stone growing warm against my chest as my ancestor's magic assisted. Time came closer to hover before me, waiting to do my bidding, and oddly enough, I knew exactly what I needed to do.

Please let this work, I thought as Ishtar launched into the air, her arms outstretched in my direction.

I molded the warping energies together with time and flung the ball of magic behind me. They landed on the ground next to Alex, and opened a warphole that expanded to gobble him up. He fell through with a yelp. The crimson magic that had been flowing out of him—still attacking demons left and right—disappeared.

"What the shit!" Eva spun from her attack position to face me. I shoved her toward the warphole.

"Go! Escape!" I yelled just as Ishtar loosed a horrible screech.

Eva snapped to attention, grabbed Hunter's hand, and jumped through the hole.

"Diana! Move! Now!" I screamed.

The headmistress's daughter shot me a desperate look.

"*Now!*" I repeated, my teeth grinding down on each other from the exertion. Even if Morgan's magic was doing most of the work, I was working harder than I ever had before. And I couldn't control something as powerful as Morgan's magic for forever. No . . . I wasn't that strong. I was just Odie, a girl who was fading fast.

"I'll follow," I insisted.

Diana gave a single nod and dove through the hole. As soon as she disappeared, I twirled toward the warphole.

Ishtar was so close that her wings beat the air at my back. I swallowed down a lump in my throat, took a few running steps, and leapt.

Heat and cold engulfed me as I hit the warphole and slipped through time.

EPILOGUE

The scent of sage and crushed berries filled my nostrils as my eyelids fluttered open.

My gaze locked on a woman across the room. She was swaying and singing, her red hair as vibrant as the fuchsia magic that swirled around her, doing her bidding.

Fuchsia.

Where was I?

As if she could hear my thoughts, the woman whirled around and caught my eyes. Then, she smiled.

"You're up! I'm so glad you survived the timewalking. Merlin will be pleased as well. It's a good omen for your friends."

Merlin . . .

Memories of paintings and drawings of this woman filtered through my mind, and recognition crashed down upon me. My heart clenched, unable to believe it although it was definitely true.

I knew this woman. I'd seen her before, heard her voice. Felt her power run through me and save my life.

I was in the home of my ancestor, Morgan Le Fay.

I stirred the cauldron with bated breath, waiting for the moment that Morgan assured me was coming.

"Any second now," my ancestor repeated, her twinkling eyes glued on the potion. The scent of bitter nettles and mushrooms wafted off the boiling liquid, herbaceous and earthy.

"Three, two, . . . Stir a little slower, Odette. You're going too fast." Diana paused, her lips parting in rapt anticipation.

Behind her, I caught a flash of motion, and dragged my gaze from the brew. Hunter had snuck back inside and was poking his head into the room. He caught my gaze, and with a trickster wink, pointed at Diana and pressed his finger to his lips.

I smothered a laugh. It was official, a week in such close quarters was too long. Hunter never would have dared to screw with Diana back home—in the future—where we lived in an expansive magical academy most of the year. But after three days of monsoon-like rains and being stuck inside a tiny cottage, it appeared that Hunter couldn't help but cause a bit of mischief.

"Almoooost," Diana cooed, her blue eyes locked on the bubbling, yellow liquid. "It's going to change n—"

"Now!" Hunter leapt into the room at the exact instant that the potion turned neon green.

Diana let out a strangled screech, and purple magic shot from her fingers as she whipped around.

"Dammit, Wardwell!" She batted at his shoulder as if he was a gross spider, which only made Hunter laugh harder. "I nearly jinxed you!"

"You should have," he replied, wiggling his fingers at her and shaking his hips in a way that made me snort out a laugh. "I need to practice my counter-jinxes."

"That can be arranged." A man with a long, brown beard shot through with white strode into the kitchen, his arms full of herbs.

A beaming Eva trailed behind him, her hair damp and arms overflowing with rocks. The rocks were from a nearby Roman site that she'd been begging Merlin to show her since he'd mentioned it two days ago. The girl looked like she'd won the lottery.

"It's been far too long since I jinxed anyone." Merlin twisted to face Hunter. "Morgan can practice too. She always came up with the best, most original jinxes. She's so clever."

"I have a few untested ones." Morgan's cheeks had pinked at her paramour's flattery, making the freckles that smattered the bridge of her nose stand out more. Usually, she appeared goddess-like and wise, but in that moment she was just a girl enjoying the praise of her loved one.

Hunter paled, and I wrapped my arms around my stomach and dissolved into full blown laughter.

"Not what you meant, my boy?" Alex's ancestor arched a bushy eyebrow.

"He can't handle you or Morgan," Eva teased.

For once, her beau didn't provide a snappy rebuttal.

Merlin's bright blue eyes ran up and down Hunter. "Not now, but perhaps one day he will be able to."

I stopped laughing and straightened to stand. Eva and Hunter blinked, stunned. The compliment was huge—even if it was a 'perhaps'. We were talking about *the* Merlin and *the* Morgan Le Fay, two of the most legendary witches in history. The witches who would eventually seal the Hellgate that I had unwittingly broken open.

The room stilled for a second, before Morgan broke the quiet, scooping a ladle of potion into a mug. "What do you lot say we get this to Alex? After that, we'll start lessons. The day is clearing up, and we should use the light while we have it."

"I'll take it to him." I held out my hand, and Morgan passed me the cup.

As I left the room, conversation began to flow again, and my lips quirked up. No matter what happened, how shocked or out of place we were in this era, M&M's cottage never stayed quiet for long.

I stepped outside and covered my head with my arm only to find that the springtime drizzle I'd expected had ceased. Morgan had called it.

A smile bloomed on my face as I approached the small outbuilding, excited to see my man for a moment. The main cottage was where we hung out and ate our meals with M&M. Like most homes of its time, the dwelling was basically one room with a small sectioned partitioned for sleeping. The older witches stayed in the cottage while the rest of us shared the shack that the legends had built after Merlin experienced a vision of us arriving.

Our quarters were about the size of a large backyard shed. A tight fit, but preferable to squeezing all seven of us in the cottage. And since it was too dangerous for us to rent rooms in the nearby village, we made it work.

I knocked on the door. "Alex? Are you awake?"

"Yeah." His tone was lower than usual.

I repressed a sigh. He'd been grumpy since we arrived in the past, and understandably so. He was stuck in a room that reeked of hay and too many bodies packed in tight. All I could do was try to be a bright spot in his day.

"Hey." I pressed the door open. Alex was still reclined in our bed of hay, a blanket draped over him, and a candle lighting the dark room. "What are you reading?"

"A healing text." He grinned, one of the first smiles I'd seen from him since he'd woken up four days ago. "I'm learning all about the humors and bloodletting."

"How interesting. Perhaps for your next birthday, you'll get a bag of leeches."

"That's love." He gestured to the cup in my hand. "Is that for me?"

"Yup. Morgan has been doing a lot of research on non-spirit walkers moving through the ghost realm. This will help to ground you in our world faster." I handed over the cup of liquid.

Understandably, Alex hated feeling as if he'd float away at any second. But according to M&M, traveling through the ghost realm often made people who weren't spirit walkers feel weightless, ill, and lethargic. Especially those who were totally unprepared. Which Alex had been when a demon-possessed ghost kidnapped him from Spellcasters and transported him through the spirit world so that he could arrive in London in mere minutes.

Add in timewalking through centuries shortly after traveling through the ghost realm and Alex was a total mess.

For now, the poor guy was allowed only one walk per day for exercise. During that walk, we had to watch after him and keep him grounded—literally. He couldn't even relieve himself unaccompanied; perhaps selfishly, I was thankful that task fell to Hunter. Until the sensation that he'd float away at any moment disappeared, Alex was stuck here.

"Bottoms up." He chugged the potion, then wrinkled his nose as he handed the empty mug back to me. "That was awful."

"You don't want to know what we put in it," I admitted.

"If dragon piss will make me better faster, I'd drink it all day." He glanced at the healing books Merlin had given him. "I'm trying to remain upbeat, but I'm missing out on so much. Especially now that your lessons are starting."

My heart broke for him. Being bedbound when there were two legendary witches around to learn from was torture for Alex. It didn't help that we'd barely had any time alone in a week.

My hand slid over his. "I know, babe. But if anyone knows how to make a potion that will help, it's Morgan. I'm sure you'll be up and running in no time." I bent down and kissed him. "In the meantime, I'll tell you about everything I learn. That way, you have something meaty to chew on."

"I can't wait to hear all about it," Alex replied with a smile that almost hid the sourness in his tone.

The door to the main cottage slammed shut, and voices grew louder as everyone stomped outside.

"Odie!" Eva called out. "We gotta go!"

"Guess that's my cue."

I felt terrible leaving him after such a brief visit, but I was also undeniably excited to get started. Although it had only been a week of resting and allowing our magic to acclimate after timewalking had screwed us all up, it had felt like a year. Not to mention, Morgan had something important she wanted to discuss with Eva and me. We'd been on pins and needles for days, wondering what it might be.

Alex tried to sit up to kiss me. I laid my hand on his

chest and forced him to lay back down again before pressing my lips to his.

"Get some rest, babe."

A sigh dripping with resignation left him. "Have fun." He reached for his book and cracked it open again.

Trying not to take his mood personally, I kissed him on the forehead and left to join the others.

ALSO BY ASHLEY MCLEO

Coven of Shadows and Secrets

Seeker of Secrets

Hunted by Darkness

History of Witches

Marked by Fate

Spellcasters Spy Academy Series (Magic of Arcana Universe)

A Legacy Witch: Year One

A Marked Witch: Internship

A Rebel Witch: Year Two

A Crucible Witch: Year Three

The Spellcasters Spy Academy Boxset

The Wonderland Court Series (Magic of Arcana Universe)

Alice the Dagger

Alice the Torch

Standalone Novels

The Alchemist of Silver Hollow (Magic of Arcana Universe)

Fanged Fae Series - A Bonegates sister series

Blood Moon Magic

Faerie Blood

The Bonegate Series - A Fanged Fae sister series

Hawk Witch

Assassin Witch

Traitor Witch

Illuminator Witch

The Royal Quest Series

Dragon Prince

Dragon Magic

Dragon Mate

Dragon Betrayal

Dragon Crown

Dragon War

The Starseed Universe

Prophecy of Three

Souls of Three

Rising of Three

ACKNOWLEDGMENTS

Thank you to my husband for being so very patient during the writing of this book, and assisting me in every way that you could. You're a freaking saint.

Special thanks to my editor, Jen McDonnell for helping me whip this baby into shape. I love working with you.

To my Facebook reader group, thank you for your support, the laughs we share even though we've never met IRL, and making writing a joy.

And finally, thank you to all my readers. Without you, I couldn't do what I love.

All the magic,

Ashley

Ashley lives in the lush and green Pacific Northwest with her husband, Kurt and their dog, Flicka.

When she's not writing she enjoys traveling the world, reading, practicing or teaching yoga, kicking butt at board games (she recommends Splendor and Dominion), and connecting with family and friends.

For most direct access to Ashley sign up for her reader group, The Coven. You can also find her Facebook group, Ashley's Reader Coven and join in on the fun there!

www.ingramcontent.com/pod-product-compliance
Lightning Source LLC
Chambersburg PA
CBHW032155180726
48284CB00001B/61